Queen
of the
Owls

Queen of the Owls

A Novel

Barbara Linn Probst

SHE WRITES PRESS

Published 2020
Printed in the United States of America
ISBN: 978-1-63152-890-3 pbk
ISBN: 978-1-63152-891-0 ebk
Library of Congress Control Number: 2019911275

For information, address:
She Writes Press
1569 Solano Ave #546
Berkeley, CA 94707

She Writes Press is a division of SparkPoint Studio, LLC.

Cover image: White Iris No. 7 (1957) by Georgia O'Keeffe
Museo Thyssen-Bornemisza, Madrid, Spain.

For the roses
had the look of flowers that are looked at,
accepted and accepting.

T.S. Eliot, *Four Quartets*

Part One:
The Photographer

One

Everyone had to meet somewhere. If Elizabeth thought about it that way, the fact that she met Richard at a Tai Chi class was no more or less auspicious than a first meeting at—say, a book store or bus stop. It was only later, looking back, that everything seemed heavy with meaning.

She had seen people practicing Tai Chi on Founders' Lawn in the center of campus—the unbelievably slow flexing of an arm or foot, the serene gaze that always made her feel, in contrast, nervous and clumsy. She had watched, entranced, as they rotated their hips and pushed effortlessly against the air. After a while, it felt odd to simply watch. Being inside the movements instead of looking at them, that was the point.

The Tai Chi studio was only a few blocks from the university and offered a discount to faculty and students. Elizabeth was both, a PhD student who taught undergraduate courses, which she took as a double sign that she ought to enroll. Besides, Ben had his squash games two evenings a week. It was only fair for her to have Wednesdays. Ben could manage. He knew how to read *Mike Mulligan and His Steam Shovel* at least as well as she did—better, according to Daniel. At four-and-a-half, Daniel was quite sure of his judgments.

Ben wouldn't begrudge her one night a week. And then, when she came home, tranquil and balletic, he'd applaud her decision. Anyway, that was the theory.

The classes were held in a converted factory, in the fourth-floor studio of a short, grave martial arts instructor with limited English. Elizabeth tried to explain that Tai Chi was new to her, but he cut her off. "You can," he said. "You try, and you can."

Really? Elizabeth wanted to say. *Tell me one thing in life that works that way.* But she nodded with what she hoped was the right combination of humility and confidence. Then she took a place in the back of the room where she could steal glances at the other pupils. Most of them, she saw, had been doing this for a long time. It was clear from the elegant, almost bored way they twisted and stretched.

She noticed Richard the moment he came in. It was hard not to, the way he strode into the dojo and placed himself right in the center of the front row, his gaze fixed on the instructor, steady as steel, as if demanding that the instructor focus on him too. Mr. Wu—that was the instructor's name, although people called him *sifu*, or master— gave a short bow, acknowledging that the class could begin, now that the person who mattered was there.

"Hey, Richard," a woman called. She gave a bright, eager wave.

Mr. Wu frowned. Then he placed his left foot parallel to the right and said, "We commence." Elizabeth tried to concentrate on imitating each of Mr. Wu's gestures, but her eyes kept straying to Richard. He was the best one in the class; that was obvious. And he was absurdly handsome. Or maybe, she thought, he just acted as if he were.

By the third Wednesday, she found herself watching for him, tracking his movements as he stepped out of the freight elevator and tucked his shoes into a cubbyhole. Adolescent, she told herself, but what was the harm? She had seven days and six evenings a week to be mature, serious, married.

On the fourth Wednesday, twenty minutes into the class, Mr. Wu grabbed his chest and sank to his knees just as they were doing *The White Crane Spreads its Wings*. Even the grabbing and sinking were fluid, composed. Elizabeth thought, at first, that they were a special part of the sequence. *I submit to the source of existence. I accept the impermanence of the body*. When she realized what was happening, she stared in horror. Mr. Wu's face turned ashen as his eyes rolled back in his head and he crumpled onto the hardwood floor. Two of the women screamed.

Richard sprang into action. He jumped forward and caught the old man before his head hit the floor. "Someone call 911." Elizabeth fumbled in her pocket. You were supposed to leave your cell phone in a cubbyhole, along with other non-Tai Chi-like items, but she'd stuffed hers into the pocket of her cargo pants. She hadn't meant to be subversive; it was only the habit, since she became a mother, of keeping her phone nearby.

"Here," she said. "I've got a phone." She pushed through the rows. Richard's arm was around Mr. Wu's shoulders, his palm cupping the back of the teacher's head. He looked up at Elizabeth. His gaze bore right into her, searing her with its intensity. She felt herself turn weak with shock. Was she going to collapse too? Only it would be from the most extraordinary swell of desire, as if someone had turned her upside-down and shaken her like a kaleidoscope, rearranging all the parts.

"Can you call?" he asked.

She blinked. "Yes, of course."

A man with a shaved head rushed forward. "Check his airways." He flung a glance at Elizabeth. "I was a lifeguard, back in high school." Richard moved aside to let the man kneel next to him, and Elizabeth punched 911 into her phone. She told the dispatcher what had happened.

"Well?" Richard looked at her again.

She shoved the phone back into her pocket and buttoned the flap.

"They're on their way." She inched closer, her knee brushing Richard's shoulder as he and the other man laid Mr. Wu on his side. She was one of the rescue squad now, a member of the intimate circle.

Within minutes, the paramedics burst out of the freight elevator, carrying a gurney. No one knew where Mr. Wu's insurance card was, or his driver's license. A woman in blue yoga pants gave the paramedic one of the postcards for the dojo that littered the top of the shoe cabinet. "It has his name and phone number," she explained.

The man with the shaved head stepped in front of her and put up a hand, as if he were halting traffic. "I think he has a daughter nearby. If you need a relative."

The EMT pocketed the card and bent to hoist the gurney. As quickly as they had come, the crew disappeared. Elizabeth watched the lights above the freight elevator until they stopped at the ground floor. With Mr. Wu gone, the studio seemed empty, pointless. She wondered if he would be all right. The possibility that he might not be, and that there might not be more classes, filled her with dismay. Was this it, then? Her Wednesdays, over already?

The students began to collect their belongings. "I'll be the last to leave," Richard volunteered. "Someone should make sure the place is locked up."

"What do you think will happen?" Elizabeth asked.

He shrugged. "No way to know." He met her eyes again. It was the same look, piercing her like a javelin. "Guess I'll come by next week and see if anyone's around with information."

"Me too," Elizabeth said. "I'll stop by too." The eagerness in her voice, audible even to her, made her flush. She cleared her throat. "I hope he's okay."

The woman in the yoga pants put her palm on Elizabeth's arm. "I'm going to visualize him radiating wellness. I think we should all do that."

One by one, the students gathered around the elevator. Reluctantly,

Elizabeth joined them. It was too early to go home. She wanted to turn around and offer to help Richard lock up, or maybe invite him for a drink. Both ideas were crazy—everyone would stare at her if she threw herself at him so outrageously. The sensation of Mr. Wu's absence washed over her anew. One minute you were doing *The White Crane Spreads its Wings*, and the next minute your life might be over.

The elevator arrived and Elizabeth got in. It took forever to descend the four flights to the street. When she stepped out of the building, she looked around for the ambulance but it was gone. There was only a wire trash basket by the curb with a newspaper caught in the mesh and a blur of tire tracks. Elizabeth buried her hands in her pockets and started to walk. The evening was clear and starry, strangely warm, even though summer was long past. The bus stop was only a block away. Without really deciding to, she kept walking. It was twenty-two blocks to the apartment, and by the time she got home, Daniel and Katie would be asleep. She loved them—beyond measure—but the reality of their dense demanding bodies, their overwhelming and exuberant love, was more than she could bear right then.

When she opened the front door, she saw that Ben was engrossed in a Vietnam documentary. He glanced in her direction, raising his chin in a quick acknowledgement before turning back to the screen. His response to her return shouldn't have been surprising and yet it was. Elizabeth didn't know what else she'd expected. A leap to his feet, an exclamation of delight, a passionate embrace? Ben never greeted her like that; why would he do that now, on an ordinary Wednesday? It was only the memory of Mr. Wu crumpling, and her knee against Richard's shoulder, and the smoldering way Richard had looked at her, that made her yearn, suddenly, for a wordless something whose absence she'd grown used to.

Blinking back her disappointment, Elizabeth bent to pick up

Katie's bunny where she must have dropped it on the way to bed. Had Katie really fallen asleep without Mr. Bunny? She glanced at Ben again, her fingertips stroking the bunny's ear, waiting, in case he decided to look up and speak to her. The thwack of helicopter blades and the rumbling of the narrator's voice filled the room. Ben's eyes were fixed on the screen. After a moment Elizabeth gathered the bunny, a pair of inside-out socks, and Katie's lime green sweater, and elbowed open the door to the children's bedroom.

The larger of the apartment's two bedrooms, the room had been partitioned into two rectangles. On one side of the partition, Daniel snored peacefully, legs flung across the Buzz Lightyear blanket that he had kicked aside, an arm dangling off the edge of the bed. On the other side of the partition, Katie lay curled in a ball, fists beneath her chin, knees pulled to her chest. Elizabeth bent and tucked the bunny next to her cheek. Katie frowned in her sleep but Elizabeth knew she'd be happy when she awoke and found the familiar comfort of its matted fur. She smoothed the blanket and kissed the top of her daughter's head.

Elizabeth closed the door softly and crossed the living room, careful not to walk between Ben and the screen, and went to the alcove where she had her desk. With the Tai Chi class out early and the children asleep, she could get some work done.

She was a doctoral student in Art History, writing her thesis on Georgia O'Keeffe's time in Hawaii. It was an interlude that most biographers and art historians tended to dismiss, and most fans of O'Keeffe's paintings had never heard of. O'Keeffe was known for her mesas and deserts, her bones and skulls—and, of course, those flowers. Yet O'Keeffe had spent nine weeks in Hawaii at a crucial time in her life, painting lush green waterfalls, exotic flora, and black lava. They weren't her best paintings but without them she might not have gone on. They had gotten her past a time of stagnation—a stalled career, a marriage in serious trouble—and prepared her for what would come next. Her transitional place. That was Elizabeth's argument.

She opened her laptop and pulled up her file of O'Keeffe quotations. The one she needed was right there, at the top of the document. *I've been absolutely terrified every moment of my life and I've never let it keep me from doing a single thing I wanted to do.*

Then she reached for her folder of O'Keeffe's Hawaii paintings and took out the four images of the luxuriant 'Iao Valley. It was the only large-scale vista that Georgia had painted while she was there, and the only Hawaiian subject she had painted multiple times. Three paintings were of the same waterfall, a jagged line cutting into the verdant slope. The first two versions were bounded, complete, a static landscape, captured at an instant in time. It was only in the third painting that she had let the valley open and pour forth, steam rising from the vortex. Or perhaps it was the fog that was entering, filling the cleft.

Elizabeth felt a stab of desire, a longing for something wide and nameless. Slowly, she slid her finger along the line in the painting where the mist parted and sliced the grey. Then she shivered, as if her own breastbone had been sliced open, expanding, like a pair of wings.

Two

Elizabeth reached across Ben's chest to turn off the alarm. He lifted his head from the pillow, grunted, and said, "Don't tell me it's 6:30 already."

"6:24. I set the snooze button."

He let out a groan and rolled onto his side. "You want the first shower?"

"I do. Thanks. I have to get the kids to Lucy's earlier than usual."

Ben pulled the edge of the blanket over his shoulders, and Elizabeth's arm slid off his chest onto the mattress. Her nightshirt was still bunched around her waist. The irritating twist of the fabric and the stickiness between her legs let her know they'd had sex during the night. Not that she had slept through it. Only that it had been, as usual, unmemorable.

She rolled onto her back, allowing herself those six extra minutes before she really did have to get up, and moved her legs under the sheet, scissor-like, until she felt Ben's calf against her toe. He twitched, jerking toward the edge of the bed. Elizabeth reached down to straighten her nightshirt.

Obviously she knew they'd had sex, the same way she knew that the rent was due or that she needed to move a load of laundry from the washer to the dryer. She'd been nudged half-awake by Ben's erection against her butt. Her first thought had been: Thank goodness. It had been a while. It was always *a while,* although Elizabeth had trained herself not to watch the calendar too closely because that made it worse. Still, an actual erection—even if it came from a particular sleep position and not from touching or seeing or anything to do, specifically, with her—was too precious to waste. She had shifted her weight carefully, nothing sudden that might startle him into limpness, and guided him toward her.

Not memorable, but duly accomplished.

Elizabeth heard the click of the alarm that meant it was about to buzz again. Quickly, she leaned across the bed to shut it off so Ben could sleep a little longer. She had a packed day but his would be tougher. Ben was a lawyer, though not the kind of lawyer with glamorous high-paying cases. Some of his clients didn't pay at all. Partner in a small local firm, Ben took on working-class clients who needed help with leases and disability claims and an occasional bequest. He was dedicated, conscientious, and saw each flat-fee case through to the end, regardless of how long it took. That included a string of tenants' rights lawsuits that were seldom winnable but, he insisted, important to the community. Elizabeth admired him for that.

"Wake me when you're done with your shower," he mumbled.

"Will do. I'll turn on the coffee maker while the water heats up."

Elizabeth folded back the blanket and eased off the bed. Ben liked to take a cup of coffee into the bathroom while he shaved. It was one of the things she knew about him, just as he knew that she liked the toilet paper to unroll from the back and not over the top. If there were other things he didn't know about her—well, she was too busy to dwell on what she didn't have.

Her priority right now was to get showered and dressed so she could turn her attention to Daniel and Katie. She had an 8:30 meeting with her dissertation adviser, who clearly had no idea what it took to get to his office at that hour. An 8:30 meeting meant that Daniel and Katie had to be settled at the babysitter's by 8:00, and *that* meant waking them by 7:00. They didn't mind going to Lucy's house. Lucy had a big yard, an endless assortment of toys, and other preschoolers to play with. It was the getting-up and getting-there that was so challenging.

Elizabeth did the seven-minute wash-and-towel-dry she had perfected after Daniel was born, slipped into her clothes, and stopped in the kitchen to pour Ben a cup of coffee. She set the cup on the bathroom sink, tucking it under the protective edge of the medicine cabinet. Ben was already in the shower. Steam billowed into the room, like the cloud that had filled the cleft of the 'Iao Valley. Elizabeth wiped a circle on the shower door and yelled, "Bye! See you tonight." Then she hurried down the hall to the children's bedroom.

"C'mon, pumpkin," she told Katie, lifting her out of bed. "Up you go." Katie rubbed her eyes and started to protest, but Elizabeth scooped up the bunny and jiggled it up and down. "Good morning," she squeaked in Mr. Bunny's distinctive soprano. "What color socks do you want to wear today, Miss Katie-Kate?"

Katie wriggled free. "Pur-pill."

"Excellent." Mr. Bunny bobbed his head.

From the other side of the partition, Elizabeth heard Daniel slide out of bed and pad across the floor. "Are we going to Lucy's?"

"We are indeed."

"Knew it."

Elizabeth had to smile at the smack of satisfaction in Daniel's voice. How nice to have the world verify, so clearly, that you were right. She opened Katie's drawer and found a pair of lavender socks. "What do you think, Tiger?" She raised her voice so Daniel could hear. "Gonna beat the world championship record for getting dressed this morning?"

"Yes!" She heard the bang of his bureau and wondered, briefly, what he was pulling out to wear. Oh, let him pick; he liked that. She unrolled the socks and reached for Katie's foot.

"*Me*," Katie said, pushing her hand away.

"Can Mr. Bunny help?" Katie shook her head, as Elizabeth had known she would. She separated the purple socks and dangled one from each hand. "Which shall we do first?"

Katie grabbed a sock and stretched it over three toes, face scrunched in concentration. She tugged, and her big toe popped free. Elizabeth could see the purple nylon beginning to tear. If that happened and Katie had a tantrum, they'd never get to Lucy's on time.

Enough. She picked up Katie's foot and snapped the sock into place. Katie opened her mouth to object, but Elizabeth threw her a *don't you dare* look and picked up the other sock. "Here you go. Purple sock number two." Then she plucked a flowered shirt from the drawer. "Up, please." Katie raised her arms. "That's my girl. Want to pull it down yourself?"

Without turning her head, Elizabeth called out to Daniel. "How's it going, Tiger? You ready, or do you need some help?"

"No," Daniel said. Elizabeth didn't know if it meant *no*, he wasn't ready, or *no*, he didn't need any help. She looked at her watch. 7:20. No time for breakfast. She couldn't let her children go to Lucy's without breakfast, but she couldn't be late for her meeting either. Getting Harold Lindstrom to chair her dissertation committee was a coup and not to be taken lightly. Lindstrom was a stickler for footnotes, MLA citations, and promptness.

"I know," she announced. She shook out a pair of overalls and made her voice as bright as she could. "Let's get Egg McMuffins on the way to Lucy's."

Ben would never start the children's day with Egg McMuffins. Of course, Ben wasn't the one in a rush to get them to daycare. Elizabeth remembered the lifted nightshirt and the way he'd jerked his leg away when she touched it with her toe. He was half asleep, she reminded herself. It was a reflex, not a rejection. Then she thought of his averted profile and absent nod when she came back from Tai Chi last night. Nothing unusual about the greeting, yet it had stung. The barrenness of their exchange—no kiss, no smile of pleasure at her return, not even a brief muting of the Vietnam documentary to ask *so how was Tai Chi?*

And what would she have answered? *The teacher opened his arms and fell to the ground. A man looked at me.*

If she'd wanted to talk about the Vietnam War, Ben would have made room for her on the couch. On another night, she might have done that; they'd had plenty of similar conversations over the years. It was what they did, analyzing and dissecting and figuring things out. The changing composition of the Supreme Court, the bioethics of stem cell research. Agreeing, in principle, about the way life should be.

Elizabeth pulled her lips together with a firm *no* to wherever her thoughts were taking her. It was after 7:30. Hastily, she collected sweaters, car keys, bag, and bunny.

Somehow she got the children into the car and settled at Lucy's by 8:03. Then she raced to campus, took the stairs in the Humanities building two at a time, and knocked on the pebbled glass door to Harold Lindstrom's office at 8:29.

As she had feared, Harold Lindstrom wasn't happy with the outline she had sent him. "You haven't convinced me," he said, eyeing her over the rim of his tortoise-shell glasses. "The whole point of a dissertation is to make a new argument, based on the evidence. Without evidence, it's wishful thinking, not scholarship. Opinion masquerading as critical interpretation."

"Yes, of course." Elizabeth tried to look grateful for the platitude without ceding her confidence. The combination of humility and assurance she'd aimed for with Mr. Wu was also, as she had learned, the proper stance for a doctoral student. "In fact," she said, "my idea is rooted in O'Keeffe's whole approach to art. She wanted to show the essence of things."

"Indeed," Harold said. He sat back, folding his arms. "But why, specifically, did Hawaii matter?" He gave Elizabeth a dry look. "Let's be honest. The stuff she did in Hawaii wasn't all that good."

"That's not the point." Elizabeth took a deep breath. Harold Lindstrom liked her, thought she had exceptional promise; that was why he'd taken her on. She was determined to be his prize student, write the most ground-breaking dissertation he had ever seen, and in record time. But first she had to make him understand her idea—no, more than understand. Admire it.

"It was Hawaii itself," she told him. "Hawaii was lush, fertile, alive. O'Keeffe had never seen anything like it. The abundance, the intensity of color and sensation. Then she went back to New Mexico and saw a whole new beauty in its starkness. It shaped her work for decades—the rest of her life, really. Hawaii was the catalyst, that's my argument. She found something new because something new had been awakened in her."

"You want that to be true," he said, "but you need the data. No data, no scholarship."

"There *is* data." People had written about O'Keeffe's time in Hawaii—not many, but a few, like Jennifer Saville in her essay for the Honolulu Academy of Arts. That wasn't the kind of data Harold Lindstrom was talking about, of course. He meant primary data, from O'Keeffe herself. Elizabeth searched her mind for an example, a painting that showed what she was trying to convey.

"Her *White Bird of Paradise*," she said. "One of the Hawaii paintings. You never see it listed as one of O'Keeffe's major pieces but it's where she brings the two things together, petals and bones, life and death." She strained forward, needing Harold to see what she saw. "Those white blades, the stalks in the Bird of Paradise? They're like the antlers and bones she painted, later, after Hawaii."

"One painting," he said.

"I don't need more than one. To make my point, convince you."

Harold laughed. "Do you give your husband a hard time too?"

Elizabeth drew back, startled by his levity. He probably thought he was being clever but it was patronizing, dismissive, maybe even illegal. None of your damn business, she thought—although, in fact, she didn't give Ben a hard time. She was careful not to. You only gave someone a hard time if you were certain they would still want you, afterward.

She thought of the way Richard had looked at her, in the Tai Chi class. Was it really just twenty-four hours ago? The whole incident— Mr. Wu's collapse, the paramedics—seemed to belong to another life, not the life of a devoted mother and O'Keeffe specialist.

She straightened her back. Better not to respond to Harold's remark. Keep his focus on her as a brilliant new scholar, the one he was grooming for a place at the elite table. "I'll start with the *White Bird of Paradise* and show you what I mean."

He dipped his head, conceding that much. "All right. Email me your work plan and we'll talk again." Then he stood, meeting over.

"I'll do that." Elizabeth rose too. All that effort this morning, for a ten-minute conversation.

On the other hand, she had free time she hadn't expected.

Elizabeth shouldered her messenger bag and clattered down the two flights of stairs to the ground floor of the Humanities building. The halls were empty; 8:00 classes were already in session, and it was too early for students with 10:00 classes to be slouched against the walls with their donuts and chai lattes, waiting for the doors to reopen.

Elizabeth herself had a 1:00 class to teach, an upper-division course called Feminist Art. It was a joke, really, when she thought about Georgia's hatred for the whole concept. But Harold had used his influence to get her the job, and she had been grateful. Doctoral candidates had to teach as part of their training, but it was rare for someone without a PhD to be allowed to teach anything other than an introductory course. The advanced class was a star in her résumé.

Feminist Art was supposed to mean art that provoked a dialogue between the viewer and the artwork, rejected the idea of art as static, and challenged patriarchal notions of what was beautiful. That was what the master syllabus said. Elizabeth planned to assign a paper on how a woman's gaze was different from a man's gaze. O'Keeffe, she was sure, would have said there was no difference. You saw what you saw, if you looked, which most people didn't. Yet O'Keeffe had also said: *I feel there is something unexplored about woman that only a woman can explore.*

It was too easy to assume that O'Keeffe was referring to her flower paintings, the ones people insisted were genitalia. Elizabeth was certain that it was something else. She didn't know what that *something else* was, and she was pretty sure that Harold Lindstrom didn't know either. She thought of the photographs Alfred Stieglitz had taken of O'Keeffe when they were first together, the pictures that had shocked the art world. Hands, breasts, the beautiful unpretty face looking straight into the camera. The nude headless torso, with a mass of pubic hair and legs like trees.

O'Keeffe had been in her thirties when she posed for Stieglitz, not an ingenue but an accomplished painter, even if largely unknown. She hadn't been a passive model for someone else's vision; she had been exploring for herself. Elizabeth had studied the photos, felt Georgia's stern unwavering gaze.

"Oops." A girl in a denim jacket, on her way out of the building, banged her knapsack against Elizabeth's arm. She ducked her head in a perfunctory *sorry* and pulled open the heavy oak door that led to the stone steps and the quad below. Elizabeth slipped behind her, into the bright morning.

Seeing the girl, who couldn't have been more than twenty, made Elizabeth feel ancient even though, at thirty-four, she certainly wasn't old. At thirty-four, O'Keeffe hadn't even begun her flower paintings. She was experimenting with shape and color. And sleeping with Stieglitz, of course.

Elizabeth flushed. Why was she thinking about all that? The Georgia O'Keeffe who had held her breasts out to the camera was twenty years younger than the woman who had gone to Hawaii. A different person, whose romance with Stieglitz had nothing to do with the subject Elizabeth had chosen for her dissertation.

Her mind skittered from Stieglitz to Ben, and the fleeting outlandish fantasy of what it would be like to face Ben the way O'Keeffe had faced Stieglitz. Really, she couldn't imagine it. Not like that, with no purpose other than to be seen. Then her thoughts shifted again, back to the moment of shocking connection in the Tai Chi studio that might or might not have been real.

Another student brushed past her, and Elizabeth realized that she had stopped walking, frozen in place on the bottom step. Embarrassed, as if her thoughts had been visible, she adjusted the strap of her messenger bag and hurried down the path that led to the library. She strode rapidly, with more purpose than she felt, her fingers scraping against the rough bark of the trees.

She rounded the corner, and there was Founder's Lawn. Five people were arranged in a zigzag across the grass, arms raised in *The White Crane Spreads its Wings*. Practicing. Or maybe that wasn't the right word. They weren't preparing for something that would happen later. They were doing Tai Chi right now.

Elizabeth scanned the faces, heart pounding like a teenager's. She made herself conjure a vision of Ben, Daniel, and Katie around the dinner table. It didn't matter because Richard wasn't there—only three young men, an older woman with cropped white hair, and the woman in the blue yoga pants.

When they finished the sequence, the woman in yoga pants ran up to her. "Want to join us?"

Elizabeth shook her head. "I can't. I don't know the movements well enough." Even if she did, she couldn't imagine displaying her body in public like that. She could see that the woman was about to insist, so she said, "Not yet. Soon. When I've taken a few more classes." Then she remembered Mr. Wu. "If we *have* more classes. Have you heard anything?"

"It was some kind of heart thing," the woman said. "He'll be okay but he needs a little time to recover." Elizabeth felt a pang. *Oh, well.* Then the woman continued. "Apparently Richard talked to his daughter last night. You know, the tall guy, the one who caught him when he fell? Anyway, Sifu told the daughter to tell Richard we should keep working together until he can return. Come to the dojo. Help each other." Elizabeth stared at her, and the woman nodded encouragingly. "It's on the website. She put a notice up."

Elizabeth wet her lip. "So we should come on Wednesday? Do what he told Richard?" She tried not to emphasize the word *Richard*, but the two syllables seemed as loud as a clarion. She wanted to say it again, more evenly. *Do what he told Richard.* Five words, of equal weight.

"Exactly." The woman offered a benevolent smile. "I'm Juniper, by the way."

"Elizabeth."

"You sure you don't want to join us?"

"I'm sure. I'll see you on Wednesday, though."

"Beautiful," Juniper said. "It's the best way to help Sifu recover. You know, work together to generate positive energy."

"Yes. Right." She gave Juniper a quick wave, then turned and headed across the quad. She passed the library, a stone edifice with carved lions guarding the front entrance, and the small modern building next to it that was used for public lectures and faculty presentations.

Beyond the library and the lecture hall was a road that led downhill, past the admissions office and three interconnected greenhouses.

Suddenly Elizabeth knew where she needed to go. The botanical garden was one of the school's showpieces, a must-see stop on campus tours for prospective students and their families. She glanced at the visitors parking lot next to the admissions office. Empty. It was early. The botanical garden would be a good place to wander, alone.

She followed the S-shaped path to the entrance at the midpoint of the central greenhouse. A woman with spiked hair and big copper earrings was unlocking the door. She looked up when she saw Elizabeth. "I'm a bit late opening up, I know. We're supposed to open at nine but it's been one of those mornings."

"Take your time. Please."

The earrings swayed, banging against the woman's cheeks. "I really apologize. My student intern hasn't arrived yet, and I'm swamped. I won't be able to help you find anything until he comes."

"It's fine," Elizabeth assured her. "I'm not a botany student. I just want to meander around in a quiet place."

"Ah. That we can do." The woman smiled. "Meander as much as you like. I'll be in my office." She gestured toward a hallway on the left. "If you need anything."

Elizabeth smiled in return. She was glad there was no one to hover and try to be helpful. The silent, moist greenhouse—like a small Hawaii—was what she wanted.

She made her way through the maze of tables and tall potted shrubs. Morning light filtered through the glass. The smells of dirt and flowers rose up around her, earthen and sweet. The woman must have turned on the automatic mister because warm vapor began to seep from invisible vents.

Elizabeth opened the plastic door to the special room where they housed the tropical plants, like the ones O'Keeffe had painted in Hawaii. She thought of *Hibiscus with Plumeria*, the painting that had become the signature piece for the Hawaii collection. A gorgeous and elegant composition, each flower rendered so differently, yet forming a single vision. Elizabeth could see the painting in her mind, as vividly as if it were right there in front of her. The utter softness of the hibiscus, and the mysterious dark place, like a hand reaching upward, calling the eye to follow. A glimpse of sky, blue shapes, exactly the right amount of blue and yellow.

The hibiscus flowers in the greenhouse were red, magenta, orange, dazzling in their glory. O'Keeffe's flower was muted, the palest pink, its folds so soft you could almost feel them, just by looking. Elizabeth bent forward to examine the real flowers more closely. Something else was different, besides the color. Her gaze moved to the sign on a post, next to the exhibit. "Hibiscus flowers," she read, "are perfect flowers, also known as complete flowers, because each has both male and female reproductive structure, consisting of both pistil and stamen, as well as petals, sepals and a receptacle."

She grew still. The hibiscus in O'Keeffe's painting had an empty center. With O'Keeffe's meticulous attention to color and form, it made no sense. If a botanical element was missing, it wasn't accidental.

O'Keeffe had stripped the flower of its sexuality. There was no thrusting blade in the center, offering its stigma and filaments. Instead, just a flimsy inverted stem, like a feather. Diminished, descending, insignificant.

Elizabeth felt the heavy wet air press down on her. Why did O'Keeffe paint the hibiscus that way? She'd studied the real flower, knew what it looked like. Was she castrating it? Making it pure and virginal? O'Keeffe's flower seemed nude, vulnerable, yet the dark center promised something more.

O'Keeffe had said: *It is only by selection, by elimination, and by emphasis that we get at the real meaning of things.*

Elizabeth was alone in the greenhouse. There were no other

visitors at this hour; the botanist was off in her office; the intern was absent. She bent over the hibiscus plant. Quickly, she pinched off its yellow center and stuffed it in her pocket.

Three

Elizabeth's sister Andrea was sprawled on their navy-blue couch, ankles crossed on the end table. A glass of Ben's good Côtes du Rhône was balanced on her stomach. "If my abs were tight enough," she told Elizabeth, "I bet I could keep this thing from wobbling without even touching it." She eyed the wine as if daring it to spill, then laughed as she grabbed the stem with a deft manicured hand.

They were having a pre-dinner glass of wine at Elizabeth's apartment while Ben and Michael, children in tow, went to pick up the pizza. Daniel and Katie loved the occasional family get-togethers, partly because they adored their cousin Stephanie, and partly because it was the only time Ben allowed them to have pizza.

Andrea gave her stomach an affectionate pat, as if it were a well-behaved child. "And my abs *are* tight, if I say so myself." She held her glass aloft and pointed it at Elizabeth, who was curled in the opposite armchair. "Here's to abs and boobs." She raised the glass another inch. "To looking good."

Seriously? Elizabeth couldn't help wincing. Of all the things a person might toast.

Well, that was Andrea. It always had been.

"Don't give me that eye-roll," Andrea said. "You have something against looking good?"

"I'm not against it. It's not what I'd toast, that's all."

"Party pooper." Andrea took a swig of her wine, then grinned at Elizabeth over the top of her glass. "Besides, looking good—and knowing you look good—is the surest way to keep those home fires stoked. And *that*, as everyone knows, is the secret to a happy marriage."

Elizabeth set her own glass on the coffee table. "That's a bit simplistic, don't you think?"

Andrea shrugged. "If it is, that's because it's true."

This time Elizabeth didn't even try to suppress her eye-roll. Really, it was such sloppy thinking. *It's how I see things, so it must be true.* Her sister wasn't stupid. It was only that Andrea had no idea—she hadn't been trained and didn't care—about unpacking the assumptions behind a declaration like that or questioning what it really meant. *It is what it is.* The philosophy of someone who pirouetted through life.

Andie and Lizzie. As different now as they'd always been, even as small children. Elizabeth, settled at a child-sized desk, studiously pushing pyramids and cubes through the proper holes in her shape-sorter bucket, while her sister draped herself in their mother's gossamer scarves, tossing the ends in the air like fairy wings. Elizabeth could remember the satisfying plonk of the blue and red shapes as they dropped through the cutouts in the plastic lid.

She gave Andrea a dry look. "Not everyone sees life the way you do."

"Everyone who wants to please her man does."

"If that's your priority."

"It's one of them," Andrea said. "I mean it, Lizzie. Men don't stray if things are interesting at home. No one goes looking for what they already have." She flung Elizabeth a quick glance. "I'm just saying."

Her sister's way of trying to be helpful, but it wasn't. Elizabeth pressed into a corner of the armchair, wrapping her arms around her knees. If she wanted help with her marriage, which she didn't, Andrea was the last person she would turn to. You didn't ask for directions to the ocean from someone who had lived in it her whole life.

"Honestly," she said, "is that all you ever think about?"

"It's all I think about when I think about Michael." Andrea flashed another impish grin. "And what about you, Lizzie? Griddle hot enough for you and Ben?"

The casual coyness of the question—as if they were college roommates having a merry exchange of bedroom tales—was like a slap. Elizabeth knew her sister hadn't meant to be cruel; it was just the way Andrea talked. Another time, she might have lobbed the quip right back. *Hot enough* was a matter of opinion, so yes, she and Ben paid their twice-monthly dues, each making sure the other got the requisite satisfaction. But tonight she couldn't pretend, couldn't even try to. A wave of dizziness swept over her as she remembered—no, not a memory but a jolt into the present, as if it were happening again, right now—the way Richard had looked at her, into her, her knee touching his shoulder as he knelt by Mr. Wu.

The hell with it. Andrea could probably tell what her sex life was like, just by looking at her.

"It's never been hot enough." She grabbed her wine glass and drained the Côtes du Rhône. Then she set the glass on the table with a defiant thud.

Andrea's playful expression was gone. "I kind of thought so." To Elizabeth's surprise, her sister's voice was kind. "I can help you fix that."

"I doubt it." Andrea had no idea what it was like to swim in such tepid water; you couldn't fix something you didn't understand. "Thanks, but no thanks."

"I mean it, Lizzie. It's dangerous to ignore a problem like that."

Elizabeth wound her arms around her knees again. "Couples are different, that's all."

"That's just psychobabble. The question is if you're happy."

"No one's happy all the time."

"Well, duh. It's what you do about it when you're *not* happy."

"You focus on other things."

"Wrong. You spice it up." Andrea gave her an arch look. "Maybe take a little side trip. Bring back a fun souvenir."

Oh please, Elizabeth thought. Andrea would never take a *side trip*, and she would never put up with Michael taking one either. She was just fishing. Or showing off, seeing if Elizabeth would react.

Well, she wouldn't. Determined to match her sister's casual tone, Elizabeth said, "You think Michael's ever strayed?"

"Oh, he might have." With a languid movement, Andrea lifted her hair away from her neck. "He does have some new little tricks in bed, so he must have picked them up somewhere." She gave a conspiratorial smirk. "Not that I mind. Might as well reap the benefits. Ramp up my own game."

Elizabeth watched as Andrea wound her hair into a twist on top of her head and then shook it free. Thick and luxuriant, it spilled down her back.

"It's all part of the allure," Andrea said. "I want Michael to look at me and not be sure what I know or what I'll do next." She caught Elizabeth's eye and grinned. "Don't look so unhappy, Lizzie. It's not some kind of terrible deception. It's all part of the dance."

Elizabeth tightened her arms, pinning her knees in place. From the hall, she could hear running footsteps and children's laughter. The door burst open. "Pizza!" Daniel announced.

Stephanie, a year older, elbowed in front of him. "With sausage *and* pepperoni." She threw her father a smug look. "Daddy said we didn't need both but I said we did, and Uncle Ben said it was okay."

"It's fine," Elizabeth said. She uncurled herself from the armchair, relieved that her conversation with Andrea had been cut short. "Daniel, can you put the box on the table and get the napkins?"

Katie wriggled out of Ben's grasp and ran to throw her arms

around Elizabeth's legs. "Napkins," she demanded, meaning: whatever he gets to do, I get to do too. Gently, Elizabeth pried her fingers away. "Will you sit next to me, sweetie? You can help me make a face with the pepperoni circles."

"I want to sit next to Aunt Lizzie." Stephanie put her hands on her hips. "Can I, Mom? Can I?"

Elizabeth turned to Andrea, her eyebrow raised in amusement. *Were we like that?* Then her gaze shifted from Andrea to Michael, and the amusement vanished. She watched Michael wrap an arm around Andrea's shoulder and pull her toward him.

Stephanie was clamoring to be heard. "I want to make pepperoni faces too. And onions. Onion eyelashes."

Elizabeth tried not to care that her sister's husband was beaming as if he'd captured the brass ring. Marriages were different. She'd told Andrea that, only moments earlier. The same way that sisters were different.

Their mother had drilled that into them when they were small. *Everyone has different gifts.* She liked to tell people: "Lizzie's our little bookworm, and Andie's our little pixie." A tidy equation, easy to capture in nine short words. The pronouncement was always followed by the ladylike coda: "But we love them exactly the same."

Elizabeth remembered being confused. Of course her parents loved them the same. She had never questioned it, so why did her mother have to make a point of saying so?

She'd thought *different gifts* meant that people gave you different prizes—except Andie always got the ones that counted, like being chosen to dance onstage, at night, in makeup and a silver tutu.

"The ballet teacher can only take a few girls for the party scene," her mother had explained. "But we are so, so proud of you Lizzie. Your story was picked for the school anthology—no other fourth grader, only you! Andie gets to be in *The Nutcracker,* and you get to be a famous author."

Her mother knew very well that there was no comparison between a dumb story about a magic bracelet and wearing a silver tutu at night on a real stage. It was mean of her to say they were the same.

Elizabeth refused to go to the performance. "I'll pretend I didn't hear that," her mother said. "You're too smart for that kind of pettiness." Then she gave Elizabeth a firm smile. "Besides, next time, Andie will come and clap for *you*."

Only it hadn't ever happened. There was one time when it might have. Elizabeth had been a junior in high school, and they needed girls for a musical version of *The Little Mermaid*. All she had to do was wear a bikini top made of pretend seashells and strike sultry poses while the girl playing Ariel did her solos. Her friend Marissa's older brother was the director, and Marissa assured Elizabeth that the part was hers. Elizabeth wanted to be in that play as much as she'd ever wanted anything. But her mother discovered that the matinee was the same time as the advanced placement qualifying test, and that was that.

Michael's jovial voice jolted Elizabeth back to the present. "Sit where you like, Stephanie darling," he said grandly. "As long as I can sit next to your mother and play footsies under the table."

Did he have to talk like that? Elizabeth thinned her lips. Then she felt a tug on her sleeve. Katie had found a box of dryer sheets. She held them out proudly.

"Those aren't *napkins*," Daniel said. "You're stupid." Katie's mouth dropped open, readying itself for a howl.

Ben looked up from cutting the pizza. "Liz. Why are those things with the food items?"

"They weren't," she muttered, although they were. She grabbed the dryer sheets in one hand, Katie's arm in the other. "Come on everyone, let's eat."

She helped Katie onto her booster seat as the others found places around the table. "There's milk or iced tea," she said. "And, of course, Côtes du Rhône."

Daniel craned his neck. "I want a coat."

"It's not a coat you wear," Ben told him. "It's a drink for grown-ups."

"Speaking of Côtes du Rhône," Michael said, "send that bottle this way." He looked at Andrea. "More, sweetheart?"

"Always, as you know."

Elizabeth bent her head as she cut Katie's pizza into eighths. *Just get through the meal*, she told herself. *Ignore them.*

Still, she couldn't help wondering what Ben was seeing and feeling. He had to be reminded, as she was, that they never flirted with each other. They never alluded to sex at all. It struck her, suddenly, that for people who loved to talk, their coupling was oddly silent.

But not hopeless. Surely not hopeless.

She raised her eyes, hoping that Ben would feel her looking at him and that something would pass between them. A glimmer, a possibility.

Ben was staring at Andrea and Michael. His eyes were hooded, his mouth pressed in a downward arc. Elizabeth assumed, at first, that he was eyeing them with disapproval—a Ben expression, full of superior aloofness. But it was a different look, complicated and unfamiliar, a troubled wistfulness that sent a shiver right through her bones, as if she'd caught a glimpse of someone she didn't know or wasn't supposed to see. Her knife hovered in the air above Katie's plate.

"Mama, pizza." Katie pulled on her arm.

Elizabeth inhaled. The air was sharp in her chest, like needles. Did Ben feel it too? Did he wonder what they were missing, grieve for something he didn't understand?

For a wild crazy instant, she wanted to push away from the table and run shrieking out of the room—or else grab Ben by the collar and make him proclaim what he loved about her—but Elizabeth Crawford didn't do things like that. Instead, she fixed her eyes on Ben's silent profile. Inconceivable that he didn't feel the heat of her gaze.

Michael handed a wine glass to Andrea. The scarlet liquid shimmered as it caught the light.

Elizabeth forced herself to turn her attention to Katie. "Pizza's all ready for you, pumpkin. Let's count the pieces."

She accompanied her daughter's happy chant, then tucked a napkin into Katie's collar and busied herself doling out extra cheese, passing out napkins, refilling the children's cups. She repeated the silent mantra: *Just get through the meal. You can do this.* Stoic Aunt Lizzie, pretending not to notice the current that still sizzled between Andrea and Michael after a decade of marriage.

"Anyone else want more wine?" Michael asked, waving the bottle.

"I'm fine," Ben said. "I've got what I need."

Really? Elizabeth thought. Do you?

Andrea set down her glass and looked around the table. "You know, we're really quite an attractive little group." She pointed a rose-tipped finger at each child. "Stephanie, you have the most perfect skin, and Katie angel, you're a total peach with those lips of yours. And Daniel—those bedroom eyes, not that you'll appreciate them for a dozen years."

Stephanie sat up straight. "I have nice eyes too, right Mommy?"

"Of course you do, my darling." Andrea's face brightened. "I know. Let's play a game. It's called, What's Your Favorite Body Part?"

"My eyes," Stephanie said promptly.

"Too many to choose from," Michael quipped, "though I'd say my pitching arm is right up there in the top three."

"We all know what Elizabeth's is," Ben said.

Andrea laughed. "Anyway, we know what it *isn't*."

Elizabeth recoiled, stung by their mockery. Andrea must have seen her shock because she added, "It isn't your *eyes*, Lizzie. That's all I meant. Stephanie already dibbed that."

But it wasn't what Ben had meant. Elizabeth felt the anger—hot, dark, so unlike her usual restraint. It spread through her body like tinder to a lit match. It was too much to bear. How hard she tried, putting his coffee cup, and her nightshirt, right where he liked it. How unloved and unbeautiful she felt. How unfair it was to glimpse something she couldn't have.

She turned to Ben. "Apparently you get the joke. Care to let me in on it?"

Seconds passed, silent and cold. Wasn't he going to answer?

Nothing. That was the answer. There was no favorite part. No part he loved.

Elizabeth gripped the edge of the table, her fingers digging into the wood. "Fine. It isn't anything. No favorite part. Everyone happy now?"

Andrea looked alarmed. "Lizzie, it's just a game."

"For you." She could feel them staring at her. Could this really be their composed and cerebral sister, sister-in-law, wife? She didn't blame them for being astonished. She'd never had an outburst like this before.

From the edge of her vision, she saw Ben slowly folding his napkin. He still hadn't spoken.

"Well, you're silly to feel that way," Andrea said, "so let's give you a brand-new body part you *can* love." Quickly, she corrected herself. "I didn't mean, like, a transplant or a nose job. I mean a new hairdo. You'll feel tons better. Really."

Elizabeth had to laugh. It was such an Andrea-like solution. Andrea was a hair stylist. She'd been offering a makeover for years, insisting that Elizabeth would be amazed by what highlights and a bit of layering could do. Elizabeth had always refused, explaining that she didn't have the time or inclination.

"It's okay," she told Andrea. "I appreciate the thought."

Then she looked at Ben. *Well?* she signaled. *Your turn to speak.*

He coughed, fingering the edge of his napkin. "Like Andie said, it's just a game."

At the word *game*, Daniel snapped to attention. "My body part is my butt crack," he announced.

Stephanie let out a peal of laughter. "Butt crack!"

Happy with his success, Daniel repeated the magic words. "Butt crack."

Katie waved a triangle of pizza. "Butt crack, butt crack."

Ben rose, hands flat on the table. "Enough. Time for bed." Daniel looked stricken, but Ben's towering figure left no doubt that he meant what he said.

"Oh dear, my fault," Andrea apologized, but she was laughing too. "Come, Stephanie, let's say goodbye."

Reluctantly, Stephanie pushed away from the table and cast a longing glance at her cousins as Ben ushered them down the hallway. Elizabeth felt a sweep of relief: the evening was over. She stood and began to gather the plates.

Michael retrieved their coats and bent to give Elizabeth a kiss on the cheek. "Thanks for hosting. Tell Ben I'll see him on the squash court."

"Our place next time," Andrea added. Then she whispered, "Don't get so upset, Lizzie. You take everything way too seriously."

"Define *too*," Elizabeth muttered, but she didn't think Andrea heard. She walked them to the door and kissed Stephanie goodbye. The click of the deadbolt was crisp and comforting.

Behind her, she heard Ben re-enter the room. "The tub's filling. I told the kids they could play till it's ready."

Without turning, Elizabeth murmured, "Okay." Wasn't he concerned, or curious, about why she had cried out?

He took a step closer, and she heard him sigh. "I know the kids got a little wired but frankly, I think you overreacted. Andie was just having a little fun."

Elizabeth wheeled around. "Oh? And what exactly *is* my favorite body part? You seem to think everyone knows. Well, I don't."

"I was making a joke."

"Let me in on it."

He hesitated, and Elizabeth saw the complicated look cross his face again, the same look he'd had as he watched Andrea and Michael. Longing and confusion, as if he were lost in a strange city. Then his features shifted, rearranging themselves into the familiar apologetic look that was part grimace and part regret. "I just meant, you know, your brain."

"That's not a body part."

"It was meant to be funny."

"It wasn't."

"I understand. I'm sorry."

Elizabeth wiped her tears with the back of her hand. "I am too."

She could feel the unsaid words linger in the space between them, all the unnamed things they were sorry for. But it was the wrong moment, the bathwater was filling. It was always the wrong moment.

"I'd better check the tub," she said. She stepped around him, wondering if he might reach out to touch her. He didn't—or, if he did, she'd missed it, already on her way out of the room.

Four

When Elizabeth stepped out of the freight elevator onto the fourth floor landing, she was surprised to see that nearly all the cubbyholes were filled with the shoes, caps, and sweaters of the other Tai Chi students. People had come, even without Mr. Wu. She tucked her purse and shoes into one of the remaining spaces on the top row. This time she left her phone. She'd worn sleek black leggings instead of baggy cargo pants, and there was no pocket for even a slender iPhone. Then, on impulse, she pulled off her knitted headband and thrust it into the cubbyhole next to her shoes.

Determined not to be nervous, Elizabeth pushed through the curtain that separated the anteroom from the dojo. Richard was standing in front of the room, legs parallel, knees flexed. A spare elegance. It wasn't, she realized, that he was classically handsome, yet there was something compelling—mesmerizing, really—about his presence. She blinked, as if clearing her vision, and slipped into the back row.

"I heard from Sifu," Richard said, "through his daughter. He needs to recuperate for a few weeks, but he wants us to keep practicing." He looked around, his eyes moving from person to person. "I'll call out the postures and we can try them together. Sound okay?" Several people murmured their assent. Clearly, Richard was the most advanced pupil, and no one seemed to mind that he had assumed the role of proxy for Mr. Wu.

"Okay, then. *Parting the Wild Horse's Mane*. We'll do it slowly." He lifted his arms. Elizabeth caught her breath. Really, it was like watching a work of art, as if one of Georgia's flowers was unfolding in front of her. She tried to copy his movements.

After forty-five minutes Richard looked at his watch. "I know we have the studio for two hours, but this feels like enough for now. What do you think?"

Juniper, the woman in the blue yoga pants, answered at once. "Agreed. The important thing is to keep the flow of positive energy."

Richard gave a polite nod. "Until next week, then. Sifu's daughter gave me the key, so I'll take care of locking up."

Elizabeth followed the others out of the studio—self-conscious, suddenly, in her sleek dance-like attire. The other students were wearing sweat pants or loose karate outfits with belted tunics. When she'd pulled her workout leggings from the drawer, relic of the days when she had time to go to the gym, she'd felt lithe and serene. Now, though, aware that Richard was watching them leave, she felt inappropriate and exposed.

She took her belongings from the cubbyhole, stepping into her shoes as she slung the purse over her shoulder. "Elevator's here," someone called.

Elizabeth hurried to the elevator, edging next to a woman in a bright knitted cap. The woman smiled at Elizabeth as she adjusted the brim. "Weather's getting cold. Anyway, my ears are."

Elizabeth gave a start, remembering the headband. "Oops, wait. I forgot something." She caught the door before it closed. "Can you hold the elevator a second?"

"Folks need to get going," one of the men said. "We'll send it back up for you."

"All right." She stepped out, and the doors slid shut. She rounded the corner, back to the wall of cubbyholes, then stretched and felt for the headband. After a minute's scrabbling she found it and stuffed it in her purse.

Then, without warning, the lights went out and the alcove where Elizabeth was standing turned dark. Quickly, she retraced her steps to the landing.

Everyone was gone except Richard, who was waiting for the elevator. "Ah. Sorry. I didn't mean to scare you with the blackout. I thought everyone had left."

Elizabeth indicated her purse. "I forgot my headband." She gave what she hoped was a casual flick of her wrist. "Anyway, I don't scare easily."

Richard met her eyes, and Elizabeth felt the same stunned help-lessness she'd felt the week before, as if her willpower was sliding down her back and pooling at her feet. It might be true that she didn't scare easily, but something in her was terrified right now.

The elevator pinged and the doors opened. Richard gestured. "You first." Elizabeth stepped inside, shivering as he reached across her. "I have to lock the floor," he explained. He twisted the key in the brass button marked with the number four. Elizabeth nodded. Was she supposed to answer?

"You're new to the class," he said.

"Very."

"Bad luck, having Sifu absent when you've hardly begun."

That smoldering gaze again—the same way he'd looked right into her, when Mr. Wu fell. It didn't feel like bad luck, not if it had led to this moment. She tried to look indifferent, though her heart was beating like mad. "Taking it slow is fine with me."

Lord. Her pulse jumped right out of her skin. That sounded like a coy little double entendre; what did he think she had meant?

Richard dipped his chin, as if agreeing with her plan. "We still have an hour of class time. I'm free if you are. Want to have a cup of coffee?"

The elevator crept along its cables. The arrow over the door moved from three to two. Richard was leaning against the side of the elevator now, hands in his pockets, ankles crossed. Elizabeth could almost touch the mysterious magnetic something that seemed to radiate from his skin. She swallowed. "Sure."

"There's a place down the street."

It was perfectly acceptable, she told herself. She had coffee with people in the Art History department all the time.

He guided her to a tiny café squeezed between a shop that sold vintage clothing and another that sold comic books and posters. There was an empty table in the back, two wicker chairs at right angles around a marble circle. A waiter gave the marble a quick swipe with a white cloth. "You guys know what you want?"

"Americano, please," Richard said.

"Same for me."

The waiter gave a sage nod, as if approving their choice. "Right back."

He left, and Richard pulled his chair closer. "I don't know your name."

"It's Elizabeth. And you're Richard. Juniper mentioned you the other day. She said you're the senior pupil."

"Years don't always translate to proficiency."

"Even so, it's hard to be proficient without them." She moved her chair closer, as he had, and propped her elbows on the table. "What else do you do, besides Tai Chi?"

"Mr. Wu would say that the *what else* doesn't matter."

"But it does to you."

"Ah yes." He smiled. "I study people, try to capture their souls."

"You're just trying to sound interesting."

"Am I succeeding?"

She felt herself blush. Was this what people did when they flirted? Whatever it was, she liked it. "I'll let you know."

He turned serious. "I'm a photographer. I do portraits, not those wedding-and-baby things. Real portraits."

"What does that mean?" *Real portraits.* It sounded arrogant, as if he thought other photographers were imposters.

Richard tilted his head. Then, almost meditatively, he touched her arm, just above the place where her elbow rested on the marble. "I try to see how people's faces and bodies reveal who they are. It doesn't have to be the whole face or the whole body. But there's an essence, everyone has it. If you can see it, you try to show it in the photograph. You pick that thing, and you show it, through a fragment." He moved his fingers, the merest inch, to the edge of the bone. "It can be anything. A jawline, a wrist. An elbow."

Elizabeth was acutely, shockingly, aware of his fingers on her skin—a place she'd never paid attention to that was, now, the most intensely alive part of her.

Say something, she told herself. Quickly. Before—what?

She cleared her throat. "On the other hand, a portrait might not be a single image. The personality, the whole person—you can't contain it in just one photo." She hesitated, afraid she had revealed too much. "Stieglitz said that, about his photos of O'Keeffe. A collective, cumulative portrait. That's why he had to take so many pictures of her. More than three hundred, over twenty years. Different parts of her, at different times."

"That's interesting."

"Oh. Am I the interesting one now?" She couldn't believe she'd said that. It was reckless, sassy.

He smiled again. "Quite."

Elizabeth felt the heat rise up in her face. She had to keep talking or she'd lose herself in the sensation of his touch. "Of course, sometimes a small part is all you need, like you said. *I often painted fragments of things because it seemed to make my statement better than the whole could.* Georgia O'Keeffe said that."

"How come you know so much about Georgia O'Keeffe?"

"I'm studying her. For my dissertation."

The waiter appeared with their coffee. "Did you need cream, milk, skim? We have almond hazelnut half-and-half."

Reluctantly, Elizabeth moved her arm so the waiter could set the mugs on the marble. "Nothing. Thank you."

"Nor for me." Richard reached for his cup. He blew across the hot surface. "Why did you pick O'Keeffe?"

"I've always been drawn to her. She painted these tiny, tiny things, and then these incredible mountains. She wanted us to take the time to look, to really see."

"We have something in common, then."

"Oh?" She could feel the place on her arm where he'd touched her, as if his fingers were still there. An inch of skin, shimmering, sizzling. "We do?"

He took a sip of coffee. "We have a passion for how art can reveal what's really there. You have O'Keeffe, I have Weston. If I could take photos like his—the beauty of a single cabbage leaf, spread like a woman's hair—I'd die a happy man."

She nodded. "The peppers and the sea shells."

"And the nudes." Richard took another sip. "It was the only way Weston, egoist that he was, could let himself adore the women he loved—Tina Modotti, Charis Wilson. Through his camera. That's my theory, anyway."

"*When you take a flower in your hand and really look at it, it's your world for the moment.*"

"Your words, or Georgia's?"

"Georgia's again, I'm afraid."

"What do you have to say, Elizabeth? For yourself."

She felt her flush deepen. "I don't know." She thought of how O'Keeffe had let herself be seen through Stieglitz's lens—hands, breasts, stomach—and then, through her own art, had made the world more visible. There was something she wanted to say about that, Richard was right. But she hadn't found it yet, that central thing. She hoped she might find it in the Hawaii paintings. O'Keeffe's transitional time, the little-known interlude that bisected her life.

Finally she said, "I guess I'm still looking for it. Pondering the paintings, her life. Waiting for that *aha*."

Richard set down his cup. "Well, don't count on the *aha* finding you. You might have to go out and look for it."

Elizabeth could hear the groan of an espresso machine, the clatter of dishes. The rich dark smell of coffee filled her nostrils.

In Maui, there had been the scent of flowers. Water dripped along the rocks.

"O'Keeffe spent nine weeks in Hawaii," she said. "That's what my dissertation is about."

"Why did she go to Hawaii?"

"That's the thing. I think she was drawn, at first, by a fake Hawaii. You know, the whole fantasy, hula dancers and palm trees and ukuleles? It was everywhere in the 1930s. That's why Dole sent her there, to paint a pineapple they could use in their ads. O'Keeffe was probably expecting the exotic paradise she'd heard so much about."

"That wasn't what she found."

"No. Not at all. I think she had to reject the fake Hawaii in order to understand the real one."

"Or accept that it was fake and enjoy it anyway."

Elizabeth began to laugh, as if Richard had made a joke. Then she stopped, unsure. "Maybe."

A long moment passed. Again, she heard the groan of the coffee machine. A shiver slid up her spine, a frisson of danger.

With a jerk, she pushed away from the table. "I really have to get going. Let me pay you for the coffee."

"No need." He gave her a slow smile. "You can buy next time."

Next time. Elizabeth's pulse shot upward. Had he noticed the wedding ring? Did he care? Anyway, why should he? It was just coffee. "Fair enough," she said.

Without saying goodbye, she turned and strode out of the café. She wondered if he was watching her walk away, her strides long and sleek. Parting the air in front of her as she moved. Parting the wild horse's mane, revealing the path ahead.

"The problem," Harold Lindstrom said, "is that you've made up your mind in advance about the Hawaii period, so you're looking for evidence that you think can prove your theory, instead of letting the theory emerge from the evidence. That's not how scholarship works." He leaned back and peered at Elizabeth over the top of his glasses. "At least, not in the dissertations that I chair."

Harold Lindstrom was head of the Art History department, a distinguished scholar, and a coveted mentor. It would be foolish to take his goodwill for granted.

"Yes, I understand. But I can't help thinking there's something there." Elizabeth remembered the words she was supposed to use. *A finding that can contribute to the scholarly literature.*

Ask him for guidance. That was her role, as the rising star she intended to remain. "How do you think I should approach the question?"

Lindstrom adjusted his glasses. "You have to widen your lens. Look at the whole of O'Keeffe's life and work, and then see how the Hawaii period fits in."

Widen the lens. The metaphor made Elizabeth think of Richard, but she pushed the image aside. "Yes. That makes sense." Then she frowned. "You know that 600-page biography of O'Keeffe you told me to read? I looked through it, and there's less than one page about her time in Hawaii. Not even one page, can you believe it? And no mention of any specific painting she did there, except that damn

Pineapple Blossom she did back in New York, after the Dole people got so mad at her. The author calls her Hawaii paintings sterile, harsh, angular." She mimed wiping her hands. "Done. Dismissed."

"And that makes you angry." The corners of his mouth twitched in amusement.

"Damn right it does. Those paintings mean something."

"And how are you going to figure out what they mean? If they mean anything. After all, they're only twenty of the two thousand paintings she did in her lifetime."

"But they're such a specific group of paintings! And she did them in such a short period of time, in a place that was the exact opposite of the desert, where she lived before and after." Elizabeth could see that she had his attention now, so she pressed on. "Stieglitz showed them at his gallery, later that year. Some of the critics were ecstatic, some were disappointed, the way it always is. I found this one review that really struck me. Henry McBride, the *New York Sun*." She rummaged through her papers. "Here's what McBride wrote: 'She annexes the islands with a glorified fishhook.'" Elizabeth looked up at Harold. "He was referring to her two fishhook paintings, of course." Then she returned to the clipping. "Anyway, then he said: 'Only the most intelligent fish would feel equal to such beautiful and reasonable bait.'"

"Meaning, the ordinary joe wouldn't understand what O'Keeffe was trying to convey?"

"It does sound elitist, but maybe that was just McBride. For sure, he thought the paintings demanded something from the viewer, a special kind of effort. And yet they've hardly been studied. Not compared to her other work."

"And you think you can bring that *special perception* to your analysis?"

"I think I can try."

"How?"

She winced, but it was a fair question. "I need to focus on the paintings. Consider them for myself, no matter what other people have written or said. Really look at them."

"That sounds a bit subjective." His skeptical look returned. "Where's the scholarship in that?"

"It'll be there. I promise." Elizabeth hunted in her bag again. "Here. You told me I could use the *White Bird of Paradise*, to get started." She pulled out a sheaf of papers. "It's a strange plant, not soft and pretty like other flowers. Like Georgia, in a way." She handed him a photo of the painting. "I keep asking myself why she chose this particular plant. Why not some other flower—Hawaii had plenty of them—or the regular Bird of Paradise, with all those gorgeous colors?"

Harold looked at the paper, then gave it back to her. "And what did you conclude?"

Elizabeth pulled in her breath. "I think it was the whiteness. That was Stieglitz's color for her. He saw her as white, pure, flawless."

"He saw her like that in 1939, when she went to Hawaii?"

"I don't know. It was mostly in the '20s, when he was obsessed with taking photos of her." She searched for the right words. "By 1939 he'd hurt her dreadfully with his infidelity. Maybe Georgia wanted to take something back that she'd given him."

"Be careful," Harold said. "You're an art historian, not a psychoanalyst."

Elizabeth knew she was treading a delicate line. "I understand. But I do think she was trying to accomplish a very specific aim."

She looked at the picture again, tracing the outline of the bracts with her fingertip. "Those long white leaves remind me of the antlers she painted later, or the ribs. So yes, the author of that book was right, there's a cold and angular quality to the painting. Yet there's more to it. Look, there's the tiny heart of the flower, right in the center, you see? Only you can't really get to it, everything around it's too sharp, like a spiked fence. Her core's still there, her female essence, but it isn't accessible, not like it is in the flower paintings she did earlier."

Harold pursed his lips. "An interesting approach, Ms. Crawford. As I said, however, your job is to make scholarly use of the evidence, not to fantasize. You're not O'Keeffe's therapist."

"I'm just explaining why I think there's something here to study." She dared to offer a faint smile. "O'Keeffe painted a heliconia again, you know, almost thirty years later. In 1967, when her eyesight was starting to fail. She called the painting *Not From My Garden*."

"I never heard of it."

"Hardly anyone has. It's a fragment of the heliconia, not like the one she painted in Hawaii. But it means she hadn't forgotten."

Harold nodded. "Well, give it a try." Then he placed his palms on the desk, signaling that the conversation was over. "As I said, put everything in context, look at the paintings she did before and after."

"Exactly. Widen the lens."

"Are you humoring me, Ms. Crawford?"

"Never, Dr. Lindstrom." Her smile deepened. "Thank you. Really."

Elated, she ran down the two flights of stairs. She could do this.

This. The word held something enormous. Larger than making her mark on art history.

This.

Find her own Hawaii.

Five

Elizabeth leaned against the heavy wooden desk that had been placed at the front of the classroom. It was a massive, authoritarian piece of furniture, like a bulkhead or a judge's bench, symbol of her command. A joke, really. She was a part-time instructor, not an actual professor. Not yet. But with Harold Lindstrom as her patron, she would be.

Arrayed in front of her were two dozen students in metal chairs with folding armrests. Behind her, a screen had been pulled down to cover the chalkboard. Elizabeth studied the class. "What do you think?" she asked. "Does feminist art depend on the artist's identity or is it a particular type of product? Can anyone create feminist art, man or woman, if they have the right intention?"

A young woman in the first row answered at once. "It's an attitude," she said. "The motivation behind the art." There was a tiny jewel above her right nostril, blinking as it caught a glint of sun. Electric blue highlights fanned out in spikes from the part in her hair.

Elizabeth gave a courteous nod. "Could we say that attitude is an aspect of identity? A set of beliefs that lead one to embrace a specific identity?" She paused. "Ms.—?"

"Pennington," the young woman said. "Naomi. And you could say it, if you want, but I didn't."

The class snickered. "A figure of speech," Elizabeth replied, trying not to react. "If you prefer, I can restate the question. Does feminist art depend on the artist's purpose or on the type of artwork that's produced?"

"It's both." The same young woman. Naomi. She thrust out her chin and the jewel flashed, a reddish flare. "You need both, or else you're saying one thing and doing another. Talking the talk instead of creating art that leads to liberation."

Elizabeth had to make an effort not to snicker herself. Art that leads to liberation. It sounded like a slogan on a coffee mug. "It's an interesting dilemma." She looked around at the class. "Think of the well-known female artists, prior to what we'd call feminist art. Frida Kahlo, Georgia O'Keeffe, Berthe Morisot, Mary Cassatt. Brilliant and independent, all of them, daring to work in a milieu controlled by men. Yet none considered herself a feminist painter."

There was a note of belligerence in Naomi's voice. "But they were, whether they thought so or not."

"Are you sure?" Elizabeth was starting to dislike the young woman. Don't, she warned herself. Letting it get personal was the surest way to lose control.

She slid off the edge of the desk and went to the podium. "Take Cassatt and Morisot. They were hardly rebels, out to challenge the status quo. They painted in the style of their time, confined to subjects they were permitted to paint—mothers, children, nature. Gorgeous paintings, certainly, but conventional. Safe. Not like this."

She pressed a button, and an image filled the screen. *Some Living Women Artists/Last Supper.* Each disciple around the table had the face of a woman artist. Georgia O'Keeffe's face was superimposed on the visage of Christ, in the center.

"Mary Beth Edelson painted this in 1972," Elizabeth said, "as a kind of feminist manifesto. At some point—I don't remember when, or who reported it—the story is that Gloria Steinem went to visit

O'Keeffe with a bouquet of roses, but O'Keeffe refused to see her. She wanted nothing to do with the feminists." Elizabeth gave a wry grimace. "That didn't stop them from turning her into Jesus, of course."

She crossed her arms, regarding the class. "Was O'Keeffe a feminist painter? She didn't even want to be seen as a female painter. Only as a painter." The next slide showed one of O'Keeffe's urban landscapes, geometric and surreal, followed by a painting of a cow's skull. "Nothing like the sweet domestic scenes of Cassatt and Morisot."

"So O'Keeffe painted that stuff on purpose? To break down a sexist barrier?" A different student this time, thank goodness. A tall girl with glasses and a tattoo that crept across her shoulder and neck, a blue-green vine that reminded Elizabeth of a snake.

Elizabeth studied the slide. "I don't know. I think she just painted whatever she wanted to paint."

"But no people," the girl said.

"No. Never." Only herself, Elizabeth thought. In the rocks and flowers and bones. She waited a moment, then continued. "O'Keeffe was the first woman to have a solo retrospective at the Museum of Modern Art, the first woman to command an enormously high price for one of her paintings. So here's my question: is it sexist and patronizing to differentiate *firsts* by gender? Should gender matter, or only the achievement itself?"

Again, Naomi answered. "It matters because it gave her power. It made people—men—take her seriously."

"True," Elizabeth said. "None of the male artists would grant her that, back when she was starting out. But she kept painting."

"They only noticed her when they thought she was painting vaginas," Naomi said.

"She insisted that she wasn't."

Naomi wrinkled her face, and the jewel sparkled. "Denying it was part of the thing. It only made the men more into it." The class laughed.

Elizabeth clicked the remote again. Judy Chicago's *Dinner Party*. "Other artists, later, were clear that they were celebrating the female anatomy. Louise Bourgeois, with her pregnant nudes. Carolee Schneemann, certainly." She could feel herself beginning to grow defensive, as if Naomi had insulted Georgia, or her. "O'Keeffe was clear that she wasn't. She was trying to examine the world around her, show it to us in new ways through color and form. Her paintings weren't symbols. They were themselves."

She knew she was talking about O'Keeffe too much. The students wanted to talk about the outrageous things the feminists had done to make their point, the performance art, the explicit use of their own bodies. It was ironic—terrible, really—that the year Edelson painted *Some Living Women Artists*, with O'Keeffe as Christ, was the very year O'Keeffe lost her vision to macular degeneration and stopped being able to paint.

"How do you know?" Naomi said. "Maybe those flowers *were* paintings about sex, even if she didn't want to admit it, maybe not even to herself."

Elizabeth fought the urge to slap her hand over Naomi's mouth. She wanted to shield Georgia from this girl with her blue hair who kept talking as if she knew her.

"Personally," Naomi went on, "I think using your own body in your art is the highest form of feminist expression. Being part of the artwork, not just a name on a plaque. Otherwise it's a cop-out, a way to play it safe."

Elizabeth frowned. "Are you saying that painters are less authentic than performance artists?"

The student with the tattoo waved her hand, and several others looked like they wanted to speak. But Naomi had the floor.

The girl kept her eyes fixed on Elizabeth's. "I'm asking *you*, specifically. How far would you go to use your own body to make a statement about what you believe? Not a lot of words on paper, but a real statement that puts you right out there, where it counts. How far, if everyone knew it was *your* body?"

Elizabeth could hardly believe what she'd heard. No instructor would be expected to respond to a boundary-defying question like that. She could feel the class watching to see what she would do.

"An interesting question, Ms. Pennington. I think I'll appropriate it, credit to you of course, for our next homework assignment. Three pages, with citations. How should an artist locate herself in her work—as creator or part of the creation? The invisible architect, holding the power, or the visible subject?" She looked around, pleased with herself. "Due on Tuesday."

She caught Naomi's eye. The young woman looked annoyed. "You turned it into words after all."

"It was a good question," Elizabeth said. She gathered her papers and aligned them against the desk with a brisk whack. "Too good to limit to a single person's reply."

She knew she'd finessed a moment that had, in fact, upset her. She had no idea how she would have answered Naomi's question.

Elizabeth hurried out of the building, headed for the library. Naomi had disturbed her, and now she had to know: was what O'Keeffe had done, in modeling for Stieglitz, different from mere posing? Was she the co-creator of the photographs he had taken of her, in charge of her own exposure, or simply his subject, like a plant or a chair? Was it his art, or theirs?

The question had nothing to do with her Hawaii thesis but she didn't care. The urgency to understand made her run down two flights of stairs and halfway across the campus before the ping of her cell phone stopped her in mid-stride.

It was a text from Lucy, the babysitter. "Can u pls call?" Lucy had written, followed by two sad-faced emojis and the word "Katie."

Katie alternated between stubborn independence and hysterical neediness, a classic case of the Terrible Two's. Elizabeth considered ignoring the text and claiming that she hadn't seen it until she was on her way home. Lucy had been told not to call unless it was an emergency; a sad face hardly qualified as an emergency, and yet—

She opened her list of contacts and tapped *Lucy*. Lucy answered at once. "Oh, thank goodness I reached you. Katie's beside herself."

"What's the matter?" Elizabeth pictured a cracked skull, blood, doctors wheeling Katie off to surgery. Then: no. Lucy wouldn't have described a cracked skull as *beside herself*.

"Her tummy hurts—way too many raisins, to be honest, plus *someone* didn't nap this afternoon—and she's worked herself into a state about how she needs her mommy to make her feel better. I've tried everything. Singing, the stroller, even that DVD she loves, you know the one."

Elizabeth closed her eyes. "I'm sure you have."

"For real, Mrs. Crawford. I wouldn't have bothered you otherwise."

Was she going to have to make Lucy feel better too? What about her trip to the library, the two hours of quiet work she was expecting, was entitled to? Elizabeth sighed as Georgia's image receded. "Why don't you put her on?"

A pause, and then Katie's plaintive little voice. "Mama?"

"It's me, sweetie."

Katie's whimper rose to a heart-rending sob. "Mama, *come*. Come *now*."

Elizabeth flipped through her mental catalogue of responses. You know Mama has to work right now, but I will be there very, very soon. And when I get there, we'll read a special story and make pasta for dinner, the kind shaped like little bows. Actually, we'll read ten stories and have ice cream for dinner. Whatever you want, as long as you stop crying and let me do what I want right now.

Yet she understood Katie's despair. Katie wanted one particular thing, and that wanting was making her desolate. Elizabeth crossed the library off the list of things she might do that day—as if Georgia had given a sigh of resignation, put on her clothes, and walked away.

"Yes," she told her. "I'm on my way right this second." Katie made a little mewling sound. It was almost a moan, but Elizabeth knew it signaled relief. "Give Lucy the phone, pumpkin, so I can let her know."

She heard the phone clatter to the floor and then, a minute later, Lucy's surprised voice. "You're coming? Really? I'm okay till five, like we agreed."

"No, it's all right."

"You know she'll drop off for her nap the second we hang up, right? She just wanted to hear your voice, but she won't know what time you actually get here. You could come at five and she'd never know the difference."

It was probably true, yet Elizabeth had to keep her word. The reason Katie would relax and tumble into sleep was because she trusted her mother. Tricking her would be unforgivable. Besides, Katie was a woman, or would be. Once a woman lost her trust in someone, it was hard to regain.

Georgia, though childless, would have understood. After Stieglitz hurt her so deeply with his infidelity, she never gave herself to him again the way she had in those early photographs. They stayed married—ardent correspondents, forever connected—but the purity of her trust was gone.

"I told her I was coming, and I will."

"Well, it's up to you. We're here, whenever."

"Daniel's okay?"

"In heaven. The Morgenstern twins are here today."

Lucy had several families with rotating schedules. Elizabeth had heard about the Morgenstern twins, a boy and girl Daniel's age, but had never met them.

"The three of them have been in the sandbox for hours," Lucy said. "Apparently they've invented a world populated by dinosaurs, Barbie, and Luke Skywalker."

Which was probably why Katie refused to nap. She'd fight to be included, no matter how tired she was. "Daniel won't want to leave, then."

"I think Phoebe's picking them up early, so it works out."

Elizabeth had never met Phoebe either, mother of the Morgenstern twins, although she'd been curious about her. Their schedules hadn't meshed until now. "Perfect. See you soon."

When she arrived at Lucy's house, Katie was sound asleep, just as she'd expected. Daniel and the twins were in the sandbox. Seeing her approach, Daniel glowered and turned his back. *If you're not really here, I don't have to stop playing.* A woman in a bright red sweater and big sunglasses strode into the yard behind Elizabeth. She had tousled light-brown hair, one side longer than the other. Elizabeth didn't know if the uneven look meant a chic expensive haircut or a working mother, like herself, who didn't have time to get it properly trimmed. Andrea, the expert on hair, would have been able to tell.

The little girl grabbed a plastic brontosaurus from her brother, checking to see if her mother was going to yell. Her brother howled, grabbing it back. The woman in the red sweater laughed. "I'm sure you two were getting along just fine until I got here. Pretend I'm still driving." Then she turned to Elizabeth, pushing the sunglasses to the top of her head. "I try to think of them as unevolved little gnomes instead of miniature humans who ought to know better. It helps me get through the day." Her smile was wide, generous. "Phoebe," she said. "Humble servant of Ruthie and Rex."

"I'm Elizabeth. And that's Daniel. Katie's zonked out somewhere."

"Wouldn't I love to join her. It's been a long day."

"Tell me about it." Elizabeth motioned to the bench, and the two women sat, a silent agreement passing between them to take a minute before collecting their children. Elizabeth felt something relax deep in her body as she settled next to Phoebe, this person who was like her. There was a comforting familiarity in the wrinkled clothes and messy hair, the dry comments and exhausted affection. Her questions about nude models seemed contrived and far-away.

She sat with Phoebe in companionable silence until one of the twins, the girl, ran across the yard demanding a tissue. "A tissue instead of your sleeve?" Phoebe declared. "What's the world coming to?" She opened her purse, her forehead creasing. "No tissues? I can't believe it. What a bad mother."

"Here," Elizabeth said. She held out a travel packet. "Would you like to pull one out yourself?" The girl nodded and plucked a tissue from the pack.

"Say thank you," Phoebe prompted.

"Thank you," the girl shouted, running back to the sandbox, waving the tissue like a victory flag.

Her brother jumped up. "I want one too."

Phoebe sighed as Elizabeth handed him a tissue of his own. Lucy opened the back door. "Want me to rouse Katie for you?"

Elizabeth glanced at Phoebe. "In a minute. It's nice to sit here."

"Sit, then." Lucy paused. "Do you need me or—?"

Phoebe waved her away. "We're good."

Elizabeth settled against the bench, oddly at peace. It was a beautiful afternoon. The birds were darts of blue overhead; sunlight glittered on the maple leaves. She could hear Daniel making happy growling noises as he banged two dinosaurs together. She smiled at Phoebe. "Do you bring Rex and Ruthie here every day?"

"Mostly when I have a big freelance job. I'm a web designer. I do the tech part."

"That sounds interesting." It didn't really—mathematics and formulas and all those strange symbols—but Elizabeth tried to sound friendly.

"Hey, it's a living."

"Well, it's good to have work that stimulates you."

"More like, work that pays the bills. If I want to be stimulated, that's what Charlie's for." Phoebe gave Elizabeth a merry sideways look. "Charlie's my husband. Sometimes we drop the kids with Lucy so we can sneak in a little afternoon delight. Of course, Lucy always thinks I have a last-minute rush job." She lowered her voice, even though Lucy couldn't possibly hear. "Makes Charlie and me feel like we're stealing a screw behind our parents' backs. All part of the thrill."

Elizabeth could tell that Phoebe was expecting her to smile in return, but her body had turned to stone.

Was everyone's marriage sizzling but hers? It was one thing to tell herself *oh, that's just Andrea, showing off.* But Phoebe too? It meant that she, Elizabeth, was the exception. Someone whose stimulation came from looking up obscure articles on Academic Search Premier and not from an hour of afternoon delight.

Mercifully, Daniel and Rex rose in unison and ran to the bench. "We can't go home yet," Daniel announced. "We're not finished."

"Guess what?" Phoebe said. "Neither are we." He looked confused, so she added, "The mommies." She gave Rex a playful poke, shooing them back to the sandbox. Then she grinned at Elizabeth, the grin shorthand for so many things. How predictably unpredictable the children were. How endearing and maddening, the little tyrants.

The secret wordless language of mothers. That much, they shared. But there was something else they didn't share. The thing Elizabeth couldn't say aloud.

The lovely relaxation was gone. Phoebe wasn't like her after all.

Her cell phone dinged inside her bag. She reached down and pulled out the phone. A text from Ben. "Can u swing by cleaners to pick up my shirts? They close at 6."

A chill spread across her body. Not even middle-of-the-night delight. Only shirts and chores and polite turn-taking, even in bed. She crammed the phone back in her bag.

"Anything important?" Phoebe asked.

Elizabeth looked into Phoebe's bright innocent eyes. Then she bolted upright, as if an unseen hand had grabbed her collar and yanked her off the bench. Anger and envy and shame surged through her veins—at Phoebe's red sweater and tousled hair and the happy marriage she couldn't possibly deserve. At O'Keeffe, the way she and Stieglitz used to run up the stairs to their bedroom at Lake George, laughing and unbuttoning their clothes as they took the steps two at a time. At the way everyone knew that her favorite body part was her brain.

"I need to get going. Sorry."

"Really?" Phoebe looked disappointed. "Well, maybe another time."

Elizabeth twisted her neck in the direction of the sandbox. "Daniel," she yelled. "Get your shoes. We need to go."

"You just *said*."

"Well, now I'm saying something else."

"Why? Why do we have to go?"

Elizabeth crossed to the sandbox and grabbed his shoes and socks. "Because we do," she snapped. "Up."

"But *why*?"

Because. Because I'm married to someone who would never dream of sharing afternoon delight, and I hate this woman whose husband dreams of it, and does it, and I cannot stay here one more instant.

"But I'm not *finished*. It's not fair."

No, it wasn't. Nothing was fair. Or maybe it was. Maybe you got exactly what you chose, back when it seemed like the right thing to want.

"Please don't be difficult. I have to get Katie."

From a thousand miles away, Phoebe asked, "You sure everything's okay?"

Elizabeth couldn't look at her. "It's later than I realized, that's all." She raised her voice. "Lucy, we're leaving." She hurried inside and scooped up the sleeping Katie. Katie fluttered her eyelashes and settled onto Elizabeth's hip. Daniel, still complaining, trailed after her.

Elizabeth pulled open the car door but Daniel, taking a belated stand, refused to get in. "You can't make me. We're not finished."

She wanted to smack him. Instead, she gritted her teeth and tried her best mommy psychology. "I understand. You weren't finished."

Daniel wouldn't budge. Elizabeth shifted Katie onto the other hip. Time for more serious measures. "I know what let's do. Let's stop on the way home and get chicken nuggets."

"Chicken nuggets?" His face lit up, and he scrambled into the car. Elizabeth placed Katie in the car seat next to his. Daniel watched her arrange the harness, then wrinkled his brow. "Daddy said we shouldn't eat chicken nuggets."

Elizabeth clicked his seatbelt. She wanted to say, "We don't have to tell Daddy." But that would guarantee that *Mommy got us chicken nuggets* would be the first thing Daniel announced when he saw his father. "He meant not every single day."

Daniel seemed to accept her answer. He settled into the car seat, dropping a plastic T-Rex onto his lap. He must have taken it from Lucy's house but Elizabeth was too tired to scold him.

We don't have to tell Daddy everything.

She started the car and veered right at the stop sign, toward the fast food restaurant, not the cleaners.

Six

It was one of Ben's squash nights, which meant he wouldn't be home for dinner. They'd agreed that it was easier for Elizabeth to cook for Daniel, Katie, and herself while Ben went out for a late supper with his gym partners. She didn't mind the separate dinners, especially tonight. The day had exhausted her—dealing with that aggressive student, Naomi, and then rushing to Lucy's house and getting blindsided by Phoebe Morgenstern's offensive happiness. Chicken nuggets in the car was the perfect meal after a day like that.

When they got back to the apartment, she let Daniel and Katie watch *The Lion King* while she folded laundry, emptied the dishwasher, and—in a burst of guilt—ironed one of Ben's almost-clean shirts. Then she gave them a quick bath and tucked them into bed with her best rendition of *Where the Wild Things Are*.

"Daddy reads it better," Daniel told her.

"I'm sure he does," Elizabeth said. "Maybe he can read it to you the next time he puts you to bed."

Tomorrow, in fact. When she went to Tai Chi. Stayed afterward for another Americano.

You can buy next time.

Once she had kissed the children goodnight and closed the door, Elizabeth went to her makeshift desk in the corner of the dining room.

She had an hour, maybe longer if Ben was enjoying his after-squash dinner. Not the two hours she had hoped for at the library, but every hour counted when you had a dissertation to write. She opened the drawer and pulled out the folder where she kept her reproductions of the Hawaii paintings.

I decided that if I could paint that flower on a huge scale, you could not ignore its beauty.

That was what O'Keeffe said, when people asked her about the flower paintings. An audacious declaration, believing that you could force people, or trick them, into seeing what you saw and loving what you loved. O'Keeffe had done that with the pelvis paintings too—made people look through the opening she had placed in the very center of the canvas, into the emptiness beyond. There was no way to look at one of her pelvis paintings without doing what she wanted and being drawn into that void.

There had to be something like that in the Hawaii paintings, Elizabeth decided. Something intentional, a secret idea that bridged flowers and bones—that connected the beauty O'Keeffe wouldn't let people ignore and the void she found later, in the desert.

Elizabeth opened the folder. She wanted to look at all the pictures at the same time—for clues, shapes, hieroglyphs that O'Keeffe began to use, specifically, in Hawaii. Delicately, she removed her copies of the two hibiscus paintings and placed them side by side. *Hibiscus with Plumeria*, elegant and stylized, with its clean sure lines. When the New York Botanical Garden mounted its landmark exhibit, bringing the Hawaii paintings together for the first time in almost eighty years, *Hibiscus with Plumeria* was the image they chose for the catalogue and posters. But there was another hibiscus painting that no one ever mentioned—missing from the show, missing from all the books about O'Keeffe in Hawaii, because no one had been able to track it down, not even the exhibit's conscientious and determined curator.

Then, three days after the exhibit opened in New York, the missing painting surfaced. Titled simply *Hibiscus*, it was the lead work at a Christie's auction, sold by one private collector to another. Too late to be included in the exhibit, even if the owner had agreed, and shown only twice in eighty years—once by Stieglitz in 1940 and once at a Memphis gallery in 1998—the painting flashed across the art world like a comet.

The other hibiscus, Elizabeth thought. This one was entirely different. Soft and dreamlike, the gentle rippling edges of the flowers flowing into each other like clouds against a glint of turquoise sky. The same yellow and pink in the two paintings, the same subject, yet utterly unalike. The carefully defined shapes in the first painting, the sunlit blur of the second.

Elizabeth grew still, noticing something else. In the second painting, *Hibiscus*, the reproductive center was there, where it belonged. Smaller than in the real flowers she had seen in the greenhouse—a gentle curve, while the stigma in the real hibiscus shot up bold and straight from a blood-red center—but there nonetheless.

Georgia had portrayed the flower both ways. *Hibiscus with Plumeria* was a painting to admire, from the outside. *Hibiscus* drew you close, asked you to soften.

Slowly, Elizabeth pulled the 'Iao Valley paintings from the stack and laid them in a neat row along the desk. The plush descending contours, folding into the center. Georgia had plunged the viewer right inside the valley itself. There were no edges, no perch where you could stand and observe the scenery. You had to enter, participate.

Elizabeth put a hand on the desk to steady herself. She was dizzy, hot, confused, as if Georgia had tricked her into an experience she hadn't agreed to. Then she shook the rest of the papers out of the folder. What was O'Keeffe's approach to Hawaii? That was the point. She was a scholar. You couldn't write a dissertation about sensations.

She studied the paintings, the ginger and lotus and papaya. There was no clear chronology, but the assumption was that O'Keeffe had started with familiar subjects, anchoring herself in what she knew— particular flowers, none of which, ironically, were native to Hawaii— before opening to a larger vista. No palm trees or hula dancers. She'd plunged right into the Hawaii she could touch and feel.

Georgia hadn't been seduced by a fake paradise. Richard had been wrong, or maybe just teasing her.

Elizabeth pushed the pictures aside and opened one of her reference books. She wanted to look at some of O'Keeffe's later work. *The Black Place*, painted four years after her return from Hawaii. It was the same composition as the 'Iao Valley paintings—a jagged streak that bisected the landscape into dark rounded hills, pulling everything into its vortex—only this time the terrain was dark and desolate, unearthly.

What had happened to Georgia between 1939 and 1943?

Harold Lindstrom told her to look at what came before Hawaii and what came after. *Before* were ripe and feminine flowers, warm red hills. *After* were arid canyons, bones and skulls. The flowers in O'Keeffe's paintings, after the ones she did in Hawaii, were tiny hollyhocks. Nothing immense. Nothing that made sure *you could not ignore its beauty.*

As if, Elizabeth thought, Georgia had shifted from lushness to dryness—from female images, bursting with possibility, to dry sexless skeletons. But why?

She thought of O'Keeffe's early work, the irises and poppies. What could be more sensuous and alive? That was how the art world got to know her.

No, she corrected herself. They learned about O'Keeffe through Stieglitz's eyes, his lens, his photos of her—exposed, robust, grave, unafraid—and carried that image back to her paintings. When they looked at her paintings, they saw the woman in Stieglitz's photos. The art she modeled for had already defined her.

It was the opposite of what that student, Naomi, was talking about. Instead of embodying her own work, O'Keeffe became the embodiment of someone else's.

Elizabeth frowned, confused. That didn't sound like Georgia, so fierce and self-sufficient. Maybe it wasn't true. Maybe she really had been the co-creator of Stieglitz's photos, collaborating on a vision that needed both of them.

Then again, she might have simply offered herself. Not passively, but consciously. That too seemed an extraordinary thing. To let oneself be seen. Not filtered through an idea or description. *Here I am. My breasts, my hands.*

They had just become lovers. She'd been a virgin until she met him.

It was clear from Stieglitz's letters that he had been obsessed with O'Keeffe. His portraits grew more and more intimate, as if his camera was learning, or evoking, the astonishing richness of her sexuality. The letters weren't published until 2011, twenty-five years after O'Keeffe's death. Elizabeth had read them, avidly at first, then with a growing discomfort. Really, they were over the top. It seemed girlish and histrionic—unbecoming, for a man of Stieglitz's distinction—to be besotted like that. Yet the letters had verified what some of the art critics had already intuited. Elizabeth remembered what Lewis Mumford had written about Stieglitz's 1921 show—forty-five photos of a single subject, O'Keeffe, an audacious and revolutionary challenge to the conventions of the art world. Mumford had called the photographs "the exact visual equivalent of the report of the hand as it travels over the body of the beloved."

Elizabeth pushed away from the desk and strode down the hall to the master bedroom. She flung open the door. On the back was a full-length mirror.

When you took time to really notice my flower, you hung all your own associations with flowers on my flower, and you write about my flower as if I think and see what you think and see of the flower—and I don't.

That was Georgia's reply to a world that believed it had the right to interpret her paintings, to reduce what she was exploring—about form and contour and the way nature revealed itself—to a metaphor for something they had selected. It had filled her with rage.

Georgia didn't need to use flowers as a stand-in for her sexuality. She expressed her sexuality directly, when she posed for Stieglitz.

Elizabeth unbuttoned her blouse and let it drop from her shoulders. In her mind, she saw the photo Stieglitz had taken of O'Keeffe with her hair loose, shirt open to reveal her breasts. O'Keeffe was languid, unsentimental, utterly present. *Here I am.*

A longing rose up in her, huge and terrible. To be the woman in that photo. To be known, wholly, without words.

"Mama?"

She wheeled around. It was Katie, clutching her bunny. "Mama." Katie stumbled forward and hurled herself around Elizabeth's legs.

"Oh, pumpkin." Elizabeth knelt and gathered her daughter close.

"Mama."

She felt the warm, impossibly tender flesh against her own. A bad dream? Or an over-wrought toddler whose sleep cycle had gone haywire from napping too late in the afternoon?

Elizabeth inhaled the purity of her daughter's scent. "Do you need a special song? A sleepy-time song?" Katie nodded. "Well, then. That's exactly what you shall have."

Pulling her shirt closed with one hand, she hoisted Katie with the other arm. She carried Katie down the hall, back to her own bed, singing softly. Just as Katie drifted back to sleep, Elizabeth heard Ben open the front door.

Quickly, she fastened the shirt buttons, all the way to the collar. "Liz?" he called.

She stepped out of the children's room and closed the door. "I was putting Katie back down. Bad dream, I think."

"Ah. All okay now?" Before she could reply, he said, "I'm hopping in the shower. The hot water was on the fritz at the gym."

Elizabeth waited in the hall until she heard the click of the shower door and the steady stream of the water. Then she slipped back into their bedroom.

The bathroom door was ajar, the sound of the shower spilling into the room. She pictured Ben soaping himself. He had a nice body, a body any woman might want next to hers. It was the body she had made up her mind to get, to have, when she met him. And she'd done it, she'd convinced him they would be good together. Elizabeth lowered herself onto the edge of the bed, remembering.

She had seen right away that the match made sense. Their taste in movies and music, their views on government and ethics and the environment. It all fit, and it was time to get started on the life she envisioned. Maybe he didn't burn for her, but he admired her—her intelligence, her principles, so much like his.

Elizabeth remembered the moment when she knew she had won. They'd been at a party, in someone's apartment. Somehow they had ended up in the kitchen, arguing. It was a tiny kitchen with white metal cabinets and grimy yellow tile. Ben was leaning against the sink, arms folded. He thought they should break up.

"It's just not there between us, Liz. I feel like we're being dishonest. With ourselves, each other. With the world."

Elizabeth's skin had turned cold. Oh no, you don't, she'd thought. You don't get to drop me like that. Her brain shifted into a hyper-alertness. She could out-think him.

"It's not dishonest if we're open and truthful with each other. We're not caught up in some Hollywood fantasy. We're clean, real. That's what matters."

Ben looked unsure. "What if that's not enough?"

"You mean, theoretically? If someone else comes along who you think would be better, just say so. But until then, it's a lot of speculation." She shrugged, feigning indifference. "I'll take reality over speculation."

It had worked. He hadn't found a way to contradict her, or maybe there wasn't anyone better, or maybe they simply got used to each other. Eight months later they were married. Elizabeth was a beautiful bride; everyone said so. She wove real flowers into her hair and wore a vintage dress made of lace the color of palest tea. They read from Rilke and Khalil Gibran. A Baroque trio played in the background.

After the ceremony they climbed into the waiting limos and headed to the reception. Swept inside the restaurant by her friends and relatives, Elizabeth laughed and lifted the lacy hem of her dress off the curb. Ben's four-year old niece looked at her in awe. Feeling regal and happy, she held up her glass for the first toast. She turned to Ben with a radiant smile.

He was holding the champagne glass in front of him, gazing at it thoughtfully. Elizabeth recognized the expression on Ben's face; he was figuring out exactly the right thing to say. He raised his head and looked out at the crowd. Elizabeth looked too, because he was.

Suddenly, fiercely, she wanted him to be looking at her, not at their guests. It was like a bell, calling to her from the distance: why wasn't he looking at her? Today of all days, his eyes should be riveted on her, his bride.

When he turned to her, finally, it was with a quiet nod. *All right, then.* A pact. Elizabeth's breath seized in her chest. His words, uttered in that tiny kitchen months before, echoed in the banquet hall. *What if that's not enough?*

She had made it enough. Until now. A chorus of voices—Georgia's, Richard's, Phoebe's—were whispering the same chant. *Maybe it isn't.*

Okay, Elizabeth told herself. You're smart. If it's not enough, do something about it.

There was a metallic thunk as Ben flipped the shower head, and the sound of running water came to a halt. She straightened the bedspread, tugging at an edge that wasn't even crooked, as he opened the bathroom door. Steam poured out, filling the bedroom like the fog in the 'Iao Valley.

Ben was drying his hair with a lime green towel. Water beaded on his limbs, matting the hair on his chest and stomach and calves. Elizabeth watched as it dripped onto the tiled floor. He wasn't a terrible man. He was a good father, conscientious and dependable. She had someone right there, if she wanted to take off her clothes and put her arms around a male body. Husbands and wives did that.

She blinked. Her face was wet. Steam, or sweat, or tears.

Ben wiped his chest. "This is the second time in a month the hot water's been screwed up at the gym. It's getting ridiculous."

Elizabeth watched the towel swipe up and down across his skin. She thought of the torsos the Greeks liked to sculpt, the nude photos of Georgia. The naked body wasn't intrinsically erotic. It was the beholder's gaze that made it so.

The words formed in her mind. *Look at me. Want me.*

A yearning swept over her. A wave cresting from its unbearable weight. An ache, exquisite and terrible, tipping her forward into an ocean of longing.

She longed—no, she needed, the way lungs needed air—for Ben to look at her and whisper, "My god, you're beautiful." The way Michael looked at Andrea. The way Stieglitz looked at O'Keeffe.

If only he would truly desire her, she was certain she would respond—a flower opening to the sun, the blades dropping away, scattering, to reveal the delicate inner core. A white crane, lifting its petaled wings.

What did a woman need to do, or be, for a man to look at her that way?

Elizabeth bit her lip. *Try.* A woman could try.

Ben reached behind the door for his robe. "Did you happen to pick up my shirts?"

It took Elizabeth a moment to understand what he was talking about. The cleaners. "No, sorry. It took forever to extract the kids from Lucy's." A half-truth. "I ironed the striped one for you, though. It was still clean."

You can buy next time. His fingers on her elbow. A slow meditative touch that could mean everything or nothing.

Stupid. A fantasy, a useless distraction.

Try. Ben was her husband, right there in front of her.

He belted the robe and crossed in front of Elizabeth to the open closet. "Speaking of clothes." He pulled a rectangular box from the top shelf. "I wanted to wait till the kids were asleep."

She frowned. "For what?"

He handed her the box, his expression sheepish. "I picked this up yesterday. After the business with Andie, and how upset you got?" Slowly, Elizabeth took the box from him. There was no wrapping, no tape. The lid came off easily. Inside, beneath a flap of tissue, was a peach-colored negligee. Ben gave an awkward shrug. "I thought it might help you feel sexier."

Elizabeth stared at the silk. She couldn't look at him, though she knew he was waiting for her to respond. And how was she supposed to respond?

With gratitude? For taking the time to pick this out. For trying, finally.

Or with shame, because they shouldn't have to try so hard.

Or with the fury that was shoving its way to the surface—a wild, blood-red rage at the way he was putting the onus on her. Tossing a Victoria's Secret costume at her like an assignment, instead of looking at himself and what he could do to make it better, what they could do together.

She jerked away from the garment, tears filling her eyes. Why now, after ten years? Because she'd embarrassed him in front of Andrea and Michael?

She didn't want the negligee. She wanted to be a woman who would wear a negligee—because of who she was, already, not because *I thought it might help you feel sexier.*

No. This was insane. Her husband had bought her a gift. Any woman would be happy if her husband gave her a negligee.

Elizabeth bit back her tears, hoping Ben hadn't seen. Then she traced the edge of the strap. It was thin, delicate, descending into a lace-trimmed V. She could stop analyzing its presence and put it on.

"It's pretty." She could feel Ben waiting, hoping for more. She lifted the garment from the tissue. It weighed nothing at all. She tossed her head, the way Andrea might. "Doesn't do any good for it to sit there in the box, does it?"

"That's what I was thinking."

She could hear the restraint in his voice, as if he didn't want to appear too eager. It touched her, made her want to assure him that the gift had been a good idea, loving and brave.

She stood, the peach-colored silk draped over her arm, and went to the bathroom to change. The air was still wet with steam. She unbuttoned her blouse for the second time that evening and pulled off her slacks. The negligee fell into place over her shoulders.

Ben was waiting for her in bed, his bathrobe folded neatly on the back of the chair. Don't think, Elizabeth told herself. Just go to him. Be Liz the Lovely. Liz the Minx.

"Hey," he said, propping his weight on an elbow. "It looks great on you." He took her arm and pulled her onto the bed. "Or off you."

His arousal surprised her. Unless it was the middle-of-the-night pressure of flesh against flesh, they had to work at it. She'd learned to adapt, get what she needed, and then focus on him. He'd accepted that, followed the choreography with meticulous attention. Their lovemaking, like their marriage, was courteous and fair.

Tonight, in contrast, Ben's ardor was startling. It was the negligee, clearly. The prop was working. He slid his palm along her hip, and Elizabeth could feel his breathing sharpen. She ought to feel happy; it was what she wanted.

And yet. She didn't know what was missing, only that something was. The very thing she craved but had no words for.

See me. Want me.

Fingers on the skin just above her elbow.

Georgia, her robe open, offering her breasts.

Elizabeth felt herself begin to retreat, away from the present. She caught the movement, like catching a door with her heel. Again, she told herself: *Try.*

She reached up to stroke her husband's back, tracing the path of his vertebrae, down to the dip in his flesh. Ben shivered, pulled at the silk, and the negligee slipped to the floor.

Then she thought: *Wait.* Let's do something different. New little tricks in bed, like Andrea and Michael. She rolled across him, straddling his chest, drawing his hand between her legs where their bodies met. Like this. Not what we always do.

Ben obliged her for few minutes, then turned her onto her back—gently, yet leaving no doubt that he preferred the pattern they could count on. Elizabeth's heart sank but she forced herself to focus. He was hard; that was the main thing. If they failed, even with the negligee, it would be terrible.

She gave a low murmur, ran her hands along his spine, the way he liked. She was playing a role now—better than usual, so that was something—but she couldn't let him know. It would hurt his feelings, and she didn't want to do that. He'd gone to a store and bought a peach-colored negligee; he deserved whatever return gift she could offer.

Shutting her eyes, she let the sequence unfold. Unless she thought too much, the response was programmed into her nerves and skin.

A certain rhythm that her nipple liked, a certain kind of touch. She knew what she had to do—deliberately, dependably—until her body surrendered to the orgasm that always left her feeling sad and alone.

Ben gave the small moan that meant he could let go and take his turn. Elizabeth wanted to cry. Maybe he'd been right, all those years ago. *It's just not there between us.* She wondered if he ever thought about it or, like her, simply kept going. Then she felt his spasm, her own relief. Two high achievers, succeeding at the task they had set themselves.

The sorrow that filled her was too huge to contain. It poured over the sheets. Surely Ben could feel it.

He was already drifting toward sleep. Elizabeth reached across his chest to the nightstand and turned off the light. After a few minutes she could feel the slow steady breathing that meant he had fallen asleep. Carefully, so she wouldn't wake him, she rolled onto her side and touched herself between her legs. A light touch, hardly anything at all. Just enough to make the ache return.

Today was Ben's squash night. Tomorrow was Tai Chi.

Seven

Richard seemed to take it for granted that they would have coffee again, after Tai Chi. He waited for her by the elevator, falling into step beside her as they exited on the ground floor, then steering her away from the others with the barest touch on the small of her back. Elizabeth gave him an oblique look, and he smiled. "You have time for another Americano? You're buying, as I recall."

"I'm buying."

The words came easily, surprising her with their lightness. A sliver of caution slid into her pleasure, but she pushed it aside. She had a right to have coffee if she wanted.

The little café was closed. "Family emergency," the sign said. "Back on Friday."

"Ah well," she said, trying not to let Richard see her disappointment. "Too bad." She began to move away, ready to return to the bus stop.

"We don't have to give up so easily, do we? Come, let's walk."

Startled, she said, "Oh." Well, why not?

He steered her again, another quick touch, as they turned from the closed café and made their way along the darkening street.

They were taking a walk, that was all. People took walks all the time.

Richard slowed his pace. Around them, the dusk darkened to a silvery-blue. "You know, I looked at Stieglitz's photos of O'Keeffe," he told her. "You got me interested in what you said, about how he wanted to record the whole of a person—O'Keeffe, that is—by accumulating fragments, moments, parts of her."

"You did?" Elizabeth stopped and faced him. It was his eyes that made him seem so handsome, she decided. They were grey, deep set, framed by dark brows. They were fixed on her now, intent, looking straight through her skin.

"I did." He smiled again, a private look that made her pulse jump. "Stieglitz called his exhibit *A Demonstration of Portraiture*, though you probably knew that."

"Yes. I did know."

Richard nodded, and they resumed walking. "Stieglitz had this idea that he could show everything about one specific person. Every side of her, from those photos where she's staring straight at the camera—you know, deadpan, in that awful hat—to those gorgeously voluptuous close-ups. It excited him, as a photographer, because it was a whole new way of thinking about a portrait. Of course, he was crazy about her, but he was crazy about his own breakthrough too, as an artist."

"Some people said it was the same thing."

Richard laughed. "It's true. He couldn't have taken those photos of just anyone. They were uniquely her, O'Keeffe, because he never got tired of trying to see her, and to capture what he saw. That's the essence of portraiture, isn't it? The effort to see someone, and to convey what you see." He flashed another smile, light and disarming. "Of course, Stieglitz was a modernist, so he was interested in form. From that point of view, the photos were impersonal, abstract, universal." He inclined his head, as if surrendering to the paradox. "So you've given me a puzzle to solve."

"Maybe it was both."

"Ah. Good answer."

He guided her across the street. Behind them, the light changed from yellow to red. The evening wrapped around them like a shawl.

"I think it was Stieglitz's genius, as a photographer," Elizabeth said. "But it was O'Keeffe's genius too, as a model. To be able to include both. Be both."

"That's why the photos are so extraordinary." Richard's steps were even, unhurried. "O'Keeffe holds her breasts and looks right at the viewer, daring us to understand. Denying and heightening the eroticism at the same time. De-personalizing the image, and claiming it. Both, like you said."

Elizabeth was grateful that they were walking side-by-side instead of facing each other across the marble table. That would have been too much to bear.

Images swirled in her mind. Georgia, grave and introspective, arms raised, the dark mass of hair in the open armpits. Georgia, holding a breast. Herself, reflected in the bedroom mirror as she unbuttoned her blouse.

She began to talk. If she kept talking, the dangerous swell of feeling would recede.

"That was how Stieglitz saw her, you know. On the one hand, as this pure, ascetic, moral ideal. He talked about what he called her whiteness, a kind of lucidity and integrity that set her above everyone else, including him. And on the other hand, as the sensuous, uninhibited essence of womanhood. You can see it in O'Keeffe's own paintings too, those contradictory sides."

This time it was Richard who stopped walking. "Is that why you picked her?"

"I was talking about Stieglitz."

"And I was talking about you."

"You're the one who brought up the photos." Elizabeth's heart began to race. "You're the photographer. I'm just focusing on Hawaii. That was years later."

Richard lifted a shoulder. "Well, I'm no professor but it seems to me that you can't yank a group of paintings out of the middle of someone's life, out of the whole body of their work."

"That's what my adviser said."

"Wise man."

Elizabeth swallowed. Her hands hung at her sides, opening and closing, fingertips pressing into her palms. "I understand why I need to look at the art O'Keeffe created before and after Hawaii. But why would I need to look at the art she modeled for? What does that have to do with it?"

It was the question that had been building in her, ever since the blue-haired student, Naomi, tossed it her way.

"If you want to understand her."

The street turned black, silent, immobile. Nothing moved, not even the air in her throat. Elizabeth knew that O'Keeffe saw Stieglitz as a collaborator, an active and essential force that allowed her to bring forth the art that was inside of her. Was she a collaborator in his work, too? Did they produce two bodies of work, jointly? It wasn't a revolutionary idea; art critics had suggested exactly that. Yet there was something about the way she felt the possibility now. It was urgent, personal.

"All right. Fair enough."

Richard's gaze was keen. "You do want to understand her, right? Not just write some PhD thing with a lot of footnotes and citations?"

"You're relentless, aren't you?"

"Am I?"

A wave of dizziness swept over her. It was too dense, too close, as if he were offering her a choice. But she couldn't choose because she didn't understand what the choices were.

They began to walk again, past a row of apartments and a

convenience store. Oblongs of amber light flanked an open door. Ahead, Elizabeth could see a maple tree and a wire fence. The silvery-blue of the sky deepened to an indigo sheen.

Richard was still speaking. "Like I said, I got intrigued and went to look up Stieglitz's work. I hadn't looked at his photos in a long time." He glanced at Elizabeth. "Me, I try to find the essence of a subject, a single image. So it was interesting to see how Stieglitz tried to portray O'Keeffe through a kind of quantity. Everything. Neck, feet, arms." He shrugged. "But you know that, of course, as a Georgia expert."

"I'm not sure I qualify as a Georgia expert." Elizabeth slowed her pace. "It's curious, though, that most of his photos of her were taken before she got famous as a painter."

"You think he lost interest in her as a subject, once she got known for her own work?"

"Well, some people think the photos were the reason she got famous. They got a lot of attention."

"Because they were shocking? Exciting?"

"People called them immoral. Of course, a ton of people came to see them."

"Of course. Wouldn't you?"

He was playing with her. And she liked it.

Elizabeth kept her eyes on the ground. "You still think a single essential photo is the way to portray someone? Or did Stieglitz change your mind?"

"It depends on the subject. Some people, like your Georgia, need to be seen in a whole range of ways."

She wanted to ask, *And what about me? How do I need to be seen?* She didn't, though. Couldn't. It took all she had to keep walking.

The buildings gave way to a small playground with an assortment of children's equipment—slide, swings, see-saw—set on foam pads bordered by a cyclone fence. It was deserted but the gate was ajar. Motion sensors lit up the ground as they approached.

"Aha," Richard said. "Much better than a coffee shop." He opened the gate, beckoning Elizabeth inside.

A playground? Playgrounds were for Daniel and Katie. Feeling foolish, she followed him into the courtyard. The gate banged shut.

"So. What'll it be tonight?" He surveyed the possibilities. "The swings?"

Elizabeth wrinkled her nose. "I don't think so."

"Don't think, then." He caught her fingers in his and pulled her gently toward the swing set. There were two canvas slings and a toddler harness, suspended by heavy chains from a metal frame. "Truth or dare. When's the last time you've been on a swing?"

"Good grief. Decades."

"Well, then."

Did he really think she'd hoist her adult body into one of those contraptions? Elizabeth began to shake her head, insist that she couldn't. Then Mr. Wu's words blazed across her vision. *You try, and you can.*

She strode to the first swing, grabbed the chains, and sat down. Her legs were too long, knees poking up as she toe-walked backward on the foam padding. When she was a child, there had been dirt under the swings, not foam. She remembered—no, her feet themselves remembered—the particular sensation of digging into the dirt as she stepped back to gain lift, then letting go as she pushed forward, legs outstretched, back arched, face turned to the sky.

She pointed her toes, ready to pump, when she felt herself raised up from behind. It was Richard, his hands on the metal chains. He leaned forward and thrust her into the air. She wanted to say *no, wait* and *not so high*, but there was no time. Again, he grabbed the chains, pulled her back, and pushed. The world flew past. Buildings, stars. She returned, and he pushed again. Higher, this time. And then she was flying, helpless to stop it. All the way to the tip of the air, the place where she would surely vault upside-down over the top of the metal frame, though she didn't, but fell back again, only to be lifted up once more and thrust into the whooshing immensity of space.

Elizabeth opened her mouth and laughed. It was delicious. To surrender, just for those few minutes. Then she yelled, "Enough! Please. My poor stomach is doing flip-flops." Richard took hold of the chains and eased the swing to a stop. Elizabeth let her feet drag on the ground. She was still laughing. "Whew. I don't know how kids do it."

"They like the flip-flops. The wildness."

"I suppose that's it." She stood and dusted off her leggings.

"What about you, Elizabeth?" Richard asked. "How do you feel about wildness?"

She froze. Sweat began to pool in the hollow of her collarbone.

He was trying to seduce her. This was what seduction felt like.

She began to tremble, a quiver rising from her soles all the way up the back of her neck. She hoped Richard couldn't see, though she was sure he could.

It was only an instant—the merest pause, as if the sky had stopped its wheeling to await her response—and then she tossed her head. "Well, I'm not a fan of anything that makes my stomach lurch." She looked at her watch. "Anyway, it's late. I'd better be going."

She almost said *going home,* but that would draw attention to the fact that she had a home. He'd never asked about that. She wondered what he thought about her life, or if he thought about it at all. Well, why should he? They weren't on some kind of date. It was just a walk, after Tai Chi.

"You still owe me an Americano, you know." Elizabeth's eyes jumped to his. He was smiling.

She stared at him. Every inch of her was alive.

"I know. I won't forget."

—

Before and after. That was how Elizabeth needed to orient herself so she could write a dissertation that would knock their socks off.

Before. In 1932 O'Keeffe painted *Jimson Weed/White Flower.* Everyone in the art world knew the painting; it sold for $44.4 million at a Sotheby's auction in 2014, making O'Keeffe the highest-selling woman artist of all time. Then, in 1939, while she was in Hawaii, she painted *Bella Donna,* a strikingly similar composition. It was because of the resemblance between the two paintings that the O'Keeffe Museum put *Jimson Weed* up for auction. The curators didn't think they needed both.

Bella Donna, one of the last of O'Keeffe's oversized flower paintings: a close-up of the white angel's trumpet, a beautiful but deadly flower, cousin to the jimson weed. Every part of the angel's trumpet was highly poisonous, as Elizabeth discovered in her research. Gardeners had to wear protective clothing, goggles, and gloves to avoid accidental poisoning. How had O'Keeffe managed to paint it, then? To get so close, without touching it?

And why? It wasn't a typical Hawaiian flower. Why hadn't she painted an orchid instead? Orchids were everywhere in Hawaii, gorgeous and intricate, with their endless shadings of lavender and purple and mauve. O'Keeffe's kind of flower. But not poisonous, not dangerous, like the Bella Donna, the beautiful untouchable lady.

Elizabeth pulled two more flower paintings from her folder and laid them side by side. The pink banana and the bright red heliconia—one girlishly sweet, the other garish—yet they seemed to have a similar intention. Both plants looked oddly staged, isolated from their natural setting, no messy undergrowth to clutter the portrait. Only a pink stalk alone against a froth of clouds, a spiky red heliconia suspended like a dancer stepping into the sky. Georgia had given them space to exist and be seen.

After. The pelvis and the desert. Dry hills, white bones. In 1940 O'Keeffe bought Ghost Ranch, her first home in New Mexico. In 1941 she painted *Red Hills and Bones*, a row of vertebrae against the rust-colored mountains. After that, more aridity. In *Grey Hills* and *Cliffs beyond Abiquiu*, painted two years later, the landscape was desolate, barren. Eroded hills, dry soil. A stark, elemental planet, all the luxuriance gone.

And yet, there was nothing about Hawaii to account for the change. Hawaii hadn't desiccated O'Keeffe; by all accounts, she had enjoyed her stay. In her letters to Stieglitz, she described the peaks and volcanoes, visible through the clouds, as fairy-like, a beautiful dream. Everything amazed and delighted her—the fantastic twists of black lava, the waterfalls and plush green slopes, the bright blue sea. She wrote to Stieglitz: "It's just too beautiful." Her notion of beauty, she told him, had been insufficient. When her Hawaii paintings were exhibited in 1940, she called them her gift to the world.

Elizabeth pored through her notes, growing more and more confused. She was supposed to immerse herself in the evidence and come up with a scholarly theory. That was what you did, when you wrote a dissertation.

She laid down her pen. She was trying to understand Hawaii with her mind.

It was never going to work.

Elizabeth dropped her papers onto the oak desk and raised her eyes to survey the class. Naomi was front and center, as usual, but there was something different about her. It took Elizabeth a few seconds to register what it was: the spikes in Naomi's hair were scarlet instead of cobalt. Good Lord, she thought. Or were the outlandish colors supposed to be some kind of statement?

Suppressing the eye-roll that would, she was certain, brand her as judgmental and uncool, Elizabeth placed her hands on the desk and looked from face to face. "So," she said, "how did you find the assignment?"

Naomi thrust out her jaw. "I opened my binder and there it was. Or did you mean, what was it like to do it?"

The girl didn't miss an opportunity, Elizabeth thought. She kept her voice neutral. "What it was like to do it."

The student with the tattoo flung her hand in the air. "I have a question."

"Please."

"We were talking about including yourself in your art, right? Like performance artists. But what about self-portraits? Aren't those, like, the ultimate way of including yourself?"

Naomi swung her head to glare at the other student, her jewel catching the light. "No," she said, "because self-portraits are static." She turned back to Elizabeth. "That's not what the assignment was about—if you're putting out something that's already set, finished, and you're, like, off somewhere drinking a Pepsi while people look at it. You aren't risking anything."

Elizabeth was intrigued. "Is art about risk?"

Naomi folded her arms. "It should be."

More hands waved in the air. Elizabeth was happy. This was what she loved about teaching.

She'd brought a lot of slides today. Self-portraits, in fact. Frida Kahlo's *Broken Column* and Louise Bourgeois' drawing of a baby inside a two-faced globe. And a photo of O'Keeffe. Not a self-portrait, technically, or maybe it was, if you believed that O'Keeffe had partnered with Stieglitz in producing it.

The hour sped past, and she didn't have time to show the O'Keeffe slide. Ruefully, she switched off the projector. "For next week," she said, "read the chapter on symbolism and think about the dichotomy between symbols of fertility and symbols of purity, both used to represent the female in art."

"How can you be both?" Naomi asked.

Elizabeth gave her a dry look. "That's the question, isn't it?"

She gathered the student essays and tucked them into her messenger bag, her thoughts already spiraling around Georgia. She had told Richard that Stieglitz's portraits captured the personal and the impersonal, the embodied and the abstract. She wasn't sure if she really believed that or had wanted to be clever. More than clever. Provocative, the way he was. To see what would happen.

She hoisted her messenger bag, shoving a hand into the pocket of her jacket. Her fingers brushed something dry and feathery. Curious, she pulled it out.

At first she didn't know what it was. Then she understood: it was the dried remains of the hibiscus center she had plucked that day in the botanical garden. Disconnected, unused, it had shriveled and turned to powder.

"Ms. Crawford? Professor Crawford?"

Elizabeth looked up. Naomi was still there, gripping the straps of a dirty yellow backpack. "Yes?"

"I think self-portraits are bullshit," Naomi said. "They're like—fake sincerity."

"Excuse me?"

"The artist is trying to control how people see her." She searched Elizabeth's eyes. "Don't you think that's cheating?"

"An interesting point." Elizabeth dusted her fingers, wiping them along the side of her bag.

"Don't you think it's cheating?" Naomi repeated. "Doesn't a person have to put herself out there, and let people see her, and then see what happens? Isn't it bullshit to do anything else?"

The girl was taking this too far. It felt aggressive, as if Naomi had crossed a dangerous line.

"We'll talk about it next time," Elizabeth said. Naomi looked unhappy. "I'm sorry," she added. "I have an appointment, that's all." She gestured toward the door. The girl went first. Elizabeth followed, kicking the door shut with her foot.

She didn't really have an appointment, although it might be smart to talk to Lindstrom again; maybe he could help her get past the impasse she'd come to. She nodded goodbye to Naomi and headed to the western wing of the Humanities building where Harold Lindstrom had his office. A long shot that he'd be available, but she took a chance.

"Dr. Lindstrom?" She gave a loud knock.

"Yes?"

Elizabeth was aware of the swift change in her role from teacher to student, from knower to novice. That was the way it worked in academia; you couldn't be both at the same time. "Do you have a minute?"

Luckily, he did. "I've boxed myself into a corner," she told him, settling into the visitor's chair and facing him across the desk. "I'm not seeing how the work O'Keeffe did in Hawaii led to the work she did afterward."

"And if it didn't?"

Then I'm screwed. "It had to. I'm just not seeing it."

Harold steepled his fingers. "What was her dominant image, afterward?"

Elizabeth didn't hesitate. "The open pelvis. The ovoid, pulling the viewer into the blueness of space."

"Were there any openings in her Hawaii paintings? Into the blueness of space?"

At first she thought he was making fun of her. Then she realized he was serious. "Well, she did those fishhook paintings. A circle of blue, floating above the horizon? I haven't really focused on them. They're not all that interesting, to be honest."

Harold eyed her sternly. "Get interested." Elizabeth gave a start. "Go where the data takes you. You didn't expect to know the road in advance, did you?"

"No." She laughed. "I mean yes, I'll do that." She thought of

O'Keeffe's painting of the black lava bridge on the Hana coastline. A bridge and an aperture, both at once.

"Let me know what you find." He dropped his hands into his lap, coughed, and rearranged the papers on his desk. It meant: meeting over.

Elizabeth stood. "Thanks for letting me stop by." She left his office and headed down the corridor. Something wondrous was swirling in her mind.

She'd been wrong. Georgia hadn't turned dry in Hawaii. She'd found an opening and walked through.

Eight

Two days later, there was Phoebe again, swinging a big leather purse as she strode down the flagstone path from Lucy's house to the street.

It was 8:30 in the morning, drop-off time. Elizabeth had said goodbye to Daniel and Katie a few minutes earlier, then made a quick U-turn when she realized that Katie's bunny was still on the back seat. Easier to return to Lucy's now than to get a frantic phone call later.

She was sliding out of the car, bunny under her arm, when Phoebe spotted her. "Hey there!" Phoebe's eyes were hidden by oversized sunglasses, but her voice was bright. "Funny how we've both been using Lucy for months now but never ran into each other. And here we are, same schedule for the second time in a week. Go figure."

Elizabeth shut the car door and held up the bunny. "Actually, I already dropped the kids off. Except Katie left The Precious in her car seat."

"Ah yes. The Precious." Phoebe gave a low chuckle. "I hate getting up this early, don't you? But I have a new client who absolutely l-o-v-e-s those sunrise meetings. You'd think we could do all this over the internet, right? I mean, since what I'm doing for him is *internet* design. But no, he likes to talk in person." She mimed putting a gun to her head. Then she removed her sunglasses and peered at Elizbeth. "Did I say something to offend you, last time? When we met?"

Elizabeth blinked. Was it that obvious? "No, of course not. Why?"

"You took off so suddenly."

"Oh. That." She released her breath in what she hoped was a casual laugh. "No. I'm sorry you felt that way. You hit a nerve, that's all."

"Ha. Got some of those myself. Like when Lucy told me you were some kind of professor? I thought you'd be, I don't know, a snob or something."

"I'm not a professor," Elizabeth said. "I just teach this one little class."

"One little class? Sounds big to me." Phoebe put the sunglasses back on and tucked her hair behind her ears. "Well, off I go. Anything to keep the customers happy."

Elizabeth watched Phoebe cross the street and get into her car. There was nothing wrong with Phoebe, not really. But just because someone was likeable, it didn't mean you had to like them.

She flattened her lips, chiding herself for being so prickly. Phoebe hadn't done anything—except toss out that breezy hurtful remark about afternoon delight. As if it was unexceptional, the kind of thing everyone did.

It was the kind of thing O'Keeffe and Stieglitz did—at least in the beginning, before he began to arrange trysts with Dorothy Norman instead. Elizabeth frowned, angry at him for Georgia's sake. Stieglitz, the hypocrite, had proclaimed his devotion to Georgia again and again, but refused to give up his mistress, insisting that Georgia was strong enough to handle it, telling her that it actually helped their marriage because it made him a more loving person.

"Mrs. Crawford?" It was Lucy, framed in the doorway. "You okay?"

Elizabeth wheeled around. "Yes, of course."

"You came back," Lucy said, "and now you've been standing there. So I wondered if maybe something was wrong."

"No, not at all. Just lost in thought. Sorry." Elizabeth hurried up the path and handed Lucy the bunny. "Can't drive away with this in my car."

"Ah. Heaven forbid."

"I'd better slip away before I'm seen."

"A wise idea," Lucy agreed. "I'll see you later."

"Absolutely." Elizabeth returned to her car and gave a farewell beep as she pulled away from the curb. Traffic was light, not much to do but steer. She signaled, accelerating into the left lane. The lane for people who didn't want to wait, who were greedy for more.

Don't think, then.

How do you feel about wildness?

Richard tugging her toward the swing, leaning his weight into each thrust, giving her no choice but to fly.

A shiver, then a scrap of memory. Wild red hair, a cracked leather jacket.

Good Lord. She hadn't thought about Carter Robinson in years.

The light turned yellow. Startled out of her daydream, Elizabeth couldn't decide what to do. Hit the gas? Brake? The driver behind her pressed on his horn. Flustered, she slowed to a halt. After a few moments the light turned red.

Elizabeth fixed her attention on the windshield. Carter Robinson. How odd to remember him, after all this time.

She'd been the youngest person in her freshman civics class, starting college when she was barely seventeen. Carter, sprawled in the chair in front of hers, long legs filling the aisle, had taken a year off to travel; that made him two years older and a decade more experienced. An aspiring actor, he had motorcycle boots, a cracked leather jacket, and a killer grin.

Elizabeth knew she wasn't his type, yet they'd ended up at the same party and, to her astonishment, he'd pulled her into a corner to talk. She could remember how she'd felt, dazzled by his attention. After a while, they left together. She'd been crazy with lust—really, there was no way to pretend it was anything else. He'd pressed her up against a wall, right there on the street. If he didn't fuck her, she'd die.

His room was a few blocks away. They walked through the empty streets, arms around each other, yet with each step Elizabeth had felt her passion fade, her doubt increase. This wasn't how she'd imagined her first time. She needed to stop, figure out what to do, but she couldn't find a way to tell him *wait, I have to think.*

They climbed the two flights of stairs to Carter's room. She followed him inside. The place smelled of air freshener and dirty clothes. There was a photo of Laurence Olivier taped above a Murphy bed. Carter saw her looking at the photo. "For luck," he said. Then he pulled on the strap and jerked the Murphy bed away from the wall.

The sound of the wood hitting the floor was like a door slamming. She couldn't do it. She made an excuse and fled, stumbling down the stairs and racing across the street, waving her arm in a frenzy until a cab driver stopped.

She had cast longing glances at Carter during civics class, but he hadn't approached her again.

Elizabeth told herself that he hadn't really been interested in her. It would have been a one-night screw, nothing more, so it was better that she had spared herself from getting hurt, later, when he stopped calling. She'd been smart to sacrifice—that was the word she used, when she thought about it—the chance for sex with Carter out of loyalty to her vision of what a *first time* ought to be like.

Her first time hadn't, in fact, been all that spectacular. A friend of her roommate's boyfriend, no one special, except that he had red hair like Carter's. It was the spring of her freshman year, and she wanted to get it over with. Other partners followed. Then she met Ben and thought *yes, this makes much more sense.*

Elizabeth eased her car into the right-turn-only lane and steered onto the cobblestone road that wound through campus. She pulled into a parking spot and turned off the ignition.

Better to think of it as a noble sacrifice, she had decided, when she ran away from Carter Robinson. Yet there was a question she had never let herself dwell on. *Better than what?*

She dropped the car keys into her messenger bag. She regretted running away. There. She'd admitted it, after all these years.

O'Keeffe's words flashed in her mind. *I've been absolutely terrified every moment of my life but I've never let it keep me from doing a single thing I wanted to do.*

That was the question. Knowing what she wanted to do.

Elizabeth was supposed to be combing the archives for references to O'Keeffe's time in Hawaii, yet she couldn't shake the idea that there was something about the way O'Keeffe posed for Stieglitz that she had to understand. Without that understanding, nothing else would make sense.

She pushed open the library's big glass door and crossed the ante-room, with its Persian carpet and dark paneled walls, and made her way to the Art History Reading Room on the third floor. She set her bag on one of the mahogany tables and paused, fingertips tapping the edge of the wood. She knew how to research a topic; that was part of being a doctoral student. But what, exactly, was she searching for? Artists who were models? Artists who posed for their lovers?

Certainly, there were women painters who had been models. Suzanne Valadon, for one, but her story was the reverse of Georgia's. Valadon had entered the male-dominated art world by posing for Renoir and Toulouse-Lautrec—naked and clothed—a full decade before she began painting herself. Valadon was a model who longed to paint, and then did. O'Keeffe was a painter who, briefly, modeled.

Elizabeth looked up Valadon, refreshing her memory. Twenty

years younger than Mary Cassatt and Berthe Morisot, the two
female painters who had been part of the French Impressionist circle,
Valadon had painted what they could not. Middle-class women like
Cassatt and Morisot were limited to painting gardens, family portraits, domestic scenes. But Valadon—bohemian, born into poverty,
and decidedly not part of the French middle class—could do as she
liked. Many of her paintings featured male and female nudes; she
even painted nude self-portraits. Her feminist students would have
liked Suzanne Valadon, Elizabeth thought, but Valadon wasn't the
example she was looking for.

All right. What about women who posed for their husbands or
lovers? It wasn't unusual for a painter to use his wife as a model.
Picasso, with his portraits of Dora Maar. Renoir and Aline Charigot.
Edouard Manet and Suzanne Leenhoff. Then Elizabeth remembered,
amused that she did, that Manet had used a different model for his
nudes. Not his wife; someone who was a painter herself.

Maybe that was what she was looking for. Hopeful, she found a
computer and looked up *Dejeuner sur L'Herbe*. Victorine Meurent,
that was the model's name. Meurent was indeed a painter, although
not famous or important like O'Keeffe. Elizabeth was disappointed
to learn that only one of her paintings had survived. Meurent had
been the model for Manet's *Olympia* too. Elizabeth studied the beautiful reclining figure—languid and indifferent, a bow tied around her
neck as if she were a present.

No, it was nothing like what O'Keeffe had done. The model stared
blankly from the canvas. An idealized version of something in
Manet's mind, more girl than woman, hairless and coy. Not Meurent
herself.

Elizabeth's head began to spin. She didn't even know what she
was looking for.

You do want to understand O'Keeffe, right? Not just write a paper
that her dissertation committee would approve.

Then it struck her: O'Keeffe had been photographed, not painted. It was different, more direct. She tried to think of photographers who had used their wives and lovers as models. Weston, for sure. Richard's hero.

She wiped her face, cleared the screen, and typed *Edward Weston*. The similarity hit her at once. Weston was twenty-two years younger than Stieglitz—a different generation—yet both men were photographing the women they loved, clothed and unclothed, whole and in parts, during the same two decades. The images were daring, voluptuous and abstract at the same time.

It was uncanny, really. Stieglitz mounted his first show of O'Keeffe portraits in 1921, introducing her to the art world as a subject before they knew her as a painter. Weston's nudes of Tina Modotti, a photographer in her own right, were done only a few years later. Elizabeth clicked through the images. She'd already known about Weston's close-ups of Modotti's face but found a series she had never seen before, Modotti posing in an open kimono, in Mexico, in 1924, sultry and exposed. Was this, finally, the parallel she had been looking for?

Yet in every photo, Modotti's face was averted, her eyes closed or covered by her hand. It was her body that Weston wanted the viewer to see, like Charis Wilson's body, a decade later. The Wilson nudes were faceless too—arms wrapped around her legs in a graceful oval, the long elegant body sprawled on the dunes. Only in the clothed photos was her face visible.

Weston had separated the two. The person, meeting the camera's gaze, or the body, erotic and impersonal. Never both.

In Stieglitz's photos, it was Georgia herself, agent of the gesture, who held her own breasts and offered them to the camera. There was nothing pornographic about the image. It was pure presence. *I am here.*

Elizabeth closed the browser with a decisive click. Enough. Not that she had done anything wrong. She'd been exploring, the way you did when you researched a topic, to see if related material could yield fresh insight.

That only a woman can explore

She needed to start over, scholarly and purposeful. Focus on her dissertation, O'Keeffe in Hawaii, instead of scrolling through irrelevant websites.

Abruptly, Elizabeth pushed her chair away from the computer. There was a women's restroom down the corridor. She needed to stretch her legs, wash her face, and get back to work.

The hallway was eerily silent, not even the clang of a radiator or the flutter of a candy wrapper on the parquet floor. Elizabeth pulled open the door to the restroom. At first she thought it was deserted too. Then she noticed a woman peering into the horizontal mirror that spanned a row of pedestal sinks. The etiquette of privacy made her avert her eyes until, without meaning to, she caught the woman's reflection. "Dr. Mackenzie?"

The woman straightened. She was tall and slender, with silver hair in an elegant twist and flame-blue eyes that matched the scarf twined in a figure-eight around her neck.

Elizabeth coughed. "I mean, hello. Good morning."

It took the woman a moment to register who she was. "Ms. Crawford. Of course." She dipped her head with a gracious acknowledgement.

Marion Mackenzie's presence on the Art History faculty was a coup for the university. Her book on American Modernism was a classic; fifteen years after its publication, she was still the reigning expert, and only the offer of an endowed chair had succeeded in luring her from a sister institution. With her publications, accolades, and impeccable reputation, Marion Mackenzie was everything that Elizabeth dared to aspire to.

Thanks to Harold Lindstrom, the great Mackenzie had agreed to join her dissertation committee. "She wants to support women scholars," Harold had explained. "Plus, to be candid, she has to serve on at least one committee, endowed chair or not, so it might as well be yours." When Elizabeth tried to express her gratitude, Harold had laughed. "Wait before you thank me. Marion's a tough one. She won't tolerate an ounce of sloppiness."

"That's fine with me," Elizabeth told him.

She had only met Marion twice, once at the introductory meeting Harold had arranged, and once at a full meeting of the committee. Elizabeth was still awed by her good fortune but didn't want to seem like a star-struck adolescent. "I didn't mean to intrude on your privacy."

Marion waved a hand, dismissing her apology. "It's a public bathroom." Then she motioned in the direction of the Art History Reading Room. "You're doing some research?"

"I am." Sort of. Well, she would be, in a minute.

"Me too. I'm giving a paper on Arthur Dove. I had one of those ideas-in-the-shower this morning and wanted to check a reference in a back issue of a journal that's not online."

Elizabeth twisted the faucet at an adjacent sink. "There's something about standing under the hot water, isn't there? Loosens the brain cells. Doesn't heat make molecules move faster?"

Marion chuckled, and Elizabeth felt herself relax. Even the great Mackenzie didn't seem so forbidding in a women's restroom.

"You know," Marion said, reaching for a paper towel. "I'm doing a sort of trial run for some of the senior faculty—you know, to see what their response is, before I present at the conference. It's a pretty select group but you should come. Dove was a contemporary of O'Keeffe, moved in the same circles. You might find it useful."

The water streamed across Elizabeth's hands. She was being invited to a *pretty select group* of tenured faculty, guest of Mackenzie herself? Doctoral students would kill for a chance like that. "I'd be honored," she said. "And yes, I'm sure I'd find it helpful."

"Excellent. Just let my secretary know and she'll put you on the list." Marion tossed the paper towel in the wastebasket and gave her jacket a quick tug. She fixed her flame-blue eyes on Elizabeth's. "Next Wednesday. At seven."

Elizabeth's hand froze on the faucet. Wednesday was Tai Chi night.

Was she out of her mind, hesitating for even an instant?

Marion must have seen the shadow cross her face. "Is that a problem? I realize it's short notice."

"No, no. I'm sure it'll be fine. Evenings are always contingent on child care, that's all."

"Oh yes, I remember those days. The good news is they do end. Eventually." Marion adjusted her scarf. "Well, fingers crossed. I'll tell Jessie to add you to the list."

"I'll keep mine crossed too." She cleared her throat. "And Dr. Mackenzie, thank you. I really appreciate it."

"My pleasure. It's a good fit with your research."

When Marion left, Elizabeth leaned against the sink, grateful for its support. She didn't know what she was going to do, and that itself astonished her. Had anyone told her that Marion Mackenzie would invite her to an intimate gathering, she wouldn't have believed him. And had that same *anyone* told her that she would consider going somewhere else instead, she would definitely not have believed him.

All she could think about—and it wasn't really thinking, more like a crazy swirl of terror and excitement—was that there was another way of understanding O'Keeffe that had nothing to do with Marion Mackenzie or her paper on Arthur Dove.

She shivered. It was because she'd spent the last hour staring at those beautiful naked forms—forgotten that she was doing research, lost her professional distance. She needed to come to her senses and tell Ben that she would be going to a faculty gathering next Wednesday instead of Tai Chi class. Luckily it was a Wednesday, when he was already planning to watch Daniel and Katie. It wouldn't matter to him where she went.

Elizabeth felt a slyness slide across her skin. *We don't have to tell Daddy everything.*

With a swift jerk, she turned the faucet full-blast and bent over the sink, splashing big handfuls of water on her forehead and cheeks. Then she snapped a paper towel from the dispenser and dried her face and hands. The restroom door slammed shut behind her.

She worked for another hour, collecting information about other American Modernists and developments in the art world while Georgia was in Hawaii. When she left the library, she cut across the campus green, toward the Humanities building. A soft breeze wafted through the scarlet and amber leaves. They were starting to turn, late this year, a mass of color that demanded to be noticed.

"Guess what?" A breathless voice, then a tap on her arm. It was Juniper, the yoga-pants woman from her Tai Chi class.

"Ah, hello," Elizabeth said.

Juniper's eyes were glowing. "I think our visualizations worked. Mr. Wu is *so* much better."

"He's coming back?"

"One more week. Not next Wednesday, the one after. Isn't that amazing?"

Elizabeth's pulse quickened. "So we have one more practice on our own, and then that's the last one? After that, our regular class?"

Juniper looked confused. "I guess. But the main thing is, we helped Sifu heal."

"Yes, of course." Elizabeth forced a smile. "Thank you for letting me know."

"We're going to practice on the lawn. Want to join us?"

"I'm afraid I can't." She pointed across the green. "I have a class to teach."

"Well, maybe next time."

"Maybe." Elizabeth gave a farewell wave. A gust of wind, rising up from nowhere, flung a crimson leaf against her shin. She kicked it aside, strangely upset. Mr. Wu's return, the Wednesday after next, was like the closing of a door. Once he was back, everything would be orderly and predictable. This was the last Wednesday when anything could happen.

For the second time that day, she thought of Carter Robinson. She had been afraid. Not of Carter or being hurt by him, but of herself. Of finding out who else she might be.

She'd been seventeen. She was twice that age now. The same Liz, because people didn't change—until they did.

Nine

Andrea rotated the salon chair so they could view Elizabeth's reflection in the mirror. She ran her fingers through Elizabeth's hair, fanning it away from her cheeks. "You see how great it looks? I'm so glad you let me do this for you."

Elizabeth loosened the collar of the nylon cape that Andrea had fastened around her neck. The Velcro was too tight, or else it was anxiety that was squeezing her throat and making it hard to breathe. For years, Andrea had tried to get her to sit in this very chair. "Let me give you highlights and a new cut," Andrea had begged. "You'd look amazing."

For years, Elizabeth had refused, and finally Andrea had stopped asking.

Now, she was the one who had asked. "If you're still willing."

"Of course I'm willing. I won't even say *told you so.*"

Andrea had a small hair salon in the back of her house, light and modern, with bright Mexican tiles and oversized mirrors on two of the walls. Another wall opened into a playroom for the customers' children. Stephanie, Daniel, and Katie were there now, busily constructing a kingdom out of blocks. Elizabeth could hear their chatter, high and musical, as Spiderman and Polly Pocket chased each other from tower to tower.

Andrea feathered her scissors through the edge of Elizabeth's hair. "Ben is going to absolutely swoon, but he won't be able to figure out what's different."

"Ben doesn't swoon." Andrea knew that. She had told her, the night they had pizza.

"He will now." Andrea twirled the chair and pulled off the nylon cape. Then she stepped back and regarded Elizabeth with a satisfied grin. "You really should have done this ages ago, Lizzie. That sixties look didn't do a thing for you. All it did was hide your beauty."

Elizabeth met her sister's eyes, touched by the generosity in her words. "Who knew you could be so sweet? I might have to report you to the sibling rivalry patrol." Then her expression turned grave. "You don't think it's weird, me doing something like this?"

"Why would it be weird?"

"Because."

"Because you've always been Miss Bookworm?"

Elizabeth winced. "I guess."

"It doesn't mean you can't look good. Anyway—trust me on this, Lizzie—just *doing* this will put you in a different frame of mind. Feeling gorgeous and sexy is the best way to make a man *see* you as gorgeous and sexy. And Ben will, I guarantee."

Why did Andrea keep talking about Ben? As if a haircut—or a negligee—would make a difference. You didn't change a relationship by putting on a costume. They'd proven that already. Anyway, she wasn't doing this for Ben.

Richard's face rose up in front of her, the smoky grey of his eyes, the carved plane of his cheeks. She felt the touch of his hand on her spine as he led her to a table in the back of the café, the firmer touch as he pushed her forward on the swing. Her gaze darted to Andrea, but Andrea had turned to wash her hands in the sink.

New little tricks in bed.

"Andie," she began. She needed to talk about Richard. Despite their differences—because of their differences—Andrea might actually understand.

Shouts rang out from the playroom, and Stephanie came running into the salon. "Mommy, Mommy, look!" She held out a plastic Superman. The figure was wearing a frilly pink dress over its molded blue tights.

Daniel ran after her. "Give it back, fart head." He grabbed the toy.

"Stop it, both of you," Elizabeth said.

"Oh, let old Superman try some cross-dressing," Andrea laughed. "Might do him some good."

"It's not funny." Elizabeth's voice was sharp. "It's about taking other people's toys." She took the action figure from Stephanie and dropped it in her lap. "Superman is in time-out. Go find something else to play with. Both of you." She shooed them back to the playroom.

"Whoa," Andrea said. "You're pretty uptight, especially for someone who just had my best salon treatment." When Elizabeth didn't answer, she reached for a towel. "I thought you had this big plan to get all blissed out. Didn't you sign up for some kind of yoga class?"

"Tai Chi."

"Whatever." Andrea wiped her hands. "So, is it working? Making you all mellow and relaxed?"

Elizabeth picked up the Superman figure. "I don't know yet." She traced the line of the red cape, moved the plastic arms up and down. "I'll have to see what happens."

"I suppose it takes a while."

"Hard to say." Again, Elizabeth longed to give words to the feeling that was pushing through her skin, clamoring to be named. Her fingertips grazed Superman's face. The handsome features were fused into place.

No, she thought. She couldn't talk about it. Not yet.

Andrea took off her smock and hung it on a hook. "Well, that's it for this morning. I have a keratin after lunch."

Elizabeth swiveled her chair to survey the salon. Two big mirrors, a hair dryer and sink, a tall cabinet made of plastic boxes. "You could do so much more with this, you know. Really make it into something."

"I like my little shop."

"Seriously," Elizabeth went on, the notion seizing her. She could help Andrea, give her a return gift. It was only right. "Some business courses, Andie, that's what you need. You could learn how to market yourself, create your own brand."

"Eh. Not my thing. I hate school and school hates me." Andrea lifted her hair, twisting it into a knot. "It's the hair part I like. I don't need business classes to do hair." She dropped her hands, and the tresses fell to her shoulders.

"But you could. Really. A lot of people get business degrees."

"Stop it, Lizzie."

"I mean it. You're smart enough."

"I'm not, and I don't need to be."

"But—"

"I said *stop*. Strange as it may seem to you with all your fancy degrees, I'm happy doing hair."

"Okay, okay." Still, Elizabeth thought, how could doing hair possibly be enough? Of course, Andrea could volley back the opposite challenge. How could sitting in libraries, writing papers, be enough? Well, it was enough for Marion Mackenzie. And she was like Marion— or would be, soon, if she worked hard and her luck held.

She hadn't replied to Marion's invitation, not yet. Marion's secretary had emailed with the location of the gathering and a request to confirm her attendance. Elizabeth told herself that the choice was obvious; she'd be crazy not to go. She started to tap *reply* a half-dozen times, ready to accept the invitation.

Of course, the talk was about Arthur Dove, not Georgia O'Keeffe. It wasn't as if she had been given a one-time-only chance to look at secret O'Keeffe papers. The point was that Mackenzie had offered a relationship. Mackenzie understood about child care; she wouldn't hold it against her if this particular Wednesday didn't work out.

Elizabeth's mind spiraled from Dove to Stieglitz, because Dove was part of Stieglitz's inner circle. Stieglitz had written to Dove: "When I make a photograph, I make love."

Andrea's words cut into her reverie. "And I'm *good* at doing hair." She gave the chair a playful spin. "Let me know if my masterpiece lights Ben's fire."

Elizabeth braced her feet on the rubber mat, halting the chair in mid-spin. "Andie."

"You act like you don't want to light his fire."

"It's complicated."

"Why is it complicated?"

Elizabeth closed her eyes.

Because I'm not sure he wants his fire lit, or if I can light it. There might be other fires.

"Mama." It was Katie this time, tired of trying to keep up with Daniel and Stephanie. Elizabeth opened her eyes, and then her arms, as Katie climbed onto her lap. "Mama," she sighed, burrowing against her.

Elizabeth pressed her cheek to her daughter's hair. "Tired, sweetie?" She expected Katie to deny it as she usually did, but Katie nodded. "You rest, then," she told her. "It's all right."

Andrea locked eyes with her in the mirror, her shrewd look letting Elizabeth know that she hadn't answered the question.

On Wednesday, as Marion Mackenzie's lecture was beginning in another part of town, Richard guided Elizabeth into the coffee shop where they had shared an Americano two weeks before. She'd imagined going back to the playground but it was raining, a cold grey drizzle. Anyway, the café had reopened.

She had emailed Marion Mackenzie's secretary to say that her sitter had come down with the flu. She hadn't mentioned the invitation to Ben. He hadn't even noticed her new hairstyle, so he had no claim—that was what Elizabeth told herself—on her decisions. She left a chicken casserole for dinner and hurried to the fourth-floor studio.

Richard led the pupils through the sequence of movements. "Mr. Wu is happy that we've been meeting," he told them.

To Elizabeth, his words were a code, a message just for her. Richard ended the practice early, and she waited for him by the entrance on the ground floor.

He greeted her with a delighted smile, his palms open wide. "Your hair looks wonderful." Then he motioned to the street. "I believe you owe me a cup of coffee."

"I do."

Richard tilted his head, studying her. Then he said, "Come. I discovered an interesting fact about your Mr. Stieglitz. I'll tell you while we have coffee."

As if Elizabeth needed something to entice her, besides Richard himself. But she nodded, pretending to agree to his terms, and waited till they were seated to ask, "So. What is it you discovered about Mr. Stieglitz?"

Richard signaled to the waiter, mouthing the words *two Americanos.* Then he leaned closer, planting his elbows on the marble. "You know how he was photographing O'Keeffe in the 1920s, right?"

"Of course."

"Well, people might think O'Keeffe was the only subject he was interested in, but she wasn't. So I checked out a hunch." He lowered his chin, teasing her. "You're supposed to ask me about my hunch."

Elizabeth flushed. "Tell me about your hunch."

"1922," he said, "the year Stieglitz started to take pictures of clouds. He wanted to photograph clouds to find out what he actually understood about photography. He said the cloud photographs were the equivalent of his most profound life experiences, a visual image of his philosophy of life. That's what he called the series, *Equivalents*, these amazing photos he took between 1925 and 1934."

"All right. And your hunch?"

Richard's face turned serious. "That he was photographing Georgia through the clouds, and the clouds through Georgia. To him, she was everywhere."

Elizabeth grew quiet, strangely moved by what he had said. "Yes, I think so too."

The waiter appeared with their coffee. Elizabeth drew back to give him room.

The corner of Richard's mouth twitched as he reached for his cup. He was teasing her again, Elizabeth thought.

"On the other hand," Richard went on, "it seems that my revered Edward Weston was a bit of a copycat. He met Stieglitz for the first time in 1922, and went on to photograph—you guessed it. Clouds. Other things too. But if you look at his cloud photos, the debt to Stieglitz is hard to miss."

Elizabeth felt the heat of her coffee cup, its curved shape between her palms. She longed to tell him what she had discovered about Weston's nudes, the way the women in Weston's photos were either faces or bodies. It was a pattern that anyone who really looked at the pictures might notice. Yet she hesitated, because it was more than that. If she told Richard what she'd seen, it would be like telling him about herself.

She edged forward, closing the space she had ceded to the waiter, and met his eyes, those grey ovals rimmed with charcoal. The smell of freshly ground coffee filled the café, wrapping her in a thick aromatic haze.

Then Richard spoke again. "I think O'Keeffe's paintings inspired Stieglitz's cloud photos. And I think modeling for him inspired her, in her own work."

Elizabeth inhaled, drawing the scent of the coffee into her lungs. "Yes, I think so too. Her work absolutely exploded after she started posing. Those flower paintings? They were all from the 1920s. She hadn't done anything like that before. She wasn't able to, until she'd modeled for him."

"Maybe posing freed her," Richard said. "Or maybe it was Stieglitz's passion."

Elizabeth felt herself redden. She caught her breath. "You mean, as a photographer? He photographed her endlessly, you know, once she came to New York."

"Weren't they lovers?"

"Not at first."

Richard eyed her intently. Flustered, Elizabeth kept talking. "It was part of how their relationship was changing. He started by photographing her hands and face, these amazing close-ups. After a while they did become lovers, and the portraits changed too. There's this quote from one of O'Keeffe's letters about how he began to photograph her with a new heat and excitement." Her flush deepened. "Those were her words. It was quite mutual, apparently. A mutual intoxication."

Richard raised his coffee cup. "Mutual intoxication makes for great art."

Elizabeth watched his throat as he drank. She thought of Stieglitz, learning Georgia's body through his camera. Deliberately, with a fire that ignited them both.

When I make a photograph, I make love.

Then Richard set the cup on the table. "So. I'll repeat my question. How are you going to actually understand O'Keeffe?"

By doing research. Obviously. That was how you got a PhD.

"Not by writing about her paintings," he said. "You know that."

Elizabeth tried to keep her tone light. "Oh? And what do you suggest?"

"You have to do what she did."

"Hardly. I'm not artistic. I can't paint to save my life."

"That's not what I'm talking about."

His gaze bored into her like a laser. She wanted to say, "Then what *are* you talking about?" But she knew. She had known from the first time they had coffee together.

The noise in the café receded. The swirl of people, the clang of the espresso machine, the coldness of the marble against her skin—everything drew back, grew silent.

She had to reveal herself. Be seen.

The very thing she wanted, and the very thing she feared.

Images of Georgia tumbled across her brain. A woman in a white skirt, looking up from her work. The same woman in an open robe, drowsy and disheveled.

The air in the coffee shop was thick as a mattress, pressing against her from all sides. Elizabeth brushed back her hair, the glinting high-lights and flattering haircut that Ben hadn't noticed but Richard had. She felt her hair against her neck. Imagined that neck bare. Imagined her whole body, bared to him.

She made herself ask. "What are you talking about, then?"

His expression was sharp and clean, like the edge of a blade. "You have to know in your whole self and not just your mind."

Her whole self. All her body parts, favorite and un-favorite.

She yearned to give words to what he was offering. A portal to another way of knowing, when nothing separated you from the thing known.

Say it for me.

As if he had read her thoughts, he told her, "You have to do what O'Keeffe did."

"You mean, pose?" Her voice cracked.

"I mean pose."

"For you."

"For yourself. I'd just be the one holding the camera."

She thought of the long hours Georgia had given over to posing—letting Stieglitz arrange her body the way he wanted, holding each position for minutes at a time. If Stieglitz was creating his art, Georgia couldn't create hers. And yet, by giving him her time and her body, she found her own beauty. Out of that, her art changed. In being seen, she saw.

Elizabeth felt the staccato of her heartbeat, pushing against its cage. The notion of posing, as Georgia had, was outrageous. No one who knew her would believe she'd consider such a thing—and yet she had already crossed a line, just by having this conversation. "Why are you doing this?" she asked. "You hardly know me."

Richard shrugged. "I'm a photographer. You've got me intrigued. You and your Georgia O'Keeffe."

That's right, it was about Georgia. Elizabeth's mind shot ahead, grabbing at words like handholds. Of course. An artistic inquiry, a joint experiment. A different kind of research, with a photographer as her guide. That's what they were talking about.

No, this was insane. She was an academic. A wife and mother. Not a person who took off her clothes for strangers.

Besides, no one really knew why Georgia had posed. It might have been private, part of their love-making, or a way to support her lover's artistic growth. Or maybe not. There were people who claimed that the photos were a deliberate image construction, to get her talked about. And it had worked. After Stieglitz exhibited his portraits of her, her own paintings started to sell.

Elizabeth's head spun. If she didn't know why Georgia had posed, how could she imitate her? It made no sense. Then again, Richard had said that posing was the way to understand O'Keeffe. If she posed, she would understand. That was the order.

For Georgia, the gradual revelation, through posing, had been a kind of foreplay. She'd been a virgin, after all.

Elizabeth shivered. She was jumping to conclusions. Stieglitz had photographed O'Keeffe in a whole spectrum of postures and moods. Austere, androgynous, in a mannish suit or a black cape. Why was she assuming that Richard meant the nude poses?

Because he did. They both understood that.

She flicked her eyes around the café. Then she was struck with a terrible thought. "You want me to hire you? I really can't afford—"

Richard cut her off. "No. It's not like that."

Elizabeth wet her lip. She hadn't really thought so, but she had to ask. She felt a swell of relief, then panic.

"Think of it as an experiment," he said.

Right. An experiment, a kind of research. "Do I have to answer right now?"

"Of course not. You can wait till you finish your coffee." As if to halt her reaction before it began, he raised his palm. *Stop.* "A joke. It's up to you."

"All right." Elizabeth lifted her cup. "I'll let you know next week."

"Mr. Wu will be back."

"Yes, I heard."

"Not that it matters. We can do the shoot whenever you want. If you decide to."

A giddiness welled up in her, saucy and reckless. "Not during class, I assume."

Richard gave her a dry look. "Certainly not. Mr. Wu doesn't want us looking at anyone but him. You'd be far too distracting."

"I certainly hope so."

Her laugh was coy, shrill, excessive. She almost spilled her coffee. He reached out a hand to steady the cup, his fingertips brushing hers.

Ten

Elizabeth wrote the words *Feminist Art* on the blackboard and drew a slash between them. "Let's look at each word separately," she said. Above the word *Art*, she added *Modernist*. "We can't really understand the feminist approach to art without understanding the modernist approach." She turned to the class. "What do you know about modernist art?"

A girl in the back of the room flung her hand in the air. She had a blonde buzz-cut on one side of her scalp, long pale strands on the other. "It's over, right? Which seems weird. I mean, I think of modern like meaning contemporary. You know, now. But it's not."

"That's true," Elizabeth said. "Modernism began at the end of the nineteenth century and lasted until 1940 or so." She drew a circle around the phrase *Modernist Art*. "It wasn't until—oh, around 1910, and up through the end of World War One—that things really began to heat up. Braque, Gris, Picasso, with their revolutionary cubist ideas, pushing at the borders of what people thought of as art."

Then she circled the word *Feminist*. "Coincidentally, or maybe not, it was also an important time for the feminists. 1913, the March for Women's Suffrage. 1916, the National Woman's Party. 1916, the first birth control clinic. Finally, in 1920, the triumph of the first wave of feminism." She looked at the class, trying to see if they knew what had happened in 1920. "The Nineteenth Amendment," she said. "Women got the right to vote."

She waited for that to register. "Two movements, feminism and modernism, blossoming at the same time. What do you think—any connection?"

Naomi spoke up, not bothering to raise a hand. The jewel flashed, just above her right nostril. Garnet, Elizabeth realized. That was the name of the stone. "They were both about breaking the rules."

"Exactly. They rejected tradition, convention. They wanted something new." Elizabeth pulled down the screen and reached for the remote. "So here's my question. What happens when you cross feminism and modernism?" She double-clicked, and two images appeared on the screen. On the left was *White Iris No. 7*, gentle and receptive, ivory petals surrounding a yellow center. On the right was *City Night*, geometric, vertical, assertive.

"What do the paintings say to you about gender?"

A pencil-thin student in a black tee shirt answered at once. "It's pretty obvious. The flower was painted by a woman and the sky-scraper was painted by a man." She rolled her eyes, as if Elizabeth had insulted the class by offering such blatant stereotypes.

"Not so." Elizabeth let a moment pass. "They were painted by the same person. A woman. A modernist woman."

Naomi threw her a smug look. "Georgia O'Keeffe."

"Yes, that's right." Elizabeth moved to the side so she could see the screen. "O'Keeffe did both paintings. In what order, do you suppose?"

Naomi frowned as if she sensed a trick. "Well, it wouldn't make any sense for her to paint a frilly little flower after she had a chance to paint a great big phallic thing like that building—you know, after they let her into the big boy club."

The student with the tattoo waved her arm. "I agree with Naomi. Women were only supposed to paint, like, nature and children, not symbols of power and technology. So, wow, no way would she give that up and go back to flowers. Especially, like you said, when women were starting to stand up for their rights."

"Actually," Elizabeth replied, "the flower you're looking at was painted thirty years after the skyscraper." She saw the students' surprise and couldn't help feeling pleased. "O'Keeffe painted whatever she wanted, whenever she wanted. Skulls, flowers, rocks. Male themes, female themes—she didn't care. If feminism's goal was to remove gender as a limitation, she was already there."

Several students looked skeptical. "I don't get it," one of them said. "Isn't feminist art about celebrating the feminine? Not about ignoring it."

"O'Keeffe considered herself an artist. Period. Not a female artist."

"But she *was* a female artist," the student insisted. "She painted stuff no guy would have painted. You know, pubes. Everyone knows that."

"It's not that simple." Elizabeth looked at the images again. "There's a story that when Alfred Stieglitz saw her drawings for the first time, in 1916, he said, 'At last, a woman on paper.' He'd been looking for a woman artist so he could show the world that their art was different."

"He could tell she was a woman by the way she drew?" Naomi made a face. "You just said she didn't want to be a woman painter."

"That's what I meant by not that simple."

The girl was sharp, Elizabeth thought. You had to give her that.

She gave Naomi an appreciative glance. "Stieglitz helped to make O'Keeffe famous precisely *because* she was a woman. There weren't any significant woman painters in the American art world in those days. There weren't, sorry. So he used that to get her noticed."

Elizabeth sensed that Naomi was about to argue, so she continued before the girl could interrupt. "Stieglitz knew how to promote artists; it was what he did. He picked up on America's infatuation with Freud and wrote this article about how women experienced the world through the womb, not the mind, and how that was the unique genius of O'Keeffe's art." She paused to let the class react.

"His comments got O'Keeffe a lot of attention, but they made her angry. She wanted to transcend gender. To be thought of as an artist, without qualifiers."

"Then she wasn't a feminist artist." Naomi crossed her arms, as if declaring *and that's that.*

"She wasn't," Elizabeth agreed. "And yet, she lived the feminist vision. She formed her identity through her work, she kept her own name at a time when women simply didn't, and she was phenomenally successful in a male-dominated field. At the same time, she totally distanced herself from the feminist art movement."

"Well, that sucks," Naomi said. "She could have helped."

"She wasn't interested in helping. She was only interested in pursuing her own vision." Elizabeth remembered what Georgia had written, early in her career, when she took the first liberating step and threw off everything she had been taught. *There was no one around to look at what I was doing, no one to say anything about it one way or another. I was alone and singularly free, working into my own, unknown—no one to satisfy but myself.*

And yet, not long after, Georgia had cared very much what Stieglitz thought. She had let him shape her identity, posing for him the very year he wrote that terrible article about how she painted from the womb.

She opened her robe to his lens. The nude torso, the mound of pubic hair.

In one of his letters, when he had just begun to photograph her, Stieglitz wrote: *You never were quite as beautiful as you are now. Yes, I'll make you fall in love with yourself.*

They weren't lovers yet. Only photographer and model.

"Why couldn't she do both?" Naomi demanded. "Be a feminist and paint whatever she wanted."

The question jolted Elizabeth back to the classroom. "It was a matter of her independence," she said. "When the feminists tried to make her their matriarch, O'Keeffe rejected what she considered their attempt to appropriate her work for their own purposes. She didn't want to be the feminists' symbol of womanhood in the 1970s any more than she had wanted to be the men's symbol of womanhood in the 1920s. Wombs, genitals—it made no difference to her. She thought both groups were trying to reduce her, rebrand her, to suit their own needs."

Elizabeth waited, letting the students absorb what she had said. Then she added, "When the Women's Caucus for Art gave O'Keeffe one of its very first awards for lifetime achievement, she was the only one of the honorees who refused to attend the ceremony. It was held at the White House with President Carter, but she didn't care."

"She didn't want to be a hypocrite," Naomi said. "White House or no White House."

The student with the tattoo looked unhappy. "It would have inspired other women."

"Perhaps," Elizabeth said. "But she wanted to inspire as an artist, not as a woman artist."

And yet, surely Georgia's identity as a woman had mattered when she posed for Stieglitz. Claiming her gender, not discarding it. Revealing the very sexuality she denied in her paintings.

Georgia, the steel-straight icon of an austere independence, and Georgia, the voluptuous nude in the photos. How was that possible? If Elizabeth couldn't understand that contradiction, how could she write a dissertation that made sense?

You have to do what she did.

Somehow, she kept talking. "It was the second wave of feminism, in the late 1960s, that led to the birth of feminist art."

Her voice rattled in the cavern of her body. Words, sentences.

There was more to being a woman than talking about it.

You have to do what she did.

—

Elizabeth was threading her way through the maze of cars in the campus parking lot, digging in her bag for her keys, when she heard the ping of her cell phone. Oh please, she thought, not Ben with another errand for her to squeeze into an impossible day. But it was a text from an unfamiliar number. She squinted to read it.

"Hey, this is Phoebe. I got your # from Lucy."

Phoebe had inserted a row of emojis. A happy face, a girl waving, and a woman in a graduation cap, presumably meant to be Elizabeth. Then she'd written, "Would you guys like to come by for a drink on Saturday, maybe around 7? You can meet Charlie, and I can meet ur honey." More emojis. A wine glass, a heart, and a honeybee.

Her honey. Phoebe's insipid cheer was starting to grate on her. Phoebe seemed to assume that Elizabeth liked her and that they were going to be friends. But she didn't, and they weren't. Besides, the couple Phoebe was inviting for a drink didn't exist. She and Ben hardly ever went out together without the children. Mostly they exchanged hours so each could do the separate things they needed, or wanted, to do. Squash on Tuesday, Tai Chi on Wednesday. A careful calculus, meticulously fair.

For yourself. I'd just be the one holding the camera.

Georgia, her shirt open.

The sweep of stars as she swung skyward.

Elizabeth bit her lip. She really needed to stop these daydreams. If she wanted something more—well, she could, and ought to, make that happen with the man she was married to. Put on the negligee again. Try something outrageous. It wasn't impossible. Relationships changed, like people changed.

On the other hand, there were things about Ben that she didn't want to change. They were the very reasons she had chosen him. He was smart, principled, supportive. She could never have embarked on a PhD without his encouragement, especially with two small children. "It's who you are," he had told her. "You should go all the way, get your doctorate."

He'd always been good like that. Elizabeth listed his virtues in her mind, as if she were an attorney arguing on his behalf.

And now, especially, she ought to be supportive of him in return. He'd just taken on a bear of a case. Wyckoff versus Solano. An old man had died because the landlord hadn't fixed a gas leak. It was complicated, Ben explained, because there was no record that the old man had ever called to let the landlord know about the problem. But he was taking the case anyway, with or without a fee, because it could set an important precedent.

That was one of the things she admired about Ben. He was idealistic, committed to the high road. Once he took on a client—or a wife—he stayed the course.

Elizabeth chirped open the car door. Then she reread Phoebe's message and typed, "Great idea. Will confirm w/Ben & let u know."

There. Done. She'd go to Phoebe's house with her husband; it was the kind of thing couples did. She threw her messenger bag onto the passenger seat, slid inside, and pulled the door shut. Then she sank forward, sagging against the steering wheel. Her shoulders twitched, and she began to tremble. Sadness and heat and shame, all scrambled together.

"We're *so* thrilled you guys could make it." Phoebe gave Elizabeth an effusive hug, then turned to Ben and hugged him too. "And kid-less, what bliss. Ours are passed out in their cave."

Elizabeth had found a sitter through the university. She'd half-hoped that it wouldn't be possible or that she could recycle the sitter-came-down-with-the-flu story, but here they were. Phoebe grabbed the arm of a tall blond man with wire-rimmed glasses and a short beard. "And this is Charlie."

Charlie offered his hand to Ben and gave Elizabeth a kiss on the cheek. "Glad you could come." He ushered them into the living room. Two overstuffed couches faced each other across a low rectangular table. In the center of the table there was a bright blue tray with four glasses and a bottle of wine. Next to the tray, a red-and-blue ceramic dish held crackers and three different cheeses. "Please." Charlie indicated one of the couches.

Ben settled into a corner of the couch, his arm stretched across the backrest. Elizabeth took the other corner. She watched as Charlie settled into the middle of the opposite couch, Phoebe next to him with her legs curled. Charlie shifted his body, adapting to hers, and rested his palm on her thigh.

Ben looked around approvingly. "This is a great space. The bay window, the high ceiling. And those crown moldings are the real thing."

"They are?" Phoebe glanced upward. "Well, the truth is we took the place because it's big and has a long hallway. You know, for running? Once the twins started running around, our old place was impossible. Way too cramped, though I was sad to leave it."

Charlie gestured at the wine bottle. "Shall we?" He removed his hand from Phoebe's leg, uncorked the wine, and filled their glasses. "Phoebe's being kind. Our old apartment was making her crazy. I was the one who hated to leave." He grinned. "My former man-cave. The place where she let me seduce her."

Elizabeth's return smile was tight. Phoebe handed her a wine glass. "How'd you two meet?"

Elizabeth answered before Ben could. "Oh, nothing remarkable. We had a class together in college." She knew she was supposed to say *and what about you?* But she didn't. It was going to be a story she didn't want to hear.

Phoebe told her anyway. "Charlie and I met in the funniest way. He crashed into me at the skating rink."

Charlie laughed. "Only way I could get your attention." He picked up two glasses, offering one to Ben and one to Phoebe. "She was wearing this foxy little butt-hugger skating skirt and a tasseled cap, and showing off like mad. I couldn't take my eyes off her, but she wouldn't slow down. A man does what he has to do." Phoebe laughed too. Charlie put his arm around her, pulling her close as he reached for his wine.

Elizabeth's cheeks were starting to hurt. She wanted to drop the tight clownish smile that was stretched across her face, but was afraid that its sudden absence would seem even more bizarre. What had she gotten herself into? Was this Andrea and Michael all over again?

Charlie drained his glass, stood, and gestured at a cabinet. "How about some music? I've got some vinyl recordings from the '50s that're unbelievable."

Ben's face lit up. "I've started collecting vinyl too. There's no comparison to the sound you can get."

Elizabeth was startled by the animation that transformed his features. Did she know he was so excited by vinyl records? She didn't think so. Yet there it was, right in front of her, the passion and delight she had assumed he lacked.

"What do you have?" he asked.

"Jazz, rhythm-and-blues? That work for you?"

"Perfect."

Charlie crossed to the cabinet in two quick strides. He took out an album. "One of the greatest ever. You're going to love this."

Ray Charles's voice filled the room. *Georgia, Georgia, the whole day through.* Elizabeth placed her glass on the coffee table and stared at Phoebe. Were they making fun of her? But no, she'd never mentioned her dissertation to Phoebe.

The road leads back to you.

Ben reached across the couch and tapped her playfully. "Liz's song." He looked at Charlie. "She's studying Georgia O'Keeffe. Ask her anything."

Elizabeth wanted to shove his hand away. He had no right to show her off, like some kind of trained monkey.

She could almost hear her mother's words. *We're so, so proud of Lizzie.* Why? Because she knew a lot of facts? The year something was painted, where and when it was exhibited. No one cared about that. Not even her. What mattered was the way the paintings made her feel.

The swollen waves of color, peeling open, pushing beyond the border of the canvas. The dark flower with its endless unfurling caverns, mauve and purple and pink. The unbearable intensity of its inner core, the utter revelation.

Ben didn't know how she felt. They'd never spoken of such things.

It wasn't what people talked about in grad school; you'd be called sloppy and subjective, and steered back to primary sources. A few weeks ago, she would have agreed.

Her eyes darted to Ben's face. Did she dare to explain?

Phoebe sat up straight, her brow furrowing. "O'Keeffe was that old lady in the desert, right?"

Elizabeth flinched. Yes, that was O'Keeffe. But it wasn't the woman who had offered her breasts to the camera.

She could feel the three of them waiting for her to answer. Her throat filled, words and silence vying for space. Could she say what she felt without dismissing all the work she had done, all that scholarship, yet without betraying Georgia? The intimacy, the breathtaking sensuality—it was real, but to speak of it risked reducing Georgia's art in exactly the way Georgia herself had despised.

"Wait." It was Charlie. "She did those flowers, the big orange poppies?"

"She did," Elizabeth said.

"They're amazing." He broke into a wide grin. "Phoebe, they're the flowers on those note cards."

"Wow. Right, they *are* amazing."

Elizabeth gathered her strength. *Do it. Speak.*

"You have to experience them," she said. "That's the point. You can't stand apart and look at them. The way she uses cropping and enlarging? It forces you to enter, like you're part of the painting."

She could hear Richard, as if he were speaking into her ear, through her mouth. She heard herself repeat his words. "You have to experience it with your whole self, not just your brain."

Then she stopped, unsure. Her gaze moved from face to face. Charlie and Phoebe seemed to understand. Ben looked bewildered. No, he looked embarrassed.

Ray Charles's music filled the room.

"The note cards. How about that." Phoebe looked up at Charlie. "Oh well, told you I was uneducated."

"Hardly—" Elizabeth began.

Before she could finish, Charlie put his hands on Phoebe's shoulders. "There are different ways to be smart, my darling. You're a genius at web design."

Elizabeth shut her eyes. She couldn't watch this.

Ben turned to Charlie, his face brightening again. "You work for a web design company?"

"We have our own business," Charlie answered. "It can be a roller coaster financially, but it's a lot of fun."

"I'd love to see some of your stuff."

"Seriously?"

"Seriously. Our firm's thinking about putting up a new site."

"Hey, that's great." Beaming, Charlie went to retrieve his laptop.

"You've made his day," Phoebe said. She picked up the red and blue ceramic plate. "More cheese?"

Ben cut a generous chunk of Brie. It wasn't like him, Elizabeth thought. He was always careful about cholesterol. Maybe it was his excitement about the vinyl and the web designs.

More and more confused, she took a sesame cracker from the plate in Phoebe's outstretched hand. If Ben could be excited about records and cheese, then maybe it was her fault there was no fire. Too owlish to evoke passion. Or maybe it was them, together, and the nature of the pact they had made—a pact she herself had crafted, that day in the little yellow kitchen.

Could they renegotiate? Strange to think of a relationship that way. Still, maybe they could.

"Here," Phoebe said. "Try some of this Manchego."

Elizabeth opened her mouth, let the taste of the cheese penetrate the whole of her. Every pore, every cell, as if she had never tasted it before. The music swelled.

The road leads back to you.

When they got home, Elizabeth waited while Ben walked the sitter to the corner. Her boyfriend was picking her up, she told them. If Ben wanted to wait till the boyfriend came, that was fine, but he really didn't need to. Ben was firm. "I'm not letting you stand out there alone."

Elizabeth paced the apartment. She didn't know what she wanted. Part of her wanted to put the negligee on again and see if she could entice him into something adventurous and thrilling. Maybe even greet him in it, when he came back. Another part of her wondered why this new agenda of hers was so important. They'd managed till now, just as they were. What was different?

She stopped, her fingertips grazing the back of the couch. *She* was different. It was Georgia, and Richard, and everything. It was herself. The mermaid in the school play, rising up out of the water and gasping for air.

Too soon, she heard Ben's footsteps in the hall. No time to change into a peach-colored surprise. If she wanted to captivate him, she needed to think fast, come up with an alternate plan.

A plan to become aroused? That wasn't how it worked between men and women.

Tears stung her eyes. Liz-the-brain, on her latest mission, her next achievement. There had to be another way to evoke desire.

Ben stepped into the apartment and closed the door behind him. "Man, I'm tired."

Intelligent, dependable, hard-working. The words drummed against her skull. A stressful case, a noble cause. Wyckoff versus Solano.

"I'm tired too," Elizabeth said. "It's been a long week." She brushed back her hair, the highlights and new layered cut that Ben still hadn't noticed.

Richard had. And he saw what she saw in O'Keeffe's art.

It wasn't like she was going to be unfaithful. She just needed to do this one thing, so she could understand Georgia.

"By the way," she said. "There's a good chance I'll be home late on Wednesday. Some of us were thinking of going out to dinner after Tai Chi, you know, like you guys do after squash?"

Ben hung up his jacket. "Makes sense to eat afterwards. Better than exercising on a full stomach."

Elizabeth watched him adjust the hanger, making sure the jacket was straight. "That won't be a problem, will it?"

"No. Of course not."

"I'll leave something for you to heat up. A casserole. I mean, if we end up going out. I don't know yet. I have to confirm it with the other people. I have to find out."

She was talking too much but Ben didn't seem to notice. That was the point.

Part Two:
The Photos

Eleven

Mr. Wu dismissed the pupils' attempts to express concern for his health or gratitude for his return, saying only, "We commence." His face was grave, impassive. To Elizabeth, his movements seemed slower and more solemn than ever.

Richard took his place in the center of the front row, but Mr. Wu motioned for Richard to stand beside him. "You say," he told him. Richard stepped forward, facing the class. Elizabeth's heart began to thud. She hadn't been prepared to look right at him for the entire hour.

Richard took the first posture, saying the names aloud as the class moved from one form to the next. *Hand strums the lute.* Elizabeth moved her arms, tried to match her tempo to his. *Grasp the bird's tail.*

She had decided to pose, to bare herself as Georgia had done, but that was back in the safety of her apartment. Now, facing him, she wasn't so sure. It was hard enough to have him look at her, one pupil among many. Dressed. Indecision seeped into her limbs, and she stumbled over the next movement. Richard caught her eye, and a silent understanding seemed to pass between them. The flare of a match, searing her. She straightened, correcting her posture.

"No tension," Mr. Wu said. "Nowhere." Then he indicated for Richard to continue. Richard nodded, scanning the rows. Elizabeth felt strangely bereft without his gaze.

Could she really do it? Posing was impossible, but so was not posing. Her stomach clenched. Which impossible thing was she going to choose?

It wasn't the posing itself, the arrangement of neck and limbs and spine. It was posing for someone. Revealed, beheld.

Regarded in its entirety. *Be held.*

Elizabeth realized that the class had moved on to the next posture. *Wave hands like clouds.* Again, she stumbled to catch up. Juniper gave her an encouraging smile.

After an hour, Mr. Wu's energy seemed to fade. He put his hand on Richard's arm, leaning close to whisper in his ear. Richard listened attentively, then said, "Sifu says it's enough for tonight. He wants everyone to practice and come back next week."

Juniper clasped her hands. "Of course, of course. We totally understand." Mr. Wu frowned. There were a few murmurs, and then Mr. Wu spoke to Richard again.

Richard looked at the class. "Maybe someone else can lock up? I need to help Sifu into a taxi. It would be good if he and I can leave first."

Elizabeth jerked to attention. Richard was leaving? He didn't know that she'd decided *yes, I'll pose. Like Georgia.* She needed to tell him, right away, while Mr. Wu was slowly, slowly putting on his shoes.

She hurried across the dojo. Richard was sitting on the bench next to Mr. Wu, putting on his own shoes. She slipped into the empty place beside him. A woman knelt in front of Mr. Wu, speaking earnestly.

Richard's head was bent as he tied his laces. Elizabeth kept her face averted. Her voice was soft. "I'll do it," she said. She didn't say what *it* was.

All she could see was the corner of his mouth. "Good."

She waited for him to tell her what to do next. How long would it take for him to get Mr. Wu into his taxi?

"Can you come Friday morning?" Richard asked. "Say, at eleven?"

Friday? Somehow she'd assumed he would photograph her right now, the instant she told him.

"I have to help Mr. Wu," he told her, "and anyway, I need light. Evening's no good."

Of course. What he said made sense, yet her disappointment was acute. She began to edge off the bench.

Richard put out a hand. Elizabeth thought, for a wild instant, that he was going to stop her from leaving. Instead, he pressed a folded slip of paper into her palm and closed her fingers over it. Mr. Wu rose. The woman who had been speaking to him gave a swift bow, and Mr. Wu turned to Richard. "We go?"

"We go," Richard echoed. Without looking at Elizabeth, he put his hand on the older man's elbow and helped him to the elevator. When they were gone, she opened her fist and unfolded the paper. Across the top, in embossed lettering, was Richard's name—Richard Ferris, photography—with his address and phone number. Heat surged into her cheeks, for anyone to see. The fact that he'd brought the paper must mean he had expected her to say yes.

Below the phone number, he had scribbled a note. His handwriting was large, bold. Elizabeth hunched over the paper, shielding it with her hand. "In 1923," Richard had written, "Stieglitz photographed the sun through the clouds. O'Keeffe was nowhere in the photo, not literally, but he named it *Portrait of Georgia*."

Elizabeth caught her breath. Why did it shock her, that he'd thought about her during the week? She'd thought about him.

She looked around. People were collecting their things, getting ready to leave. Someone had already dimmed the lights. She looked at her watch. The class had been short. She'd be home early, instead of late, as she had told Ben. Well, she'd make up a new story.

She pulled her jacket and shoes out of the cubbyhole. The man with the shaved head, the same man who had helped Richard when Mr. Wu collapsed, was standing by the elevator and waiting for the stragglers to leave. "I'll lock up," he told her.

"Yes, all right." She stepped into the elevator. The doors closed. It felt strange to be going straight home instead of out for coffee with Richard, but she couldn't think of anywhere else to go. She walked home slowly, postponing her return.

The wind rose up in the empty street. A gust lifted her hair, throwing it across her face. Her mind raced. She'd have to arrange to leave the kids with Lucy, since Friday wasn't one of her regular days. Actually, she hadn't agreed to Friday aloud, only in her mind. Did he assume she would come, or did she need to confirm? And for how long? Lucy would want to know.

Was this something a person like her could really do?

Yes. It was. She just had to organize it.

When she walked in the front door, Ben looked surprised to see her. "Wasn't this the night you were supposed to have burgers with the Tai Chi people?"

Elizabeth turned her back as she pulled a hanger from the closet and hung up her jacket. "It didn't work out. We'll do it another time."

"Well, if you're hungry, there's some of the casserole you made for the kids. It's in the refrigerator."

Elizabeth felt a flare of anger. She had no idea why she was angry but there it was, ready to burst out of her skin. "It's fine," she said. "I grabbed a sandwich."

She hadn't, though. She was ravenous; she could eat cardboard, mud, anything. Instead, she clamped her lips shut and let herself feel the raging hunger.

"I hear you made a conquest," Harold Lindstrom drawled. He was tilted back in his leather chair, fingers laced together, in the tweed jacket and tortoise-shell glasses that lent him the vaguely avuncular look that Elizabeth assumed he was aiming for.

Across from him, she shifted uneasily in the smaller chair. How could Harold have found out about Richard?

"Marion Mackenzie," he said. "She's taken a liking to you. Told me she was disappointed you couldn't make it to her talk."

Mackenzie. Of course. Harold didn't know about Richard. Anyway, there was nothing to know. He certainly wasn't a conquest.

"I was disappointed too," Elizabeth said. "I'm in awe of her, to be honest."

"A worthy object of your awe." Harold eyed her keenly. "Marion's a formidable ally. A word to the wise, though. If you get her invested in you, you'd better not let her down. She takes it personally, especially when it comes to rising young female scholars."

"I don't intend to let her down. Or you."

A smile flickered across his face. "I happen to know that Marion's old university is on the lookout for someone to fill her vacant spot. They want someone young, with a promising future. It's being advertised in the usual ways, but the truth is that whoever Marion recommends will get the job."

Elizabeth's eyes widened. "You're joking."

"Not at all. But you didn't hear it from me."

"Of course not."

A job at Marion's former university, filling Marion's place, was a prize Elizabeth hadn't dared to dream was within her reach. Yet Harold had said it might be. Her mind began to spin. They would have to move. A new apartment, a new babysitter. Ben's job.

"No promises," he said. "But keep doing what you're doing."

Elizabeth pushed her concerns aside. She'd deal with those details when—or if—she was offered the job.

Harold refolded his hands and peered at her over the top of his glasses. "So. What have you come up with, since we spoke?"

Everything.

The events of the past week came roaring back. The realization she'd had about the photos—how Georgia had given herself to the camera, face and body together. How Stieglitz had seen her everywhere. Her presence in the clouds, the very air. The slip of paper Richard had pressed into her palm.

Harold coughed. He was waiting for her to talk about her dissertation.

Elizabeth adjusted her position in the chair. "You told me to think about themes that emerged after Hawaii, and whether there were any indications in the Hawaii paintings. Like an experiment, a foreshadowing?"

He nodded, and Elizabeth continued. "So I thought about the next group of paintings O'Keeffe did, after Hawaii. The pelvis series. She started them in 1940, right when she got back to New Mexico. The same image, that empty ovoid, again and again. In her next show, nearly half the paintings were pelvises. Shocking, in a way, after the living subjects she'd depicted before. Just an open bone against the flat blue sky."

Her voice dropped. "I did the math and, well, O'Keeffe was fifty-three in 1940, fifty-nine when she completed the series. She was probably going through menopause. She'd been clear about her desire to have a child but Stieglitz wouldn't allow it; he said it would interfere with her painting. And now it was too late." Elizabeth spread her hands. "I think O'Keeffe had to reclaim her center. Take it back and redefine herself. Pure, down to the bone. Beyond flesh, beyond desire. Beyond all the things people projected onto her work."

Harold was quiet, his eyes fixed on the desk. Elizabeth grew anxious. "You think I'm psychoanalyzing her? Making things up?"

"I don't see how it's anything you can verify."

"But I can. I can show you the first intimations." Elizabeth tried to contain her fervor. If he thought she was getting ahead of herself, he wouldn't listen.

"You can see it," she went on. "If you look at the Hawaii collection as a whole, you can see that O'Keeffe was saying farewell to her old themes, painting those giant flowers for the very last time, and preparing for what would come next."

"You're rather passionate about this, I must say."

"I guess I am."

"Why?"

Elizabeth stopped, wondering if she had gone too far. Then she thought: might as well go all the way.

"I think O'Keeffe was trying to understand what it means to be a woman. She did that her whole life, but people kept misunderstanding."

"And you think you've got the missing piece?"

"Ouch. That sounds arrogant."

"Not if you actually do."

"I don't know. Everyone seems to dismiss the Hawaii paintings, as if they never happened. The enormous retrospective at the Tate, a few years ago? Not one painting from her time in Hawaii, and only one tiny reference in the whole 250-page catalogue." Elizabeth shook her head. "Sure, there was that exhibit at the New York Botanical Garden, when they showed the Hawaii paintings all together—well, most of them. But it was a flower show, really. At a garden, for heaven's sakes, not an art museum."

Harold looked amused. "Does the venue really matter?"

"It does. It means the art world didn't take them seriously."

"They were paintings of flowers and plants." He gave a loose shrug. "It's not so far-fetched to exhibit them at a garden. Besides, I seem to remember that the show was a success."

Of course they were paintings of plants, but they were plants seen through O'Keeffe's eyes. Harold knew that.

Elizabeth thought of the Hawaiian flora she had seen online. The garish stripes of the croton and cordyline leaves, magenta and crimson and chartreuse—splattered, surely, across Georgia's vision. So much color, gaudy and chaotic, everywhere on the islands, yet not in the paintings. Georgia's limited palette seemed strange. Carefully orchestrated pink and white and bright red, not the wild juxtaposition of color and abundance she must have encountered in the real landscape.

Georgia had been watchful, selective. A step at a time, she had cleared space for what she wanted to convey. Maybe she'd understood that there was only so far she could travel in nine weeks. The rest of her journey had to take place somewhere else, after she left.

Elizabeth edged closer, determined to make Harold see. "I understand that the Hawaii paintings weren't her best work, Dr. Lindstrom. But they mattered. They were a passage."

"To?"

Again, she hesitated. Then she said, "To emptiness."

"That's a bold proposition. You're sure you can support it?"

"I'm sure."

"Well then." His face creased in a smile. "Looks like you're on your way."

Elizabeth sat back, letting the relief sweep over her. She had taken a risk, and it had worked. Her career was about to launch, the fulfillment of everything she'd been working toward, ever since the day she took the advanced placement test instead of dressing up as a mermaid. She could already see it, the academic robe and cap she would wear at graduation. Her own office, her name on a brass plate.

To be safe—to assure Harold that she hadn't forgotten her place as his student—she added, "Do you have any other suggestions?"

She meant *about the dissertation*, but Harold answered a broader question. "Stay close to Marion. That's my best advice. The dissertation's your currency, but Marion's in charge of an important turnstile. Don't underestimate her influence."

Elizabeth got the message. The job possibility was real.

The light glinted on Harold's glasses. "Play by the rules," he said, "but don't let them box you in. Knowledge comes in surprising ways."

His words startled her, as if he had known about Richard after all.

"Mama stay, Mama stay." Katie kept repeating the three syllables. She latched onto Elizabeth's leg as tears ran down her cheeks.

Elizabeth turned to Lucy. "I don't know what's gotten into her. I'm so sorry."

"No worries," Lucy said. "I'm sure she'll be fine once you leave."

This sort of thing was happening more and more often with Katie—fierce and independent, pushing Elizabeth away when she tried to pick her up, then pathetic and clinging.

"Well, you may have to put up with her misery the whole time I'm gone." Elizabeth chose her next words with care. "Unless it's a real emergency, please don't call me. I think it's better for everyone." She knelt and gently pried Katie's hands from her leg. She held them between her own. "I have to go, pumpkin, but I'll be back later."

Katie whipped her head from side to side. "No, Mama, no."

"I know you're sad," Elizabeth said, "but I'm giving you my solemn promise that I'll be back exactly when I said I would. Lucy will show you on the clock."

Katie turned her face away, refusing the promise. Elizabeth told herself that even if she hadn't been going to Richard's studio, she would still have had to stand her ground. It was bad practice to let a two-year-old manipulate you. Her destination was irrelevant. For all Lucy knew, she had a shift in her teaching schedule or a special meeting. She hadn't told Lucy why she needed childcare on an off-day. After all, Phoebe didn't explain.

She gave Katie a squeeze, then stood and put her palm on her heart. "My solemn promise," she repeated. "Because I never, ever break my promises."

She kissed the top of Katie's head, even though Katie squirmed away. Then she called, "Bye, Daniel. See you later."

Daniel glanced up from a mound of Legos. "Okay. Bye."

Elizabeth waved to Lucy. She closed the door behind her and hurried down the path to her car.

The drive to Richard's studio took less time than she had expected. Ten minutes, and there she was. The studio was on the second floor of a cedar-shingled building, above a store that sold candles, crystals, and handmade jewelry. On the right was a Peruvian restaurant; the left side of the building opened onto an alley. Lots of windows, with the light he had said was important. There was a sign in the front window. *Richard Ferris, photography.*

Amazingly, there was a parking space right in front. Elizabeth slid into the spot and shut off the engine. Her eyes flew to the rearview mirror, checking her mascara. Not that it mattered, of course. It was for her dissertation.

She grabbed her purse and pushed open the car door. There was a buzzer outside the entrance to the consignment store, with *Ferris* in small black letters on a white rectangle. Elizabeth pressed the button, and he buzzed back right away. The door clicked open.

She could see him waiting for her at the top of the stairs. The steps were made of a dark wood, worn in the center. Elizabeth felt her mass shift as she found the next tread, and the next—as if her body was changing shape, growing lighter as she ascended.

"You came." He sounded happy.

"I did."

He put out his hand to guide her inside, fingers grazing her elbow, the same way he had guided Mr. Wu to the elevator. Elizabeth felt a twinge of disappointment. What had she expected? A hug? Applause?

"My studio." He pulled the door shut.

She could see lights, a stool next to a tripod, a chair in front of a white screen. Dark shades were rolled up at the tops of the tall windows. She turned in a slow circle. "There's nothing on the walls. None of your photos."

"It's a studio, not a gallery."

"You'd rather not see what you did before, when you're shooting something new?"

A smile lit his face. "You've very perceptive. That'll help us work together."

Elizabeth met his eyes. Then she crossed the room and touched the screen. "An empty backdrop. Nothing to distract from the subject, the person in the portrait."

He came to stand next to her. "It depends." He crossed his arms, tilting his head as he regarded the blank surface. "When Stieglitz photographed O'Keeffe, he tended to use a dark backdrop. Or else a very specific background, like a curtain to show her body against the light, or one of her paintings. Sometimes there wasn't any background at all, since the whole picture was a close-up. He liked to crop his portraits of her, as if she kept going beyond the frame."

Elizabeth turned to face him. "You've studied Stieglitz."

"Mostly in the last few weeks, since you decided to re-enact his photos."

"I only decided that a few days ago."

He arched an eyebrow.

Elizabeth flushed. "You think I decided earlier."

"I know you did. Your mind just had to catch up." Then he opened his hands. *We have nothing to hide, you and me.* "And here you are."

Here I am.

She walked to the window. "Why do you have those dark shades?"

Again, Richard followed her. He reached up and pulled the cord. The shade snapped down, covering the window. "Sometimes the natural light's too harsh. Or I want to play with artificial lighting and can't let the sunlight interfere."

Elizabeth went to the next window. She wanted to cover it too, block out everything except the two of them in the bare room. The intimacy, or the possibility of intimacy, was so close she could taste it. She touched the cord. If she pulled it, it would be a signal.

Richard's voice startled her. "I have a client at noon," he said, "so we should probably get started. Try a few angles, see what might be a good sequence."

She whirled around. He was pointing at the chair in front of the screen. "We could start with some close-ups of your hands, or maybe your neck. Just to see how it feels."

She stared at him. What had she thought would happen? She didn't really know. But she would show herself. That, at least.

As if he'd seen her disappointment, his face changed. "There's no hurry," he said. "It's like Tai Chi."

Elizabeth shuddered. It was the gentleness, right on the heels of the business-like reminder that someone else—another woman?—would be taking her place at noon. The way he stood, arms at his side, relaxed.

Shame sliced into her like a scythe. She'd paid a babysitter—for what? A fantasy that she hadn't even admitted she was constructing, counting on?

Then she tensed, struck by a new concern. She pictured the line of people—clients, models, whatever he called them—who would follow after she left. "Each of your sessions is private, right? No over-lap, no one else sees what you've done?"

"Of course," he answered. "This is our project, yours and mine." He gestured at the bare walls: *See? I'm discreet. I guard my work.* "Let's try this, to begin with. Let me get to know your face."

"My face?"

"Your face. It's a good way to start." He indicated the chair again. "You have such a lovely face, Elizabeth. Surely you know that."

Shame splashed over her again, then a spark of danger. Lovely face. Oh, he was smooth.

She sat down. "What am I supposed to do?"

"Nothing. Not till I tell you." He went to the tripod and loosened the camera. Holding it in front of him, he circled her seated form. She could hear the soft clicks as he moved closer, then further away. "That's good. You look very stern, just like Georgia."

"Stern," she echoed. "It's better than telling me to say *cheese*."

He crouched in front of her, shooting up into her neck and jaw. "If you look at the portraits he did of O'Keeffe, she never smiled. She was very confident and deliberate. Head high, strong, distinctive, even when she was naked."

The word *naked* made Elizabeth jump. He'd said it on purpose, she was certain. To see how she would react.

Richard kept talking. "The more I think about it, I don't think those photos would have had the same power without her collaboration, the way she used them to construct the identity she wanted to present to the world."

"It's not clear that she meant for *the world* to see the photos. She posed for him. Stieglitz."

"Because he was her lover."

"Not in the beginning, when he first started taking pictures of her."

"It depends on how you define lover." He lowered the camera. "I want to shoot your collarbones. Unbutton your shirt."

Elizabeth froze.

"There's a wonderful closeup of O'Keeffe's neck and collarbones. I want to try it."

She swallowed. "All right." She undid the top two buttons. The shirt dropped, baring her shoulders.

"Perfect." He moved in closer. "Ah, yes. I had the feeling your collarbones would be beautiful." Before she could react, he touched the center of her sternum. "From there, Elizabeth." She could scarcely breathe, pinned by his touch. "Let yourself open, right from here."

Elizabeth filled her lungs, trying to do what he said. "Yes. Good."

He undid one more button. "Another inch. Like a hint, an invitation to the viewer." He took a step to the right, angling his camera. She heard the click of the shutter. Another click.

Richard circled her again, his steps light, defining her by his gaze. If he looked at her shoulder, the shoulder existed. Midas of the flesh, beckoning her into sensation.

Was this what she wanted? What he wanted? With a hoarse cry, she grabbed her shirt, pulling it tight. "I can't." Her voice caught, terror mixing with apology and regret.

"You can," he said quietly. "But not yet." He let the camera drop to his side. "It's all right. We'll try again."

The word flew out of her mouth. "When?"

"Whenever you're ready." His face was grave. "It's up to you, Elizabeth."

She could hear Mr. Wu's words, before her very first Tai Chi class, when she wanted to excuse herself in advance for her slowness, her clumsiness, her lack of experience. *You try*, he had told her. *You try, and you can.*

"Whatever you want," Richard repeated.

"And if I don't know what that is?"

He smiled. "You will."

Twelve

Elizabeth had just settled Daniel and Katie in front of a rerun of *Curious George*, promising herself that she wouldn't use TV to keep them occupied for at least another week, when she heard a determined rapping on the front door.

She needed a half-hour to finish grading her students' papers—that was the point of *Curious George*—so she gave herself permission to ignore whoever was knocking. Someone with a menu for Chinese takeout or an earnest neighbor collecting signatures for a petition. She settled onto the couch, tapped the stack of papers against the coffee table, and gave Daniel and Katie a quick glance. An occasional TV show, like an occasional burger-and-fries, wouldn't really hurt them. Besides, it was a lovable monkey, teaching them about friendship and forgiveness.

Instead of stopping, the rapping got louder. Growing annoyed, Elizabeth dropped the papers onto the couch. She crossed the living room and yanked open the front door. Andrea stood in the hallway, extending a bag of overalls and tee shirts as if it were a bouquet. "Maybe Katie can use these?"

Elizabeth took the bag from her sister's outstretched hand. They didn't show up at each other's homes like this; visits were negotiated, planned. Puzzled, she stepped aside so Andrea could enter.

"Hardly worn," Andrea explained. "Stephanie wouldn't be caught dead in anything but a frilly dress—a frilly *pink* dress—when she was that age. Maybe Katie can get some use out of them."

Elizabeth peered into the canvas bag. "She might, if she thought it would make her look like her brother. She yearns to catch up with him—except when she's yearning to climb back into the womb." She lifted a blue-and-white striped tee shirt from the stack of neatly-folded garments. "When I potty-trained her, she insisted on standing up to pee because, of course, that's what Daniel does."

Andrea laughed, and Elizabeth dared to hope that, errand accomplished, Andrea would leave. She still had twenty-six minutes to get the essays read and reviewed. Then she heard the brittleness in her sister's laugh and knew something was wrong. There was another reason for the surprise visit.

She set the bag on the floor. "What is it, Andie?" Andrea bit her lip, and Elizabeth saw that it was quivering. "Come," she said, leading her to the couch. She scooped up the student essays and tossed them onto the floor.

Andrea sank into the cushions. "Today's lesson. Be careful what you joke about. It might not be funny."

Elizabeth sat down next to her. "What do you mean?"

"Michael."

She started to ask *what about Michael,* but suddenly she knew. She remembered Andrea's quip about new little tricks in bed, picked up somewhere. Her confidence that an affair, if Michael ever had one, was a challenge she could handle by turning up the heat at home. "Shit."

"In a word."

Elizabeth thought of the way Michael had looked at Andrea when they had pizza. "It's not possible."

"Except that it is."

"You really think he's playing around? Cheating on you?"

"I know he is."

"Oh sweetie." Elizabeth wanted to gather her sister into her arms, but Andrea's proud icy glare sent a clear warning. *Don't you dare feel sorry for me.* "What makes you so sure?"

"Everything." Andrea looked irritated now, as if she shouldn't have to list her reasons. "The usual. Working late, quote unquote. Little things that someone else might not notice, but I do."

Elizabeth's mind was reeling. She never seen her sister like this, acting hard yet clearly vulnerable, and in the very area that had always been her domain. Every possible response felt stupider than the next. *You poor thing. It will be all right. He's a prick anyway.* Michael had punched a hole in her sister's world. Words couldn't knit it back together.

She glanced at Daniel and Katie again, hoping they weren't listening. They didn't seem to be. Their attention was fixed on the TV at the other end of the room.

Get curious (curious) and that's marvelous (marvelous)
And that's your reward, you'll never be bored

Was that really what she'd chosen for her children to watch this morning? Go ahead, leap before you look. It's all too marvelous to resist, so don't.

Less than twenty-four hours ago she was unbuttoning her shirt in Richard's studio. *Curious Georgia.* Wanting to be marvelous, but afraid to take the next step. Michael, apparently, hadn't been.

As if on cue, Katie gave a gleeful laugh. "Curie," she chirped, pointing at the screen.

"Curie-*us*," Daniel said smugly. "He's like a person, only he doesn't wear any clothes."

Elizabeth closed her eyes. Who was writing their dialogue?

Then she blinked, returning her focus to her sister. Andrea, who had done the unimaginable by appearing in her doorway with wet eyes and trembling lips.

Andrea was twisting her hair into a tight coil. Her mouth was twisted too. Again, Elizabeth wanted to pull her into an embrace, and this time she did. Andrea's back was stiff, her arms unyielding, and after a moment she broke away.

"Don't baby me. I needed to vent, that's all."

More words crowded into Elizabeth's mind. *Whatever you need. I'm here for you.* More useless phrases, because something huge and unthinkable was happening—as if gravity had reversed itself and tables, chairs, cars, were flying off into space. As if things had lost their names.

Because this was *Andie,* charming irresistible Andie, with her rhinestone barrettes and midriff-baring halters, her lowered eyelids and the foxy toss of her head.

Those things hadn't protected her, after all. She might as well have been Lizzie-the-owl.

Elizabeth struggled to take it in. Andrea was afraid. And Michael, who'd thought his dalliance was undetectable, had been mistaken. There were consequences, if you were curious.

"What are you going to do?" she asked.

"Besides vent?" Andrea shook out her hair. "I don't know. Maybe nothing. Let him get it out of his system."

"You mean, pretend you don't know?"

"I could," Andrea said. "Because I don't totally *know.* I don't have, like, security tapes. Only what I know about him." She sniffed. "Which is plenty, trust me."

Now Elizabeth was confused. "You don't have any evidence?" She couldn't help thinking of what Harold would say. *Without data, it's just conjecture.*

Andrea frowned. "Maybe I should do that, get actual evidence."

"It might be helpful. So you'd know, for sure."

"So he can't tell me I'm being paranoid."

"Would he do that?"

"Who knows what a person would do, if they thought they'd been caught?" Andrea flipped her hair behind her shoulders. "If I have proof, I can decide when to use it, or if I want to use it. I'll have some power in this shit storm." Elizabeth could see the sheen of tears on her sister's cheeks.

My turn to help, she thought. Andrea had given her highlights and a layered haircut. She could give her this, in return. Her skill, as an investigator.

"If you want to get real evidence," she said, "you have to think it through."

"I wouldn't know where to begin. That's your specialty, Lizzie, thinking things through."

Elizabeth pursed her lips. "You need a plan."

"Right. To catch him in the act."

"You want to confront him?"

"No, not yet. He doesn't know that I know, and I want to keep it that way." Andrea's face hardened. "I need to set a trap."

"You mean, spy on him?"

"Fine. Spy on him. Whatever it takes to get what I need without him knowing." Her expression was beseeching and demanding at the same time. It must have been the way she looked, Elizabeth thought, when she cajoled teachers into giving her extra time on assignments or finessed her way out of being grounded for coming home late. "You're clever, Lizzie. You can think up a good scheme. I know you can."

Clever. That meant sly enough to figure out how to sneak behind a husband's back.

It was just so she could understand O'Keeffe. She wasn't having an affair, like Michael.

Andrea inched closer. "You know me, Lizzie. I do whatever's in front of me. I don't know how to think like that—two steps ahead, like someone who'd cook up a smart lie as a cover for sneaking around."

A pang of guilt stung Elizabeth in the chest, in the very spot Richard had touched. *Whenever you're ready.*

She glanced at the clock. The TV show would be over soon. "Well," she said, "what sort of things does Michael do with his time—you know, something you'd never dare to question?"

"Something above suspicion?"

"Exactly. You'd look possessive and neurotic if you questioned it."

"Ha. That's good, Lizzie. Keep going."

Elizabeth's eyes darted to the bag of clothes. Her heart skipped a beat, as if she had already betrayed the person who would soon be wearing those neatly folded shirts. "Not squash," she said. "Ben would rat on him if he used that as a cover."

"Unless they're covering for each other."

Elizabeth snorted. "I don't think so."

"You think Ben's immune?"

"No one's immune." Her jaw tightened. "But no, they aren't bad-boy pals like that. It would have to be something else that Michael does with his time. Something altruistic."

"You're right." Andrea grew thoughtful. Then she brightened, looking almost happy. "I know *exactly* how the little sneak is playing me. It's that damn coat drive at his office. I kept wondering how there could be that many fucking coats to organize." She grabbed Elizabeth's arm. "You're the best, Lizzie. I always did love that steel-trap mind of yours."

Elizabeth flinched at her sister's grip. Andrea's elation scared her. She wanted to caution her: "Don't count on my mind so much. It doesn't know everything."

Instead, she kept her reply mild, noncommittal. "Don't be so quick to draw conclusions, that's all. Life's complicated."

"Aha." Animated now, Andrea pounced on the remark. "I get to ask you, *again*, why it's so complicated. And you get to answer me this time."

"Me?"

"You. Something's up. I can tell."

Elizabeth hesitated. She'd wanted to talk about it. Well, why not now? Maybe it would take Andrea's mind off her own concerns. "You really want to know?"

"Duh. So you'd really better *tell*."

Again, she wavered. Once said, it couldn't be unsaid.

Oh, who cared? Hadn't the impossible just happened to Andrea? That meant anything could happen; the world could flip inside-out. "I'm kind of interested in someone."

"Other than Ben."

"My turn to say duh."

"Who?"

"He's in my Tai Chi class."

"The plot thickens."

"It's nothing, really."

"How do you know? Is he interested back?"

Elizabeth thought of the way Richard had undone the button on her shirt. *Let yourself open, right from here.* "He might be."

"So. No sizzle with old Ben, even with your new haircut?" Andrea thrust out her chin. "Then I say, go for it. If they can, we can." Her tone grew sharp. "Men. Husbands. We can do it too."

She's angry, Elizabeth thought. She wants to get back at Michael.

"We'll see." She glanced at Daniel and Katie again, saw that they were still enraptured by the monkey's antics, and turned back to Andrea. "And what about you, Andie? What are you going to do about Michael? I mean, how?"

"Pooh. That's the easy part, now that you've broken the code."

"You need to think it through—" she began, but Andrea cut her off. "I got it. I'm not a complete moron, you know."

The brassy chorus filled the room. *And that's your reward, you'll never be bored.* "I think the show's over," Elizabeth said.

Andrea stood and dusted off her jeans. "That's my cue. I'll keep you posted."

Elizabeth rose too. Don't, she thought. She didn't want to know if Andrea had caught Michael in his secrets and lies.

But she gave her sister a hug, saying only, "Thanks for the clothes. And good luck."

Mr. Wu's daughter was waiting on the fourth-floor landing, at a respectful distance from the curtained archway that led to the dojo. "I have a cab waiting," she announced. Within moments, she had whisked her father into the elevator.

Elizabeth went to get her purse and shoes from the cubbyhole. Around her, the other students were collecting their own sweaters and shoes. She could hear fragments of conversation, Juniper's high-pitched commentary. She wasn't sure what she was supposed to do. Wait for Richard again? Could they still sip Americanos, after the hour in his studio? Not that anything had happened. She had fled before it could.

She drew her shoes out of the cubbyhole and bent to slip them on. She could have tossed them on the floor and stepped into them quickly, but every second she took before leaving the dojo was another second before she would have to find out—or decide—if she would see Richard tonight.

He'd have to lock up. Should she wait for him on the street? What if she did, and he walked right past her? What if she didn't, and he wished she had?

The lights flickered, and the dojo turned dark. Only a splatter of light remained from the waiting area in front of the elevator. Her heart throbbed against her ribs, a fat red muscle she couldn't fool.

"Anyone back there?" Richard called.

Voices rang out from the far end of the landing, near the

restrooms. "Coming!" It was one of the older women, a wiry elf with a grey pony-tail.

A bearded man, her husband, hurried to join her. "Sorry to keep you waiting."

Elizabeth hoisted her purse onto her shoulder. She'd walk out with them, a protective flank. That way, Richard wouldn't think she expected anything. She caught up with the couple, trying not to look at him, but her lashes lifted, on their own, and she looked into his eyes.

He wanted her to wait. The message was right there, in those smoky grey irises. "We'd better go down together," he said. "I have to turn off the access to the floor, once we're all out."

"Good security," the bearded man said. "Can't be too careful, these days." He motioned for his wife to precede him.

Elizabeth followed them into the elevator. Richard was the last to get on. He leaned against the side, near the panel of buttons. There was an empty spot in the front but he settled near the back corner, only inches from where she stood. She could see the planes of his face, a shadow of stubble on his cheek. The elevator growled to a halt, and the couple got off. "See you next week," the woman called. Her husband fished in his pocket, pulling out a set of car keys. He gave a quick salute, and they hurried across the street.

Elizabeth and Richard were alone in front of the building. The streetlight flickered. If she did the wrong thing, it would all be over.

"So," he said. He slouched against the building, hands in his pockets. "I did some more reading about your Mr. Stieglitz."

Elizabeth tried to match his nonchalance. "And?"

"And he had an interesting approach to photography." He smiled, and her pulse began to race. "He'd go out into the world with his camera until he came across something that excited him. He'd take the picture, and then he'd manipulate the print, make it into a kind of abstraction, an evocation, of what he felt when he looked at the scene. It was pretty radical for those days. Because he wasn't trying to be accurate. He was expressing, creating."

"Learning," Elizabeth said. "He was always learning." About photography, and about Georgia. The way Georgia was learning about herself, by posing for him.

"O'Keeffe said the same thing," she told Richard. *"I had to create an equivalent for what I felt about what I was looking at, not copy it."*

"You think one of them imitated the other, or they both saw it the same way?"

"It would be nice to think they were that attuned, wouldn't it? But they probably talked about it."

Richard's voice was low, unhurried. "They had a lot of time to talk, you know, while he was taking his pictures. The exposures were really long in those days, up to four minutes. Think of it. The two of them waiting together, not moving, all that time."

Elizabeth held his gaze. Not four minutes, but longer than two people ought to, who were standing in public like that.

"Of course, maybe he was just wrapped up in his own creativity. O'Keeffe once said that Stieglitz was always photographing himself."

Richard stared at her in surprise, then let out a roar of laugher. Elizabeth flushed, pleased with herself. Then, abruptly, he grew serious again. "What do you think, Elizabeth? Is the photographer always taking his own portrait, or can he see and capture someone else?" The grey eyes penetrated hers. "Really see them?"

"I guess it would depend on how carefully he looked." She cleared her throat, trying not to fly out of her skin. *"When you take a flower in your hand and really look at it, it's your world for the moment."*

"More quotations?"

"I'm afraid so."

"Are you?" He caught her fingers in his hand. "Afraid?"

"A little."

"Are we going to try again, anyway?"

Elizabeth drew in her breath. "Yes. We are."

After all, her sister had told her to.

Thirteen

awaii. Elizabeth typed the word into the search engine of her laptop. She needed to know about the real things O'Keeffe had seen and touched while she was there, the raw material O'Keeffe had transformed into her paintings.

Most of O'Keeffe's time had been spent on Maui, with Patricia Jennings as her guide. Jennings, a young girl whose father managed a sugar plantation, took O'Keeffe to her favorite places, introducing her to a verdant landscape that must have taken Georgia's breath away. Elizabeth scrolled through the websites designed to lure travelers to the islands. Rainforests, cascading waterfalls, the freshwater pools of the Ohe'o Gulch. The massive Haleakala volcano. The hairpin turns of the Hana Road, with their heart-stopping view of cliffs plunging to the sea. The Wai'anapanapa coastline, black sand beaches, arches, and caves; the white sands of Palauea. The 'Iao Valley, inspiration for four of O'Keeffe's paintings. Hawaii's exotic flowers: Plumeria, Bird of Paradise, Ginger, Heliconia.

Everything about Hawaii was the inverse of what Georgia was used to. Breathing itself must have been strange and new. In New Mexico, Georgia had breathed air that was crisp and dry; in Hawaii, the very oxygen was thick and soft, heavy with a different kind of heat. Volcanic mountains replaced New Mexico's bare red hills. High and craggy, emerald and jade against an azure sea. A landscape lush and fecund and wet, unlike anything in Georgia's experience.

How had Georgia coped, a desert creature flung into the tropics? The weight of the air, hot and moist on her skin—it must have pushed at her with the relentless question. *Who am I, here, in this place?*

Elizabeth could almost feel it. The sensuality, everywhere. Georgia had to paint. It was the only way to keep from drowning in sensation.

She turned to her folder of prints, flipping through the pictures, looking for something she had missed. *Hibiscus with Plumeria*, with its flimsy diminished sexuality; the mysterious golden *Hibiscus* that never got included in the art books. *Cup of Silver Ginger*, a complicated painting that she had found difficult to like.

She drew *Cup of Silver Ginger* from the stack and laid it next to her laptop. The white petals, tinged with lime, seemed to bulge outward—begging her to fit her palm over the white mound, press her thumb into the dense green swirls, trace the frayed edges of the petals. She could almost feel the soft mysterious mass of palest orange, like cotton or smoke, the silk of the lavender corners. She wanted to crawl inside and lie down.

And then she understood. The understanding had begun earlier, when she looked at the 'Iao Valley paintings, but now it opened wide, revealing itself to her stunned comprehension.

Georgia's paintings weren't meant to be looked at, from the outside. They were meant to be entered, experienced.

Elizabeth remembered what Richard had told her about Stieglitz. Stieglitz would use cropping and lighting to transform an object into something universal and abstract. In control, always. Georgia was different. She used her art to draw the viewer inside. Whether it was a flower, a pelvis, a fissure in the hills—it was the same gesture. *Enter. Participate.*

After Hawaii, the openings were cleaner, starker, nothing that could be mistaken for mere beauty. A pelvic opening against the flat blue sky. A doorway, a window.

Elizabeth sat back, staring at her folder. She had figured it out, what she wanted to say in her dissertation.

Lindstrom would be happy. Marion Mackenzie too, because her dissertation would be about a female artist claiming her own form of knowledge.

There's something unexplored about woman that only a woman can explore.

Hawaii had transformed Georgia through her body, not just her eyes or her paintbrush.

Instead of elation, Elizabeth felt a grief so immense that it made her grab the edge of the desk. She had her idea now. She didn't need to do what Georgia did, in order to write about her. The whole point of posing for Richard was gone.

They had an agreement: posing was a way to jolt her into understanding how O'Keeffe related to the world. It was audacious, provocative, but it had a purpose. Without that purpose, there was no reason to continue.

Unless she just—wanted to. Wanted to take her clothes off and let him look at her, the way Stieglitz had looked at O'Keeffe.

They hadn't even started. It wasn't fair to stop now.

Elizabeth let out a cry. She tried to stifle the sound but it was too late. There were no walls between the dining room, where she had her desk, and the living room, where Ben was watching a basketball game. "Liz?" He turned around. "You okay?"

"I jabbed my elbow, that's all."

"Be careful." Elizabeth didn't know if he was being critical or concerned; it didn't matter. He made a vaguely sympathetic sound and returned to the game.

No, she told herself. Just because she had a good idea about the ovoid motif, it didn't mean she was finished with her quest. She needed to understand O'Keeffe in any way she could. Harold had told her not to limit herself. She could experiment. Pose, if that was part of her research.

Good Lord. She was on her way to a gold medal in the self-deception Olympics. You didn't need a graduate degree to figure that out.

And yet, it was true. Something had shifted. She didn't want to imitate Georgia any more. She wanted this for herself.

Elizabeth closed the laptop and stood. "Ben," she said. "I meant to ask you."

He muted the sound and turned around again. "Ask me what?"

She leaned against the arch that separated the dining alcove from the rest of the room. "If you can watch the kids on Saturday morning. I said I'd do a tutorial session for some of the students who're falling behind."

Saturday, Richard had told her. She could try again on Saturday.

"On your own time? Seems a bit exploitive."

"I'm just trying to help. Anyway, they aren't making me. I offered. If you can watch the kids, that is."

Ben shook his head. "It's not the greatest timing. I was hoping to meet with the leader of the tenants' organization on Saturday morning. He works Monday to Friday."

Elizabeth tried to mask her disappointment. She didn't want to pit her good deed against his, even if hers was a fabrication. On the other hand, he hadn't actually refused.

"I'm a little confused," she said. "You were hoping, or you already arranged it?"

He sighed. "Fine, I'll do it another time." His eyes darted to the TV as someone in a white-and-green jersey pushed a basketball through the hoop. "I'm sure your students will appreciate it."

Something altruistic, above suspicion—that's what she had advised Andrea, who wanted to unmask her husband's deception. "Thanks. It'll only be a couple of hours."

Oh, she was learning fast. That was one good thing about being an owl.

Richard had a stack of prints, reproductions of Stieglitz's portraits of O'Keeffe. "We'll start with the top one," he said, "and work our way through, as far as you want."

Yes, that was better, Elizabeth thought. A trail to follow, a plan. No Richard, wanting to see her collarbone when she wasn't prepared. She examined the pile of photos he had placed on a wooden table in the center of the studio. The top photo was a close-up of O'Keeffe's hands, one above the other, bent, like cranes poised in a *pas de deux*. The others were hidden below it.

He touched the picture, then gave a soft shrug, as if to say: *You see? You're in control. Nothing's going to happen that you don't want to happen.*

Like the cranes, in a delicate dance. If one crane wanted to stop, the dance ended.

She considered asking to see all the pictures, to know what lay ahead. But Richard was already in motion, pointing her toward a dark screen. "Stieglitz tended to use a dark backdrop, so we will too." He grabbed a camera with one hand, using the other to steer her to the screen. "He did a half-dozen shots of her hands, all of them gorgeous. Always both hands, never just one." He gave Elizabeth a sideways look. "I think he was in awe of her hands. His art was all from his eyes and his mind. Not from his hands the way hers was, as a painter."

"That's interesting."

"It's all interesting." He pulled a metal stool in front of the screen. "Here. You can sit. It'll be easier for you to hold your hands up."

Elizabeth climbed onto the stool while he adjusted the settings on his camera. She began to feel nervous—not because he was trying to seduce her, but because he wasn't. No smoldering looks or slow stroking the curve of her finger. He was serious now, professional. Well, that was the idea, wasn't it? A photo shoot, not a date.

She wanted to ask him why he was doing this. She had never really asked, only accepted that he understood what she needed. But he didn't really know her. He didn't even know about Daniel and Katie.

"I'll position your hands," he said. "Just hold them where I put them."

"Not for four minutes, I hope."

He laughed. "No, it'll be quick. We're a hundred years past the technology Stieglitz had to use." Delicately, he bent her hands and placed them the way O'Keeffe's were in the photo. Then he stepped back and snapped the picture. "You see? Easy." He took a step to the left and clicked the camera three more times. "Hold it, just like that." More shots, from different angles.

"I can drop my hands now?"

"You can drop them." He walked to the table, placed the photo of Georgia's hands to the left of the stack, and picked up the next photo. "This one is wonderful too." Elizabeth waited. He returned to where she was sitting and handed the picture to her.

Georgia's face was in profile, her hair pulled back. Her bare upper arm filled the bottom of the frame. Both arms were raised, fingers open like the fronds of a fern. "She looks so strong" Elizabeth said. "Like a priestess."

"That's good. Try to feel that way yourself, when you take the pose."

Elizabeth studied the picture. Georgia's shoulder, round and powerful, was cropped at the base of the composition. There was no way to tell if she was wearing anything. There might have been a strap, hidden by the curve of flesh, or there might not.

"Take your shirt off," he said. "You can leave everything else. All I need is your arm."

Elizabeth wet her lips. "Right." She drew the blue jersey over her head and let it fall to the floor. She kept her bra on. He hadn't told her to take it off, not yet.

"I need your hair back." He came up behind her and smoothed her hair from her face. "Like that. Just a part of the ear, and a scallop of hairline. The rest won't show." Elizabeth felt his palms against her scalp, their loss when he stepped away. "Look down," he told her. "Inward. You're quiet and alone. Nothing can distract you."

He raised her arms, opened right hand into a fan. She felt regal, pure, poised in an ancient ritual. A queen, sure of her power.

"Don't move." He took two shots, then a third. "Perfect." She held the pose as he tried different angles, closer and further away. Then he met her eyes. "Another?"

"Yes. All right." She lowered her arms and started to reach for the blue jersey, then thought: why?

"I thought we'd focus on hands today." He took the next picture from the stack. "Hands and faces. There were so many ways he tried to portray O'Keeffe, just through her hands and face."

"Yes. I want the pictures that show her face. So we know it's her."

Richard stood behind her as she examined the photo he had placed on the table. Georgia looked pensive and lovely, dark hair loose across her shoulder. One arm framed her face while the other, cropped, entered the portrait from outside. The fingers were spread, palms facing the camera. Elizabeth noted the thin white strap of a camisole. It meant she would be covered. She felt a flicker of relief, yet the dark mass of underarm hair, so raw and exposed, seemed unbearably erotic.

"This one was taken against one of her paintings," Richard said. "We'll have to make do with a dark background."

Elizabeth was still looking at the picture. She didn't have a camisole, just a bra, but only the strap would show. Like a bathing suit. People wore less at the beach.

"Take the pose," he told her. "Don't think about it."

Elizabeth looked closely. "I think she was leaning against the painting."

"You're right." He looked around. "Pick a wall." Seeing the question on her face, he added, "You can't lean against the screen. It's not sturdy enough."

Leaving the jersey on the floor, Elizabeth walked to the far wall. A strange new boldness filled her limbs as she walked; she hoped he was watching. "Show me the picture again. Or do you want to arrange me?"

"I want you to take the pose yourself. However you feel it."

"All right." She pressed against the wall and raised her arms. Her armpits were shaved. She wished they weren't, wished she had that raw mass of hair to reveal to him.

"How do you feel?" he asked.

The word spoke itself. "Beautiful."

"Yes. Beautiful." He watched her, his eyes shrouded. "Show me."

She held the pose. Her expression was private, like Georgia's. She could feel her skin tingling, alert and alive. She couldn't believe she was doing this. It was unreal, yet realer than anything she'd ever done.

She heard the click of the shutter. Then again, as he circled her. "Yes, good."

She dropped her arms. "What's next?"

Richard walked to the little table. He ruffled through the stack of prints. "Do you want to see what we've got so far? I can load the photos onto my laptop."

Look at the pictures, with Richard? No. She didn't want to see them. It would make her into a looker instead of a woman in a body; it would break the spell. "No. Let's keep going." She followed him to the little table.

He moved the portrait she had replicated to the side of the stack. There were three photos on the left now, completed, and a dozen remaining on the right. "Have a look at these. They're all from the same day, the same series. We can do one, or all, or none." He spread three new photos across the table.

Elizabeth leaned forward to look. The first was of Georgia in a white robe, dreamy and disheveled, her left thumb resting inside the open V of the robe. In the next, her chin was held high, her expression austere and ethereal, the robe open to reveal the top of her breasts. In the third, she was looking into the distance, the robe fully open, hands cupping her breasts, the edge of a dark nipple between her splayed fingers.

Her boldness dissolved. The sense she'd had, only moments before—of being more fully herself, imitating Georgia, than she was in her own life—fell away like petals from a dry rose, like the dust of the stolen hibiscus. What game did she think she was playing? She was supposed to hold her breasts and offer them to Richard? It was sick, a delusion. The pathetic fantasy of a lovesick adolescent. And what did it have to do with her dissertation? Was she planning to tell Harold, "By the way, I'm adding another kind of data?"

Her neck and face were wet. She wiped her hand across her forehead.

Richard's voice was quiet. "Or none. Whatever you want."

Why did she have to decide? She wanted him to decide.

Georgia would have decided for herself. That was the point. That was why she had to do this—so she could understand how to be like Georgia, who did what she wanted.

"This one," she said, touching the middle picture. A compromise.

Richard looked at the photo. "I don't have a robe but I can get you one of my white shirts. Stay here. I'll be right back."

Did he really think she would leave, now that she'd come this far? Again, she wondered why he was doing this. Shouldn't she ask? She watched him disappear through a door at the other end of the long room. Maybe she didn't want to know. She shivered and wished, for an instant, that she had picked the third photo.

Richard returned with a white shirt. "We'll use the light backdrop this time." He handed her the shirt and went to retrieve the metal stool. When his back was turned, Elizabeth unhooked her bra, slipping it off her shoulders, and put on the shirt. Holding it closed with her fist, she followed him to the other side of the studio.

She sat on the stool, and he lifted her chin. "Your hair needs to be loose, down your back." Then he moved her hand, gently, and the shirt fell open.

She began to tremble. In a moment he would look at her, see everything. The tender nipples, the sensitive skin. An offering that felt, just then, more intimate than anything she had ever offered to Ben or her children.

"You have nothing to be afraid of," he told her. "Your breasts are lovely. Your skin, and that beautiful collarbone."

She squeezed her eyes shut. Yes. No. She couldn't bear it.

"Don't disappear," he told her. He picked up the camera.

The trembling grew stronger. And then, suddenly, it stopped. She opened the shirt all the way. She looked right into the lens. A series of clicks, like raindrops, or a heartbeat.

"The third one," she said. The one where Georgia took her breasts in her hands, loving them. She wanted Richard to see her doing that.

His hand was steady as he snapped the picture. Each snap, another heartbeat.

Elizabeth looked at the wooden table. There were more photos in the pile; these were only the beginning. As if he had read her glance, Richard drew a photo from the middle of the stack. "I know you want pictures with her face, but I want this one too." It was a close-up, cropped, of Georgia's hand between her breasts. One breast faced into the camera, heavy and full, the nipple like a child's eye. "Can you do this?"

Elizabeth looked at his hand, holding the photograph. "Yes. I can do this."

—

She lay next to Ben, listening to the low *pfft* of his breathing as he slept. The room was dark, only the yellow glow of the night-light in the hall and an oblong of moonlight, slanting from the window onto the hardwood floor. Elizabeth lay on her back, staring at nothing. The quilt was impossibly heavy. She kicked it off.

Memories of Richard's studio swirled in her mind. Watching him watch her. Herself, inside her body. The pictures of Georgia spread on the table. She'd thought of asking Richard if she could see the photos he had taken, after all, but she didn't, and he didn't offer again. She didn't really want to see them. If she did, she might feel foolish and want to stop.

Lying in the dark bedroom, she relived the morning, pose by pose. An ache rose up in her to be seen, ever more fully.

She propped herself on an elbow and studied the slope of Ben's shoulder as he lay on his side, the slow rise and fall of his chest. He had touched her many times, yet never with the intimacy she had felt in Richard's studio. Had she betrayed him? No. There was nothing to betray.

Then she rolled away, pulled up the quilt, and tried to sleep.

Phoebe was helping Ruthie and Rex out of their jackets when Elizabeth arrived at Lucy's house. Rex squirmed out of his jacket as he and Daniel slammed into each other, half tackle, half embrace. "I have *Bat*man," Daniel shouted.

"I have *Spider*man," Rex countered, holding up the action figure like an Olympic torch. They raced off to the playroom.

"Don't cry," Ruthie told Katie. "I'll play with you." Katie dropped Elizabeth's hand and followed Ruthie down the hall.

Phoebe blew her daughter a kiss, then burst out laughing. "Go figure. Just when I've written Ruthie off as a hopeless diva, she goes and does something lovely like that."

"Katie will be her slave forever."

Phoebe turned to Elizabeth. "So how are you?"

How was she? Elizabeth longed to tell Phoebe what she had done. It was so extraordinary, so far outside anything that mothers talked about. Yet she needed to talk, she needed to tell someone.

Lucy hurried into the foyer, wiping her hands on a dishcloth. "I thought I heard you."

"You did," Phoebe answered. "It's us. The conjoined moms."

"You do seem to be on the same schedule these days."

"It must be a conspiracy." Phoebe gave a merry grin, and Elizabeth considered, again, whether Phoebe was someone she might confide in. They were women, weren't they? Mothers, professionals, members of the same generation.

"Well, now that the troops have landed, I'd better see what they're up to." Lucy slung the towel over her shoulder. "See you later, ladies. Enjoy your day."

"You too." When Lucy had vanished into the playroom, Phoebe turned back to Elizabeth. "Really. How *are* you? You look a little—I don't know, wired?"

Wired? Maybe. Like a guitar string that had stretched further than it ever imagined.

I want this one, too, he had told her. Not a question. The ripe naked breast. The single faceless portrait among all the photos he had taken, but it was still her.

Oh, she had to speak, right now, before she started to think of all the reasons she shouldn't. "How am I?" she echoed. "In transition. A work in progress."

"Hey, aren't we all?"

"I mean, I really am."

"Well, of course. You never know what's up next. Charlie and I are, like, so what's today's insanity?"

Elizabeth felt her conviction dim. Even if she tried to tell her, there was no way Phoebe would understand. She had Charlie.

Phoebe picked up the jackets and hung them on pegs by the door. "Wine and cheese was fun, by the way. We should do it again. The four of us. We have a lot in common."

No, we don't. But Elizabeth nodded politely. "Absolutely."

Phoebe blew an air kiss at each of Elizabeth's cheeks. "Well, got to fly. But text me, we'll find a good time to do it again." She yelled, "Bye, Lucy! See you later."

Elizabeth watched Phoebe stride down the flagstone walkway to her car. It was Phoebe's fault. If she hadn't flaunted her relationship with her husband, Elizabeth wouldn't have had to bare herself to Richard.

Phoebe, Andrea. There was always someone reminding her that what she had wasn't enough.

If she wanted more, she had to take it.

Fourteen

Marion Mackenzie's office was bigger and grander than Harold Lindstrom's. Marion had written textbooks, had an endowed chair; that was how these things worked, so many square feet for each line in your c.v. Tall shelves were jammed with art books and spiral-bound university publications. A framed print of Dove's *Me and the Moon* hung above the glass-topped desk. A bright rug in matching tones of black and grey and gold covered the floor.

"I'm glad you could stop by," Marion said. "I thought we should get to know each other a little." She crossed her legs, graceful in real stockings, and arranged her hands in her lap. A silk scarf was twisted around her throat, a swath of coral that matched her lipstick. "Harold sang your praises—which is, of course, why I agreed to join your committee—but there's no substitute for a personal connection, don't you think?"

Elizabeth wasn't sure which part of the sentence to respond to. The last part seemed safest. "Definitely," she said. "And truly, I'm honored to have you on my committee, Dr. Mackenzie."

Marion waved an elegant hand. "Please. Call me Marion. We're on the same team."

"Yes, thank you." She didn't think she could say *Marion*, though. It seemed indecent, unearned.

Marion ran her palm across the glass figurines that lined her desk. They were cobalt, lime, amber, curious abstract shapes. "A shame you couldn't make it to my talk but I'd be glad to send you a copy of the paper."

Elizabeth resisted the impulse to repeat the story about the babysitter with the flu. "I'd love that. Thank you." Was she thanking her too much? Humble plus confident, she reminded herself. The best stance for a budding scholar.

"It might be useful, who knows?" Marion dropped her hand and eyed Elizabeth sternly. "So what do you think, now that you're deep into your research? Georgia O'Keeffe, matriarch of American Modernism, or Georgia O'Keeffe, matriarch of female artists?"

It was the same question Elizabeth had posed to her students. "We know what O'Keeffe herself would have said. There's this story about how she had a request for an interview about women artists, and she said, 'A silly topic. Write about women. Or write about artists. I don't see how they're connected.'"

"Maybe she was just being ornery. She had to know it was a legitimate question."

"I don't know. She stood her ground about that, over the years."

"Phooey. She used her identity as a woman in her art. She used it to get noticed, for heaven's sake."

"At last, a woman on paper." Elizabeth hoped Marion would recognize the quote.

She did. "Exactly. Stieglitz was desperate to be the first person to showcase a woman artist—an American woman artist, in particular." Marion gave a disdainful sniff. "Even if it meant showcasing her as the subject of his own art. Showing *off*, I should say."

"You think it was self-serving? A way to promote himself, not her?"

"I think it was for their mutual benefit." Marion brushed her fingertips across the amber figurine. It was a glossy curved mound, like a sleeping cat. "They knew perfectly well what they were doing with that photography show. He wanted to create a demand for her art, which would benefit them both— it was his gallery, after all, and his reputation for spotting artists who were ahead of their time. Plus, they needed money. If generating public fascination with O'Keeffe as a woman—a scandalous woman—was the best way to achieve that, it was fine with him. And her." Marion gave a grimace of distaste. "There was no way he could have pulled it off without her collusion. She knew precisely what kind of attention those nude photos would get her. It's disingenuous to claim that she didn't."

The amber figurine cast an oval shadow across Marion's desk. Elizabeth watched as Marion moved it an inch to the right.

"It's true," she conceded. "Stieglitz told everyone that her art was the first truly female art—you know, drawing its energy and expression from her secret female essence. But the idea was already out there in the public consciousness, long before he showed her work. For sure, it shaped the critics' response. They'd already decided what her paintings meant, before they'd even seen them. The exotic wellspring of repressed female sexuality, never before revealed in art. It came from what Stieglitz wrote about her, not from her art itself."

"What he wrote with her permission."

"Maybe."

Marion shook her head. "O'Keeffe posed nude for an ambitious man whose mission in life was to promote work he believed in, including his own. You don't think she deluded herself about that, do you? No matter how upset she claimed to be, she had to have known what he was doing. What *they* were doing."

Elizabeth stared at her. Was Marion implying that Richard was ambitious, with his own agenda? That she was colluding with him, the way Marion thought O'Keeffe had colluded with Stieglitz?

No, that was crazy. There was no way Marion could know about Richard. Her remarks were academic, not personal.

The blue eyes flashed, electricity glinting on snow. "What do you think, Elizabeth? Wasn't O'Keeffe trying to have it both ways?"

"You mean, disavowing how she presented herself in those photos, while also benefitting from it?"

"Exactly."

Elizabeth hesitated. Marion was interested in her; that's what Harold had told her. *A formidable ally.* Someone who could help her vault right to the top of the academic ladder. A hasty response, challenging or offending Marion, could jeopardize that alliance.

"It's hard to say," she answered. "A lot of people gave Stieglitz all the credit, as if he'd created her. He did have the status, the connections. At the same time, O'Keeffe was pretty tough and independent."

"Later. Not when she was starting out." Marion shrugged. "We'll never really know, of course. But that's why I don't like O'Keeffe, genius that she was. I can't stand hypocrisy."

Elizabeth straightened her back. Marion's words were a warning. "Well, I'm focusing on Hawaii, as you know. It's a pretty specific aspect of her life."

"Indeed." Marion reached across the desk and switched two of the figurines, moving the smaller one behind the larger. "She was already a major figure in American art by the time she went to Hawaii."

"True. But she went there in 1939, just when she was starting to break free from Stieglitz."

Marion looked up with interest. "Personally or artistically?"

"I think they were the same thing."

Marion smiled. "I imagine that's right."

Elizabeth dared to return her smile. "Just a couple of years earlier, Elizabeth Arden—you know, the cosmetics entrepreneur and, really, one of the few women with that kind of stature in the business world—commissioned O'Keeffe to do a huge flower painting for her New York salon. It was O'Keeffe's first commercial commission. Stieglitz didn't like it because she took the job without consulting him. She'd never done that before, but it was a big success. A giant composition of four jimson weed flowers."

"He'd always managed her career."

"Always. There was even a big four-page story in *Life* Magazine, less than a year before she went to Hawaii, that gave Stieglitz all the credit for her fame—as if, without him, she'd still be a schoolteacher in some backwater town in the middle of nowhere. I think O'Keeffe was sick of it. Then she got the Dole offer. A free trip to an island paradise five thousand miles from Stieglitz, in exchange for a picture of a pineapple."

"So the Dole job was well-timed?"

"That's part of my argument."

Marion nodded. "I think you have a good topic. It hasn't been studied much, which works in your favor. Originality plus good scholarship makes an unbeatable combination. It's what departments look for, when they hire."

Elizabeth understood the reference but didn't think she was supposed to know about the opening at Marion's former university. Better to assume that she wasn't.

Yet she couldn't keep the image from rising up and filling her mind. Her own office, with a framed print of Georgia's *Abstraction, White Rose* on the wall. A brass nameplate, like Harold's. Sitting on the dais at university events in her academic robe.

Marion switched the figurines back the way they had been. When she returned her attention to Elizabeth, her face was composed. "One thing at a time. For now, let me know how I can help with your research."

"I will. Thank you."

"I'll send you that Arthur Dove paper."

Elizabeth remembered what Harold Lindstrom had told her. Don't disappoint Marion Mackenzie. Marion doesn't like it when people let her down. "Hearing you read aloud would have been wonderful," she said, "but I'm excited to read it, in any form."

Marion extended her hand. "Always glad to help another woman scholar. The world needs more of us."

"O'Keeffe would have said, 'The world needs more scholars. Not more women. I don't see how they're connected.'"

Marion laughed. "I like you, Elizabeth Crawford. I'll see you soon."

Elizabeth practically danced down the stairs of the Humanities building. Having the great Mackenzie *like you* was a phenomenal piece of luck. She'd read that Arthur Dove thing, and then she'd prove to Marion Mackenzie that she was someone worth liking. She'd write an immaculate and impressive dissertation, a work of scholarship that Marion would respect.

Re-enacting Georgia's poses had nothing to do with it, not any more. Maybe she had really believed, at first, that *doing what she did* would open the portal to a truer understanding of O'Keeffe's art. Maybe it even had. But she was past that now.

She had her thesis, her central idea. That was for Marion, and Harold.

And she had the stack of photos on the table in Richard's studio. That was for him.

And for herself.

Two hours later, Daniel had a colossal episode of impossible-ness at pickup time, refusing to leave the Lego spaceship he had built because he didn't want anyone to touch it. There were other children—shadowy, malevolent aliens—who came to Lucy's house on days that he didn't and played with the Legos behind his back. They would ruin his masterpiece.

Lucy tried to remind him that the Legos, like all the toys, were for everyone to enjoy, returning to the bins at the end of the day. Not hidden, as Daniel had suggested, and definitely not taken home.

Elizabeth was well aware of Lucy's rule. Racetracks, battlegrounds, villages, everything had to be dismantled. And she understood Lucy's logic. Without it, there would soon be nothing to play with, just a museum of private untouchable creations. Part of her was mortified by Daniel's behavior. She wanted her children to be generous and easy-going; surely all the other children Lucy watched were like that. Yet another part of her thought Daniel was right. Didn't the fact that he'd created the spaceship—his vision, his work—count for something?

Daniel was gripping the spaceship, his face growing redder and redder. The seconds ticked past. Think, Elizabeth told herself. Use that big IQ of yours.

With a swift decisive movement, she unzipped her messenger bag and pulled out her cell phone. "Let's take pictures of the ship. That way, if anything breaks or gets moved, which it *won't*, you'll know exactly how to fix it." She handed him the phone.

Daniel's mouth dropped open. She was offering him her iPhone? "Can I take the pictures myself?"

"Of course. I'll show you how."

He was tapping away, his misery forgotten in the thrill of taking pictures with his mother's magical iPhone, when Phoebe burst through Lucy's door. "Yikes, what a day," she announced. Then she spotted Elizabeth. "Goodness, we *are* the Bobbsey Twins. Same schedule, once again." She dipped her chin in Daniel's direction, indicating the iPhone that he was pointing at the spaceship. "You're brave."

"Desperate," Elizabeth said. "He needed a diversion. Nothing like a bit of photography to take your mind off the world's injustice."

As soon as she said the word *photography*, her mind leapt to Richard. An irresistible need grabbed her in its talons. To say his name aloud. To hear it said.

She made her tone as casual as she could. "I met a terrific photographer, by the way, in case you ever need one. In my Tai Chi class."

Ruthie came running into the foyer. "Mommy, Mommy."

Elizabeth kept talking. "His name's Richard Ferris. I'm not sure if he does kids, although he does do portraits." Ruthie was trying to explain something, but Elizabeth raised her voice and talked over her. "Richard Ferris," she repeated. "You should look him up."

Phoebe gave Ruthie a *just a second* signal. "Okay. Let me write it down." She reached in her purse and pulled out a notebook. "Ferris? Like the wheel?"

Elizabeth gave a start. "Right. Like the wheel."

"Okay." Phoebe scribbled a few words. "It's true, you never know. I try to keep a file. Someone who fixes shower doors, someone who knows about gutters."

"This isn't like that. He's more of an artist than a repairman."

"Down girl. It was just an example." Phoebe gave her an amused grin. "I got it, okay? Ferris."

Ruthie pulled on her mother's arm. "I want to take pictures, like Daniel. Why can't I take pictures too?"

Phoebe rolled her eyes as she dropped the notebook into her purse and searched for her phone. "Stay in here, please. Don't take it outside."

Elizabeth shuddered. The need to talk about Richard pounded against her temples. And yet, as much as she needed to, another part of her wanted to keep their time in the studio away from foreign eyes and ears. It was private, a language only the two of them knew.

She turned to Daniel. "I think you've got it, buddy. A perfect documentary." She extended her hand for the iPhone. "Let's get Katie and scoot on home."

"She's not going to get a doctor-mennery too, is she?"

"Documentary. It's like a movie. And no, she's too little." Daniel gave a satisfied grunt and handed her the phone.

A wave of exhaustion swept over her. Having to tread so carefully with Marion, and with Ben. Her sister's crisis. The children, the dissertation. How was she supposed to keep all those plates spinning at the same time?

She had to, that was all. "Come, Tiger," she said, putting a hand on top of Daniel's head.

"Can I show Daddy my doctor-mennery?"

"Of course you can. Daddy will love it."

He would. Ben was a good father; he had embraced fatherhood with dedication and joy. If he hadn't brought the same effortless delight to their marriage—well, neither had she.

"Do I still have to leave my ship here, like Lucy said?" To Elizabeth's amazement, Daniel's words held a glimmer of hope.

She wanted to tell him, *No, you don't. It's yours, and you take it if you need it. Screw Lucy's rules.* She couldn't say that, obviously. Not if she wanted to be a responsible mother.

But she was more than a mother. She was a woman, and she was tired of being so responsible.

The next time Elizabeth entered Richard's studio—Saturday, when she told Ben she was holding a student tutorial—she saw that the shades had been pulled down. Instead of natural light from the windows, there were two complicated lamps on movable poles. The dark screen was still there at the back of the room, and a gauzy curtain had been draped across a paler screen in the opposite corner. "I didn't want you to worry that someone might look in," Richard told her. The corners of his mouth curved in a smile that seemed, to Elizabeth, both assuring and amused. "Not that anyone could. We're on the second floor. The only thing out there is sky."

Elizabeth hung her jacket on a hook and walked to the wooden table. The stack of photos, shorter now, was waiting for her. She knew which ones they were. She had studied Stieglitz's portraits of O'Keeffe until she knew them like pictures of her own children. Georgia's face, cropped or whole, hair pulled back or wearing that ridiculous hat. Georgia clothed in black or seated by the leaves in a white skirt, turning to the camera. Beautiful headless torsos, close-ups of her stomach and breasts.

Elizabeth wanted the face and body together. The woman, claiming her whole self.

She met Richard's eyes, locking them to hers, before she looked down to examine the pictures he had chosen. Her heart was a jackhammer.

Yes. He'd understood. Georgia, naked except for a thin white shawl, holding her left breast. Georgia, silhouetted against a window.

Could she do this? She had to.

She picked up the first photo. Georgia was caressing her breast, her face inward and mysterious, letting the viewer watch. Not like Weston's nudes, their faces hidden. "This one," she said.

Richard dipped his head in acknowledgement. "We'll use the light backdrop. I can blur the background when I make the print."

A tiny bell, like the tap of a spoon against a cup, sounded in Elizabeth's mind at the word *print*. She didn't need a print, a physical reminder that today had happened. All she needed was for it to happen.

She handed him the photo and strode across the room, stopping in front of the screen. Then she faced him and pulled off her sweater. No bra this time. Only herself, the air against her skin. He tossed her a white cloth. It was sheer, like the filmy curtain he'd spread across the backdrop. "Use this." She draped it over her arms and opened her jeans, pulling them an inch below her navel, baring her stomach the way O'Keeffe had. The long plane of skin disappearing below the bottom of the frame. She took her breast in her hand.

The surge of arousal shocked her. Richard reached for his camera, his eyes hooded. "Like that," he said. "Hold your breast as if you want me to understand exactly how it feels to you."

Elizabeth was dizzy, weak with the desire that flooded her body, but she did what he told her. Open your fingers. Raise your chin. The shutter clicked twice, then a third time, and a fourth.

"Let's do this one now." He went to retrieve another photo from the stack on the table. Barely breathing, Elizabeth bent her head to look. The shawl had fallen. Georgia, against the window, lifting both her breasts with her right arm. Again, the photo was cropped just below the navel.

He adjusted the lamp, selected a different camera. Then he reached out and tilted her face to the right. "There. Good."

She looked at him, not trusting herself to speak. His voice was soft. "Enjoy it."

Elizabeth held still, inside her body, as he took shot after shot. He hadn't asked her how she felt this time. He knew.

She ached for him to touch her; surely he saw that. Instead, he rolled the lamp behind the screen. "The next one needs to be lit from behind." Elizabeth watched him adjust the light, experiment with the illumination, then lower the curtain so it covered the bottom portion of the screen. "You'll see it in the print," he told her. "He has Georgia framed in front of the window, as if she's about to pull the curtain aside."

"And be revealed."

"Stieglitz was very deliberate. There's nothing accidental in his compositions."

He met her eyes, then crossed the room to get another picture. Elizabeth began to cover herself with the shawl. It felt strange to stand there, half-undressed, while she waited. Then she dropped her hand and let go of the shawl.

Richard returned and held out the photo. She had seen it on her computer, but it was different on paper, in person. The beautiful body with its heavy breasts and mound of pubic hair, one arm extended like the branch of a tree. The whole body.

Silently, she handed the photo back to him.

"Are you ready?" he asked.

A vein beat against her temple. Trembling, she stepped out of her shoes and removed her jeans and underwear.

Here I am.

Yes. It was all right. Taking off her blouse had been harder, maybe because it was the first step, the transition from concealment to exposure. This was just more flesh. The rest of the portrait.

Richard leaned close, pointing to the photo. "You see how her body's so beautifully curved? The way her right arm echoes that curve? It's holding on to what's behind her while her left arm is stretched forward, ready to seize whatever's next."

Elizabeth looked. Yes, she could see that. The figure was bare, unadorned, arced like a bow in the space between past and future.

"Take the pose."

She pulled in her breath. Then she took the posture, all at once— as if her body had been waiting, ever since it was formed, to inhabit that very shape.

"Yes, that's it. Perfect."

Perfect. No costumes, only herself.

"One more," he said. Georgia's whole body, again. The same curtain, both arms outstretched, her head thrown back in prayer, ecstasy, exultation. Elizabeth opened her arms.

Richard snapped picture after picture. "You're amazing."

She laughed. "I am, aren't I?" She wanted to ask him, "What next? What are we going to do now?" She could do anything. Whatever he wanted her to do.

He lowered the camera. "You are, Elizabeth. Quite amazing." Then he stepped behind the screen and shut off the light. She waited for him to say something, do something, the next thing. She would respond. He knew that.

He turned to her and nodded. She was still naked. "Good session. I think we did it." He pulled the fabric away from the screen, no longer needed, and flipped up the shades. "I'll see you at Tai Chi, then?"

At Tai Chi? Elizabeth felt as if she'd been slapped.

She'd done what she set out to do. But it wasn't enough. She was farther from *enough* than she'd been when she started.

She fought to keep her voice steady. "Of course. Wednesday."

She grabbed her clothes. It took her four tries to get her foot through the pants leg.

Fifteen

Then it was Wednesday, but Richard wasn't at Tai Chi. Elizabeth kept scanning the pupils' faces, unable to believe that his wasn't among them. Richard was always right up front, the first to arrive and the last to leave. She wanted to ask Mr. Wu where he was but couldn't bring herself to meet the return question: *Why you ask?*

Her limbs moved through the postures, obedient to Mr. Wu's instruction, but her mind careened from one impossible thought to the next. She didn't really think anything terrible had happened, yet Richard had never missed class before. Why tonight? And why hadn't he let her know? It was the least he could do, after what they had shared.

Then it hit her, nearly toppling her off-balance as she shifted her weight for *The White Crane Spreads its Wings*—the movement they'd been doing when Mr. Wu collapsed and everything began.

Richard had no idea how to reach her. He'd never asked for her phone number, only given her his. He might not even know her last name.

Worry collided with doubt, then confusion and shame, a kaleidoscope of emotions. What did he think she was, without a name?

No, it was meaningless, just as his absence tonight was meaningless, nothing to do with her or the photos.

His visage filled her mind, those smoky grey eyes locking into hers, the way he'd looked at her across the marble table, telling her that the only way she could understand O'Keeffe was by doing what O'Keeffe did. A great seduction line. Except he hadn't tried to seduce her.

Fear seized her like a fist. How was she going to make it through the class? Mr. Wu rotated his hips. *Wave hands like clouds.*

She stumbled. Juniper, next to her, threw her a concerned look. Elizabeth gave a reassuring smile and tried to focus on Mr. Wu.

Finally, after minutes that felt like lifetimes, the class ended. She had to get out of there, away from the studio where Richard's absence felt as large as his presence. She rushed to the door, but Juniper's hand on her arm made her stop.

"Hey Liz," she said, her eyes bright. "There's a new vegan place down the block. Great smoothies. A bunch of us are going. Want to come?"

Elizabeth stared at her. A bubble of hysterical laughter swelled in her throat. *A bunch of us might go out to eat after class.* The cover story she had planned to use with Ben. Juniper's face tightened. "They have more than smoothies, if that's an issue."

"No, no, I'd love to, if I didn't have to rush home to my kids. Maybe another time."

Juniper gave a murmur of agreement. "Don't have any kids myself, but I get it. So sure, another time."

Elizabeth couldn't leave without asking someone. "You know Richard, the guy who helped while Sifu was sick?"

"Of course. We've both been coming here since, like, forever."

Elizabeth tried to keep her voice low. She didn't want anyone wondering why she was so interested in Richard's whereabouts. "Seems odd for him to miss a class, don't you think?"

Juniper shrugged. "Oh, he gets like that every so often. He'll get totally engrossed in some new thing he's working on and won't come up for air till it's done."

"Ah yes. The artistic temperament." She wanted to ask how long his immersion usually lasted but that would be too much. It was an explanation, anyway.

"You should check out his work," Juniper added. "He puts his stuff up at that gallery right by campus—you know, next to the old firehouse? He's got this great series up now, all these close-ups of old people's faces. Ears, noses, things like that. It's really cool."

Elizabeth had stopped listening. Juniper said Richard might not *come for air*—meaning, she assumed, that he was holed up in his studio, alone. The question was: what was she going to do about that?

Juniper seemed to sense that Elizabeth's mind had wandered. She adjusted her collar. "Well, see you soon."

"Yes. Have fun." Elizabeth went to retrieve her jacket and shoes. Nowhere to go now, but home. Or Richard's studio. She thought of going there, surprising them, and for a moment that seemed entirely possible, maybe even the right and brilliant thing to do. Then her sanity returned. *Don't chase boys.* She got out of the elevator, stepped into the street, and began walking.

Hands in her pockets, she bent into the autumn wind. Her body was hunched, cold, nothing like the body she had shown to Richard, so glorious and unafraid. She reached the end of the block just as a bus with green letters and a familiar logo eased into place. The doors whooshed open. Elizabeth hesitated. It seemed as if there was something else she ought to do, besides getting on the bus and going back to her apartment, but she didn't know what it was. She thought of walking, just to fill the time. The wind bit into her skin.

"You coming, miss?"

She looked up at the bus driver. Disappointment, doubt, desire—a tangle of emotions, like the colors of a painting, splashed across her face.

"Yes. Sorry." Elizabeth climbed the step, swiped her card, and took a seat. The bus swung away from the curb.

She pressed against the window, hugging her elbows, and thought about how she'd felt in Richard's studio. Opening her shirt, the fabric sliding down her arms like water. The air on her flesh. He'd meant it to be erotic. How could it be anything else?

O'Keeffe had insisted that people were projecting their own desires onto her work. *When people read erotic symbols into my paintings, they're really talking about their own affairs.* On the other hand, Marion Mackenzie thought O'Keeffe knew very well what her paintings suggested. Judy Chicago had said the same thing, accusing O'Keeffe of refusing to articulate her commitment to a female art—a female erotic art—even though her own work embodied it.

Elizabeth gazed at the darkening streets. Had Richard done that too, pretending not to know, pretending it was all about helping her with her dissertation, when it was really about—what? Getting her to take her clothes off? But why? Altruism, voyeurism, an artistic experiment—none of the possibilities made sense.

No matter which way she tried to force her thoughts, they circled back to the same fact. He hadn't tried to seduce her, even though she was clearly seducible.

Her stop was just ahead. It was too soon; she wasn't ready to face Ben and her life with him. She'd gone to Tai Chi and Richard wasn't there, even though he had told her he would be, and now the class was over. She stood. Her feet were huge, heavy, alien limbs, as she walked to the front of the bus and descended the steps to the pavement. Then she crossed the street and entered her building.

Ben was gathering the sections of newspaper when she turned her key in the lock and pushed open the apartment door. "The day's chaos," he said, indicating the newspaper. "Did you want any of this, or should I put it with the recycling?"

Elizabeth blinked. Who cared? "No, I don't need it. Go ahead and recycle it."

She opened the closet and took out a hanger for her jacket. Ben hadn't commented on her early return, any more than he'd commented on her haircut. Maybe he didn't care when she came home. She shoved the hanger back on the pole and slammed the closet door.

Ben lifted his head. "You okay?"

"Of course. Why?"

He tossed the newspapers into a bin by the front door. "You seem upset, that's all. Did something happen at Tai Chi?"

"What could happen at Tai Chi?" Part of her wanted him to insist on knowing, even though there was nothing to tell. "Of course not," she repeated. "I'm fine. Like I said."

Be nice to him, she told herself. He was her children's father, the one who watched them when she saw Richard. "What about you?" she asked. "How's the case?"

Ben gave an exasperated sigh. "The case is impossible. The landlord keeps changing his story, and then Solano's family keeps upping their demands, even when it doesn't make any sense, even if it actually hurts the case. I feel like I'm chasing my own tail."

"Oh dear. I'm sorry to hear that."

"Me too." He picked up the TV remote. "In the end, I think it'll come down to the judge's impression of me, personally, which isn't the way the law is supposed to work."

Elizabeth made what she hoped was a sympathetic murmur.

Ben pressed a button, and a newscaster's face filled the screen. "Oh," he added. "There were two messages for you on the land line. Lucy and Andrea."

Lucy? She wasn't obsessing about Daniel's little fit, was she? He wasn't even five, for goodness sakes. Besides, she'd handled it with her iPhone. *Richard Ferris, photographer.*

"What did she say? Lucy."

Ben's eyes were on the screen. "I was getting the kids out of the bath. I didn't pick up."

"Well, what was the message? You said she left a voicemail."

"Something about an idea she had, I didn't listen to the whole thing. She wants you to call her back."

Honestly, Elizabeth thought. Couldn't he have listened and called back himself? They were his children too. Then she checked herself. She was the one who dealt with Lucy. She'd set it up that way; it was easier to juggle the duties you'd chosen.

"Fine. I'll see what she wants." She grabbed the phone and pressed *messages*.

"Hi there, folks." Lucy-like, she got right to the point. "I didn't mean to interrupt your evening, but I was thinking about Daniel and that Lego rocket, and how upset he was that some unknown enemy might ruin his creation?"

It *was* about the spaceship, then. Elizabeth let out a sigh of her own.

"Not a major incident," Lucy continued, "but it got me thinking because that sort of thing can happen when kids are creative, which Daniel is, and which I try to foster. But I also need to foster their sense of community. So I had an idea, a way to make the kids feel like they're part of a little tribe. Call me back and I'll tell you about it."

Not as bad as she'd feared. Elizabeth took the phone to the couch and sat down next to Ben. He lowered the volume. "What do you suppose her idea is?" he asked. "Taking them to Disneyland for a week, her treat?"

Elizabeth smiled. "Guess I'll have to find out."

Lucy's idea was to organize a project that all the children could work on together, a cooperative endeavor uniting the Monday-Wednesday and Tuesday-Thursday cohorts. "I thought maybe we could do a play—well, more like an excuse for everyone to dress up in costumes, say a few lines, maybe do a song? Something even the little ones like Katie can manage." She chuckled. "A surprise for the parents. They'll like that."

"It's a wonderful idea," Elizabeth said. She caught Ben's glance and gave a thumbs-up. "When were you thinking of doing it?"

"Give us a week or so. Say, a Monday at noon? Not this Monday, but the one after. Would that work for you?"

"I'll make it work."

"I was thinking Katie might like to be a snowflake."

"She'll be in heaven."

A play, Elizabeth mouthed, and Ben signaled *sounds good*. When she hung up, he said, "Put it on my iCal, okay? I don't want to miss it."

"Will do. It sounds adorable."

Then she pressed *messages* again. Andrea's voice, unlike Lucy's, was urgent and tight. "I need to talk. Call me."

Elizabeth remembered their last conversation—the canvas bag of clothes, *Curious George* babbling in the background, Andrea's certainty that she would figure out a way to ambush Michael and unmask his lie about a coat drive.

She glanced at Ben. This might not be a conversation she wanted him to overhear. "I'll take it in the other room," she said. "Let you have your peace and quiet, especially after such a tough day." She took the phone into the bedroom and shut the door. She tapped on Andrea's number.

"Lizzie?"

"It's me. What's up?"

"Everything. Nothing." Andrea's voice rose, cracked. "This whole thing is making me completely in*sane*."

Elizabeth lowered herself onto the edge of the bed. "Is Michael there?"

"Of course not. He's quote, working late, as usual. When he's not busy with his firm's beloved coat drive, that is. How many coats are there in this fucking town?" Andrea gave a harsh, humorless laugh.

"You told me to spy on him at that coat thing, but how am I supposed to do that without him noticing?"

"I said it *could* be a cover story. There's no way for me—"

"It's absolutely his cover."

"Andie. Things aren't always what they seem."

"Which is why *you* have to spy on him."

"Me?"

"You. All you have to do is show up on Sunday with some old jacket and ask around. He won't be there, of course." Andrea cut off Elizabeth's objections before she could raise them. "I can't do it myself, someone from his office would recognize me. But they don't know you. You can look around, ask if he's there or when they expect him. They'll tell you no, and I'll have proof that he's lying. Simple."

"Andie," Elizbeth repeated. It wasn't simple at all. Even Andrea— for whom obstacles dissolved and penalties were waived by the flash of a saucy grin—even Andrea didn't get to decide what was simple and what wasn't. Elizabeth was sure her sister had forgotten what she'd told her about being attracted to someone in her Tai Chi class, and her advice to *go for it*. If Andrea remembered, she couldn't possibly think Elizabeth was the right person to spy on Michael.

"I don't see how—"

"You *have* to, Lizzie. I can't stand this a second longer." Her voice caught. "There's no one else I can ask."

That was the impossible part. Her sister's misery, her need. Andrea didn't know what it was like for her charm to fail.

"Please." And again, heart-wrenching. "Please."

Elizabeth tightened her grip on the phone. She was certain this was a bad idea. There were too many loose threads that couldn't possibly add up to the kind of evidence Andrea wanted. No serious investigator would endorse such a half-baked idea.

From the other room, she could hear Ben's footsteps. She didn't have much time. "All right," she said. "Fine. Just tell me where and when."

"Thank you, thank you, Lizzie darling. I knew I could count on you."

Andrea's gratitude only increased her conviction that the whole thing was a mistake, but she had already agreed. The door creaked as Ben pushed it open. "I'll do my best," she said, and hung up.

"What'd she want?" Ben asked.

"Oh, another favor. She has a new customer on Sunday morning and wanted me to fill in for her at the food co-op." Elizabeth waved a hand. "You know Andie. It's hard to say no."

The lie came easily. She didn't actually need to lie, yet she didn't want to tell Ben the whole story. It was all connected, somehow. Michael, Tai Chi, her sessions with Richard.

"Sunday morning? Does that mean you're asking me to watch the kids?" She heard the unsaid *again*. He was right, she'd been asking more often than usual. But she couldn't let her sister down.

"It's only for an hour."

Ben looked unhappy, and Elizabeth retreated quickly. It would be foolish to spend her limited currency on Andrea when she might need it for Richard, later. "I'll take Katie with me," she said. "Daniel can occupy himself with his Legos, and you won't have to do anything except be home. You can work on your brief, talk to clients on the phone, whatever you need to do."

"Divide and conquer."

"Exactly."

"All right," he said. "If you really need me to do it, that can work."

Elizabeth tried not to feel guilty—and, really, she had nothing to feel guilty about. All she was doing was checking on Michael. She rose and smoothed the nonexistent creases on the leggings she'd worn to Tai Chi. "I'm going to peek at them before I go to bed."

She opened the door to the children's bedroom, engulfed at once by the sweetness that seemed to radiate from their sleeping forms. Oh, she loved those two. It overwhelmed her, sometimes, the realization that she'd created these perfect little beings—well, she and Ben, as if they'd loved each other best through their children, a lavish and generous feast of love they couldn't seem to bestow on each other.

When Daniel was born, she had been giddy with happiness, entranced by watching him yawn and twist and flail those fierce little fists. She hadn't cared about the sleepless nights, the howls, the spit-up, the spray of urine right in her eye or the mustard-yellow shit that oozed out of his diapers. It didn't matter; she loved it all. His first gummy smile, the first time he held up his head and looked around. Impossible to imagine feeling the same way about a second child, but she had. Katie was a different kind of baby, delicate and watchful where Daniel had been round and exuberant, yet just as enchanting. She'd look right into Elizabeth's eyes and melt against her chest with a blissful sigh.

Elizabeth knelt by Katie's bed. She still slept in a toddler bed, low to the ground, with padded bumpers made of pale green flannel. Katie was scrunched in the center of the mattress, her round little rump high in the air, the bunny under the chin. Tiny sleep sounds, like bubbles, punctuated the air.

Elizabeth watched her daughter sleep, marveling at how complete she seemed. Was it easier when you were the only girl, no sister to get half the gifts? She and Andrea had divided the available traits—or maybe their mother had divided them, and they had taken what they were given. It was so long ago, she couldn't remember how it started, but once established, the division was immutable. *Lizzie's our little bookworm and Andie's our little pixie.* Every time she ventured out of her assigned role, she had been reminded of who she was.

She lifted a strand of hair from Katie's cheek, smoothing it behind her ear. And what about Andrea? Had she ever resented being cast as the pixie, the daughter with the lightweight gifts? Elizabeth had always felt like the one consigned to the least attractive role, but maybe Andrea had felt that way too, barred from the more valuable spot because her sister had already claimed it. She longed, suddenly, to call Andrea back and ask if she'd ever wished they could trade roles.

Then she sniffed, dismissing her own thought. Who would possibly want to be solemn straight-A Lizzie, when you could be a minx, a butterfly, a vamp?

Either way, though, it was only half a person.

As if sensing her mother's presence, Katie stirred in her sleep. Elizabeth bent closer. "Ssshh," she whispered. She put her palm on the curve of her daughter's skull and bent her head until her lips brushed the pink-and-white edge of Katie's ear.

Don't be half, she told her.

Be everything.

Anything less was wrong, the same as being nothing.

Sixteen

"**I**'m in a *play*," Daniel cried, rushing toward Elizabeth when she arrived at Lucy's house. "I'm going to be a super hero. With a *cape*."

"Oh my goodness!" she exclaimed. Lucy had, apparently, scooped the children into a whirlwind afternoon of costume-designing and song-learning.

Katie pulled on her sleeve. "So fake," she whispered.

Elizabeth's heart jumped. Her daughter was calling her a fake? Katie had seen through her lies about running a student tutorial and having to stay late for a special Tai Chi class?

Of course not. What in the world was wrong with her? Snowflake, that's what Lucy had told her.

Elizabeth knelt and took Katie in her arms. "Yes, my darling. You're going to be the most wonderful snowflake." Then she turned to Daniel. "And you have a real cape? That's awesome. What color?"

"Yellow," he said proudly. "And a sword."

"Wow. I can't wait." She hoisted Katie onto her hip and took Daniel's hand. "Come, let's rocket on home and you can tell Daddy about it too."

"Rex has a red cape, but I wanted yellow. Like gold."

"Who wouldn't?" Elizabeth laced her fingers through his.

181

"Know what else?" Daniel said.

"What else?"

"The play is a surprise," he confided. "For the parents."

"That makes it even better."

Elizabeth adjusted Katie's legs around her hip and guided Daniel down the path to the curb where she had parked the car. "Into your car seat, my dove," she told Katie, who let herself be tilted into place. Daniel climbed in after her.

"Elizabeth!"

It was Phoebe. Elizabeth suppressed a groan. The woman was always there, like a new part of Lucy's child care program. Pick-up time, drop-off time. Wherever she turned, there was Phoebe's too-cute asymmetrical haircut and insipid grin.

Elizabeth lifted a hand in greeting, then checked Daniel's seat belt and closed the car door. "We're about to leave, but hi." The message was obvious, maybe even rude, but Phoebe didn't seem to notice.

"Soon as I round up the twins, I'm right behind you." Phoebe's voice dropped to a conspiratorial whisper. "Isn't it the sweetest thing *ever*, their little performance?"

Elizabeth couldn't help smiling. "The surprise for the parents?"

"The very same. Good thing we don't know about it."

"Lucy's a genius. Somehow she's managed to combine Star Wars, Robin Hood, and *Frozen*." Elizabeth shook out her car keys.

Phoebe kept talking. "Wine and cheese was fun, by the way. We should do it again. Maybe we could try a movie or a concert, or something like that?"

Elizabeth gave a noncommittal murmur. "After the play's over would probably be best."

"Sure. Let's pencil in the Saturday after."

God, the woman was pushy. There was no getting out of this. Elizabeth threw her bag onto the passenger seat. "Sounds good. I'll check with Ben, see what he's up for."

"Oh, the men are useless." Phoebe laughed. "Let's you and me set it up. They won't care what we do."

"All right. Fine."

"I'll see what's on and let you know."

Daniel rapped on the car window. *Hurry up,* or *hi Rex's mommy.* Elizabeth gave an apologetic shrug. "I'd better get going. I'm running late today."

"Me too. See you later." Phoebe blew a kiss and hurried into Lucy's house.

Elizabeth watched her disappear. Phoebe was probably used to people liking her, with her adorable combination of tech wizardry and foxy little skating skirt, but her cuteness was getting on Elizabeth's nerves.

She slid into the car, her eyes darting to the rearview mirror as she clicked the seatbelt into place. Daniel was flicking the wheels of a tiny sports car as Katie gazed out the window, singing to herself. Elizabeth wondered what she saw.

Or didn't see. The notion stopped her cold.

Katie never saw her father wrap his arms around her mother or give her a spontaneous kiss or tell her she looked beautiful. She wouldn't think that was something men and women did.

Her daughter was already watching, taking note. This is how a woman acts. This is what a woman expects. This is what a woman is.

Not a fake. Not a super-hero. Real.

Two dozen students faced Elizabeth the next afternoon, eager to talk about art, power, and the feminists who had incorporated their own bodies into their work. *Her Body as Art,* that was today's topic. It was the highlight of the syllabus, and no one was absent.

Naomi's challenge rang in Elizabeth's ears. "I'm asking *you,* specifically. How far would you go to use your own body to make a statement about what you believe? How far, if everyone knew it was *your* body?"

How far, indeed.

Elizabeth surveyed the class. "Since the early 1970s," she began, "feminist artists have been challenging our notion of what constitutes art by disrupting the distinction between creator and creation. By using their own bodies as the medium—the canvas, as it were, the clay—they're stepping into the art itself, insisting on their right to be an active part of the viewer's experience." She paused, leaning against the oak desk. "A lot of them did that by taking the objectification of women to an extreme. It's the opposite of what you might expect. Why do you suppose they did that?"

"To take control." It was Naomi, before anyone else could answer.

Elizabeth turned her head. The spikes in the girl's hair were now a neon orange. "How so?"

"It's like, if *we* do it, instead of letting *you* do it, then we own it, not you." Above her nostril, the jewel sparkled.

"Good. Any other ideas?"

More students raised their hands. "To show how ridiculous it is to objectify women like that?"

"To show they didn't care?"

Elizabeth nodded. "They're trying to shock the viewer, aren't they? And then, through that shock, dismantle our notions of the feminine, undo our perception of a woman's body as a thing."

"People don't want to admit they have those perceptions, but they do." Naomi again. "When you take it to an extreme, you can see it."

"Well said." Elizabeth flipped on the projector. "Let's look at four women from four different countries, all working with conceptual photography and feminist performance, back in the 1970s. As you'll see, none of their work is static. It's in movement. A chronicle of transformation."

The first slide lit up the screen. *Her Body as Art, Act, and Agency.*

"Let's see how these artists used their bodies as the vehicle for what they wanted to say." She waited, letting the students settle in. "It was a rejection of the way women's bodies had always been the passive subject of male art—from Titian in the 1500s to Renoir in the 1800s, and all the way to the present. Men were the artists, the makers. Women were the models, the subjects, like apples or boats."

She thought of Weston's nudes, faceless and exposed, stretched out on the sand devoid of agency—worse, really, than the voluptuous Venus of Urbino, or Goya's coy and strangely awkward *Naked Maja*, or the fleshy pink bathers of Rembrandt and Renoir.

Georgia, unlike all of them, had claimed her portraits. Stieglitz may have composed the photographs, but it was Georgia who entered them and made them hers.

When I make a photograph, I make love.

Elizabeth bit her lip. A ripple of longing filled her body.

She brought up the next slide. "Renate Eisenegger," she said, "from West Germany." A woman's face filled the screen, eyes darkened like a raccoon's, mouth taped shut. "*Isolation*, 1972. Eisenegger started by taping cotton over her mouth, depriving herself of speech." Elizabeth clicked through a series of eight pictures. "In each frame, you can see how her senses are eliminated. Each one, in turn, is bound, restricted, obscured. Even her hands. Finally, her face is gone. She can't take in impressions, and she can't act. She's completely dehumanized."

Elizabeth waited for the class to absorb the final disturbing image. "It was meant to convey a message about the oppression of women, but apparently it was a profound experience for Eisenegger herself. She said, afterward, that it made her feel as if she'd been purified, free from everything that had gone before, just by submitting to the enactment—which she herself had devised, of course."

One of the students recoiled. "That's creepy."

Another student waved her arm, the girl with the blonde buzz-cut on one side of her face. "Objectifying the body means de-personalizing it, cutting yourself off from it, right? So I don't get it. You're saying these artists did it on purpose, to make a point?"

"Yes, Exactly."

"They disconnected from their own bodies?"

"They did it to make a point, just as you said. Because they thought it had been done to them." She pulled up the next slide. "Ewa Partum, from Poland."

Partum's face, grave and Madonna-like, was bisected down the middle. "In a 1974 performance that she called *Change,* Partum had a makeup artist work on half her naked body in front of a live audience. By artificially aging only half her face, Partum wanted to show—and protest—the standards of beauty, established and perpetuated by men, that equated desirability with youth." Elizabeth angled her head to study the photo. "She plastered the image on posters all over Poland, with the words: 'My problem is the problem of a woman.'"

Naomi gave a loud sniff. "1974? Nothing's changed."

"You don't think so?"

Naomi gave Elizabeth a secretive look. "In general. Not for people who aren't afraid to stand up and be seen."

Elizabeth wanted to ask Naomi what she meant but the class was waiting for her to continue. She turned back to the screen. "Let's look at the next artist. Karin Mack. Austria."

The slide showed a 1950s-style woman against a floral background, cradling a jar of jam tenderly against her cheek. Pins pierced her face and body.

"*Demolition of an Illusion,* 1977. Mack used self-portraiture to investigate the constructed self. We can see how the false image of a contented housewife is systematically torn to shreds until only a few bent pins remain." Elizabeth clicked through five more slides. "In her preface to the exhibition catalogue, she wrote: 'The death of the image, the destruction of the photograph, is at once the end of an illusion and an act of liberation.'"

The girl with the buzz cut waved her hand again. "That's cool. It's like she's demolishing people's illusion that women love domesticity. You know, the way she's hugging the jam?"

"You think the nails are supposed to mean she's a martyr?"

"I think they're, like, sewing pins. Destroyed by domesticity."

"One more," Elizabeth said. "Hannah Wilke, from the United States." The next slide was a collage of ten images of the same woman—in a cowboy hat, sunglasses, necktie—her naked torso covered with darkish blobs. "Wilke's body art, *S.O.S. Scarification Object Series,* 1974 through 1982."

"What's that stuff on her body?" one of the students asked. "Does she have a disease?"

"It's chewing gum," Elizabeth said. "If you look closely, you can see that each piece is folded into a shape meant to resemble female genitalia. She was juxtaposing a kind of pin-up girl seductiveness with tribal scarification. The idea was to invite the male gaze while disrupting it at the same time."

"It doesn't work," Naomi said, folding her arms. "She's too gorgeous. You can't disrupt anything if people can't get past how hot you look."

"That was exactly the problem Wilke encountered. No one wanted to take her seriously, especially when she started using her own nude body, because they said she was too beautiful. They accused her of being narcissistic and inauthentic. They said her self-portraits looked more like Playboy centerfolds than feminist nudes."

Naomi flicked a strand of orange hair from her cheek. "When you put it that way, it's not fair. It's not her fault she's so great looking. It's just another way of dismissing her."

"What do you think?" Elizabeth asked, looking around. "Is the body simply a container for the person inside, or does it have its own meaning?"

Naomi gave Elizabeth another private look. "You know better than any of us."

"So what did she do?" someone asked. "Hannah Wilke?"

Elizabeth returned to her notes. "Let me read this to you. It's what Wilke said when critics complained that her body was too beautiful." She read slowly. "'People give me this bullshit of: what would you have done if you weren't so gorgeous? What difference does it make? Gorgeous people die, as do the stereotypical ugly. Everybody dies.'" She looked up from the paper. "Wilke was oddly prescient, as it turned out. Because the critics shut up about all that in the early 1990s when she began documenting the ravages of chemotherapy on her own cancer-ridden body."

Elizabeth could feel the class's stunned silence. She clicked the remote. The next slide showed a bald, naked woman on a commode, her body sagging forward. She clicked again. A woman with a bloated and bandaged torso, her left breast clamped with an IV. A naked woman with gauze pads taped to her hips, hands framing an absurd flower arrangement. A bald head, palms covering the mouth and cheeks—a visage that could be man or woman, old or young, it didn't matter. The face of someone dying, solemn and terrified and resigned.

"When Wilke was diagnosed with lymphoma, she decided to document her degenerating body in a series she called *Intra-Venus*. The last photo in the series was taken in August of 1992. She died in January of 1993."

"Jesus," a girl whispered.

Elizabeth's voice was quiet too. "I think Wilke just wanted to be seen. It wasn't political any more. It was personal."

Naomi shook her head. "The political is always personal."

"I suppose it's up to the individual," Elizabeth said. "If they want to be taken that way."

"No," Naomi answered. "You're responsible for the political impact of whatever you do." She lifted her chin, pointing the jewel at Elizabeth like a laser. "Anyway, you have nothing to worry about on that score."

Elizabeth's discomfort was acute. She had no idea what Naomi was doing, with her hints and innuendos, but she wasn't going to take the bait. She looked at her watch. "I see we're out of time. So, for our next class, pick an image that speaks to you from what I showed today—the Power Point will be on the class web page—and write a paragraph about what you think the artist is trying to denounce and what she's trying to affirm."

She gathered her papers, shut down the podium. She was done talking about women who had incorporated their bodies into their art.

Georgia hadn't stuck gum or pins or tape on her body. She'd shown it to one man. That was enough.

It was Sunday morning, the day Elizabeth had promised Andrea that she would play undercover agent at the coat drive. Now that Sunday was here, the ruse filled her with distaste. Leave Michael in peace, she thought, irritated with her sister and with herself for getting involved. Why did Andrea have to know everything her husband was up to?

She'd told Ben that she needed to cover for Andrea at the food co-op. Before he could ask why Michael couldn't do it, since it was a family membership, she spun a vague story about a family event in honor of one of Michael's cousins. Ben didn't press her for details; he was used to the endless baptisms and weddings and confirmations of the extended Silvestri family. Nor did he ask what she intended to do with Katie while she stacked produce and sorted boxes. People brought their kids to the food co-op all the time. It was part of the natural food, natural parenting philosophy—principles she and Ben agreed with, in theory, but hadn't had time to actually practice since Elizabeth started graduate school.

At the last minute she grabbed a frayed parka Daniel had outgrown and tucked it behind Katie in the stroller. She couldn't very well show up at the coat drive without a coat.

Michael worked at a small advertising agency, a progressive firm that promoted solar energy and organic cleaning supplies. A community coat drive was their kind of project, and it wasn't so farfetched for Michael to be involved. Still, Elizabeth had promised Andrea that she would try to catch him in a lie, so she pulled into the parking lot, flipped open Katie's stroller, and entered the building.

The lobby was full of people, boxes, and racks on wheels—a bigger and more disorganized event than Elizabeth had expected. Maybe Michael really did have to put in all those hours. She looked around, trying to decide what to do.

"Can I help you?" A man with a parrot-like profile was standing in front of the stroller. He had a clipboard and a plastic badge with the logo of Michael's firm.

"Oh," she said. "Yes. I'm looking for Michael Silvestri. I don't suppose he's here?"

She was sure the man would say *haven't seen him since Friday* or *who's he?* Instead, he craned his neck and pointed to a table in the back of the lobby. "He's over there, with his laptop."

"He is?" Elizabeth looked where the man was pointing. It really was Michael. There was a woman seated next to him but she was typing away on her own laptop and Elizabeth didn't think they looked like people who were having an affair.

Andrea had been wrong, then. The coat drive wasn't a cover story for an illicit tryst. Well, that was an answer too. "You want me to get him for you?" the man asked.

"No. Please don't." Elizabeth was sure she sounded ridiculous after telling him that she was looking for Michael, but the last thing she wanted now was for Michael to see her and ask why she was there. "It isn't really necessary."

"No problem—" the man began.

Katie stood up in her stroller and pointed in the direction the man had indicated. "Un-ca My-ca!" she shouted.

Michael looked up. He seemed confused, then pleased when he recognized them, and then confused again. But not guilty, Elizabeth thought. Not like she would have looked if someone had caught her coming out of Richard's studio.

Katie was trying to climb out of the stroller. "Sit," Elizabeth ordered. "We'll go say hi to Uncle Michael when you sit down."

She angled the stroller across the room, toward the folding table where Michael and the woman were sitting side by side. Up close, the woman was more attractive than Elizabeth had realized. She had dark hair cropped close to her skull, a high forehead and perfectly arched brows.

"Liz," Michael said, his voice rising in delight. "Caro, this is Liz, my sister-in-law."

Katie raised her arms. "And *Katie*," Michael said. "Katie is my absolute favorite niece. Especially now that she can say my name so beautifully." He bent to lift her from the stroller, then turned to Elizabeth. "What brings you here?"

Spying on you. She stole a glance at the woman, Caro, and something seized in her stomach. She didn't want to be the one to catch Michael flirting behind his wife's back. And even if he was flirting, it didn't mean he'd been unfaithful. A person could do a lot of things without crossing that line.

She watched as Caro brushed her index fingers across her eyebrows. Her fingernails were dark blue, almost black. A dozen silver bracelets circled her wrists. *Flair*, that's what she had, Elizabeth thought, and a slinky feline appeal. She could imagine Michael wanting to take Caro to bed, but that didn't mean anything. Both people had to take the step, together.

She reached into the stroller and pulled out the matted parka. "I wanted to drop this off. Daniel's outgrown it." Caro gave her a wary look. "In person," Elizabeth added. "I thought it would be nicer that way."

"Why didn't you just give it to Andie?" Michael asked.

Just give it to Andie? Because we wanted to catch you in a lie. Only they hadn't. Elizabeth scrambled for an answer that made sense. It really was a half-baked scheme; she couldn't remember why she had agreed to it. "I didn't have it with me when I saw her." A stupid excuse. Why was she acting so nervous, as if she was the one who'd been caught?

"Anyway," she added, "I figured it would be interesting to see the coat drive."

She cringed at the inanity of her words. She could almost read Michael's mind. Since when was Liz, his hyper-intellectual sister-in-law, so fascinated by seeing people sort jackets into small, medium, and large?

Katie wiggled in Michael's arms. "Un-ca My-ca," she repeated. "Katie Un-ca My-ca."

The skepticism on Michael's face was hard to miss. After a moment he returned his attention to Katie. "I am, indeed, the famous Un-ca My-ca. How smart of you to find me."

Elizabeth grabbed at the opening. "That was another reason for stopping by. Katie wanted to show you how beautifully she can say your name."

Jesus. What was wrong with her? Every idiot knew that giving a second reason, when no one had questioned the first, meant there was something you were trying to hide.

Caro gave a snort of amusement. "We'll have to put it in the firm's newsletter." Then she looked at her phone. "I have ten minutes, max. Then I have a Pilates class."

"Ten minutes?" Michael quipped. "Max may be that quick, but I prefer to take my time." Caro rolled her eyes. Elizabeth understood, then, in the very tartness of their banter, that nothing was going on between them. Lovers wouldn't joke like that. Not that she'd had a lover.

"I have less than ten," she said. "I just wanted to drop the coat off."

Michael arched his eyebrow again, and again Elizabeth could tell what he was thinking. *Fine, we'll let it go. But you and I both know there's some major bullshit going on here.*

He returned Katie to the stroller. "And now, your famous Un-ca My-ca has work to do."

It could be someone else, Elizabeth thought. Not Caro-of-the-sculpted-haircut, but someone else.

Not her problem. She'd done what she promised Andrea she would do. Time to get out of here. "Of course," she said. "We're on our way."

"Tell Ben I'll see him at squash," Michael said.

Tell Richard I'll see him at Tai Chi.

Elizabeth's steps were slow as she entered the Tai Chi studio. For the second Wednesday in a row, Richard wasn't there.

Seventeen

She hadn't seen Richard in twelve days. The last time she saw him was in his studio, her naked body silhouetted against a white curtain.

"I'll see you at Tai Chi." That was the last thing he had said to her.

Those Wednesday meetings, with their danger and their promise, had been a path. She had followed the path, all the way to the white curtain, exactly as he told her to.

She'd been certain there would be more between them, after the photos. He'd let her believe that. And he'd felt it too. She had felt his desire, all the way across the room. Maybe he hadn't planned to want her, but he had.

This was insane. Unbearable. It took everything Elizabeth had not to run to his studio and up those stairs and through that door, tearing off her clothes as she ran—the way O'Keeffe had done, at Lake George, laughing as her clothes flew behind her like birds, because she and Stieglitz couldn't wait another second.

Instead, she climbed the two flights of stairs in the Humanities building, her hand tracing the groove in the wooden bannister, and rapped on Harold Lindstrom's door. This time, she was on his calendar. A scheduled meeting.

Harold leaned back in his leather chair and studied her across the desk. "So, Ms. Crawford. What have you come up with?"

Elizabeth collected her thoughts. She needed to show him, step by step—the idea that would catapult her dissertation straight to publication, and from there to a tenure-track position and an office like his, with a view of the campus green and her nameplate on the door.

It was simple, really. Georgia had spent nine weeks in Hawaii. It was long enough, and different enough, for something new to happen. And it had.

After Hawaii, Georgia had turned from the lushness of living forms to the beauty of the void. A pelvic bone, opening to an azure sky. A doorway, a window. None of it was an accident, because everything Georgia did was intentional.

Elizabeth cleared her throat. "I've been looking at O'Keeffe's timeline, like we said? Well, turns out she bought her first house in New Mexico in 1940, six months after she came back from Hawaii. It was a commitment to a new life, separate from Stieglitz."

Harold seemed unimpressed. "They'd already been living apart. That doesn't mean Hawaii was a seminal influence on her work."

"Here. I'll show you." Elizabeth opened a folder and drew out a dozen prints, spreading them across his desk.

Pink Tulip, painted in 1926. The vibrant colors, a living plant in the very act of opening. *Pink Ornamental Banana*, painted in 1939. The same colors and shapes, but closed now, tall and proud against a lavender sky. "O'Keeffe painted the first one when she was living in New York with Stieglitz, the second one when she was in Hawaii by herself. They're similar, right? Like they're part of a series—except the second flower is shut, contained. No one can see what's inside."

She pointed to the next two prints. *Waterfall No. 1*, another Hawaii painting, and *The Black Place*, painted four years after O'Keeffe's return to New Mexico. The same composition, but the landscape in *The Black Place* was stripped of life, dark and lunar, the waterfall reduced to a desiccated crack.

"It's as if she had a final burst of sensuality in Hawaii, and then she began to withdraw, renouncing all that ripeness and vitality, so she could come to something stark and pure." She touched the print of a hollow pelvis that she had placed next to *Hibiscus with Plumeria*. It was one of O'Keeffe's last flower paintings, pretty and pale, like a girl's cupcake. Its lushness was already fading.

"After O'Keeffe bought her house in New Mexico, she started painting the empty pelvis. No more flowers." Elizabeth paused, wanting her words to have the gravity they deserved. "And then, after Stieglitz died in 1946, all she wanted to paint were doorways. In the end, it was all geometrical, abstract."

"That doesn't prove Hawaii was the catalyst."

"Of course not." Elizabeth scooped up the prints, tapping the edges into a neat stack. "Things aren't provable in art, as if they were math problems. But if you line up the evidence—the paintings, the dates, the facts of her life—it all makes sense." She slid the papers back into the folder. "That's what I intend to argue. A fresh argument, like you said, supported by data."

Harold dipped his chin, a smile warming his features. "You're good, Ms. Crawford. Well said."

Elizabeth beamed in return. "I hope so." Then she grew pensive. "There's a curious aspect to her time in Hawaii, you know. O'Keeffe was very precise about everything, right down to the color of her linens, and definitely about how she presented herself. Neutral colors, always. So the photos of her in Hawaii are strange, because they depict an entirely different woman. You'll see, if you look at them, that she's happy and relaxed, in this big straw hat, with a patterned shirt—completely different from the way she dressed in nearly every other picture."

"And?"

"And it's odd. For someone who loved color and line, the curve of a petal or hillside, there was nothing soft about the way she looked and dressed. Her hair pulled tight, in a black cape or a black suit. That Zen-like dress she wore in New Mexico." Elizabeth's voice dropped. "It's almost like she refused personal beauty. Or only let herself be beautiful when she was nude."

As soon as she heard herself utter the last four words, Elizabeth knew she had taken a risk, maybe even a stupid one. But she yearned—suddenly, desperately—to talk about the photos. If she couldn't talk about the photos Richard had taken of her, she could talk about the ones Stieglitz had taken of Georgia.

She began to speak rapidly now, driven by an urgency she couldn't seem to halt. "If you look at O'Keeffe's early years, the more the art world raved about how erotic her paintings were, the more she presented herself as this stern, austere, almost androgynous figure. Like she was trying to project a counter-image of someone harsh and sexless, the exact opposite of the sex goddess everyone assumed she was, and wanted her to be—all because of what Stieglitz had written about her in the beginning, and how he'd portrayed her in his photographs."

Elizabeth stopped to catch her breath. She could tell from the look on Harold's face that she'd gone too far.

"I'm not sure why we're talking about all this," he said. "Your dissertation is on O'Keeffe's paintings, not Stieglitz's photographs. On Hawaii in 1939."

Elizabeth snapped to attention. What the hell was she doing? Harold had singled her out—from a cadre of equally smart and ambitious doctoral candidates—and become her champion. He'd recommended her to Marion Mackenzie; he was grooming her for academic stardom.

"Yes, of course. I was just putting Hawaii in context. Before and after."

"That's my point," Harold said. "Can you make a convincing case that Hawaii was the crucial juncture? The pivot, if you will. Otherwise it's wishful thinking, not scholarship."

"I can. And *my* point is that, after Hawaii, O'Keeffe's work was stripped to the bones. Literally. As if she'd left everything else behind."

"She changed, matured. All artists do."

"True, but for O'Keeffe it was a complete contrast. Once she started her patio series, the curves and whorls completely disappeared. Everything became sharp and geometrical. Stylized, reduced to its essence."

After Stieglitz was dead. After the nudes ceased to matter.

She held Harold's gaze. "Only the doorway, the passage. That's all she cared about, in the end."

"And it began in Hawaii?"

"I think so."

He nodded. "All right. You have your idea. You'll be challenged when you defend it—Marion, especially, is quite the stickler—so you'll have to line up your sources. But if you can do that, you'll be off to an impressive start as a top-notch scholar."

"Thank you, Dr. Lindstrom. That means a lot to me." Elizabeth let out a sigh. "I do love it, you know." She gestured at the bookshelves that lined his office. "Research, teaching. The academic life."

"I know you do." Harold pushed back his chair. "Actually, I have a book that might interest you. It's about the doorway in contemporary art." He rose and went to the bookcase. "It's quite valuable, both in itself and to me personally, since it's signed by the author." He pulled a heavy volume from its place on the top shelf. "I'll loan it to you if you promise to guard it like one of your children."

"I will. Thank you."

"Monday," he said. "I need you to return it to me on Monday morning."

She took the book from him. "Monday morning. And thank you again, Dr. Lindstrom."

"Let me know if you find it useful."

Lucy's play was at noon on Monday. Fine; she could drop Daniel and Katie at Lucy's house to get ready while she ran over to campus to give Harold his book.

Finding time to read the book over the next few days would be more of a challenge than returning it. At least there were no secret trips to Michael's advertising agency, no double dates with Phoebe and her husband.

Just life. Her ordinary life that she would have to get through, somehow, until next Wednesday.

He had to come back to Tai Chi. See her. Want more.

It was another of Ben's squash nights. Elizabeth made Daniel and Katie's favorite meal, pasta with baby tomatoes, and read *Where the Wild Things Are* before kissing them goodnight. They were sound asleep by the time she heard Ben's key in the lock and the click of the front door. She set down Harold's book, the cover drifting shut over the single page she'd read, and went to greet him. "How was your game?"

Ben eased out of his windbreaker, dropping it onto the back of the couch. "Not bad. Michael was in rare form." Then he sank onto the cushion to take off his shoes. "He got a kick out of Katie knowing his name, by the way. He didn't think she'd ever said it before."

"Yes, that's right. It was her very first time."

Ben glanced up from untying his laces. "What were you doing at Michael's office? I thought you were going to the food co-op because he had a big Silvestri family baptism or something."

The food co-op? That stupid lie. Why had she wasted a lie on Andrea's ridiculous scheme? No wife, even one as clever as she was, could pull off an endless number of deceptions and half-truths. She needed to spend hers more carefully.

Elizabeth rearranged her features, though she could feel the tell-tale heat rise into her cheeks. "I got mixed up, that's all."

Ben kept looking at her—not suspiciously, Elizabeth assured herself, merely waiting for her to explain. There was no reason for him to be suspicious, since she'd never done anything she had to keep from him. Until now.

"Andrea was telling me about the baptism," she said, "and then she asked me to sub for her at the co-op. Some new customer who absolutely *had* to have a Sunday appointment. It was all part of the same conversation, so I got the two things confused."

Did her story make any sense? It might, if she didn't trap herself in too many details. But it still didn't explain what she was doing at Michael's office.

"Anyway," she added, "that's why Michael couldn't sub her for her. He's one of the people in charge of the coat drive. It's a big deal, apparently, part of their whole image. So I stopped there on the way home, you know, to drop off a few things."

Ben gave her an odd look, and Elizabeth tried not to react. She'd kept a deadpan face when she lied about going to Richard's studio but she was flushing now, as if she had an important secret to hide, not a silly fib about an hour at the co-op. She was sure Ben didn't believe her, yet the whole thing was absurd. She'd had Katie with her, for god's sakes. What could she possibly have been doing with Katie in the stroller?

She tried to turn it into a joke. "Andrea will be green with envy that Katie said his name before hers. Actually, I think Daniel did the same thing." She gave a crisp, stilted laugh. "We'd better not tell her just yet. Let's wait till Katie says *Aunt Andie* and pretend that came first."

She really had to stop babbling. It was unlike her, excessive. The same way she had acted with Michael.

Deflection, that was the best strategy. Plus, Ben looked exhausted.

She reached across him to retrieve the windbreaker. "How's that case going? The *pro bono* one?"

"It's not supposed to be *pro bono*," he said. "In theory, I get a percentage of the settlement. Only there are too many plaintiffs and they're all broke, so who knows?"

"Isn't the landlord evil and loaded?"

"Wyckoff? Evil, anyway."

Elizabeth shook out the jacket and arranged it on a hanger. It smelled like Ben, a scent she'd gotten so used to that it hardly registered, sweat and soap and something that reminded her of rosemary, wafting into the air when she changed the sheets. It had been a long time since she'd been close enough to breathe it straight from his skin.

Since she began to pose for Richard, in fact.

For the first time in weeks, she thought about the peach-colored negligee and wondered if she ought to put it on. Before she could decide, Ben stood, gym shoes dangling at his side. "At least they fixed the hot water at the gym. Finally. But I'm fried. I'm going to pour myself a shot of Maker's Mark and watch the news."

Elizabeth shut the closet door. Never mind about the negligee. Not tonight. "I think I'll do some reading. Harold loaned me a book so I'd better skim it or he'll feel unappreciated."

She brushed past Ben on her way to the desk, tensing as their arms touched. Then she reached, again, for the book Harold had loaned her. *The doorway in contemporary art.*

He hadn't said it was an open door.

Only a passage, a possibility.

Either Ben had forgotten the incongruity in her story about the food co-op or else he hadn't cared. But it bothered Elizabeth. She worried that he had made a comment to Michael, which meant that Michael might make a comment to Andrea—*What was Liz doing, snooping around my office?*—and then Andrea's plan would backfire.

Andrea's whole point had been to gather evidence without Michael knowing—so she'd have power, that's what she had tried to explain. If Elizabeth had attracted attention when she was supposed to be invisible, it meant she'd bungled the whole thing, ruined Andie's one advantage, maybe even put her sister in a humiliating position.

She needed to talk to Andrea, confess, and offer to do whatever she could to minimize the fallout. It was a non-Lucy day, so she took Daniel and Katie with her to Andrea's salon, telling them, "Why don't you play with Stephanie's toys while I talk to Aunt Andie for a minute?" Stephanie was at kindergarten and wouldn't be happy that her cousins were using her toys. But Elizabeth needed the two of them occupied and out of earshot.

Weary of all the subterfuge, she sank into the salon chair and began to explain. Andrea put up a palm to silence her. "Never mind, Lizzie. It doesn't matter anymore."

"You don't need to be so nice. I take complete—"

"Stop. I told you. It doesn't matter."

"What doesn't matter? That Michael might—"

"All of it." Andrea's voice was firm. "I fixed it. It's over. Problem solved."

Elizabeth didn't understand. Had Andrea confronted him, given him an ultimatum?

"I decided to preempt the whole thing," Andrea said. "To forget all that worrying about what he *might* be doing and make sure he didn't *want* to do it." She gave Elizabeth a smug, cat-like smile. "I told him the only reason I was suspicious was because he was so damn attractive. That turned him on, like I knew it would. Apology followed by make-up sex. A sure-fire remedy."

"You didn't."

"Of course I did."

Elizabeth stared at her. "You apologized? For what? You didn't do anything wrong."

"Don't be such a prig, Lizzie. I did what I had to do to preserve my marriage."

"What about facing what happened, talking it through?"

"Not everyone's like you, Lizzie, with your precious talk, talk, talk. I don't have your great big IQ. I have to use what I have."

Apology sex. How could Andrea do that?

No, she'd called it make-up sex. Affirmation that they were rejoined in body and spirit.

Not fair, Elizabeth wanted to cry. Not fair for her sister to be allowed to fix everything so easily. She wanted to tell Andrea about that Caro woman, show her that everything might not be as wonderful as she thought. But what was there to tell? Your husband sat next to someone with a laptop, and then she had to go to a Pilates class.

She wanted there to be more; it would mean that Andrea's marriage was no better than hers. But Andrea's marriage *was* better than hers. Her husband loved and wanted her.

There it was, the unadorned truth. Ben might think he loved her—and in his own way, he did—but he didn't desire her. He had to work at the task, the way he worked at his job, or hope for the pressure of flesh against flesh in his sleep—anyone's flesh, not *God, you're beautiful, Elizabeth.*

Undesired, she had turned to dust, like the center of the hibiscus.

Who was she to say that Andrea was wrong, using what she had? A long moment passed, and then Elizabeth said the only thing that seemed safe to say. "If it's what you want."

"It's what I want." Andrea's face softened. "And what about you, Lizzie? What do you want?"

Elizabeth looked at Daniel and Katie, kneeling on the playroom rug, surrounded by trains and blocks and plastic animals. "Obviously," Andrea said. "I meant, what else?"

Elizabeth inhaled, filling her lungs with the acrid scent of mousse and hair spray. What else? She wanted what Andrea and Michael had, but she wanted what Marion Mackenzie had too. Georgia had gotten both. Why couldn't she?

"What do I want?" She tried to make it into a joke. "Oh, I want it all. Don't you?"

"No, I don't," Andrea said. "The way I see it, you get what you get, and it's up to you to make it work."

Elizabeth's forehead creased. "Then why did you ask me what I wanted, if you think people just get what they get?"

The sound of crashing blocks filled the room. Elizabeth wheeled around, just in time to catch Katie as she threw herself against her mother's legs. Daniel raced after her, indignant. "It was her fault. I *told* her not to put the giraffe on top of my tower. I *told* her it would knock it over."

Elizabeth shut her eyes for a brief, steadying moment. "Yes, I'm sure you did. She didn't understand that it really would topple." Then she put a hand on Katie's head and extended her other arm to Daniel. "Let's pretend a volcano erupted and the tower exploded."

"What's erupted?"

"Blew up. With a lot of smoke and hot bubbly stuff."

"*Two* volcanoes."

"Two *huge* volcanoes." Gently, she pried Katie's arms away. "Go play for a little longer, and then we'll clean up and head home."

Daniel and Katie ran back to the play area, and Andrea laughed. "I probably should have had a second child. Then Stephanie wouldn't be on me all the time." She gave another cat-like smirk. "On the other hand, making arrangements for one child is easy. Which I just did."

Elizabeth pushed her hair away from her face, the glinting strands that Andrea had coaxed into existence. "What do you mean?"

"A little weekend getaway, grownups only. Stephanie's having her first sleepover, so she couldn't be more thrilled. As I intend to be too, thank you very much."

"You and Michael are going away for the weekend?"

"We most certainly are." Andrea lifted her hair, twisting it into a knot and letting it tumble back down in a glossy heap. "Like I said, I know what I have to do, and I do it."

"It's not that simple."

"For you."

"For me."

Andrea didn't answer, and Elizabeth sighed. She'd wanted to fix the complication she had caused, but Andrea had beaten her to it. She had nothing to offer—only, as her sister pointed out, her precious talk.

She gave the salon chair a half-spin and stopped in front of their joint image in the oversized mirror. Lizzie, grave and concerned. Andie, sassy and smug. As usual, Andie had solved the problem by wielding her charm. Elizabeth wished her own problems were so easily solved.

Even so, she needed to come clean about how she'd bungled things at the coat drive and pinged Michael's radar. Better for Andrea not to be blindsided, just in case. She cleared her throat. "There's something I should probably tell you."

"Oh?" Andrea gave the chair another half-spin so their real selves were facing each other.

Elizabeth looked at her sister, wishing she didn't have to confess her ineptness. "I'm glad you and Michael are working things out, I really am, but no thanks to me. I pretty much screwed up my assignment. You know, when I went to spy on him at the coat drive?"

Andrea frowned. "What about that?"

"I was—well, a total moron. Made up all these lame excuses about why I was there, and it was obvious he knew I was lying." She opened her hands in surrender. "With Ben too. I made up one story after another, got them all mixed up. I'm sure he thought I was out of my mind or else hiding something. What I worry about is if he said something to Michael. You know, made him suspicious."

The change in Andrea's face was swift and brutal. "What the fuck."

"Andie—"

"Are you telling me that you gave me away, did the one thing I asked you *not* to do?"

"It wasn't like I—"

"You did it on purpose."

"Of course I didn't."

"You must have. You're not that stupid."

"I am. I was."

"Since when?"

Since that first Americano with Richard. Elizabeth opened her mouth, not knowing how she could possibly explain, but Andrea cut her off. "I *trusted* you."

"I'm not perfect, Andie. I make mistakes."

"You don't. You don't screw up, ever. It's your job not to screw up."

"What's that supposed to mean?"

"You don't. You're too smart for that."

Elizabeth bristled. "That's not fair. Why do I always have to be the wise, noble, reliable one?"

"Because you like it that way." Andrea's eyes narrowed into angry slits. "It makes you feel superior."

Superior? A joke to think she had ever felt that way. Bitterness seeped into her words. "It was the only role left, after you took the role of everyone's favorite. The one people wanted to do things for, and give things to. The cute, delightful, *desirable* sister, who got away with everything."

Andrea's voice was cold now. "Don't blame me if you don't have the life you wanted. No one kept you from getting what you wanted except you."

Elizabeth could hardly believe this was happening. As if a cork had been pulled out of a bottle, and now all the demons were hissing and kicking and spitting out their poison. None of this would have happened if she hadn't started lying to Ben. She'd never lied to him until she took up with Richard.

The ugliness between them was too big now. It couldn't go back in the bottle.

But it had to. She couldn't bear one more shaking block in the precarious tower of her life. "Look, Andie," she began. "We're both—"

"Don't tell me what I'm feeling." Then Andrea, too, seemed to be wrestling with herself. "Just leave it, okay? Drop it, forget it."

How could she? But what was the alternative? Elizabeth could hear Daniel and Katie in the other room, shrieking with glee as another stack of cubes and cylinders crashed to the floor. "Volcano!" Daniel yelled. The sound of tumbling blocks filled the silence.

After a minute Elizabeth cleared her throat. "I'd probably better get going, errands and all. Anyway, I'm sure you have customers."

"I do have customers." Andrea raised her voice. "Hey guys, put Stephanie's stuff back now. Your mom has to go."

Elizabeth put her hand on Andrea's arm. "Have a great time this weekend. Really."

"Like I said, I intend to." Andrea didn't specifically remove Elizabeth's hand, only stepped away to retrieve the children's jackets.

Quietly, Elizabeth took the garments from her. The weather was cooler now, the season for fleece; there had been frost on the windshield this morning. Soon it would be winter, and the end of the semester.

Daniel and Katie came running from the playroom. As she held out their coats, Elizabeth's gaze darted to the window. The long naked arms of an oak tree reached across the glass, moving together against the curtain, reaching upward, as if in supplication.

Eighteen

Katie insisted on wearing her snowflake costume on Saturday morning. Within minutes, she had opened the refrigerator, removed a carton of orange juice, and spilled its contents all over the white fabric. Between making a new costume and assuring Katie that it was even more beautiful than the first one, and then helping Daniel make a cardboard-and-tin-foil sword, since he now wanted a new costume too, Elizabeth barely had time to open the book Harold had loaned her.

On Sunday evening Phoebe called, wanting to pin down a plan for the four of them to go out for what she kept describing as *grown-up fun*. "Next weekend, right? Like you said, once the kids' play is over."

"I'm trying to survive *this* weekend," Elizabeth told her. "Lucy's extravaganza has Daniel and Katie beyond wired."

"Us too. The twins are beside themselves with excitement. Translation: they won't stop whining and fighting. Naturally it's right when Charlie and I have two new clients and another one with an oh-so-emergency update. Good thing I'm such an amazing multi-tasker. I've figured out how to do web design with one hand while separating punching siblings with the other."

Elizabeth had to laugh. "Yep, I get it."

"All the more reason to take time for our grownup selves."

There was no getting out of this. "Well, you're more plugged into things than I am," she said. "Why don't you find something that looks interesting and let me know?"

"Okay, I'll see what's on. A reward for surviving."

"Survival is good."

Phoebe gave a soft chuckle. "I'll see you tomorrow. At the play."

On Monday morning Ben told her that he wouldn't be able to come. "We finally got the landlord to agree to a face-to face meeting. Today, naturally, and I have to be there. There's no way around it."

"Oh dear. The kids will be so disappointed."

"I know. I can't tell you how sorry I am."

Daniel was crushed when Elizabeth told him that Daddy wouldn't be there, but rallied when she added, "I'll film the whole thing, and we'll watch it with Daddy after dinner. Then you can see exactly how you looked."

"A doctor-mennery. Like my ship."

"Just like your ship." Elizabeth knelt and put her hands on Katie's shoulders. "And you, my pumpkin, are going to wear your gorgeous new snowflake dress. I can't wait to see it on you."

"Mama come?"

"Of course I'll come, you silly. Have I ever, ever not done what I promised?" She gave Daniel a reassuring smile. "I'm going to drop you guys at Lucy's for a little while so I can run over to my school, okay? But I'll be back in plenty of time for your play. So let's all scoot into the car and you can show Lucy how amazing you look in your costumes."

Elizabeth knew Harold would want to talk for a few minutes, and then she had to go to the admin building to copy some hand-outs for her class, but none of that would take long. She grabbed the shopping bag with Daniel's tin-foil sword and Katie's tiara—a new addition, since Daniel had a sword, and why couldn't a snowflake have a tiara?—and flung it onto the passenger seat. As she drove, she rehearsed what she planned to say about the book Harold had loaned her, even though she hadn't actually read it.

But Harold cut off her effusive remarks and tossed the book onto his desk as if it were an irrelevant parcel. "Don't reference it more than once or twice in your paper, especially not to please me. The doorway's an over-used motif."

Elizabeth smiled. "O'Keeffe would have appreciated the warning. She hated ready-made images."

"Not entirely," Harold said. "Didn't she use familiar images in her Hawaii paintings? Fall back on painting flowers that reminded her of ones she'd already done?"

Elizabeth thought of the *Bella Donna* O'Keeffe had painted in Hawaii, so similar to her *Jimson Weed* that the O'Keeffe museum didn't think it needed both. And *Cup of Silver Ginger*, an elaboration on the camellias and petunias she had painted fifteen years earlier. It was true that Georgia began by turning to what she knew. But she'd kept going, moving toward what she didn't know.

Elizabeth remembered the hibiscus Georgia had painted in Hawaii, its gaudy reproductive core shrunken to a thin and childish frill. A private message, perhaps, to the critics who claimed that her flowers were the outpouring of a repressed sexual fervor. Impossible to know Georgia's intention, yet nothing she did was accidental.

"I think O'Keeffe started out doing that," Elizabeth said, "but then she painted the ocean, the lava caves, things she hadn't ever painted before."

"Not quite successfully."

"Perhaps not. You can see that in the black lava paintings. They have an unfinished quality that's unlike her other work." Elizabeth flashed another smile. "I think it probably frustrated her no end, not to be able to capture the roiling ocean the way she saw it. She wasn't used to falling short."

"It's a challenge to render something totally new. Even for the esteemed O'Keeffe."

"Even for the esteemed O'Keeffe." Elizabeth tented her hands, fingertips touching her chin. "When she came to Hawaii, O'Keeffe wrote: *One sees new things rapidly everywhere, when everything seems new and different.* But she also wrote: *Maybe one takes one's own world along and cannot see anything else.* So yes, she understood that it might not be possible to begin entirely fresh, to work without old associations and ideas."

"In life, as in art." Harold's voice was dry. Elizabeth took his words as a concluding epigram and prepared to leave, but he motioned her to stay in her seat. "One more thing."

"Yes?" She tensed. Was something wrong?

"This whole Hawaii business." Harold eyed her over the rim of his glasses. "It's an original idea and I think you can make it work, as long as you don't imply that O'Keeffe's Hawaii paintings were anything other than a bridge. In other words, don't inflate them. They weren't masterpieces. You'll get ridiculed if you imply otherwise."

Elizabeth nodded, relieved that he wasn't bringing up—what? Her obsession with the photos? He didn't know about that. "Yes, I understand. And no, I'm not arguing that they're some sort of under-appreciated artistic treasure. Only what I told you—that they were how she worked her way from her old themes to the art that came next."

"Her transitional relationship."

"Exactly. She was just passing through."

"Very good." Harold placed his palms flat on the desk, shorthand for *we're done, then.*

Elizabeth was about to stand, as she knew she was supposed to, but she didn't. Instead, she moved closer.

"At the same time," she said, "I don't want to oversimplify anything about O'Keeffe, including her time in Hawaii. That wouldn't be fair, since she rejected everyone's attempt to pin her down—you know, the quintessentially female artist, beyond epochs. Or else the epitome of a modern artist, beyond gender. A painter of the flesh, or a painter of symbols. She hated to talk about her art. She thought it was something you had to experience directly." Elizabeth gave a soft shrug, as if conceding the limits of her own vision. "So who knows? I could be wrong."

"You don't have to be right," Harold said. "You just have to be scholarly."

Elizabeth smiled, as she knew she was expected to. Then she heard Richard's voice, as if he were right there, lifting his coffee cup in a challenge, or a benediction.

If you want to understand O'Keeffe, you have to do what she did.

Well, she had. And?

"You've done fine work," Harold told her. He pushed against the desk and rose. This time, the signal couldn't be ignored. "You might want to confer with Marion Mackenzie, just to cross your *T*s. If she likes your argument, no one in the department is going to challenge it. She's our resident maven." He gave Elizabeth an amused look. "And she likes you. Consider yourself fortunate."

"I do." She stood. "Thank you, Dr. Lindstrom. For the book. And the advice. For everything."

"Glad to help." He held the door, and Elizabeth stepped into the hallway. A bell sounded, the end of one class period. Elizabeth hurried to the staircase before it filled with students. Sliding her hand along the oak railing, she sped down the two flights to the ground floor. She would slip out ahead of the crowd, cross the quad, make her copies, and hurry back to Lucy's. She was nearly at the bottom when she felt a tap on her arm.

"Professor Crawford?"

She turned to see who had spoken and recognized the young woman, a student in her Feminist Art class. The blonde hair, buzz-cut on one side, long on the other. Her mental roster of names stopped at Sutton, Isabelle. "Hello, Isabelle," she said, pleased with herself for matching face to name.

The young woman was out of breath. Clearly, she'd been running down the stairs to catch up. "I just wanted to let you know," she gushed, "that I think it's totally awesome."

"Awesome? I'm not sure what you're referring to."

Isabelle gave her a knowing look and edged out of the way to let others pass. "I get it that you wanted us to find it for ourselves, instead of, like, announcing it in class. That makes it even cooler."

Find it, announce it. What *it* was the girl was talking about?

Students passed them on the stairs, hurrying in both directions. The clattering of feet, a swirl of colors and sounds. Around the noise, a deadly silence. Something thick and cold dropped into Elizabeth's stomach.

"What is *it* you've found?"

Isabelle's expression reminded Elizabeth of the arch look Naomi had given her after the last class, as if they shared a secret. "A bunch of us have been over to the gallery," Isabelle said. "And all I can say is—wow, what a totally awesome way to make your point."

"My point?"

"About Feminist Art? Putting your own body on the line. Using your own body, instead of hiding behind words and impersonal forms. Like you told us." Isabelle inched closer. "Naomi didn't think you'd actually do it, but she was, like, the first person to find out. She was the one who told me."

No. Not possible.

The staircase turned black. Airless.

Using your own body.

No, he couldn't have. *It's our project.* That's what he'd told her. A collaboration, just the two of them.

She wanted to grab Isabelle by the throat. The girl was cruel, evil, messing with her in that sly fucked-up way.

Or else it was Naomi, spreading a crazy rumor to show what a hypocrite Elizabeth was. Some kind of sick little enactment, her demented idea of performance art. Elizabeth could almost see it: Naomi's idea of dismantling the academic power structure and exposing them as cowards who taught one thing but lived another.

"Naomi?" she hissed. If Naomi was behind this disgusting hoax, she'd rip her to shreds.

Isabelle's grin widened. "She's so, so impressed with you, Professor Crawford. Me too. I just had to tell you." Her face grew serious. "What you did took guts. You're a model for all of us."

A model for all of us. A bad pun, or was the girl too naive to realize what she'd said?

No, it wasn't a hoax.

"You saw the photos?"

"They're amazing," Isabelle said. "And putting those little pictures of Georgia O'Keeffe next to them? Like, you can take something famous and embody it, claim it for yourself? It's like the ultimate empowerment. So—wow. Really."

Elizabeth's fingers groped for the railing, wrapping themselves around the oak as if its realness would undo the unreality of what she was hearing.

She'd never thought about the photos as having an existence separate from the taking of them. It was the act of being photographed that mattered.

Richard had tried to tell her. *I can blur the background when I make the print.* She hadn't listened. She hadn't wanted to hear about what he would do later. Only about what he was doing right now.

She needed to ask Isabelle where she had seen the pictures. Then, in the next instant, she knew. Juniper had told her. "He always has stuff up at that gallery right by campus—you know, the one next to the old firehouse?" Some kind of permanent showcase, the exhibit changing whenever he had a new concept.

Somehow she got out the next five words. "How did Naomi find it?"

"She was googling O'Keeffe," Isabelle said, "because of that thing you said, about how O'Keeffe painted whatever she felt like? You know, just random googling? And then this link popped up about how O'Keeffe was, like, still inspiring people, and one of the things they talked about was this show right here in town. They had a photo of O'Keeffe with her shirt open, and then a picture of you doing the same thing, and then they had a link to the gallery website. So Naomi texted me, 'Hey, let's go see it.'"

Elizabeth could hardly breathe. "It's on the internet?"

"Only that one picture, in the article. But the gallery website had, I don't know, three or four. They picked some of the really good ones. That's what Naomi said."

Elizabeth didn't know what she meant by *really good ones*. She didn't want to know. "Who else has seen it?" Her voice cracked.

"Who else?" Isabelle echoed. "I wouldn't know. But Naomi did a post. Crawford rocks, that was the headline. And you do. Totally. Not like the other professors around here."

Elizabeth met Isabelle's star-struck gaze. This was insane. She didn't need the girl's adoration. She needed to get those fucking pictures off the wall.

The bell sounded again, its shrillness slicing right through her flesh. The next class period. As if Isabelle's tap on her arm had been a *pause* button and the bell had unfrozen a suspended world, the staircase was filled, once again, with the blur and cacophony of bodies on the move. "I better run," Isabelle said. "I have a class over in the Math building. But I'll see you tomorrow."

Elizabeth didn't answer. Before Isabelle had finished waving, she was out the door and on her way to the gallery.

—

"You need to take them down," she hissed. "Now."

Those were O'Keeffe's first words to Stieglitz. He had mounted a show of her drawings without her consent, and she told him: *I'm the person who made them, and I didn't give you permission to hang them. You have to take them down.*

He didn't. Determined as Georgia was to maintain control, Stieglitz was equally determined that the world needed to see her work. What persuaded her, finally, was her feeling that Stieglitz actually understood what she was trying to convey. The possibility of being seen, so fully, was irresistible.

But this wasn't like that. Elizabeth was the model, not the artist. And the man facing her, the gallery owner, didn't care what she felt.

The gallery, called *On View*, was owned and managed by a sculptor named Joaquin Ventana. Ventana's work—mid-sized abstractions in bronze and wood—was mounted on pedestals in the center of the room. He needed something interesting on the surrounding walls. Bare walls were too cold, he explained; customers didn't like them. Richard, a long-time friend working in black-and-white, had suggested an arrangement that suited them both. For Joaquin, original art on the walls that complemented his sculptures and changed often enough to sustain attention. For Richard, a reputable and well-trafficked place to hang his work—a place where he could be seen and talked about, without having to pay rent, as long as Ventana's sculptures were the only work for sale.

Richard had been showing his photographs at *On View* for several years. From there, he'd picked up commissions, a one-man show at a major gallery, and a coveted spot in a museum exhibit on American portraiture.

His new show was called *Re-Visions*. Georgia's body was the vision. Elizabeth's body, re-enacting the poses, was the re-vision. She wasn't sure what it meant. Revising: improving the first draft? Or re-visioning: seeing anew?

It didn't matter. Whatever Richard had in mind, the photos had to go.

Joaquin Ventana laughed.

They were in the anteroom of the gallery. Elizabeth could glimpse the exhibit off to the left, the light reflecting off a curved bronze form in the center of the room, the rectangular shapes of the photographs on the walls, illuminated by spotlights but not discernable from where she stood. "It doesn't work that way," he said. "You can't storm in here and demand that I remove my exhibits."

Elizabeth glared at him. He knew it was her in Richard's photos. She had insisted on face and body together; that was the point. "I never gave permission."

"You didn't have to. You posed for an artist. He's showing his work. End of story."

"I didn't know he was going to show it. I just—" She stopped. She'd just—what?

"Did he take the photos covertly, without your knowledge?"

Elizabeth dropped her eyes. "No."

Ventana wouldn't shut up. "You went to his studio, then? Freely, without coercion?"

Oh, she hated both of them. "I get it. Freely. Yes." Then she tightened her jaw. "But it was a private matter. He never said he was going to put the photos in a public gallery."

Ventana shrugged. "They're his, to do with as he wishes."

No, that couldn't be right. "There must be some law against that, when it's a recognizable person."

"Actually, no, since the photos aren't for sale. He's simply showing his art." She began to argue, but Ventana cut her off. "That's the way it works. As long as it's not for commercial use. They're his work, his property, and he's the only one who can put them up or take them down. Not me, and not you."

"You don't understand." She tried to quell her rising panic. "I can't let them be seen."

"Like I said, it's not my decision."

Her voice sank to a whisper. "Please."

Ventana's irritation was obvious now. "I don't know what you expect me to do. I'm not going to shut my gallery down while you and Richard work this out."

Richard. The thought of seeing him, begging him, was almost unbearable. But there was no other way.

Elizabeth looked at her watch. 10:43. Thank goodness she had left Lucy's with plenty of time to spare. Forget making copies of her handouts; she'd wing it in class tomorrow.

Richard's studio was less than ten minutes away; that gave her half an hour to confront him, convince him, and get out. She wouldn't need half an hour, because his violation was so egregious and so wrong. As soon as he saw her, he'd know there was no way to spin what he'd done. She'd been pathetic with Ventana, but now she was angry. She wanted to grab Richard by the hair and scream, "What the hell did you think you were doing?"

She hurled the words at him like hailstones, pummeling the Richard in her mind. What. The. Hell. Are. You. Doing.

Did he have any idea what his exhibit would do to her? He couldn't, or he wouldn't have done it. No one could be that careless, that naive, or that cruel.

She wanted to twist that hair, hurt him back. The blithe confidence that had attracted her was her enemy now.

I didn't say you could let anyone else see them. They were for you.

She could already hear his reply. *You didn't say that I couldn't.*

Did it have to be said? Wasn't it obvious?

Well, he'd hear it soon enough. And then she'd rip his hateful photos right off the walls.

Part Three:
The Woman

Nineteen

Elizabeth didn't stop to wonder if Richard might be in the middle of a shoot—if another woman might be there, taking off her clothes for him. She slammed the car door, crossed the street in three quick strides, and jammed her finger on the buzzer next to the little white card. Ferris.

He buzzed back. The door clicked, and she pushed it open. His immediate response seemed odd. Had Joaquin Ventana called to warn him? Or was he expecting someone else? Or maybe he just let people in, not caring who they were.

Elizabeth grabbed the iron railing and started up the stairs. The first time she came here, he'd been waiting for her at the top, watching her ascend. Letting her come to him. Her heart had been pounding with the knowledge of what she was about to do.

Her heart was pounding now too, but it was a different kind of pounding, full of rage and desperation.

The stairs were planks of dark wood, steep, and worn in the center. There was a water stain shaped like South America on the right-hand wall. She'd never noticed it before—too eager to get to the top, to begin. A Styrofoam coffee cup had been left on the third step, the plastic tab pointing upward like a flag.

She climbed the rest of the stairs to the second-floor landing.

Richard's door was shut. She waited, listening for the sound of voices or footsteps. Finally she knocked.

More than two weeks since she'd seen him. Would he be glad to see her? Would he touch her? Oh, she was demented. She was there to yell and demand and scream, not to swoon. He'd done something unforgivable, and he had to undo it.

After endless seconds, the door swung open. "Elizabeth." He did look glad. "Come in." He ushered her inside the studio, fingertips light on the small of her back, and pulled the door shut.

A woman in a burgundy turtleneck was perched on the stool. She was older than Elizabeth by at least a decade, with a long neck and an aquiline nose. Fully dressed, Elizabeth thought, relieved, and yet disappointed because now she couldn't be angry at Richard about that.

"Elizabeth, Teresa," he said. He turned to Elizabeth. "Teresa's a physical therapist. She's showing me how the different muscles work."

His face lit up. "I have this idea for a new series. I want to capture the point of transition when a movement begins, when the body starts to do what the mind's decided, or maybe *before* it's decided—it's an interesting question, isn't it? I might shoot a few athletes, dancers, people like that. But first I have to understand the anatomy."

Teresa lowered her head in a regal nod. Elizabeth didn't give a shit. "You need to leave," she spat. "Richard and I have to talk. Alone."

The woman's chin shot up. "Excuse me?"

"You heard me. Get out."

Richard looked amused. "It's okay," he told her. "We were finished anyway." He ushered her to the door, closing it firmly.

At least he had let her in, Elizabeth thought. He could have refused to answer the buzzer, if he'd wanted to be alone with Teresa. "You always buzz people in," she challenged, "without knowing who they are?"

"It could be a pleasant surprise. As it was."

Elizabeth had fantasized about doing this very thing—showing up, without warning. In her fantasy she had taken her clothes off as she strode through the door. He had taken his off too.

Relaxed and handsome as ever, Richard was acting as if he'd done nothing wrong. Even Daniel, when he was trying to look innocent, had a crooked little dent in his grin. But Richard offered no sign that he knew why she was there or that anything had changed since her last visit.

Then again, maybe it hadn't.

A gust of wildness rose up in her. What if she didn't know about the gallery? If she hadn't run into Isabelle on campus today? Another minute talking to Harold, a few more sentences, and everything would have been different. Isabelle would have been on her way to math class instead of tapping Elizabeth on the arm. It was just chance that it worked out one way and not another. She could just as easily not-know about Joaquin Ventana and his damn gallery.

What if she let that be true—forgot about Naomi and Isabelle and Joaquin? Not for long, just long enough to live out her fantasy?

She looked into the grey eyes that seemed to see her more clearly than she saw herself. It seemed possible, for a moment. To be a person who could do that.

Then she shuddered. What was she thinking?

She straightened her shoulders and snapped, "I doubt you're all that surprised to see me. You could hardly expect me not to get wind of your little show."

"I wasn't trying to hide it. I figured you'd come across it."

His casualness caught Elizabeth off-guard. She'd been ready for a fight, for a flimsy excuse she could demolish with the swipe of a claw, leaving him in the wrong and eager to placate her. But he seemed almost indifferent.

"And that didn't concern you? How I might react when I saw it?"

"I hoped you'd like it, if that's what you mean."

Elizabeth couldn't believe what she was hearing. Was he a moron?

What kind of person wouldn't understand that she would be horri-fied? "Like it? Are you out of your mind?"

"You ought to like it. You look gorgeous."

She wanted to smack him. She'd wanted to look gorgeous for him. Not for Naomi and Joaquin Ventana and everyone else in this fuck-ing town.

"You need to take those pictures down. Right now."

Richard took a step back. "Excuse me?" The same phrase that Teresa person had used. It meant *are you insane?*

"Now," she repeated. Literally, because she really didn't have much time, and she damn well wasn't going to leave without know-ing she'd gotten what she came for. "I never said you could make them public."

"Not to be rude, but it wasn't your call."

"My *call*? I'm the one in the pictures."

He waved a hand, as if waving away her objection. "I offered to show them to you. You didn't want to see them. You didn't seem to care what happened to them."

"I care now. Take them down."

"It doesn't work like that, Elizabeth."

"It can."

"No, it can't."

She didn't understand why he was acting so obtuse. They should have settled this by now. She had to get out of there, get back to Lucy's. "It's about consent. I didn't give it."

"Of course you did. You knew exactly what you were doing. What we were doing."

The same thing Marion had said about Georgia. But did she? No. She had assumed—a jumble of assumptions. "What were we doing? You tell me."

Richard gave her a long hard look. *Flirting*, Elizabeth thought. *Foreplay.*

The silence was thick, connecting them, separating them. Then he said. "I think we both understood. It was for our mutual benefit."

What was that supposed to mean? A shared benefit, or two individual benefits, of equal heft on a scale that only he could understand? "I guess I'm stupid. Spell it out for me."

Richard sighed. "Let's not argue, Elizabeth. Here. Sit down."

She began to protest *I have to get going*, but he touched her arm and led her to a folding chair. Then he pulled up a second chair so he could face her.

They were sitting at the little wooden table, the same table where he had stacked the photos of O'Keeffe. He regarded her evenly. "Did it help you, to pose?"

"Don't patronize me."

"I'm serious. Did it help you?"

Help her—to what? Elizabeth wanted to fling the words back at him, insulted by his arrogance. But the knowledge was there, right in front of her. Yes, it did.

"It freed you to feel your own beauty." He leaned forward, his face close to hers. "And it helped me too. I'd been stuck, in my work. I had this idea—I think I told you?—that each person has one particular part of their body that captures the essence of who they are. I wanted to show that, through my camera, and I did. I was good at it. But I kept doing the same thing. I didn't know how to let it go and move on."

Despite herself, Elizabeth listened. Yes, she remembered him telling her that.

"Then I met you. You wanted to be photographed. I could feel it, even before you told me about O'Keeffe." Idly, he reached out a hand to trace the line of her neck and shoulder. Elizabeth wanted to jerk away but she couldn't.

"It was my chance," he went on. "To try something new. A whole person. You were that person, because it was what you wanted too."

He dropped his hand. "A serendipitous occurrence. For our mutual benefit, like I said."

Her neck felt empty, abandoned. That was all?

Seconds passed as his words sank in. "It was for your art?"

"I'm an artist. I told you that when we met. We talked about Weston and Stieglitz, what I was searching for. What you were searching for, in your study of O'Keeffe." His gaze was disarmingly candid. "What did you think it was about?"

She could kill him. He knew what she thought it was about. Proof that she could be someone other than Lizzie-the-owl. A way out of a marriage and a life that was choking her to death. And yes, a slow seduction. Obviously.

He had tricked her, twice. Making her believe she was beautiful and alluring, and then mocking her by putting her delusion on display.

She couldn't believe that she'd never asked why he was giving her so much time and attention. She'd accepted the gift, blindly, preferring not to question his motives. Carried away by her fantasy, like a dumb schoolgirl. Ignoring the fact that he'd never asked to see her away from Tai Chi and their studio sessions, never asked about the wedding band on her left hand, never even asked for her phone number—she'd still thought it was a prelude to becoming lovers. Or maybe it was because of those facts, because their encounters were a world of their own, separate from the rest of her life.

Oh, who knew? All she knew was that he had humiliated her.

He lifted a shoulder. "It was good timing. For both of us."

Elizabeth was sick with revulsion and shame. Revulsion, that he could pretend to be so innocent, as if it was some kind of business transaction. And shame, that she could have been demented enough to believe she'd become a fox at last.

Her failure was as bright and clear as Naomi's jewel. If she'd been sexier, he would have wanted more than a new phase in his artistic development.

"I do understand," he said, "that it might be a little shocking to see yourself as an artist's model, but you look beautiful, trust me. It's a good show. And it needs to stay right where it is, where people can see it."

Now she was angry. "Please don't play dumb. I can't have people seeing me like that. This is a small town. I'm a doctoral student, for god's sake."

Richard gave another dismissive wave. "None of those professors are going to see your pictures. They never leave their little academic bubble. You ought to know that. There's the campus, and there's the town."

Was he cruel, or just stupid? "You don't think people are going to know? I have students, and some of them have already seen it. I have children—"

She stopped. Her eyes widened in horror. No, please. When had she lost track of the time?

She looked at her watch. It was 11:56. Lucy's program was about to start. She was going to miss Daniel's superhero and Katie's snowflake.

Her lie about a broken-down delivery van that stopped traffic for twenty minutes until a tow truck came to drag it out of the way—and her distress, which wasn't a lie—worked with Lucy, but it didn't work with Katie. Katie screeched when Elizabeth tried to touch her. Still screeching, she twisted away and fought to tear off her snowflake costume. When she couldn't get it off, she began ripping it apart. The lacy pattern, painstakingly cut by Elizabeth only two days earlier, made it easy to shred. She stood in the corner of Lucy's dining room, face to the wall, as bits of white costume fluttered to the floor.

Daniel wasn't much better. He pretended not to care but kept going up to other parents and announcing, "You smell like poop." Elizabeth told herself that she ought to reprimand him, but she didn't have the heart. He was talking about her, and to her. She wanted nothing more than to erase the entire horrible day.

Phoebe's sympathy only made it worse. "It's not your fault," she whispered. "It could have happened to anyone. Everyone understands, and your kids will too."

No, Elizabeth thought. It was entirely her fault, it couldn't have happened to any of the other parents, and no one actually understood, least of all her children. She had betrayed them as badly as Richard had betrayed her.

She knelt by Katie, who refused to come out of the corner. "Katie my love, I am so very sad. I can't tell you how sad I am." She put a hand on Katie's shoulder, but Katie swatted it away. She looked to see if Katie was crying, but her little body was rigid, pressed into the V where the walls met, like the crack in the center of Georgia's painting, *The Black Place.* Elizabeth wanted to cry herself.

"I know you're sad too. And mad. You have every right to be. I let you down terribly." She sensed Daniel coming up behind her, listening. "I didn't mean to break my promise, but something happened and I didn't get here in time." She waited. The wait took forever.

Finally Daniel said, "I hate that delivery van."

"Me too."

"It's made of poop."

"It's definitely made of poop."

"Stinky poop." Elizabeth could see him watching to see if she would react. When she didn't, he added, "Stinky fart poop."

Katie turned around and gave Daniel a deadpan look. "Fart poop."

Elizabeth wanted to pull the two of them into her arms and never let go. "Now, now," Lucy said. Elizabeth hadn't realized that she was nearby. "Is that how we talk?"

Ruthie, trailing behind Lucy, imitated her voice. "No, it isn't." She threw a smug look Elizabeth's way. Elizabeth didn't care. All she wanted was for her children to forgive her.

"Stop," Phoebe said, taking Ruthie by the arm. "Focus on yourself and how you talk to your own brother." She shook her head, including Elizabeth in her silent *kids*.

Elizabeth felt worse and worse. Was everyone crowded around this one little corner of the dining room, watching her display of terrible parenting? She reached for Katie again, but Katie flung her hand away. *Fart poop* had been for Daniel, not a sign that she forgave her mother.

"All right, everyone," Lucy said. "Cookies on the porch. And coffee for the parents." She gave Elizabeth a reassuring nod. "Come, have some coffee. Katie will relent in her own good time."

Reluctantly, Elizabeth stood. Lucy was right, of course. Katie would grow tired of pressing her face to the wall. As the afternoon wore on, she would want to play and then, sleepy, she would climb onto Elizabeth's lap and grant her the reprieve she didn't deserve. Yet Elizabeth knew she had let Katie down in a far deeper way than missing the performance. She'd been the opposite of the woman she wanted her daughter to see and become.

"I took pictures," Phoebe whispered in her ear. "I'll send them to you."

Elizabeth tried to blink back her tears. Everyone was being so kind. They wouldn't be kind if they knew the real reason she was late. Phoebe, especially, made her want to weep. After the way she had rebuffed Phoebe, again and again, she was absurdly grateful for Phoebe's generosity.

"Of course," Phoebe added, "my pictures suck. I always miss the best shots." She gave a lopsided grin, like her haircut. "Maybe we should have hired that friend of yours to take some photos? You know, that Ferris wheel guy? The one you told me about?"

Elizabeth froze. How did Phoebe know? Phoebe kept smiling, and she realized: of course Phoebe didn't know. Yet her words brought Richard right there into the room, where he didn't belong.

"What's a Ferris wheel?" Daniel asked.

She whirled around. Why hadn't Daniel run after Lucy, first one at the cookie platter, the way he usually was? She tried to steady her ragged breathing. "It's big wheel that turns," she said, when she was able to speak. "You sit in a special seat and it takes you up and around, up into the sky."

"I want to go on it." He crossed his arms, his eyebrows a stern line. Elizabeth got the message: If you want to redeem yourself, take me on it right now.

"And you will," she told him. "The very next time we see one."

"You promise?"

She had told them *I never, ever break my promises.* Next to her, Katie stirred, tired of sulking against the wall if no one was paying attention. Elizabeth put a hand on the top of her head, lightly, so Katie could pretend it wasn't there. "I promise," she said. That was what you had to do, when your child asked.

"Now let's go get some cookies, pal. How's that sound?"

Daniel broke away and ran to the porch, shouting, "I'm going on a Ferris wheel!" Katie pushed past Elizabeth and ran after him.

Twenty

Elizabeth knew that Ben wouldn't be as understanding about the broken-down delivery van as Phoebe and Lucy had been. He'd mask his reaction in front of the children but later, when they were alone, he'd be furious. Elizabeth could already hear his angry hiss. "You couldn't have gone to campus *after* the program, instead of trying to squeeze it in when you knew that time was tight?"

Of course she could have returned Harold's book in the afternoon. But she knew, as Ben didn't, that Harold liked to reserve afternoons for his own writing, which was why he had specifically asked her to come first thing in the morning—and that Daniel and Katie would need to get home and cool down after the play, instead of being dragged to campus—and that she couldn't possibly have predicted what the morning would bring. So yes, in theory, she could have made sure she was there. But things didn't always work out the way they did in theory.

Daniel and Katie were buckled into the back seat of the car as Elizabeth drove home from Lucy's house. Katie, predictably, was sound asleep. Daniel was looking out the window and humming to himself as he rubbed his thumb against the metal clasp of his seat belt. Elizabeth cleared her throat.

"Hey buddy," she began. "You know how sad Daddy was that he

couldn't be there today?" Daniel met her eyes with an oblique look that could have meant anything from *you should talk* to *what's your point?* Carefully, Elizabeth went on, "He'd be even sadder if he thought I wasn't there either."

She hated what she was doing. Saying *thought I wasn't there* when she and Daniel both knew that the correct wording was *knew I wasn't there.* But she couldn't handle one more terrible conversation today.

Daniel didn't answer, so she kept going. "Daddy works so hard, and I really don't want him to be sad. Will you help me?"

"I can tell him a joke," Daniel offered. He brightened, then inserted an experimental finger into his nose. "Rex told me one."

"That's a very good idea," Elizabeth said. "And maybe we can also, you and me, make Daddy happy by telling him all about the play. But maybe we don't have to exactly say that I wasn't there—that I was *late*—because it would make him too sad."

"You mean a secret?"

Daniel was sharp. She really didn't want to call it that. All the parenting books said that was one of the worst things you could do. But she was trapped. "Kind of."

Daniel twisted the finger for a while before withdrawing a piece of dried snot. He inspected it with interest. "Okay."

Okay what? Elizabeth thought. *Okay* you won't say anything, or *okay* secret was the right word to use for the sly little maneuver she was suggesting to her four and a half year-old son?

Too late to back out now. Keeping her voice mild, she said, "We can show Daddy the pictures, like I promised him. I have a lot of great pictures from Rex and Ruthie's mom."

Elizabeth said a silent thank-you to Phoebe for her kindness. Then her words boomeranged back, stunning her with their irony. *A lot of great pictures.* Those other pictures, still on the walls of Ventana's gallery, weren't great at all.

"Okay," Daniel repeated. Absently, he flicked a yellow trapezoid of snot across the back seat. It landed in Katie's hair. Elizabeth saw, but said nothing. That was the least of her concerns. Katie, snoring quietly, didn't notice.

"What's gotten into Katie?" Ben asked, gesturing at Katie across the dinner table.

Katie was refusing to let Elizabeth cut up her food or come near her chair. She shook her head from side to side, jaw clamped.

"Oh, more Terrible Two's," Elizabeth said. "You know, devoted one minute, snobbish the next."

"I get that," Ben began. "But I've never seen—"

Before he could finish, Daniel looked up from his plate and said brightly, "She's mad at Mommy because Mommy didn't come. She ripped up her snowflake dress. It's a secret."

Elizabeth wanted to melt into a puddle and disappear. She should have known that Daniel, who had proudly told her about the "surprise" play, would say exactly that. It would have been more startling if he hadn't.

Ben looked at her. "Didn't come?"

She sighed. "Just my luck. A horrible backup, thanks to a stalled van." Oddly, she almost believed the story now. She'd told it three times at Lucy's house and it felt more real than the awful encounters with Joaquin and Richard that really did happen. "There was nothing I could do."

"You didn't even go?"

Indignant now, she snapped, "Of course I *went*. I was late, that's all."

He looked puzzled. "Why didn't you call Lucy and ask her to delay a few minutes?"

Elizabeth stared at him. It had never occurred to her. She'd been too full of everything else—panic, shame, rage, the pain of

thwarted desire. There hadn't been room in her mind for a practical thought like calling Lucy. She considered making up another
story about a dead cell phone, but there were so many lies already.
"I don't know," she said slowly. "I was too upset to think." That, at
least, was true.

Ben set down his fork. "Honestly, Liz. Thinking is what you *do*."

Oh, that was cold. A terrible, unlovely way to describe her. Lizzie
the brain—and a failed brain at that, someone who hadn't even had
the sense to call Lucy and say she was running late.

Daniel looked from parent to parent. Ben reached across the table
and gave Daniel's arm a quick squeeze. "I know you were disappointed, buddy, but Mommy got there as fast as she could."

Elizabeth tried to salvage something from what had been a stun-
ningly disastrous day. "At least Phoebe took some good pictures.
She was nice enough to email them to me, so we can look at them
together after dinner."

Daniel sat up straight. His voice was full of authority. "The Ferris
man wasn't there either," he told Ben. "Or else he would have taken
pictures, instead of Rex's Mommy. From the sky."

Ben swiveled his head. "What Ferris man?"

Elizabeth tried to suppress her alarm. Daniel missed nothing. It
was all stored in a memory bank organized into Daniel-specific cat-
egories and retrieved, hours or weeks later, according to a Daniel-
specific logic.

"He wanted to know what a Ferris Wheel was," she explained. "So
I told him how you got to ride up into the sky." She prayed that Ben
wouldn't ask what that had to do with taking pictures. One more
twist, and whatever was holding her together would split apart.

Ben threw her a dark look. It was only an instant, and then he
turned back to Daniel, his features shifting into the encouraging
expression he'd had before. Yet Elizabeth saw the contempt in the
way he had glared at her; he would never have let a stalled truck keep

him from his children's play. Or maybe it wasn't contempt, but suspicion. The stupid lie about the food co-op, her obvious agitation after Tai Chi, and now a conveniently timed traffic jam.

Katie pushed her plate across the table to get Ben's attention. "Pity," she told him. "Pity Katie."

"Yes, pretty," Elizabeth answered, before Ben could wonder if her daughter was asking him to pity her for having such an terrible mother. "You were so, so pretty in your snowflake dress."

Katie gave her a disdainful glance. Elizabeth could imagine that look breaking hearts in fifteen years. Right now it was breaking hers.

"I had a sword." Daniel said.

"Indeed you did." Elizabeth pushed out her chair. "I know. Let's look at the photos on the computer right this very minute. I'll put my laptop on the table and we can eat our applesauce while we look at them." Ben raised an eyebrow. *A laptop on the dinner table?* She didn't care. Anything to end this conversation.

She plucked a napkin from the center of the table and bent over Katie, giving her mouth and cheeks a decisive wipe. She was still the mother, even if Katie wanted to keep punishing her.

"Hands, please." Katie looked up, her mouth falling open into a startled O. She extended her hands and let Elizabeth clean them. A small concession.

Elizabeth dared to let herself feel a glimmer of relief. Katie would come around. It wasn't in her nature to reject her mother forever. Ben—well, that was more complicated.

One thing at a time. Right now, the priority was repairing her daughter's trust. Tomorrow, it would be getting rid of those damn photos.

Hanging them up in Ventana's gallery might not be illegal but it was wrong. She'd tell him that. No apologies, no begging.

Tomorrow was Tuesday, a Lucy day. Unencumbered by Daniel and Katie, she'd rush over to that gallery and be there before

Joaquin Ventana unlocked the doors. The pictures would be gone by Wednesday.

Before the next Tai Chi class.

"I already explained," Ventana said. Elizabeth could tell that he was trying not to lose his composure. "I have no authority to remove someone else's work."

She tried, equally hard, not to lose hers. "I understand." She forced herself to smile. Determination was good, but she had to get him on her side, make him want to help her. "Your hands are tied, in terms of doing anything directly. Of course. So it's a matter of convincing Richard to remove them. That's something you *can* do."

Joaquin eyed her coolly. They were standing in the entrance to the gallery; he had barely let her cross the threshold. "Why would I want to? Richard's an old friend. There's no benefit to me in pissing him off."

Elizabeth's mind shot ahead. Thinking was what she did; Ben had told her that. "Well," she said, scrambling for a new approach. "I can't imagine it would be good for business if there was a lot of negative attention. An irate model. Protests. Maybe I'll talk to a lawyer." Ben was a lawyer—the last person she would go to for help, but Ventana wouldn't know that.

Joaquin's face turned hard. "Please don't threaten me. Especially when you don't know what you're talking about. No one's going to stage a protest in front of my gallery because you posed nude." His eyes locked onto hers. "Voluntarily."

Elizabeth blanched. Of course he was right. What was she thinking—a student protest, with signs, chanting, candles? Her students thought what she had done was heroic. They weren't going to link arms around the gallery and demand that Ventana take the pictures down.

"Look, I'm sorry." She put out her hand, then quickly withdrew it. "Please. Can't you just talk to Richard, out of humanity? Let him know how damaging this could be for me. Ask him to reconsider."

Instead of relenting, Joaquin stepped back. "I really can't get in the middle of this. And frankly, I resent your trying to put me in that position."

"Please." She hated to throw herself at his mercy like this, but she was growing desperate. "I'm begging you."

He winced, as if her plea was in bad taste. "I think I've tried to be civil but, frankly, I'm reaching the end of my patience. If you keep badgering me, I'm going to have to complain to Richard that you're interfering with his work."

"You wouldn't."

"I most definitely would." He narrowed his eyes. "So you decide."

What sort of decision did he think she had? Walk away, which was impossible, or tell him, "Sure. Instead of helping me, why don't you complain to Richard so you can join forces against me?"

To her surprise, a hint of compassion crossed Joaquin's face. "I understand that you're upset. But I can't have you standing here ranting at me. Customers are going to walk in, it's bad for business." Then the compassion faded. "In any case, I'm not interested in being a go-between, particularly when one person's a friend and the other's a stranger. I'm sure you can appreciate that."

When Elizabeth didn't answer, he opened the door and motioned toward the street. "It's time to end this conversation. Nothing personal, but I don't see a point in continuing."

Elizabeth's eyes darted to the gallery's name. *On View*, etched onto the glass. That was her. It might even be funny, if it wasn't so horrible. She remembered a sign she'd seen in the window of a bar. *Live Nude Girls*, in pink neon. As opposed to what—dead nude girls? She had pointed it out to Ben, marveling at people's inanity.

Ventana was waiting for her to leave. Reluctantly, she bowed her head and stumbled onto the sidewalk. He closed the door behind her.

Elizabeth looked around, staring at the once-familiar street that now seemed alien and unwelcoming. The blare of horns, the smell of diesel, the beeping of a truck as it backed up. The sunlight was absurdly bright, like yellow paint splattered across the buildings.

She'd been as stupid as Andrea, trying to recruit someone else to intervene and solve her problem. It hadn't worked for Andrea and it wasn't going to work for her.

"Sorry." A teenager on a skateboard tossed the two syllables her way as he angled past. Elizabeth jumped to the edge of the sidewalk, then hurried across the street to her car. Her feet moved by themselves, lifting and falling, like the turning of a wheel. A Ferris Wheel. A bad joke, sickening her with its mixture of desire and remorse. She remembered how she had watched Richard at Tai Chi, long before they spoke. That regal, animal presence—as if the very space of the room was defined by the shape of his body, the others in the class existing only in relation to him. And then, once he had touched her elbow in that coffee shop, how she herself was shaped and situated by his presence. Knowing herself by how far apart they were in the room, how many days until she would see him again. Moon to his planet, tide to his gravity.

It was the same force that had drawn her to the photos of O'Keeffe. Four-minute exposures, Richard had told her. How was it possible to stay there, being seen, for that long? A moment at a time had been as much as she could bear.

She yearned to undo everything. To reel back time and let the pile of photographs stay as they were on the wooden table, never plucked from their places in the stack he'd prepared.

Let the coffee stay un-poured, safe in its carafe. Let the swing hang on its chains.

She yanked open the car door, jerking it shut as she got in. How was she supposed to show up on campus now, as if nothing had happened? What if she ran into someone else who had seen the exhibit? A fellow doctoral student, another instructor?

Her hands slick with sweat, she pushed the hair off her face. Damn highlights. Who did she think she was, anyway, with a hairdo like that? Some kind of runway model?

Shit. The double meanings were everywhere. Run-*away* model, that's what she wanted to be. Elizabeth grabbed her hair in her fists, hating the falseness of its shimmer, the sleek sophisticated way it framed her face.

She didn't want it any more.

She couldn't get Ventana to pull those photos off the walls, but she could do this. Would Andie agree to help her, after the awful way they had parted? She couldn't believe her sister would refuse. Anyway, she was asking Andie to take something back, not do her a new favor.

What the hell. The worst Andrea could do was say no.

Elizabeth jammed the key into the ignition and screeched away from the curb.

Twenty-One

There were two women in Andrea's salon, one with foil packets covering the left side of her head, the other under the dryer. Andrea was bending over the first woman, a brush thick with blue cream poised over the woman's scalp. She halted in mid-gesture when she saw Elizabeth. "Lizzie? What're you doing here?"

"An unscheduled stop. Can you fit me in?"

Andrea looked puzzled, but she said, "Of course. Give me half an hour."

Elizabeth looked for a place to wait. There wasn't one, except in the playroom. She perched on the edge of a child-sized chair and tried to contain her impatience. Behind her, she could hear the women talking. One was saying, "What I do, when I need to zone out, is I knit. And let me tell you, it definitely works."

"Well, what *I* do," the other woman answered, "is I go and pull the crabgrass out of the flower beds."

"I don't know. At least with knitting you're making something."

"What I'm making is a nice flower bed. Anyway, the one thing doesn't, you know, stop you from doing the other thing."

Preclude, Elizabeth thought. You mean it doesn't preclude the other.

She turned around, wanting to tell them that there was a word for what they were talking about. It seemed important to let them know, but their attention had shifted to Andrea, who was adjusting the hair dryer and explaining, "I'm going to let you air-dry for a few minutes, Lois, okay? Then I'll brush you out while Mary sits under the dryer."

Elizabeth lost interest in their conversation. She planted her elbows on her knees, took out her phone, and typed: *Can you stop someone from using a photo of you?* All the links were about Facebook and Instagram. Nothing about art exhibits.

Still, there must be some kind of law. She tried *model's legal rights* but the sites had to do with working conditions for professional models. Then she tried *model's right to photos* and *model's release for photos*. Damn. Ventana was right. Unless she had paid Richard, which she hadn't, he owned the photos. And unless he used them for a commercial purpose—sold them or incorporated them into a commercial product—he didn't need her permission. "*Under U.S. copyright law,*" she read, "*copyright in a photograph belongs to the person who presses the shutter on the camera.*"

She had nothing. Richard had everything.

Dimly, she heard the two women leave. Andrea joined her in the playroom. "What's up?"

Elizabeth extracted herself from the too-small seat. "I want to get rid of these." She flicked her fingers through her hair. "The highlights. It's not me."

"You're kidding."

"I'm not. It was a stupid idea."

"It was not stupid. You look fabulous." Andrea put her hands on her hips and gave Elizabeth a shrewd look. "Is this a way of telling me to piss off, I don't want any of your damn favors?"

"Good Lord, Andie. Not at all."

"Well, what is it, then? You have a fight with Ben or something?"

Elizabeth gave a bitter laugh. "Ben never even noticed my haircut. Not that I cared."

"Maybe you need a more dramatic look."

"Forget Ben. This has nothing to do with him."

Andrea frowned. "If it has nothing to do with Ben, then it's just some bad mood you're in, and I'm not going to pay attention to anything you're saying."

"Are you refusing to help me?"

"I'm refusing to take back what I gave you." Andrea's glare was a stubborn as Elizabeth's. "Don't be a moron, Lizzie. You never looked better."

Such a lovely face, Richard had told her. *Surely you know that.*

Pushing past her sister, Elizabeth crossed the playroom in three quick strides. She grabbed the nylon cape that one of the women had tossed onto the counter and fastened it around her neck. Then she dropped into the salon chair and pulled her hair off her face. She looked pure, severe. Like Georgia, swathed in black.

"Never looked better than what? Than myself?"

"Oh please," Andrea said. "Don't do some philosophy thing on me. Just leave the highlights alone. You look good."

"I don't care what you think. It's my hair."

My image. My body.

Andrea eyed her warily. "Look, Lizzie. Let's not make this into some kind of battleground for whatever's going on between us. You know, instead of the stuff we're actually mad about."

"No, it's not that." She tried to sound calm, even though she wasn't. "Look, I know there's a lot going on right now. But I need to do this one thing, and I need you to help me. Will you?"

"You mean, will I take back my gift?"

Elizabeth didn't answer.

"I won't," Andrea said. "Because you gave *me* a gift."

"Me?" Elizabeth remembered the angry words she had flung at her sister. Where was the gift in that?

"You." Andrea sank into the opposite chair. "You made me realize that I wanted to keep my husband and I'd better focus on that, instead of trying to pull off a dumb *gotcha* that would only make him furious."

"I didn't make you realize that."

"Maybe not on purpose, but you did. When you screwed up my little scheme, I figured I could either be pissed off or relieved. So I picked relieved."

Elizabeth tried to make sense of what Andrea was telling her. "You decided you'd rather not know?"

"I decided I'd rather be hotter than Miss Whatever." The corners of Andrea's mouth twitched in an impish grin. "And I was. Our weekend getaway?"

"Oh." Elizabeth looked down. She smoothed the nylon folds of the cloak across her lap. "I take it your weekend went well."

"Very."

"So you two are good?"

"Better than ever."

Like her hair—which, clearly, hadn't been good until Andrea intervened.

Don't, Elizabeth told herself. Don't resent Andie for making sure she got what she wanted. Her sister had already delivered the bittersweet truth. *No one kept you from getting what you wanted except you.*

"Why are you giving me such a sour look? Aren't you glad Michael and I worked things out?"

"I am glad."

"I think you're a little bit not-glad. A little bit disappointed."

"You mean, a schadenfreude thing?"

"Stop showing off."

"I'm not," Elizabeth said. "It means pleasure at another person's misfortune."

"That's a shitty attitude."

"I didn't say I felt that way. I just said what it meant." Then she sighed. "It hurts, sometimes, when you remind me of what you and Michael have. That's all."

"You could have it too, you and Ben."

"No. It's either there or it isn't. Candles, music, props—they don't make the chemistry happen." Elizabeth sniffed. "He actually went out and got this skimpy little negligee, can you believe it? Like if I put on a costume, everything would be different."

"Oh, Lizzie."

"He probably read it in some magazine. How to fix your wife."

"Look, he was trying," Andrea said. "That's a good thing."

No, it wasn't. A man shouldn't have to try so hard to desire his wife.

Elizabeth dug her toe into the mat. "Anyway, none of this is about Ben. Yes, I want to change my hair back. And yes, I'm glad you and Michael patched things up."

"And yes, a little bit of schaden-whatever when you thought we wouldn't."

"I suppose."

"But why?"

Why? Because Andie got to be in *The Nutcracker*, dancing onto the stage without a hint of effort or doubt. Because she pranced through life, confident that boys would honk at her from their cars and fling her compliments and whisk her away for romantic weekends. Because, for Andie, charm solved all. And if that charm seemed to fail her, even briefly, what bookworm-sister could resist a flicker of satisfaction?

"Oh, sibling rivalry, I guess." Elizabeth extracted a strand of auburn hair from a crease in the cape. "Everything was so easy for you."

"Easy? All that stuff was agony. Times tables, French verbs—"

"I don't mean school," Elizabeth interrupted. "I mean life."

"What's that even supposed to *mean*? It's all life."

"It isn't. You wouldn't understand."

"No?"

"No." Elizabeth's voice hardened. "You always got the best, the first."

"Oh, please."

"You did. You got the silver tutu."

"The silver tutu?" Andrea let out an astonished hoot. "I got to wear a cheap little piece of netting and be in a crowd of kids around a fake Christmas tree. You got a story in the school anthology with your name on the damn cover. Mom and Dad kept the anthology on the coffee table. Me? I was in alphabetical order with eleven other kids at the very bottom of the program." Andrea shook her head. "That's how it always was. You were the one with the big future."

Elizabeth's mouth fell open. No. Andrea was the star. It was her light that filled a room.

"Seriously," Andrea said. "You look like I just dropped a raw egg on your head."

"Good Lord, Andie." There were too many years and too many incidents that proved Andrea was the sister who'd gotten the better gifts. The idea that Andie had seen it differently was too bizarre to believe.

Elizabeth stretched the nylon across her lap, flicking away the curls of russet and silver that dotted the fabric like galaxies scattered across the night sky. Every researcher knew there were different perspectives. One set of data, but multiple truths. If Andrea's truth was different from hers, then hers wasn't the single immutable version of reality after all. There weren't cubes and pyramids and spheres, each fitting neatly into its proper cutout in the shape-sorter bucket. There were other possibilities.

Elizabeth the beautiful. Andrea the wise.

"Andie." Elizabeth sat up straight. An idea bloomed in her mind—so wonderful that her sister had to see it too. The solution to the terrible fight they'd had.

She put her palm on Andrea's. "You could go further, have a bigger future of your own. Go for that business degree, like we talked about."

Andrea made a face. "Like *you* talked about. I never said I was interested."

"But you could! It'd be so good for you. A way to improve yourself."

"I don't want to improve myself. I'm happy the way I am."

"You could be so much—"

Andrea cut her off, removing her hand. "That's your thing, Lizzie. Not mine."

Elizabeth stiffened. Her idea had seemed so right.

Then Andrea sighed. It was a complicated sound, weary and impatient and proud. "I don't need to be everything. I've made my peace with being one thing, and being good at it, like I told you the other day. So please don't badger me."

Not a magical solution after all. She'd miscalculated.

Elizabeth grew quiet. Then, with a decisive flourish, she jerked the cape from her neck and tossed it on the floor. "On second thought," she said, "leave the highlights. What the hell."

Andrea's eyebrows shot up. "Lizzie?"

Elizabeth rose from the chair. "It's my hair. And I like it this way."

Screw Ben, who hadn't even noticed.

And Richard, who had.

The next day was Wednesday. Tai Chi night. No doubt Richard would be back, Elizabeth thought, *coming up for air*. The pictures of her pretending to be Georgia were finished and hung, and his new series was still in the planning stage. He was too devoted to Tai Chi to stay away for long.

As dreadful as Tai Chi had been without him, it would be worse with him back. Watching him next to Mr. Wu, in front of the class. Watching him get into the elevator and walk away. Or did he imagine they'd continue their flirtatious little cups of coffee? She had no idea what he imagined.

The thought of going to Tai Chi made her ill. She wasn't lying when she told Ben, "I don't think I'm going to go tonight. I'm not really up to it."

He looked surprised. "I thought you loved Tai Chi."

Elizabeth's cheeks burned. "I did. Do. I just don't feel so great." She put a hand on her abdomen. "My stomach's off, that's all."

Daniel, marching his plastic dinosaurs along the coffee table, turned to her with interest. "What a *stomach's off*?"

Elizabeth hadn't known he was listening. "It means your tummy hurts." She rubbed her stomach and made a face.

"Not off and on. Like the TV."

Elizabeth couldn't help smiling. "No, not like that. Just that it hurts."

Daniel banged the dinosaurs together. "Sometimes my tummy hurts."

"I know. It happens to everyone."

She felt a tug on her sleeve. It was Katie, her eyes round. "Mama sick?" She put a chubby hand on Elizabeth's forehead.

Daniel, not to be outdone, jumped up. "I'll get some ice," he shouted. "And a Band-aid." Abandoning the dinosaurs, he raced to the bathroom, Katie at his heels. Within moments, they were back. Daniel had the box of Band-aids, the hot water bottle, and her deodorant. Katie held out an arm, offering her bunny.

Elizabeth wanted to burst into tears. They'd forgiven her for missing their play. Their baby hearts so large and open, wrapping her in their astounding generosity.

Did she dare to accept their forgiveness? To hope that life might go on?

Surely, if she was patient, Richard would move on to another set of photographs. The origin of movement—he'd already told her what he wanted to work on next. Get them done, she thought. Quickly. Do a brilliant new series and put it up on Ventana's wall.

All she had to do was to survive until then.

Twenty-Two

arold's email was seven words long. "Please see me first thing
tomorrow morning." No word of explanation, no apology for
the last-minute notice, no expression of hope that she could make
herself available. Not even a salutation.

Elizabeth ran through the list of reasons that Harold might need
to see her. Someone else's publication had preempted her idea about
O'Keeffe in Hawaii? There was a problem with her class? It couldn't
be about the photographs. There was no way he could know about
them, she was being paranoid. Anyway, they had nothing to do with
her dissertation—even though, of course, her dissertation had been
the reason for posing. *The only way to truly understand O'Keeffe.*

Somehow she got Daniel and Katie dressed and settled at Lucy's
in time to knock on Harold's pebbled glass door at 8:45. As soon as
she saw his face, she knew.

"Congratulations," he told her. "You've come up with a new infrac-
tion that's not in the Graduate School Code of Ethics. Apparently we
couldn't foresee every stunt a doctoral student might pull."

Elizabeth couldn't tell if he was disgusted with her or was inviting
her to join him in a moment of sarcasm, a shared eye-roll at the university's endless regulations. For an instant she thought of replying
with a joke of her own. Then she saw the flatness in his eyes. No, he

didn't think it was funny. And there wasn't a shred of doubt what he was referring to.

"How did you find out?"

He removed his glasses and cleaned them with a pale grey cloth. "It seems you have quite a fan club, Ms. Crawford. One of your students thinks you're the only instructor around here with, I quote, balls."

Naomi. Elizabeth remembered the sly looks, the thumbs-up, the coy allusion to how she *of all people* should understand what it meant to invite others to notice your body. A bunch of students had been to the gallery to see the photographs, that's what Isabelle told her on the staircase. But it never occurred to Elizabeth that any of them would tell the department chairman.

"She went to you? To tell you about it?"

Harold inspected the glasses for spots and then, satisfied, returned them to his face. "Hardly. She posted it on the student Facebook page." He picked up a sheet of paper and read aloud, enunciating each word. "Finally, a professor who walks the walk instead of hiding, literally, behind the Emperor's New Clothes. Crawford has more integrity than all the tenured professors put together. The hypocrites around here could learn a lot from her. The woman's got balls." He lowered the paper and regarded Elizabeth over the top of his newly polished glasses. "Followed by a couple of snapshots—her favorites among the portraits, I presume—and a link to the gallery's website where, evidently, there are additional photos."

"She wrote that?"

"Indeed. And a hundred and eleven other students have *liked* it."

"Oh my god."

"That's the problem with social media. It's impossible to contain something once people start to *like* it."

"You looked on the student Facebook page?"

Harold sighed. "We have to monitor these things. We can't have students posting material that might be construed as racist or revolutionary. You know, pornography, overthrow the government, that sort of thing. We try not to interfere unless it's really egregious." He pushed the paper to the side of his desk. "The dean's secretary keeps an eye on the student Facebook page and lets us know if there's anything we should be aware of."

"The student thought she was doing me a favor."

"The very definition of naiveté."

His dry tone, with its hint of humor, gave Elizabeth hope that it might be a matter of a *pro forma* reprimand and a pointed request to Naomi that she delete the post. She wouldn't want to, of course. Harold might have to engage in a bit of censorship, which could provoke a reaction. But that wasn't Elizabeth's concern.

"I know which student it is," she said. "I'll speak with her, ask her to remove the post."

"Ms. Crawford." Harold cleared his throat. "It's not that simple. Removing the post doesn't remove its effect."

Like the photographs. The sooner they came down, the less damage they would cause. She drew closer, eager to explain that she hadn't sanctioned the exhibit any more than she had sanctioned Naomi's praise. "Dr. Lindstrom—" she began, but he stopped her.

"There are two issues," he said, "and it would be a mistake to conflate them. One is the student's decision to compare your integrity to what she deems the lack of integrity in tenured faculty members—based, apparently, on the sole criterion of one's willingness to pose naked. The other is your decision to pose in the first place. Without the latter, the former wouldn't exist. But the former is the issue I have to deal with."

Elizabeth's mind reeled. This was more complicated than she had thought. To Harold and the rest of the faculty, her worst transgression might have nothing to do with baring her breasts.

That damn Naomi, admiring her for all the wrong reasons. And

Richard, telling her that it was good for her to pose, that it freed her
to feel her own beauty. Slick. Manipulative. The same kind of bullshit
Stieglitz used on O'Keeffe to justify his affair with Dorothy Norman.
Love enriches a marriage, he'd told Georgia, whether it comes from
inside or outside the relationship. A nice rationalization for doing
what he wanted.

"You've put us in an unfortunate situation," Harold continued. "As
I said, you haven't done anything that's explicitly against university
policy because there isn't any policy that applies. Your activities may
reflect bad judgment, but they're not illegal."

Again, Elizabeth dared to hope. Was he implying that there
wouldn't be any consequences—other than, perhaps, the loss of
his respect, which was bad enough? She searched Harold's face but
couldn't tell what he really felt. Clearly, he was displeased. But she
didn't know if it was because he was disappointed in her, maybe even
disgusted, because of the position she had put him in, as her mentor.

She tried to explain. "Dr. Lindstrom, no one wants those photographs to come down more than I do. I'm not trying to make a
statement about art or academic freedom or a woman's right to her
body, or anything like that." It was the students, she wanted to tell
him, who were projecting all that onto her. The same way that the art
world, and then the feminists, had projected their own agenda onto
O'Keeffe.

"But you did consent to pose for them."

To pose, that was all. For Richard. She'd never thought beyond
the photo sessions themselves—ignoring the fact that Richard was
a professional photographer, dismissing the caution that any sensi-
ble person would have exercised. She'd been as naive as Naomi, and
Richard had taken advantage of her trust. He'd let her unbutton her
shirt and step out of her jeans, knowing very well that she assumed
no other eyes would see.

Oh, he was slick. He'd been careful to do nothing except watch and, once in a while, adjust her pose. She couldn't accuse him of impropriety. She could only accuse herself of stupidity.

She met Harold's eyes. "Yes. I consented."

He nodded. "The issue at hand, even if there's no specific policy against what you did, is that the university has standards to maintain. An image, if you will. If that image is sullied, everything we do and stand for is at risk." He straightened his glasses. "That includes prospective students, alumni gifts, all of it. Like you, Ms. Crawford, we need to have integrity. We need to be impeccable."

"I understand."

"As impeccable as Marion Mackenzie."

Yes, that was how she would describe Marion.

"Who won't countenance your behavior." Harold flattened his lips. "Marion's withdrawn from your committee. You know how she feels about women's scholarship. To her, what you did turns scholarship into a self-indulgent gimmick."

Elizabeth sat back, stunned. "That's not what I intended."

"Nonetheless." He gave a philosophical shrug. "If it had just been nude portraits, who knows? But it was the fact that you imitated O'Keeffe's poses. To Marion, that was a mockery of the very topic you were purporting to study."

Elizabeth could hardly keep up with everything Harold was telling her. Losing Marion's goodwill—and, clearly, the recommendation for a plum job that was no longer within her reach—was a blow she had never expected. Then she squared her shoulders. All right. If Marion's support was the price she had to pay for her foolishness, so be it.

"I'm so sorry," she said. "I'd like to think she might give me another chance, but I respect her principles." She drew in her breath. "Should I try to replace her on the committee?"

Harold's hesitation sent a spike of fresh alarm up her spine. "It goes a bit beyond that," he replied. "I'm sure you can understand that

it involves more than a slight shift in the composition of your dissertation committee."

Elizabeth's fear mounted. "What are you referring to?"

He clasped his hands, right over left, and propped his elbows on
the dark green blotter that covered his desk. "A compromise. Marion
wanted you gone immediately. But I reminded her that there's no
legal ground to prevent you from finishing your dissertation and
your degree. Plagiarism, failure to progress—we have policies for
things like that. But not this."

Her pulse slammed against her temples. She could feel it coming,
another blow.

"We have to let you finish," he said, "but we can't have you standing in front of a class. Again, Marion wanted you removed right now,
today, but one of the faculty members pointed out that it would only
make you into a martyr, since the students are so intent on praising
what you've done. Frankly, we don't need a lot of turmoil that could
inflate the whole thing into some sort of radical feminist, freedom-
of-speech showdown. Make it into a political event, when it's merely
an act in bad taste."

Elizabeth yearned to explain. There hadn't been anything political
about the way she had bared herself to Richard. Yet the alternative
that Harold was suggesting—bad taste—wouldn't save her either.

Harold opened his hands, laying them flat on the green felt. "I
worked out a compromise. You can finish the term with your
Feminist Art class, that's the best way to keep things from escalating.
But you won't be rehired. And you won't get a recommendation for
another position." There was a glimmer of sympathy in his eyes. "I'm
sorry. It was the best I could do, given the factors at play."

Tears stung her cheeks. The years of classes and papers, the hefty
tuition, the hours away from her children—all to prepare her for a
future like Harold's or Marion's. It had seemed so certain, so close.
How had her infatuation with Richard possibly led to this?

"But I love teaching," she whispered.

"I'm sure you do. Your students' admiration, albeit misguided, attests to that. Nevertheless."

Without a letter of recommendation, her chances of getting hired anywhere—never mind for a coveted job like the one at Marion's former university—would plummet, dissolve. If she couldn't teach, her dissertation was a stepping-stone to nowhere.

"Should I fight it?" she asked. "Try to keep my job, instead of going quietly? Since I haven't broken any actual rule."

She tried to picture it. Naomi, Isabelle, and the others would support her. If that was what she wanted.

She had threatened Joaquin Ventana with the possibility of a student protest, but he'd told her she had it backwards. The students weren't going to protest that he had put the photographs on display. They might protest, however, if the administration punished a fellow student—a doctoral student, like her—for their existence. They'd call it the suppression of a woman's right to make decisions about her own body.

A protest would attract more attention to the photographs, not less. She'd become notorious. Her private mayhem would be splashed all over the community.

"If you're asking my opinion," Harold said, "you don't have a case. The university isn't obligated to rehire you as an adjunct instructor. If you recall, they offered you this upper division class at my specific urging. They don't need a reason not to repeat the offer." He adjusted his glasses once more, settling them on the bridge of his nose. "I don't regret my intervention, by the way. I think you've done well as an instructor. But that's of minor relevance, from the administration's point of view." Then he paused, emphasizing his point. "They can't condone, or even appear to condone, your choice to dress up—or undress, I should say—and pretend to be O'Keeffe. Whether you intended it that way or not, it looks frivolous and self-serving." He flicked his hand across the paper he had read from. "It doesn't help that your fans are holding you up as an exemplar that we tenured faculty ought to emulate."

Elizabeth fought to contain her despair. Never, ever had she foreseen any of this. Images tumbled across her vision, each blurring into the next. Herself, Dr. Crawford, walking across the stage in an academic robe with its blue-and-scarlet hood. Liz, a person she hardly recognized now, in a peach-colored negligee. Elizabeth, in a kimono like Georgia's, open and loose on her arms.

"By the way," Harold said, "have you actually seen the exhibit?"

Elizabeth shivered. "I don't have to. I know what's in it."

"Well, I have," he told her. "I went yesterday, so I'd know what we're talking about." His face softened. "Officially, it's a serious problem. But personally, it's quite powerful. You should go to see it."

She didn't need to go to Ventana's gallery to see the photos. They were burned into her skin. The light behind the white screen. The way Richard had crouched, shooting upward. The click of the shutter as he circled her body.

Because of her stupidity, her career was crumbling—the career she'd been preparing for, ever since she took the advanced placement test instead of dancing onstage in a mermaid costume. They would let her finish her dissertation, there was no way to prevent her, but she wouldn't be part of their world. That was her punishment for not thinking—proof that she should have used her brain, been her reliable Lizzie-self, instead of imagining she could be someone different.

She looked at Harold, and a fresh wave of horror washed over her as she understood that *I went yesterday* meant that he had seen her naked. Was that how he was seeing her now? The sympathy she'd glimpsed on his face, the softness. Maybe it was something else.

For a desperate instant, she wanted to grab his lapels and scream, "Tell me. What are you really thinking?" Was he disappointed in her, angry, ashamed? He'd invested a lot in her, it had to feel personal. But this was a university and those weren't questions she could ask.

Somehow she managed to offer a courteous response. "In any case, thank you for being so candid with me."

"Give yourself a bit of time to mull things over," he said. "It's a lot to take in."

Elizabeth dipped her head, the obedient acolyte. She wanted to run—or linger, in case he changed his mind—but she kept her steps measured and steady as she left his office. She made her way down the stairs and through the big oak door that led to the quad.

The paths that crisscrossed the campus were dappled with shadows. A boy sped past on a bike, a black dog at his heels. A bird swooped low, startling her; she'd thought the birds would be gone, now that the weather had grown chilly and the trees were bare. Maybe she ought to go to the botanical garden, just to see something colorful and alive. She remembered the day she'd gone there and taken the yellow center of the hibiscus for herself. She had put it in her pocket and forgotten about it; untended, it had dissolved and disappeared.

No, not the garden. Maybe the library, the place that had always welcomed her. She had to go somewhere. Numbly, she began to walk, following the path that cut across the center of the green, to Founders' Lawn.

A half-dozen people were standing in a row, arms lifted for *Wave Hands Like Clouds*. Juniper, at the end of the row, motioned for Elizabeth to join them.

Elizabeth began to shake her head, the way she always had, but the absurdity of her diffidence made her laugh. Was she really worried that passers-by might look at her? That she might be revealed to students and strangers?

You try, and you can, Mr. Wu had told her. Oh, what the hell. She hurried across the grass.

Juniper stepped back to give her room. "Let's start over, guys, okay?"

Elizabeth slipped off her shoes and arranged her body into the first form, feet parallel, arms relaxed. *We commence.* One posture at a time, she moved through the forms, surprised by how much her body knew. When they were finished, she went to retrieve her shoes. Two students were standing at the edge of the lawn, watching her. One was a tall skinny boy in a red sweatshirt with Che Guevara's face emblazoned across the chest. The other was a girl with waist-length braids in a #MeToo tee-shirt. Elizabeth didn't recognize either of them.

The girl beamed at her and gave a vigorous thumbs-up. "You go, Professor!"

"Crawford rocks," the boy agreed. His voice was unnaturally loud, as if he meant for passers-by to hear.

Elizabeth blushed; their praise made her feel awkward and shy. "I'm not very good at this yet," she wanted to explain.

Then she stopped. Were they referring to the way she was doing Tai Chi?

No, of course not.

Word had already spread.

Twenty-Three

Elizabeth broke away from the group on Founders' Lawn, anxious to distance herself from the admiring students. It was obvious that they had seen the exhibit or, at the very least, Naomi's post.

Who else had seen it, by now? Other adjunct instructors, members of her doctoral cohort, the people she saw at department meetings and seminars? What would they think—what did some of them already think—if they'd been to the exhibit or tagged in a post? That was how news spread these days. Anyone could forward a link, re-post to another Facebook page. Elizabeth's head began to throb as the radius of potential ripples grew wider and wider. Sweat beaded on her forehead despite the end-of-autumn chill.

The irony was hard to miss. Her students were making her into an icon of what they admired and needed her to be. She'd wanted to be like Georgia, but not this way.

The throbbing in her temples grew worse. A dog barked as it raced across the grass, chasing a squirrel that gave a taunting chitter before scampering up a tree. Its owner yelled, "Zero, come right back here!"

Elizabeth opened her messenger bag, searching for the bottle of Advil that she was certain was inside. She fumbled beneath her wallet and felt the buzzing of her cell phone. What now? Ventana, telling her that a national magazine was going to do a story on the exhibit?

Harold, telling her that they had come up with another way to punish her?

By the time she found her phone, the buzzing had stopped. She grabbed the Advil, twisted the cap, and shook three pills into her palm. As she swallowed the tablets, she heard the *ding* that meant the caller had left a voicemail. She didn't really want to know what the call had been about, but knew she'd better listen. Delaying bad news wouldn't make it less bad.

To her relief, the message was from Phoebe. It wasn't about the photos. Elizabeth tapped to listen.

"Hi there, it's me, and great news! Lucy can take all four kids on Saturday evening. Perfect, right? I'll check out the possibilities, like we talked about, and let you know what looks interesting. I'll try your land line too, maybe I'll catch you there. TTYL."

Elizabeth threw the phone back in the bag. A Saturday evening double-date was the last thing she cared about right now. Grimacing, she hoisted her messenger bag and hurried down the path to the library. She made her way up the tiered steps, trying to ignore the headache that still hadn't gone away, trying to focus on the Hawaii paintings, O'Keeffe's choice of colors and shapes.

The smack of another body jolted her into awareness. Embarrassment turned to disbelief as she realized that she had slammed right into Marion Mackenzie, who was striding down the stone steps in the opposite direction.

Elizabeth backed away in horror. Incredible that Marion was in this very spot, outside the very building where she had first offered her friendship. "I'm so, so sorry," she stammered. Then she turned crimson. "For crashing into you, I mean."

Did Marion think she was apologizing for posing naked? Elizabeth tried the words in her mind. *I'm sorry for pretending to be Georgia O'Keeffe. For going to Tai Chi instead of your talk on Arthur Dove. For letting you down.*

Only she wasn't sorry. Despite everything.

The knowledge shocked her, but there was no time to think about what it meant. She had to make things right with Marion. This might be her only chance.

She waited for Marion to say *it's all right* or the ubiquitous *no problem.* Maybe Marion would ask how she was doing or offer an apology of her own. *I really had no choice.*

Even a curt *look where you're walking* would have been better than Marion's icy silence as she brushed off her clothes. What was she brushing off? Elizabeth's presence?

Elizabeth's heart began to hammer. She needed to say something, to explain how persuasive Richard had been—anything, so Marion wouldn't hate her. She clenched her fingers, pleading for a sign. Before she could decide which words to use, Marion flicked her jade green scarf, stepped around Elizabeth's frozen form, and strode down the steps.

She stared at Marion's disappearing back. If she hadn't understood before, she did now. She'd done the one thing Marion couldn't forgive. Posing nude would have been in bad taste, but posing nude as Georgia O'Keeffe was beyond redemption.

For the second time that day, Elizabeth's eyes filled with tears. Warring emotions collided in her chest. Anger at being double-crossed—by Richard, Naomi, Marion herself, who had laughed and said *I like you, Elizabeth Crawford.* And then shame, because of the self-delusion that had made the betrayal possible. Fear of what would happen now. Anxiety, gripping her in its beak, because she didn't know what that might be.

Then she thought: No. She didn't have to wait, like a model holding a pose, to find out what would happen. She could act.

The Legacy of Feminist Art, that was the title of today's lecture. According to the syllabus, they were supposed to talk about post-feminism in contemporary art—whether millennial women saw art as a means of social protest or simply a form of personal expression, whether all-women shows were necessary or patronizing or both. Elizabeth had slides of installations done by post-feminists and trans artists who sought to undo the very gender lines that had shaped the early feminists' vision.

Instead of warming up the projector or taking out her notes, she pressed her palms against the oak desk and surveyed the students—a sea of bodies in torn jeans, Indian tunics, and oversized hoodies. She hadn't planned what she would say or do, beyond the certainty that she had to say or do something. She had to face them. Dressed, but revealed.

After a long silent moment, she let go of the desk and straightened her shoulders. "We're not going to talk about emerging women artists. Not just yet. First, we're going to talk about me."

No one moved. Even Naomi was quiet, the jewel in her nostril motionless as an unblinking eye.

"I know that many of you are aware of the exhibit in town," Elizabeth said, "and some of you may think I was trying to make a statement about how to relate to art, or the autonomy of women's bodies, or the repression of women in academia. Those are all important topics but they have nothing to do with my intention in posing." She moved her gaze from face to face. "Whatever the photographs mean to you, it's fine. Feel free to take them as you wish. But it's your meaning and not mine. Just to be clear."

Naomi looked as if she wanted to speak. Elizabeth could almost see the *yes, but* forming on the girl's lips. *Yes, but* weren't you really telling us to claim women's art for women instead of letting the men in power tell us how to view it—as something separate from ourselves, the way they do?

No, she wasn't. No more than Georgia was trying to do anything but let her lover see her exactly as she was. Georgia had been adamant.

Interpretation was just a way for people to project their own needs onto her art.

The girl with the tattoo raised her hand. "Are the admin people giving you shit?"

Elizabeth could feel the students waiting to see how she would answer. If she said *yes*, they would sympathize and support her. She wouldn't be alone; she'd be surrounded by an ardent, admiring crowd. Maybe their response would be dramatic enough that the department would reconsider and rehire her.

She could do that, just a small shift in emphasis. Nothing she'd said had foreclosed the possibility.

She tried to envision what would follow if she gave the answer that she sensed the students wanted to hear. She would become a martyr, the leader of a worthy and inspiring cause. People would cheer for her—the way her mother had promised all those years ago, when Andie danced across the stage in *The Nutcracker*. She would make something noble out of the humiliation, transform a private failure into public acclaim. She would be saved.

Not really. It would be a false salvation.

That was the price for being so smart. She knew better. Pretending to be a heroine would turn the photographs into exactly the kind of stunt Marion had accused her of.

It would be like putting on a costume. She didn't want the mermaid costume, or Georgia's kimono, or anyone else's clothes. She wanted her own skin.

If the students needed a cause, someone else would have to provide it.

"No," Elizabeth said. "It's a private matter."

She waited for the next question, surprised when it didn't come. Had she defused the situation that easily? Then Naomi leaned forward, frowning.

"I don't get it," Naomi said. "If it wasn't about deconstructing the border between the viewer and the viewed or showing us what education is really about—why *did* you do it?"

Responses arrayed themselves across Elizabeth's vision like a fan. Because she wanted to be Georgia instead of Lizzie. Because she was tired of being invisible and unloved.

She remembered how Richard had touched the place in the center of her sternum. *Open. From here.* She had. For him. To him.

Her voice was soft. "I wanted to."

Elizabeth had only skipped one Tai Chi class, yet it felt like much longer than two weeks. Mr. Wu looked stronger, more substantial. He was standing in front of the class, legs apart, feet parallel. Richard was next to him, facing the pupils. Elizabeth slipped into an empty spot. Not in the back this time. In the center.

"We commence," Mr. Wu said. He looked straight at her, and Elizabeth felt a shift in her posture, as if someone had put a hand on top of her head and drawn her upward, lengthening her spine, opening her chest. The lightest touch, barely perceptible. But it changed everything.

For the first time, the movements made sense. Not a sequence of instructions to memorize and will herself to reproduce, but a natural expression of her body's relation to the air, the space, its own shape. Inhale as you lift up, exhale as you push out. Draw the silk up. Raise the leg and step out. As if the form was already there and she was simply filling it.

Her body. Beautiful. Perfect, with a language of its own. No wobbling or hesitation, only an obedient grace. She could feel Richard watching her.

The hour flew past, and then the class was over. Elizabeth waited for Richard outside the entrance to the building. He might, of course, have another plan. He might be taking Mr. Wu home or inviting another woman to share an Americano at the little café. But she didn't think so and she didn't care. She was going to talk to him tonight, no matter what.

She watched the pupils come out of the building, knowing that Richard would be among the last. Juniper, flanked by two other women, spotted her and broke into a smile. "Hey, Liz. Want to come to that smoothie place with us?"

"Thanks, but not tonight."

Juniper's smile twisted into a smirk. "Otherwise occupied?"

Elizabeth flushed; she hadn't realized that her interest in Richard was so obvious. "Another time," she repeated.

"Have fun, then." Juniper's voice was jaunty, as if she and Elizabeth shared a secret. She bent close to one of her companions as they strolled off, laughing loudly.

Elizabeth leaned against the side of the building. Her pulse jumped each time the door opened. He had to appear eventually. Finally Mr. Wu and his daughter emerged, followed by Richard. Richard gave a short bow. Mr. Wu bowed in return and took his daughter's arm as she ushered him into a black car that had been waiting by the curb.

The car pulled away, and Richard turned to Elizabeth. She didn't know what she had expected—annoyance, defensiveness, disdain— but he looked as pleased to see her as ever. The last time she saw him, she had raced out of his studio as she realized she was about to miss her children's play. She hadn't explained why she had to leave; she'd simply fled, his words ringing in her ears. "You look beautiful, trust me. It's a good show. And it's not coming down."

"Elizabeth." He put his hand on her waist.

The gesture was shocking, intimate. She wanted to fling off his hand, and she wanted to move it down the length of her hip. Oh, she hated him, hated him for exciting her like that.

"I need to talk to you."

He didn't move his hand. "Of course."

She had assumed they would go to the café but there was no reason, really, not to say what she had to right there in the street.

He was waiting for her to speak, letting her decide. Elizabeth was acutely, achingly, aware of his hand on her waist. She knew he wouldn't remove it. Not unless she told him to.

Then she straightened her shoulders. "I don't care what story you're telling yourself," she said, keeping her eyes on his, "about how I consented to your little exhibit, just because I didn't say: 'Oh, by the way, in case you were thinking of displaying my body at some art gallery, please don't.'"

His fingers burned through the fabric, all the way to her skin. She could hear Georgia's words, like a distant call: *I've been absolutely terrified every moment of my life, and I've never let it keep me from doing a single thing that I wanted to do.*

"Obviously I didn't say no," she went on, "because you never bothered to ask. You assumed."

"I didn't have to ask. They're my photos."

"They're photos of me."

"You were the subject. The subject doesn't own the art."

A cold, cold thing to say. As if she were a vase or an pear in a still-life. Not a woman.

He dropped his hand. Elizabeth felt its absence, as if someone had snatched a child out of her arms.

She wouldn't let him turn her defiance back into longing. "You might own the photos," she said, her voice sharpening, "but you don't own the person in them. Not my hopes, my sensations. Not any part of me." She felt her spine stretch, pulling her upward, the way it had during the Tai Chi class. "You act like you do. Like you had the right to play with me." She took a step closer. "Why? Why did you do that?"

The street was quiet, only the whoosh of a passing car, the grinding of brakes. The streetlamp threw a circle of orange onto the pavement.

Then he shrugged, an ironic *oh well*—and Elizabeth understood that he had known exactly how she was responding when she posed. It hadn't been innocent flirting. It couldn't be innocent, because he'd seen what it was doing to her and he'd let it continue.

"It was a collaboration," he said. "Like Stieglitz and O'Keeffe. That was what you wanted, right?"

Elizabeth narrowed her eyes and didn't answer.

"We were partners," Richard went on. "I saw how you were letting yourself open, savoring your own sexuality, enjoying your desire. It was beautiful to see, and it was good for you. You know that, Elizabeth."

She waited, daring him to put the rest of it into words. "And yes," he admitted, "it was good for my photos. It made them quite extraordinary. My best work yet."

She wanted to slap him then. His best work yet. Achieved by using her, stealing from her, humiliating her in a way that even exposing her body hadn't done.

Richard tilted his head, studying her with those smoldering grey eyes. "You did go to see them, didn't you? You saw for yourself?"

Elizabeth couldn't believe his obtuseness. "No, I did not. And I don't intend to."

"Are you afraid of them?"

"I'm angry about them."

"Don't be," he said. "It was a good experience, for both of us."

"Don't speak for me."

"Then speak for yourself. Say what you really feel."

"How about what *you* really feel?" She took another step, closing the distance between them. "Do you like objectifying women? Does it make you feel big and powerful?"

"I didn't objectify you. I showed you to yourself."

"And to everyone else."

"Does it matter?"

"It matters to me."

"Then you might try letting it matter in a positive way," he said. "Being proud of what you did, of who you are."

Oh, for god's sakes. Was the man living on another planet?

Why had she let herself get pulled into this? It was Andrea's fault. *Go for it*, she had urged. *If men can do it, so can we*. And Phoebe's fault, for flaunting what she had. Or Georgia's, because she'd done it first. Ben's fault. Someone's.

No. No one else's choice. She'd wanted it. That was what she had told her students, and it was true. She had wanted to pose, to be seen and known. By Richard. By someone. But she hadn't wanted him to put her body on a gallery wall. They were two different things.

She drew herself upward again. "Your turn to be honest, Richard. During that *good experience*—the one I should be so proud of, the one you captured in your *extraordinary* photographs—what was going on in you?" She lifted her chin. "Did you want to have sex with me?"

"I want to have sex with every woman I see naked." Another smile, innocent and disarming.

Then he held up his palm, halting whatever she was about to say. "I don't mean to be flippant. It's just a fact. It doesn't mean I do have sex with them. In general, I don't."

"How noble of you."

"It's not personal, Elizabeth. I've just learned not to complicate things when it comes to my art."

How could it not be personal? She was a person, and that made it personal. She wasn't part of some vague *them* that he wanted to fuck, but didn't.

And yet. There was a new awareness, opening slowly. It spread through her like water.

If it really wasn't personal—his seductive behavior, as well as his ultimate restraint—it meant there was nothing lacking in her, specifically, that made him hold back. She was just as foxy and alluring as the unnamed *them* who were too complicated to sleep with.

You were as foxy as you let yourself be. Georgia knew that. She had told the world: *You get whatever accomplishment you're willing to declare.*

Richard was watching her. She could feel the keenness of his interest, as tangible as a touch. Her skin tingled from where his palm had been. That hand on her waist had been deliberate. It hadn't been intended to uncomplicate things.

"Of course, we're not making art anymore." His words were soft, languid, belying the shock of their meaning.

A black car glided past, silent as an eel. The silence seemed to spread, filling the street, as Elizabeth felt something gather inside her. A sensation of her own existence, her mass, spacious and full. This very body, the container of herself.

She could feel her desire, pushing through her limbs. And her desirability. That was why he was looking at her like that.

The sensation was lovely, delicious. But that wasn't what was making her feel so extraordinary. It was a new understanding, blooming for the first time, like one of Georgia's flowers.

She was desirable whether he saw her that way or not. Richard's gaze didn't determine her desirability, nor did Ben's. They had nothing to do with this quality that was hers, part of her.

I claim this.

The car's tail lights threw a red shimmer across Richard's elegant form. Elizabeth released her breath. "You're not going to remove those photos, are you?"

Of course not. She had known that from the moment she faced him in the street.

She looked at him, taking in everything. "Nothing more to talk about, then."

With a nod, almost a bow, she brushed past him, the way Marion had brushed past her, and walked away.

Twenty-Four

As soon as Elizabeth opened the door to the apartment, she knew something was wrong. It was the quiet. Ben was in his usual spot on the couch but the TV was off, not even the rustling of a newspaper or the rattling of ice in a glass to break the stillness. He wasn't doing anything except waiting for her.

Cautiously, she circled the couch and sat down across from him. "Kids asleep?"

"Of course they're asleep." Elizabeth could hear his irritation. It was long past their bedtime. Did she think he'd forgotten to put them to bed?

She smoothed the edge of the upholstery, her discomfort growing. Maybe he had figured out that there was something fishy about her stalled-delivery-van story and was angry at her for missing the play. Being Ben, maybe he had gone on some traffic accident website, googled the date and location, and caught her in a lie. Or maybe her ridiculous explanation about the coat drive had nagged at him until he brought it up with Michael, who confirmed his suspicion that she had something to hide. Ben hated people who tried to cover up what they had done. That was why this whole Wyckoff-Solano business had gotten to him.

Ben's next sentence sliced through the air like a scythe. "For fuck's sake, Elizabeth, what were you thinking?"

She scrambled to catch up. Her mind was still on the play, the times she'd been late coming home from Tai Chi, the landlord-tenant case—

"Your little modeling career," Ben snapped. "It's not much of a secret. Except from me, of course."

The photos. Harold and Marion finding out—it made sense, because of that damn Naomi and the student Facebook page. But she'd never imagined it would get back to Ben. How in the world had Ben learned about Naomi's post?

"Your dear friend Phoebe," he said, answering the question that must be written across her face. "She left quite an interesting message."

Elizabeth's eyes flew to the phone, upright in its perch on the end table. Ben clamped a hand over the receiver—a harsh, possessive movement that shocked her almost as much as his words. "I'm sure it didn't occur to her that I'd listen to the message before you did. It was supposed to be a bit of girl-to-girl chatter. Made me feel like calling her back and spoiling her fun."

"Why are you being so nasty? It's not like you."

"Really? You're sure you know what's *like me*? Apparently I don't know what's *like you*."

Elizabeth tried to calm her racing pulse. This strange, aggressive Ben frightened her. "You talked to her? Phoebe?"

"I couldn't get to the phone. I was too busy putting our children to bed."

Oh, fuck you.

"Just tell me what she said."

Ben's face was dark. "Phoebe called with an idea about what we could do on Saturday. For fun." He pressed the button for *messages* and folded his arms. Phoebe's cheerful, bell-like tones invaded the room.

"We do a monthly maintenance check on our clients' websites— you know, to monitor usage, see if someone's been trying to hack in? Well, one of our clients has this fabulous art gallery. He does the updates himself, but we do the security stuff."

Elizabeth's skin turned cold. She knew what was coming.

"So I noticed he had a couple of new exhibits. One of them was photography, and I remembered the photographer's name from when you told me about him, that guy from Tai Chi? Mr. Ferris Wheel. Seems his show has something to do with Georgia O'Keeffe, so I figured, wow, that's right up your alley. There's a link to Ferris's website but I didn't have time to check it out. Sounds cool, though. We could get a glass of wine, do the art thing? Anyway, see what you think—the gallery's called *On View*—and let me know."

End of message. To listen again—

Ben clicked the button, and the recording stopped.

"So you did," Elizabeth said. "You checked it out."

"Oh yes."

She braced herself for the rest.

"It was the reference to Tai Chi that piqued my curiosity," he said, "and the whole furtive way you've been acting lately. And then the Ferris Wheel. I remembered Daniel talking about a Ferris Wheel man who took pictures. I figured he must have overheard something. So I looked up *On View*, and I found Mr. Ferris." He curled his lip. "And you."

There was no point in protesting that the model wasn't identified. Ben knew what her body looked like.

"I'll repeat my question, Elizabeth. What the fuck were you thinking?"

She wanted to laugh. That was the irony. She hadn't been thinking. For once, she had been responding from pure embodied longing, not from thought.

"You think it's funny? A big joke? My clients aren't going to think so." His eyes blazed with anger. "I don't suppose it ever occurred to you—how this insanity of yours would affect me, my credibility, my whole reputation. People seeing my wife on display like some kind of sleazy centerfold."

Elizabeth drew back, stunned. With everything that had happened, *how could you do this to me* was the last response she'd expected. "Really? That's your biggest worry? Your image?"

"My ability to argue my cases."

"You mean: what people will think."

"What people will think affects you too. Our friends, our families."

She couldn't believe what she was hearing. "What about you, Ben? Not other people. You." She could see anger and humiliation contort his features. Good. At least she'd made him feel something.

"What the hell am I supposed to think," he spat, "when my wife acts so flat-out adolescent and inconsiderate?"

Elizabeth struggled to put herself in his shoes. Shocked, embarrassed, confused—those reactions made sense. Hurt that she hadn't told him what she was doing. As if she could have. But this nastiness, the way he was judging her as if she were his enemy—she'd never dreamed that would be the first emotion she would make him feel, after ten years of polite coexistence.

"Look," she began. "I'm sorry if I blindsided you."

"If? What kind of bullshit is *if*?"

She flinched, and Ben threw her a look of disgust. "You might have talked to me before you decided to ridicule me in front of the whole community."

Elizabeth told herself that none of this was his fault, he'd done nothing to deserve it—until her empathy gave way to exasperation. Why did he keep sounding this one petulant and self-righteous note, making it all about him? Surely, he felt something besides rage. A glimmer of curiosity about how and why the cerebral wife he knew could have done such a thing?

Ben had asked what she was thinking, when she posed. *What the fuck were you thinking* was more of an accusation than a question, and yet—what if she told him, tried to make him understand? It was an astonishing idea, but it filled her with hope.

His next words cut through that hope. "Did you sleep with him?"

Elizabeth didn't know whether to laugh or cry. It was a question any husband would ask. And Ben, like any husband, probably assumed that she had. After all, the photos she'd imitated were a testimony to Stieglitz's passion for the woman who was his lover. The woman in the photos knew that. Proud, unapologetic, she proclaimed her sexual power, just as Stieglitz, behind the camera, proclaimed his.

That was why the photos had drawn her. Richard had seen that. But unlike Stieglitz, he hadn't entered the portraits himself.

No, she hadn't slept with Richard. Had it been up to her, all those weeks, she would have. If that was Ben's real question, then the answer was *yes*. Yes, everything in her that mattered had been unfaithful. She yearned to say *yes*, to have the right to say *yes*.

If she lied and said she had, it would confirm what Ben already believed. She could own what she had longed for.

On the other hand, if she told the truth, *no I didn't*, he would think she was lying. He saw her as a liar now. He wasn't wrong; she had lied.

There was no good response. Finally she sighed. "Does it matter?"

It was the question Richard had asked when she protested that others had seen her, without her agreement. She had told him, "It matters to me."

She thought Ben would say the same thing. *Yes, it matters to me if another man touched my wife. Saw her. Entered her.*

To her surprise, he didn't. "What *matters*," he said, "is dealing with the mess you've created."

He must have seen the shock on her face because he glared back. "I'm being practical, even if you won't be. We need to contain the damage. If Phoebe knew about the exhibit, others will too."

This calculating stranger unnerved her. He was acting like a crusader, not like a husband—moving right past his concern that she might have slept with another man, straight to damage control. A man who loved her would never have been able to do that.

Elizabeth stared at him, incredulous and beseeching. *Don't you love me at all? Doesn't it hurt to think of someone else seeing me?*

Something flickered across Ben's face—a stab of pain, as if he'd heard her unvoiced question. Because yes, it did hurt, and he couldn't bear it? Or no, it didn't, not really, and that realization was just as terrible?

His expression shifted again, too swiftly for Elizabeth to know which it was. Then he thinned his lips. "It never crossed my mind that you could do something so irresponsible. In all the years I've known you, I've never seen a hint of that kind of careless exhibitionism."

You've never known me.

He gave a humorless sniff. "I'd be curious to know how he got you to step out of character like that. It must have been the O'Keeffe business, though I wouldn't have expected you to fall for something so derivative."

Derivative. A spiteful way to put it. Well, no one wanted to be the betrayed spouse.

Elizabeth understood. Another man might have struck a wife who had humiliated him, or thrown a lamp, or stormed out of the house. But Ben was using words as his weapon because words were how they related to each other.

Sorrow wrapped itself around her like a cloak. "Ben," she began. He knew she wasn't an exhibitionist. Surely, that fragment of truth could be salvaged from their conversation. "I never meant for those photographs to be on public display. No one wants them taken down more than I do." It was what she had told Harold.

But Ben asked the question that Harold hadn't. "Then why the hell did you pose for a professional photographer?"

Naomi's question, too. It echoed in the stillness of the apartment. And Elizabeth's answer. *I wanted to.*

She hadn't thought, when she walked away from Richard, that she was walking back to Ben, yet she had believed in their essential kindness toward each other. She'd even imagined, only moments earlier, that she might tell Ben what she had discovered about herself, standing in front of Richard on the sidewalk. It had felt like an extraordinary idea, yet utterly possible. Ben cared about her. He would want this for her.

But now, in the wake of everything they had said, and not said, she couldn't imagine telling him what the photos meant to her. It was too intimate.

Ben tightened his jaw and stood. "I'm going to bed. I can't talk about this anymore, not right now."

Elizabeth rose too. She started to reach out her hand, but he recoiled and she let it drop. His voice was cold. "I'm still trying to fathom your moronic audacity and figure out how we're going to deal with its aftermath. I'll talk to someone at the firm, see what our legal options are." He stepped around her as he left the room, flinging open the door to the bedroom. She heard the thwack of his shoes hitting the floor.

Elizabeth stood by the couch, unable to move. Ben was right about one thing: she hadn't thought about him when she posed. He belonged to one life, and Richard, along with the Georgia-like person she might become under Richard's gaze, to another. Ben was like the apartment or the car, a fact of her daily existence.

She could hear him moving around in the bedroom. She tried to picture her own movements. Turning off the living room lights, getting undressed, climbing into bed, her back to his. Sleeping or not sleeping. His words lingered in the air. Moronic audacity. How *we're* doing to deal with it. A crisis to get through, like the time Katie swallowed one of Daniel's Legos and had to be rushed to the emergency room.

We weren't going to deal with anything.

It was her body, her life.

Joaquin Ventana was bending to unlock the door of the gallery. It wasn't due to open for fifteen minutes, but Elizabeth had hoped he might arrive early. She tapped his arm. When he saw it was her, his face darkened. "I thought I made it clear. If you continue to harass me—"

"No. Please. That's not why I'm here."

He glared at her. "Why *are* you here?"

Elizabeth wet her lip. "I need to see the photographs."

"So you can—what? Rip them down yourself?"

"No. I just need to see them. Without anyone else around."

Joaquin gave a barking laugh. "Right. Trust you alone with the photos. Sure, honey. No problem."

"I mean it. Please. I need to look at them."

He stopped laughing. "Why?"

"I've never seen them. I need to." She paused. "Alone."

He waited, as if taking her measure. They were outside, on the sidewalk. The sun glinted on the etched glass of the gallery door, igniting the oversized O and V. *On View.*

"That's why I came early," she said. "Before you opened. So I wouldn't be in the way."

"You've never seen them? Really?"

"I never wanted to."

"And now?"

"Now I have to." She held his gaze. "All I want to do is look, I promise. By myself."

The seconds seemed endless. Then he sighed. "I hope I don't regret this."

"You won't."

"Fifteen minutes." Pulling open the door, he ushered her inside. "I won't open up till then. After that, if someone else wants to come in, they can."

"Thank you. I really appreciate it."

Joaquin waved her toward the interior gallery. Slowly, Elizabeth crossed the foyer and entered the adjoining room. She heard him flick a switch, and the room was flooded with light.

In the center were four bronze sculptures on pedestals, Ventana's art, and on the surrounding walls were Richard's photographs. Next to each was a small reproduction of the Stieglitz photo she had re-enacted. A sign, white lettering on a black rectangle, was propped on an easel. *Re-Visions: Seeing/Being Seen. Richard Ferris, photographer.*

She didn't turn to check, but she was sure Ventana had kept his word and left her alone. For an instant she was tempted to do exactly as he'd said—grab the photos, slash them, rip them to shreds. But she didn't.

Because they were beautiful.

She knew it at once. The woman in the photos was extraordinary. Utterly revealed, through Richard. The arising of desire, and the way she had ached for satiation yet reveled in the desire itself, vulnerable and confident, surprised and pleased by her own body. The arousal and the mystery. The intelligent eyes in the beautiful face.

She moved around the room, gazing at each photo for a long time, seeing herself as Richard had seen her. It was uncanny, how he'd captured the heart of her experience. Exploiting her, perhaps, yet without him she would never have felt that glory and wholeness. It was there in every photo.

She had thought, at the time, that she was doing it for him. Without him watching her, there would have been no possibility and no point.

Yet, now, all thoughts of Richard fell away. There was only her astounding, embodied self. Revealed, as Georgia had been—but not through imitation, outside matching outside. Her unique self, traveling outward through the tracery of the postures, like in Tai Chi. That was what Richard had drawn from her, no matter what his motive.

Elizabeth stood in the center of the room and turned, a heart-beat at a time, to absorb the panorama of the portraits. There were faint lines on one of the nudes, stretch marks, from her children, the people she and Ben had made. A scar on her right leg from the time Andrea had shoved her off her bicycle. A map of her life.

Joaquin Ventana was going to leave them up. She had to accept that, not reluctantly, but with her whole heart.

Yes. I accept the gift.

Mahalo.

That was what Georgia said in Hawaii. To Hawaii.

Mahalo.

Thank you.

Twenty-Five

Katie held Elizabeth's face in her hands, fingers splayed like a starfish on her mother's cheeks. "Pity Mama," she crooned.

Elizabeth broke into a delighted grin. She could take Katie's words as an expression of compassion for her unfulfilled life or as a declaration of her beauty. It was up to her. "Yes, my darling," she said. "I *am* pretty. And so are you."

The rosebud mouth, the long-lashed eyes, the porcelain curves of her round little face. Katie's perfection took her breath away. "And you are very, very smart too. Just think of all the words you know, all the things you know how to do."

As if to demonstrate, Katie dropped her hands, climbed down from Elizabeth's lap, and went to the silverware drawer. Gravely, she extracted four spoons and carried them to the dinner table. She laid a spoon in front of the chair where Ben always sat, and Elizabeth stiffened.

She and Ben had barely spoken since he confronted her about the photographs. His phone call with Tim D'Agostino, the intellectual property lawyer, hadn't yielded any useful ideas, not that Elizabeth had expected it to. The photos weren't her property; Richard had told her that. After dismissing the conversation with D'Agostino, Ben had announced, "I'm going to try the defamation of character angle, see if there's anything there we can use."

We. Elizabeth had bristled at the pronoun. Ben was no better than Richard, appropriating her life without her consent. Yet the shared concern in that plural formulation came from a true feeling. Ben had called her moronic and careless, in need of rescue by a fast-acting attorney. It had felt presumptuous and unfeeling—but it was a Ben-like way of caring.

Katie distributed the other spoons to three random spots on the table and turned to Elizabeth with a satisfied *so there.* "Thank you so much," Elizabeth told her. "I had no idea you could do that."

"Do dat," Katie said.

Elizabeth swept her into a hug. Her daughter was growing, changing. She couldn't stop Katie from leaving babyhood behind, any more than she could stop the change that was happening in her-self—because she *was* changing, had already changed. Like Katie, she wasn't finished.

Katie squirmed off her lap, heading back to the silverware drawer. As Elizabeth watched her daughter amble across the room, her gaze fell on the telephone, upright in its cradle. The memory flashed across her mind. Ben, clamping his fist around the black rectangle, assert-ing his claim on the message it contained.

Then she realized: *Damn.* She'd never returned Phoebe's call. The last thing she needed was for Phoebe to call again and ask her—or Ben—if they'd had a chance to check out the exhibit.

"You're doing such a good job," she told Katie. "But Mommy has to make a phone call. Can you go play for a few minutes?"

Katie nodded and ran off. Elizabeth reached for the phone, scroll-ing through the call-back numbers until she found Phoebe's. Phoebe answered right away. The bright, musical lilt was unmistakable.

Elizabeth could feel her irritation spike, the way it did when-ever she heard Phoebe's voice. How could anyone be that absurdly chipper?

Then she froze, struck by a thought that seemed both obvious and astonishing—because what was so absurd, really, about Phoebe's cheerfulness? She'd always taken that kind of perkiness as the sign of a shallow mind, an indication that the person wasn't worth knowing. Based on what, though? As a researcher, she ought to know better.

With a flutter of shame, Elizabeth remembered how Phoebe had told her, when they first met, "When Lucy told me you were some kind of professor, I thought you'd be, I don't know, a snob or something."

She *had* been a snob. Phoebe had offered an easy friendship, but she had rejected the offer without trying to know who Phoebe really was. Had she truly not seen that?

"Hey there," Phoebe said. "I left you a message the other day."

"Yes, I know."

All Elizabeth could think was: *I'm sorry.* She seemed to be apologizing to everyone. To Marion, her children, Andrea. Not to Ben, although she supposed he wanted her to.

"So what do you think?" Phoebe asked. "The Georgia O'Keeffe thing? It looked cool, from the little write-up."

Was it? Maybe.

Elizabeth fought the urge to tell her: *Don't go to see it. Don't open the link. Ever.*

Of course, Phoebe might go, with or without them. Ventana was a client; she might be curious or happy to lend support.

The Georgia O'Keeffe thing. The old lady in the desert, that was how Phoebe had known who she was. Yet, equally, a woman at the edge of the shimmering Pacific, swathed in the humid Hawaiian air. A woman lifting her arms.

Somehow Elizabeth found the words she needed. "Turns out we can't do it after all."

"Oh no." Phoebe's voice rose in dismay. "I'm totally bummed."

"I know. I'm sorry." She swallowed, then said again, "I'm so sorry. Please forgive me."

"Hey, no problem. We'll do it another time."

"Sure," Elizabeth managed to say. "I'll be in touch."

She wouldn't, though. Once the semester ended and she submitted her dissertation, she wouldn't need Lucy anymore. She and Phoebe wouldn't run into each other, and whatever thread had connected them would fray. That was what happened when two people weren't really friends.

And yet, oddly, Phoebe had altered her life.

That guy from Tai Chi, Mr. Ferris Wheel?

Phoebe had no idea what her words had set in motion, just as Ben had no idea what the photos—and Richard—had meant to her. Elizabeth thought back to their conversation, when Ben had confronted her about the exhibit. She had thought of trying to explain, but she hadn't. Things had veered in a different direction, and she'd never given him a chance to understand.

Maybe she could, even now.

But not in words.

She could show him.

She waited until Daniel and Katie were asleep, and even then, she almost didn't say anything. The newspaper in front of Ben's face was like a banner, proclaiming *Keep out.* From the opposite armchair, Elizabeth watched as he flipped the page. There was a hiss of steam as the radiator switched on; the evenings were chilly now, as fall faded into winter. From faraway, she could hear the wail of a siren. The *Journal of Art and Art History* lay face-down on the armrest.

It would be easy to pick up the journal and retreat to her desk. She and Ben would stay in separate ends of the apartment until one, then the other, went to bed. It wouldn't be the first evening they had spent like that. Maybe that was the best thing to do. Let the tension dissipate, wait till the crisis had passed.

Yet Mr. Wu had told her: *You try, and you can.*

Elizabeth flexed her fingers. "Ben," she began.

Reluctantly, he lowered the newspaper.

"About the exhibit."

She could see his mouth tighten. She wondered if he thought she was going to offer an excuse, a retraction, a form of penance—something he would tell her was unnecessary, when he really meant that it wasn't enough.

"I told Phoebe that I don't want to go to the gallery with her and Charlie. I want to go with you." Elizabeth straightened her back, committed now. "I want you to see the photos with me."

He gave her a sour look. "Really, Liz. Why rub salt in a wound?"

"It doesn't have to be a wound."

"You can't be serious."

"I am. It's important."

Their eyes locked. Elizabeth knew he didn't understand her request. She wouldn't have believed it herself if someone had told her, only twenty-four hours ago, that she'd be pleading with Ben to see the very photos she had wanted to destroy.

"I need us to see them together. Please."

"I'd rather spend my time undoing the havoc they've caused."

"Please, Ben." She needed to tell him that this was their chance. That whatever he had missed, all these years, could be his now. Theirs.

Better that he saw for himself. It was right there in the photographs.

He gave a weary sigh. "If it means so much to you. At least I'll know the extent of the disaster."

Elizabeth bit back her response. He'd said *yes*, that was what mattered. "Maybe we can meet there at five tomorrow, if you can get away a little early? Before I pick the kids up from Lucy's?"

Ben shook the newspaper open again. "Fine." He gave her a pointed look, then returned to the paper. "Tomorrow."

She remembered the first time she had pushed him until he gave in. The little kitchen with the white metal cabinets and dirty yellow tile, when she'd convinced him not to break up.

Ten years ago, she had made her case, and won. Tonight she had won again.

She sat without moving, unsure of what she felt. It might be relief, or it might be dread.

Elizabeth led Ben through the etched glass door, across the foyer, and into the room where the photographs were displayed.

She stopped in front of the photo with her arms raised above her head, fingers wide open, clinging to nothing. Her face, like Georgia's, was grave and inward. Ben didn't comment. After a while she moved to the photograph that showed her holding her breasts, one in each hand, framed by the open kimono. Still he said nothing. Slowly, Elizabeth moved from picture to picture. Breasts and collarbone, chin held high, hair streaming down her back. Her whole body against the white curtain. The photo Richard had wanted to take, a close-up of her breasts and stomach and pubic hair. No head, but it was still her. Beautifully, still her.

She turned to Ben, pleading with him to see. For a moment she thought he might have understood—a softening of his expression, a hesitation. But the moment passed, and he frowned.

"Honestly, Liz, it's even more tawdry and inappropriate than it was online. You've embarrassed yourself. And me. All I can hope is that none of my clients—or opposing counsel, worse yet—get wind of this." The frown deepened. "Well, really," he said, looking almost annoyed. "What did you expect me to say?"

The words burst from her. "But what do you *see*?"

His annoyance was unmistakable now. "I see a careless woman, whose lapse of judgment I'm going to have to deal with."

That was his response? As if she were a stupid child, instead of a woman who had made her own choices. "I don't believe you," Elizabeth said. "That can't be all you feel."

"You're telling me what I feel?"

Maybe she was. It was what she'd done from the beginning, when she told him that his feelings for her were stronger than he believed. Or, in any case, strong enough. She had out-thought him, won the debate, won the husband and marriage she had decided to have. Lizzie the planner, the achiever, the brain.

"No," she said. "I just want to know what you really *do* feel."

Ben shrugged. "Like I told you the other day, I think a clever photographer roped you into imitating Georgia O'Keeffe. There are a lot of manipulative people out there, and I suppose none of us is immune if the right button gets pushed." He reached in a jacket pocket for his cell phone. "My guess is that it had to do with your wanting some kind of original take on O'Keeffe. You know, something that would advance your career."

Elizabeth was too stunned to respond. Was Ben right? Had Richard manipulated her by appealing to her ambition, her determination to write a knock-em-dead dissertation?

She could say *yes, that's right, it was about my career.* The narrative Ben was offering fit with his image of her, made her vulnerable in a way he could understand and forgive. Not quite as noble as the narrative her students had offered, but plausible. If she embraced Ben's version of the story, she could save her marriage.

Yet Ben's version wasn't the whole truth. An ocean of meaning lay in the difference between his description and her experience.

He scowled as he scrolled through his messages. "Can we go now? You wanted me to see the pictures, and I've seen them. It's been a long day. I'm sure the kids are ready for dinner and, frankly, so am I."

She wanted to grab the phone out of his hand. His vacillation between hostility and indifference was making her crazy.

Ben looked up from his phone. "I don't think you slept with him, by the way, if that's what you're worried about. It's not something you would do."

Elizabeth wanted to burst into tears. Not just because of the way he had reduced her, shrunk her back into a cautious little person whose disrobing had been an aberration instead of a transformation. But because the whole conversation was so arid and cerebral and sad. Like their marriage.

Understanding hit her like an ax against a tree. She had cheated Ben in a far worse way than if she had slept with Richard—because she'd coerced him into marrying her when she knew they didn't love each other. She had robbed him of the chance to be truly loved by someone else. To feel the desire, naturally, that had eluded him for all these years.

Her hand flew to her mouth. Ben glanced at her, then away. He hadn't seen what she was feeling now, just as he hadn't seen what she was feeling in Richard's photos.

"Anyway," he said, "we have other things to deal with." He gestured at the walls. "Suppressing any further publicity. Or, if worse comes to worse, making sure the exhibit's spun as part of your dissertation."

The same half-truth she'd told herself in the beginning. Had she come full circle?

Elizabeth followed the arc of his arm as he indicated the portraits of her neck and stomach and face. She could still accept Ben's version of what had happened. Maybe he was hoping that she would. But she couldn't. The price was too steep.

There was nothing more to say. Elizabeth stood in the center of the room, surrounded by images of herself, and knew that her husband would never see her.

Elizabeth read through the final pages of her dissertation. She still had to defend it to her committee—that was part of the process, an oral defense, revisions, a final submission—but she knew they didn't want to prolong her stay on campus by requesting extensive changes. They wanted her gone.

She would submit her manuscript, complete the semester of Feminist Art, grade the students' final papers. She and Ben would step politely around each other, as they'd done since the hour in Ventana's gallery, held together by a complicated web of shared arrangements and, she supposed, a reluctance to upset the equilibrium.

O'Keeffe had told Ansel Adams, her close friend, that spending time in Hawaii was one of the best things she had ever done. The place enchanted her, not only because of its visual splendor—the shimmering waterfalls and extravagant flowers—but because it was a place that was utterly new, free of memory and association. Starting with small things—a spikey red crab-claw, a white lotus with its bright yellow heart—she had engaged with ever-larger aspects of the strange and irresistible islands, hiking, sketching, painting. In her statement to accompany the 1940 exhibit, O'Keeffe had written: "If my painting is what I have to give back to the world for what the world gives to me, I may say that these paintings are what I have to give at present for what three months in Hawaii gave to me."

What was it, exactly—the new *something* that three months in Hawaii gave to her? Georgia never explained.

To Elizabeth, the key words were *at present*. The paintings captured what O'Keeffe had been able to absorb and express while she was in Hawaii. But her time in Hawaii hadn't finished unfolding. That would take more than nine weeks.

O'Keeffe never painted in Hawaii again. She went forward, to a new stage of work. *Making your unknown known is the most important thing,* she had written, *and keeping the unknown always beyond you.* As soon as the artist rendered her vision in a knowable form, it was finished, replaced at once by a new unknown. A field in movement, constantly emerging.

O'Keeffe kept searching, painting, even when her eyesight was nearly gone, returning at the end of her career to an abstract purity that echoed the way she had begun—not a repetition, but a fulfillment of its promise. O'Keeffe's journey took her from the swollen fecundity of flowers to the stillness of bones, from the pelvic ovoid to the angular doorway, from a rounded landscape of undulating color to the stark geometry of space and form.

Road to the Ranch, painted in 1964, breathtaking in its perfection. The Zen-like *Winter Road*, with the same elegant simplicity as the painting she had called *Black Lines* half a century earlier. The formless energy of the compositions O'Keeffe had entitled, simply, *Blue,* or *Blue Abstraction,* painted between 1916 and 1959, with their coiled potential.

O'Keeffe had said, years later: *When I look at the photographs Stieglitz took of me, I wonder who that woman is.* Elizabeth wished she could ask Georgia if posing had been a transformative experience—if she had been right to think of it that way. Then she had to laugh, because it was so obvious. Posing for Richard hadn't helped her understand O'Keeffe. It had helped her understand herself. The question was what she planned to do with that understanding.

Richard's studio was her Hawaii, her place of transition. But not her destination.

She would submit her dissertation. Defend it. A strange term, as if the dissertation had enemies. And after that? She had no idea.

Twenty-Six

The answer to her question came from Harold Lindstrom.
When Harold emailed to say that he needed to meet with her
again, as soon as possible, Elizabeth wondered what else had gone
wrong. Was her dissertation that bad? Did Marion want her ousted
from the entire program?

But Harold's expression was gentle as he opened the door to his
office and motioned for her to take a seat. "I have an offer for you," he
said. "Something to consider."

Elizabeth took one of the chairs that faced his desk. Instead of
circling back to the big leather chair, Harold sat down next to her.
"I'll get right to the point."

"Oh dear. Sounds ominous."

"Not at all." He leaned forward, and she was struck, again, by the
kindness in his eyes. "You're an excellent teacher, Ms. Crawford. I'd
hoped, candidly, that there might be a place for you on our faculty
once you completed your doctorate. However, I'm sure you understand that it's not possible now."

Elizabeth gave him a wry look. "I do."

"Nonetheless, you should be teaching somewhere. It would be a
crime to let that gift go to waste. So." He placed his hands on his
knees. "I have a colleague, an old friend from my undergraduate days,

who's dean at a small liberal arts college. I told him about you and he's prepared to offer you a position. Not to give you a swelled head, but this is the first time I've advocated for a student like this. He knows that, and that's why he's taking my recommendation seriously. The job's yours if you want it."

The job's yours. Elizabeth could hardly absorb the three simple words. The rest of the sentence didn't matter. Elation, followed by astonishment and gratitude, nearly made her jump up and hug him. Then her brow furrowed. It didn't make sense.

"Why are you doing this?" she asked.

After I've embarrassed the department. Pissed off Marion Mackenzie. Caused so much trouble.

Harold seemed to understand the complexity of her question. "Lloyd—that's my colleague—was impressed by your fearlessness in entering the art, as it were, instead of viewing it from a safe intellectual distance. He's a champion of what he calls the need to rethink how we engage with art and what an art history department ought to be doing—cultivating a twenty-first century sensibility instead of dwelling in the past. Teaching students to explore what art means, for them, instead of merely writing papers." He smiled. "Your story appealed to him. He said you were exactly the kind of innovator and risk-taker he'd like to bring on board."

Elizabeth tried to take in what Harold was saying. The generosity. The surprise. The implications of his offer—which she couldn't possibly accept.

The person Harold was talking about wasn't her. She hadn't been fearless, revolutionary, out to challenge the conventions of art history. She had been drawn by Richard, the man, and the possibility of being a different kind of woman. It hadn't been about art, not for her, although she understood now that it had been about art for Richard. Then, when Richard made her private exposure into a public event, she'd been desperate to suppress the photos, not a partner in promoting them.

Harold shouldn't give her credit for something she hadn't done. And Lloyd, whoever he was, shouldn't offer her a position based on a falsehood. It wouldn't take long for him to discover that she wasn't the innovator Harold had described.

"It's a small college," Harold went on, "not a big research institution like this place. But it's a start and you might, in fact, be happier there."

Yes, she might. Another reason it stung to have to turn it down. But she had to, because Elizabeth-the-innovator was just one more made-up story about who she was and what she had done.

Everyone, it seemed, had a narrative to offer. There was Naomi's version: the proud and feisty professor, champion of a woman's right to use her body as she damn well pleased. And Ben's version, less flattering but equally convenient: naive and bookish wife, victim of a clever manipulator. Now this one: a free spirit with a bold new educational vision.

It was all nonsense. She'd rejected the first two stories, even though each had its benefits, because they weren't true. Harold's story wasn't true either. She was finished with stories.

Elizabeth was about to explain why she had to decline his offer, generous as it was, when something in his eyes made her stop. There was an understanding, a silent pact—as if he knew, or suspected, that she hadn't really been the person he described but was giving her a chance anyway.

A chance to choose, intentionally, the identity she wanted. Even if it had been thrust on her, at first, by others—it didn't matter. She could consent, actively, to a way of being. A woman who entered the art she loved. A woman who entered and lived in her own body.

Georgia had been furious at the art world's response to the photos Stieglitz took of her, yet the photos had opened a door, spurring interest in her work. Maybe it could be like that for her too. Richard's use of the photos had made her angry, but they could open the door she needed.

That had been the theme of her dissertation. The doorway. The opening.

Harold cleared his throat, waiting for her to answer.

"I'm a bit dumbstruck," she said, finally. "I had no idea what I'd do after graduation, frankly, or be able to do." Now that she'd lost Marion's sponsorship. She didn't have to say it. Harold knew, at least as well as she did, the consequence of that loss.

"It's an intriguing opportunity," he said. "Perhaps not what you originally envisioned, but if you're willing to focus on teaching instead of research—which, again, might be more to your liking—it could be a good fit."

Elizabeth studied his face. It was open, encouraging. She wasn't sure, then, that she'd been right about the tacit understanding she had seen on it a moment earlier. Maybe he did think she'd meant to take some sort of stand when she posed. Or maybe it had less to do with sympathy for her and more to do with his relationship to Lloyd. An opportunity to help an old friend and colleague, repay a favor or put one in the bank, to be redeemed later in the bizarre academic calculus that she was just beginning to comprehend.

"You're being incredibly kind."

Harold gave a small sigh. "I was in your shoes once, about to get my doctorate. I had a chance to do something bold and exciting that I truly believed in. But I didn't. I took the safe route, told myself it was the mature thing to do, but there was always that *what-if.* So I thought, well, why not help someone else do what I didn't have the courage to do myself." He opened his hands. "And here we are. I'll pay it forward and hope that one day you will too."

Elizabeth was touched by what he had shared, after all those months of meticulous adherence to their advisor-advisee roles. They sat in silence, and then she asked, "Where's the college located?"

"It couldn't be more idyllic." He named a small town about two hundred miles northwest. It was well-known for its pristine lake and vibrant community of artists and craftsmen. The perfect place for a non-conformist art history professor who didn't mind taking her clothes off to make a point.

But not a place Ben would want to move to.

He wouldn't want to move anywhere. He had a law practice and, of course, those squash games.

Harold handed her a folder. "Here's a packet about the college and the program. Read it over and give Lloyd a call, his number's on the top sheet. No doubt you'll have questions—salary, teaching load, tenure requirements, all of that. I'll leave it to the two of you to work out the details." He coughed. "If you're interested, that is. I don't mean to assume."

Elizabeth inhaled. Then she took the folder. "Yes, I'm interested."

"Excellent. I do think you'd thrive there. Certainly they'll appreciate your, shall we say, eclectic approach."

"I'll try not to disappoint." Rising, she tucked the folder under her left arm and stretched out her right. "Thank you, Dr. Lindstrom. For everything."

"My pleasure." He took her hand in his, his clasp firm. "Let me know how it goes."

"I will."

She left his office, closing the door softly behind her.

"You want to *what*?" Ben said. "Are you out of your mind?"

"Maybe I am." Elizabeth willed herself not to flinch. "Maybe for once I'm out of my mind and into my whole self."

"Oh for god sakes, Liz. You really think you can just decide, unilaterally, that we're going to uproot ourselves and move to some pretentious little hippie town on a goddamn *lake*?"

She'd been afraid Ben would respond like this, but she had dared to hope that he might see it as a chance for a new beginning—for them, not just for her. Improbable, perhaps, after all that had happened, yet it didn't seem entirely foolish.

Ben had always supported her career, and he'd been the one, in the end, to help her across the threshold of her dissertation. She had wanted to give up after losing Marion and her teaching job and, she assumed, Harold's goodwill. It had seemed masochistic and pointless to finish a manuscript that wasn't going to be an entrée to academia after all. But Ben had been adamant. "You've worked so hard on this, Liz. It's been your goal for as long as I've known you. You can't quit now. It's who you are."

Elizabeth had wanted to say, "It's not all I am." Yet she'd been touched by his belief in her, in the side of her that he knew and understood. She double-checked her references, formatted her table of contents, and emailed Harold to schedule the oral defense. And then Harold offered her a gift she had never expected.

Ben was glaring at her now. There was no mistaking his reaction.

Elizabeth steeled herself. She hadn't known when the moment would arrive, only that it would. "If you don't like the idea, you don't have to come."

"What's that supposed to mean?"

"You know exactly what it means. Don't come."

Ben's eyes were blazing. It was the same fire she had seen that evening, when Charlie started talking about jazz, or when a principle Ben believed in was under siege. It was arrogant and myopic to think Ben wasn't capable of passion. Of course he was. Only not toward her.

"Is this some kind of game? What is it you want, Elizabeth?"

Freedom, she thought. The freedom to walk through the passage, the opening, into whatever might come next.

"I want to take this job, and I want to have a life where I can be everything I need to be."

"Christ. Where did you read that? On a Hallmark card?"

"Fuck you, Ben."

"Would you, if I bought myself a camera?"

She slapped him, as hard as she could. Then, just as swiftly, she covered her face with her hands. She'd wanted there to be fire between them, but not this kind.

"Please," she whispered. "Let's not do this. We've never been ugly with each other."

"We've never been anything with each other. That's the problem, isn't it?"

Elizabeth raised her eyes. His gaze was flat, the anger gone.

He'd said it. Finally. She didn't know if she felt relieved or cheated that he had been the one to utter the truth she had tried so hard not to know.

Ben's shoulders slumped. "I never understood why. I got used to it, I guess."

Sadness seeped into her limbs, as heavy as the Hawaiian air. "Me too."

"I blame myself," he said. "I never should have married you. You were so sure, so convincing. I don't know, it just seemed like the easiest thing to do."

The words made Elizabeth want to smack him again. He made her sound like a lousy job he'd settled for, the only car he could afford.

"Don't look at me like that, Liz. I'm taking my share of the responsibility, that's all."

Oh yes, that was the Crawford way. Fair and reasonable, equal portions of blame. Then Elizabeth shook her head, sick of analyzing every gesture and phrase. What did it matter—her fault for talking him into a loveless arrangement, or his for accepting it? They'd made a calculated alliance, and their calculations had been wrong.

Richard had shown her that.

She'd faced her students, Richard, Harold. Her own image, there on the gallery wall. She could face Ben too. "You're right," she said. "We're both responsible for our lives. But we're not trapped."

"Meaning what?"

"Meaning that I'm taking the job." Then, to be sure there was no misunderstanding, she repeated, "I'm moving. And I'm taking the kids with me."

"They're my children too."

"Of course they are. They need you, and they need to spend as much time with you as they can."

Elizabeth braced herself to say the last and hardest thing. "But they don't need how we are together. It's not good for them. They need to see what it's like for a man and a woman to love each other."

She wasn't prepared for the swell of tears, big and bright. Somehow, she hadn't thought she would cry. She tried to blink them back but there were too many, falling too fast.

"You really think it's that simple to break up a family?"

Elizabeth wiped her cheek with the back of her hand. "It's not simple at all. But we have to."

She knew it was hard for Ben to believe she was doing this. It was the surprise, that's all, and the upheaval. It wasn't as if he couldn't bear to lose her.

And yet there was a shared sadness, surrounding and uniting them. She could feel it; she was sure he could too. As if they were closer, in this terrible moment, than they had ever been.

His eyes glistened, his tears matching hers. "I'm sorry, Liz. I'm sorry we couldn't do better."

"We will do better," she told him. "Only it will be a different kind of better."

Elizabeth let the big oak door to the Humanities building hiss shut behind her as she stepped out into the winter afternoon. The trees were covered with a layer of snow, lace against a cobalt sky. The air was clean and cold.

Dr. Crawford. That was her title now. Her defense had gone smoothly, no last-minute challenges from the panel that faced her across the conference table, just as Harold had promised. They had asked her to wait in the hall while they conferred and then, as was the custom, they had called her back into the room. Harold had given the official benediction. "Welcome to the Academy, Dr. Crawford."

She wondered what Georgia would have thought about her dissertation. Had she gotten it right, about Hawaii? The committee had declared her argument sound, her scholarship solid, but that didn't mean she was right. Only Georgia could have told her that.

Then she had to smile. Georgia would never have responded to that sort of question. "Look at the paintings," she would have said. "Let them speak for themselves."

Elizabeth made her way down the steps, along the path that bisected the quad. Ahead was Founders' Lawn. She remembered how she had yearned for the balletic grace she'd seen in the people doing Tai Chi on the grass, all those months ago. Her vision had been of something that could move inward, becoming hers—the possibility of watching, learning, and then doing it herself. Now she understood. Grace began from the inside, radiating outward.

If it hadn't been for Tai Chi, she wouldn't have met Richard.

Thankfully, she had.

The afternoon, surrounding her, was lit with its particular beauty, the sunlight glittering on the branches, the fine white mist of snow that rose up as she walked. She wove from tree to tree, reveling in the luxuriant pleasure of swinging her arms, moving her legs.

She thought of what O'Keeffe had written to Stieglitz, from Hawaii. *My idea of the world had not been beautiful enough.* In Hawaii, Georgia had seen that her vision was too small, despite everything she'd accomplished up till then, and had dared to go beyond it.

Elizabeth stopped at the edge of the path. There was one more thing she had to do. She took her phone out of her messenger bag, swiped through her contacts, and tapped the first one on the list. *A*, for Andrea.

The photos of her were coming down. She had kept an eye on Ventana's website, watching to see when Richard's new series of people on the brink of movement would take their place. The new exhibit was slated to open, finally, on Monday. Today was the last day her image would be on display.

Elizabeth opened the door to the gallery and held it so Andrea could enter first. It was her third visit. The first time she had been alone with the photographs. The second time she had brought Ben, who didn't understand. This time, she was with her sister, who might.

Andrea spent a long time in front of each photo. Then she turned to Elizabeth, her eyes shining. "They're absolutely beautiful, Lizzie. Like you."

Elizabeth's throat filled with emotion. She didn't know the name for what she felt, but it didn't need a name. What mattered was the experience itself.

"You know," Andrea said, "you've always been lovely. The only one who didn't know that was you."

Without stopping to think, Elizabeth opened her arms, and Andrea stepped into them. The movement was effortless, natural, like Tai Chi. "I love you, Andie," she whispered.

"Well, *duh*." Andrea squeezed her, then stepped back and grinned. "I knew that. That's why I decided not to be pissed off at the way you kept nagging me to take a business class."

"I shouldn't have—"

"No, it's okay." Andrea's grin widened. "I signed up for Small Business Management 101. It's dry as the Mojave, but oh well."

"You really did?"

"I did."

Elizabeth smiled too. "You'll do fine. You're smarter than you think. I just acted like I was the only smart one."

"Eh." Andrea waved a hand. "We each had our role."

"Back then."

Andrea's face turned serious. "You think we still do?"

"Maybe. But we're more than that. Each of us is more than that."

Elizabeth felt the truth of what she'd told her sister. Her own knowledge, not something she'd read in a book.

She turned around, slowly, and looked again—one last time, before it disappeared—at the final picture Richard had taken of her. Her whole body, adorned with nothing but itself, arms spread wide, face open and full of light.

Reader's Guide Questions

1. Did Richard use Elizabeth? What did you think of his declarations about consent and ownership of one's art? Did Elizabeth have the right to demand that he take down the photographs?

2. A turning point for Elizabeth is when she finds the theme for her dissertation and thus no longer "needs" to pose in order to understand O'Keeffe. She decides to pose anyway. Do you think that her motive for posing actually changes in that moment, or was that her real motive all along? Might she have more than one motive, whether she was aware of it or not?

3. What do you think of Elizabeth and Ben's marriage? Were you hoping they might work things out? What would have it taken for that to happen? At what point did you begin to know that it wasn't going to happen? Do you think Elizabeth tried hard enough?

4. Elizabeth juggles many roles, among them wife, mother, sister, and academic. How well do you think she fulfills each of them? Does her understanding of each role change over the course of the story?

5. Do you think O'Keeffe was a feminist? What role does feminist art play in the novel?

6. Various groups—from the early art critics to the later feminists—have told stories about who O'Keeffe was and what she stood for, although O'Keeffe repudiated all their attempts. Do you think Elizabeth understood something important about O'Keeffe, or did she make up her own story about O'Keeffe, to suit her own needs?

7. At the end of the book, Elizabeth is offered various narratives to elevate or explain what she did. Ultimately she decides to embrace and enact the narrative she wants. Do you think a person can live without some sort of narrative? What does it mean to live an authentic life?

8. Naomi, a student in Elizabeth's class, declares that an artist ought to put herself out into the world, the person and the art together, inseparable. She goes even further, stating that professors—as teachers and scholars—ought to embody what they believe. How far would you take this principle? Which characters in the book live what they believe? Is there a cost for doing that, or for failing to do that?

9. Elizabeth states that Georgia O'Keeffe was searching for what it means to be a woman—which, of course, she herself is also doing. There are many female characters in the book. In their physical descriptions, how are hair and clothing used to convey aspects of being a woman?

10. Elizabeth wants to tell her young daughter to be everything. "Anything less was wrong, the same as being nothing." But Andrea, her sister, believes that you have to find out the one thing you are, and are good at, and just be that. How do these two attitudes or premises play out in the story?

11. At the end of the novel, Elizabeth states that: "The committee had declared her argument sound, her scholarship solid, but that didn't mean she was right. Only Georgia could have told her that." Then Elizabeth chides herself and decides that Georgia would want the paintings to speak for themselves. Do you agree? Does a work of art benefit from interpretation by others? Do you think artists always know or can analyze their influences and intentions?

12. Early in the book, Elizabeth states that she wants to find "her own Hawaii." Do you think she did? If so, at what point in the story? Where?

Acknowledgments

I had the good fortune to have two brilliant and generous mentors during the writing of this book. Kathryn Craft guided me through its early stages, when I was searching for my story and finding my way. Sandra Scofield pushed me to go further—and further still—until the book grew into what it was meant to be. Boundless gratitude to these wise teachers.

And huge thanks to Brooke Warner, Crystal Patriarche, Tabitha Bailey, Lauren Wise, Julie Metz, and the loving community of She Writes sisters who shared this journey with me.

Thanks also to others who helped along the way:

Theresa Papanikolas, formerly of the Honolulu Academy of Arts, curator of the exhibit of O'Keeffe's Hawaii paintings at the New York Botanical Garden, who shared her insights into O'Keeffe's work.

Cody Hartley, director of Georgia O'Keeffe Museum in Santa Fe, New Mexico, who graciously answered my endless questions, and Tori Duggan, research associate, who made a wealth of material available to me at the Georgia O'Keeffe Research Center.

Sylvia March, who shared stories of her mother's 40-year friendship with O'Keeffe and her own "lunch with Georgia."

Teri Goggin-Roberts, the first one to understand that Elizabeth had to face the photos alone in the gallery.

Kay Scott and Dianna Sinovic, early readers whose insights into what the book still needed were exactly right.

Maggie Smith, for her unwavering support and belief in this project.

Tom Steenburg, whose patience, love, and respect gave me the space I needed to bring Elizabeth's story to life.

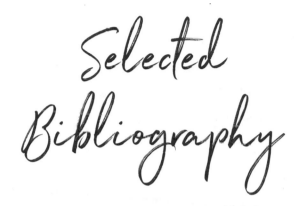

Georgia O'Keeffe's Hawaii Paintings

Jennings, P. & Ausherman, M. (2011). *Georgia O'Keeffe's Hawaii*. Koa Books: Kihei HI.

Papanikolas, T. (2013). *Georgia O'Keeffe and Ansel Adams: The Hawaii Pictures*. Honolulu Museum of Art: Honolulu HI.

Papanikolas, T. & Groarke, J.L. (2018). *Georgia O'Keeffe: Visions of Hawaii*. Prestel Publishing: New York NY.

Saville, J. (1990). *Georgia O'Keeffe: Paintings of Hawaii*. Honolulu Academy of Arts: Honolulu HI.

O'Keeffe and Stieglitz

Buhler Lynes, B. (1989). *O'Keeffe, Stieglitz and the Critics, 1916-1929*. University of Chicago Press: Chicago IL.

Burke, C. (2019). *Foursome: Alfred Stieglitz, Georgia O' Keeffe, Paul Strand, Rebecca Salsbury*. Knopf: New York NY.

Greenough, S. (Ed.). (2011). *My Faraway One: Selected letters of*

Georgia O'Keeffe and Alfred Stieglitz, Volume 1, 1915-1933. Yale University Press: New Haven CT.

Pyne, K. (2007). *Modernism and the Feminine Voice: O'Keeffe and the Women of the Stieglitz Circle*. University of California Press: Berkeley CA.

Georgia O'Keeffe, Art and Life: Books

Barson, T. (Ed.) (2016). *Georgia O'Keeffe*. Tate Publishing: London UK.

Castro, J.G. (1985). *The Art and Life of Georgia O'Keeffe*. Crown Publishers: New York NY.

Corn, W.M. (2017). *Georgia O'Keeffe: Living Modern*. Prestel Publishing: New York NY.

Cowart, J. & Hamilton, J. (1990). *Georgia O'Keeffe: Art and Letters*. New York Graphic Society: New York NY.

Grasso, L.M. (2017). *Equal Under the Sky: Georgia O'Keeffe and Twentieth-Century Feminism*. University of New Mexico Press: Albuquerque NM.

Robinson, R. (1989). *Georgia O'Keeffe: A Life*. University Press of New England: Hanover NH.

Georgia O'Keeffe, Art and Life: Articles

Boxer, S. *New York Times*, March 27, 2019. Book Review: "The Two Artist Couples Who Helped Start American Modernism."

Brenson, M. *New York Times*, November 8, 1987. Art View: "How O'Keeffe Painted Hymns to Body and Spirit."

Crisell, H. *New York Times*, July 6, 2016. *Style Magazine*: "A Collaboration Between Georgia O'Keeffe and Alfred Stieglitz, Captured over 20 Years."

Lahue, A. *The Guardian*, July 1, 2016. Art and Design: "The Wild Beauty of Georgia O'Keeffe."

Messinger, L.M. *Metropolitan Museum of Art Bulletin*, 42(2). Fall 1984. "Georgia O'Keeffe."

Perrrottet, T. *New York Times*, November 30, 2012. Travel: "O'Keefe's Hawaii."

Tomkins, C. *New Yorker Magazine*, March 4, 1974. "Georgia O'Keefe's Vision: The Painter Considers her Life and Work."

About the Author

© David Heald 2018

Barbara Linn Probst is a writer, researcher, and former clinician living on an historic dirt road in New York's Hudson Valley. Her novels (*Queen of the Owls* and *The Sound of One Hand*, forthcoming in April 2021) tell of the search for authenticity, wholeness, and connection. In both novels, art helps the protagonist to become more fully herself. *Queen of the Owls*, Barbara's debut novel, has been chosen as a 2020 selection of the Pulpwood Queens, a network of more than 780 book clubs throughout the U.S.

Author of the groundbreaking book on nurturing out-of-the-box children, *When the Labels Don't Fit*, Barbara holds a PhD in clinical social work and is a frequent contributor to the major online sites for fiction writers. To learn more about Barbara and her work, please see http://www.barbaralinnprobst.com/

SELECTED TITLES FROM SHE WRITES PRESS

She Writes Press is an independent publishing company founded to serve women writers everywhere. Visit us at www.shewritespress.com.

The Geometry of Love by Jessica Levine $16.95, 978-1-938314-62-9
Torn between her need for stability and her desire for independence, an aspiring poet grapples with questions of artistic inspiration, erotic love, and infidelity.

A Drop In The Ocean: A Novel by Jenni Ogden $16.95, 978-1-63152-026-6
When middle-aged Anna Fergusson's research lab is abruptly closed, she flees Boston to an island on Australia's Great Barrier Reef—where, amongst the seabirds, nesting turtles, and eccentric islanders, she finds a family and learns some bittersweet lessons about love.

Play for Me by Céline Keating $16.95, 978-1-63152-972-6
Middle-aged Lily impulsively joins a touring folk-rock band, leaving her job and marriage behind in an attempt to find a second chance at life, passion, and art.

Anchor Out by Barbara Sapienza $16.95, 978-1631521652
Quirky Frances Pia was a feminist Catholic nun, artist, and beloved sister and mother until she fell from grace—but now, done nursing her aching mood swings offshore in a thirty-foot sailboat, she is ready to paint her way toward forgiveness.

Shelter Us by Laura Diamond $16.95, 978-1-63152-970-2
Lawyer-turned-stay-at-home-mom Sarah Shaw is still struggling to find a steady happiness after the death of her infant daughter when she meets a young homeless mother and toddler she can't get out of her mind—and becomes determined to rescue them.

Center Ring by Nicole Waggoner $17.95, 978-1-63152-034-1
When a startling confession rattles a group of tightly knit women to its core, the friends are left analyzing their own roads not taken and the vastly different choices they've made in life and love.

Praise for *Queen of the Owls*

"A nuanced, insightful, culturally relevant investigation of one woman's personal and artistic awakening, *Queen of the Owls* limns the distance between artist and muse, creator and critic, concealment and exposure, exploring no less than the meaning and the nature of art."
—**Christina Baker Kline**, #1 *New York Times* bestselling author of *A Piece of the World* and *Orphan Train*

"This is a stunner about the true cost of creativity, and about what it means to be really seen. Gorgeously written and so, so smart (and how can you resist any novel that has Georgia O'Keeffe in it?), Probst's novel is a work of art in itself."
—**Caroline Leavitt**, best-selling author of *Pictures of You, Is This Tomorrow* and *Cruel Beautiful World*

"*Queen of the Owls* is a powerful novel about a woman's relation to her body, diving into contemporary controversies about privacy and consent. A 'must-read' for fans of Georgia O'Keeffe and any woman who struggles to find her true self hidden under the roles of sister, mother, wife, and colleague."
—**Barbara Claypole White**, best-selling author of *The Perfect Son* and *The Promise Between Us*

"Probst's well-written and engaging debut asks a question every woman can relate to: what would you risk to be truly seen and understood? The lush descriptions of O'Keeffe's work and life enhance the story, and help frame the enduring feminist issues at its center."
—**Sonja Yoerg**, best-selling author of *True Places*

"Readers will root for Elizabeth—and wince in amusement at her pratfalls—as she strikes out in improbable new directions … An entertaining, psychologically rich story of a sometimes giddy, sometimes painful awakening."
—*Kirkus Reviews*

"A gifted storyteller, Barbara Linn Probst writes with precision, empathy, intelligence, and a deep understanding of the psychology of a woman's search for self."

—**Sandra Scofield**, National Book Award finalist and author of *The Last Draft* and *Swim: Stories of the Sixties*

"Barbara Linn Probst captures the art of being a woman beautifully. *Queen of the Owls* is a powerful and liberating novel of self-discovery using Georgia O'Keeffe's life, art, and relationships as a guide."

—**Ann Garvin**, best-selling author of *I Like You Just Fine When You're Not Around*

"A beautiful contemporary novel full of timeless themes, elegantly portraying one woman's courage to passionately follow the inspiration of Georgia O'Keeffe and brave the risk of coming into her own."

—**Claire Fullerton**, author of *Mourning Dove*

"Obsession, naivety, seduction, desire, self-deception, love, and courage—all emotions subtly and powerfully revealed in this story of Elizabeth, mother, wife, and intellectual, as she follows her idol, artist Georgia O'Keeffe, along a path to herself. A thought-provoking novel that readers will want to savor and share."

—**Jenni Ogden**, author of Nautilus Gold and multiple award-winning *A Drop in the Ocean*

QUEEN OF THE OWLS will be the May 2020 selection for the Pulpwood Queens, a network of more than 800 book clubs nationwide. In the words of founder and CEO, Kathy L. Murphy: "An absolutely wonderful book that every woman should read!"